THE SHADOW ARCHIVE

THE SACRED VEIN

Book Two

Brian Young

This is a work of fiction. Names, characters, places, and incidents either are the product of the author's imagination or are used fictitiously. Any resemblance to actual persons, living or dead, events, or locales is entirely coincidental.

The Sacred Vein Series:

Book One: The Sacred Vein
Book Two: The Shadow Archive

For Kaylie, Owen, and Kara

The real treasure was never hidden in a chamber. It was you, all along.

Seek wisely. Protect fiercely. Love completely.

PART ONE

THE DISCOVERY

PROLOGUE

Hidden Secrets

Snow was falling when the phone rang—the kind of call that separates life into before and after.

"Ammon." Dr. Chen's voice had a quality he'd never heard from her before—the careful control of someone trying not to sound like they'd just discovered fire. "We've finished the preliminary translation of the first codex. You need to come see this. Today, if you can. It's about Hathenbruck."

He was in his car within the hour.

The drive took two hours, the winter roads slowing him down, headlights cutting through falling snow. By the time he reached the reservation, the mountains had disappeared into darkness, only their absence visible against the gray-black sky.

Chen met him at the door of the cultural center. She was still wearing her reading glasses pushed up on her forehead—the way she did when she'd been working too intensely to remember to take them off. Her usual composure was cracked just enough to show what lay beneath.

"This way. Thomas is already inside."

The secure translation room was windowless, thrumming with climate control, the air carrying that particular stillness of spaces built to protect fragile things. The codex lay open on a padded table at the center, its ancient pages glowing amber under conservation lights.

"This codex is different from the others." Chen's fingers hovered over the glass. "It's a record of guardianship going back centuries. Each guardian added their own testimony." She turned to a section near the end. "Hathenbruck is the last entry."

Thomas stood at the edge of the table, his weathered face unreadable. "The journal he left for his descendants told one version of the story. This tells another." He paused, and his expression shifted—a guardedness Ammon had never seen before. "A version with secrets he kept even from us."

"He mentions instructions," Chen said carefully. "Hidden with someone he trusted completely." She exchanged a glance with Thomas—something passed between them that Ammon couldn't read. "A woman named Anna." A pause. "His wife."

Anna... The name unlocked something buried so deep Ammon had forgotten it existed. Hathenbruck and his wife, Anna, had a daughter, also called Anna.

Ammon recalled his great-grandmother's hands, worn and gentle. A gold locket, warm from her skin. On it, a tiny, engraved symbol—nested circles radiating outward like ripples in still water. A hidden mechanism inside that she'd shown him once, when he was seven, whispering *someday, when you're older, I'll tell you what's inside.*

She'd died before that someday arrived. The locket had passed to her youngest daughter—Ammon's great-aunt Clara, who had always been distant, disapproving of the family's treasure-hunting obsessions.

"The locket," he said, and the words came out strange—too steady, as if speaking from somewhere outside himself. "Anna's locket. My great-grandmother had it. She showed me the hidden compartment when I was a child."

"Where is it now?" Thomas's voice was sharp.

Ammon's mind flashed through the years—his great-grandmother's funeral, the reading of the will, the locket passing to his great-aunt Clara while he stood at the edge of the family he'd never quite belonged to. He hadn't thought about it in decades. Hadn't known to think about it.

"My aunt. Denver." He was already reaching for his phone, his heart pounding with recognition. Like pieces finally falling into place after nearly three decades.

He had to go to Denver.

CHAPTER ONE

The Locket

The drive took six hours. Aspen Rhoades drove the first half—the former park ranger turned guardian security lead, whose quiet competence had become one of the few constants Ammon could rely on. Aspen left him alone to his thoughts. He stared out the window at mountains giving way to high desert, high desert giving way to plains. They stopped once for gas in Green River, shared a package of peanut butter crackers without really tasting them, said almost nothing.

Some silences were comfortable. This one was too heavy for comfort— weighted with everything that might be waiting at the other end.

Clara's house was a tidy bungalow in a quiet Denver suburb, the kind of place that spoke of careful maintenance and deliberate order. A life built in opposition to the chaos that had defined the Lundquists for generations.

Ammon stopped at the front walk, his feet suddenly unwilling to carry him forward.

"She won't be happy to see me. She blames my father's death on the family obsession. Blames all of us, really, for not letting the search die when it should have."

"And yet here you are." Aspen's hand found his, squeezed once. "People can disagree about the past and still work together in the present. Come on. Let's see what your great-grandmother wanted you to know."

Clara opened the door before they could knock. She looked older than he remembered—grayer, the lines around her eyes deeper—but with the same sharp Lundquist features and stubborn set to her jaw. Fifteen years since his father's funeral. Fifteen years of silence between them.

"Ammon." Her voice was flat. "I wondered when you'd come."

Inside, the house was aggressively orderly—furniture arranged with precision, surfaces free of clutter, not a single family photograph in sight. Clara had spent decades building a life that contained no reminders of what the family obsession had cost her.

She led them to a living room more like a waiting room than a home and settled into an armchair with the rigid posture of someone preparing for battle.

"So. You found it. The treasure everyone wasted their lives looking for." Her voice was bitter, but beneath the bitterness, Ammon heard exhaustion. The weariness of someone who had spent years waiting for this knock on her door. "And now you want something from me."

"The locket," Ammon said. "Anna's locket. The one with the concentric symbols. There's something hidden inside—instructions from Hathenbruck himself."

Clara went still. "What about it?"

"I found the chamber, Aunt Clara. I protected it. I helped create a partnership between the guardians and the academic world. Whatever test Hathenbruck set up, I think I've passed it."

"You know," Aspen murmured. "You know what's in the locket."

Clara's composure cracked, tears spilling down her cheeks. "My mother showed me before she died. The most important secret in the family, passed down from mother to daughter for five generations, waiting for the right person to claim it." Her voice broke. "I watched the family obsession destroy your father, just like it destroyed his brother Marcus. I haven't seen you since Brock's funeral—fifteen years ago. I swore I'd protect what was left of this family by keeping the secret buried."

"The situation has changed," Ammon said gently. "The treasure hunt is over. What's in the locket isn't a path to more obsession. It's the final piece of a puzzle that's already been solved."

Clara looked at him—really looked. She saw a man who had found what generations had sought and chosen to protect rather than exploit.

For a long moment, she didn't move. Her hands gripped the armrests of her chair, knuckles whitening. Then her face released—not surrender, but decision.

"Wait here," she said.

When she returned, she carried a small velvet box—the kind meant for jewelry, aged and worn with handling. She stood before Ammon, holding it in both hands like an offering. Her face had changed—the bitterness drained out of it, leaving her older and more tired but also, somehow, lighter.

"My mother made me promise to pass this on when the time was right." Her voice had steadied, as if the act of surrendering the secret had released a burden she'd been holding for decades. "I never thought the time would come. But if anyone has earned this, it's you."

Ammon took the box with trembling hands. He looked at Aspen, saw his own anticipation reflected in their eyes—and something else too. Pride, maybe. Or simply the quiet certainty of someone who had always known he would get here.

He opened the lid.

Inside, resting on faded satin, lay a gold locket—small and delicate, its surface worn smooth by generations of handling. The front was engraved with intertwined letters: A and F. Anna and Friedrich.

He lifted it carefully. It was heavier than he expected, as if the secrets it held gave it physical mass. He found the clasp, opened the face, and Anna Hathenbruck looked out at him from a tiny portrait—her expression serene, her eyes holding secrets she had kept for a lifetime.

"There's a mechanism," Clara murmured. "On the back. Press the center of the engraving."

His hands were trembling. He turned the locket over, found the raised letters, pressed.

A soft click—the sound of a secret finally ready to be told. The hidden compartment sprang open.

Inside was a tiny roll of paper, yellowed with age but remarkably well-preserved. He extracted it with the care of someone handling a holy relic, unrolled it, and found himself looking at Hathenbruck's handwriting—cramped and precise, German words packed into every available space.

His great-grandmother had shown him this locket when he was seven years old. He was thirty-five now. Twenty-eight years, waiting for this moment.

He began to translate.

"To whoever holds this message: You have found the chamber, and you have chosen wisely. Now I give you my final gift—the location of the shadow archive. Go to the place where I first met Walkara, where the river bends like a serpent beneath the watching stone. There, in the hollow of the ancient tree where the cat watches, you will find what I have left for the future."

The description was vivid enough. Ammon saw it in his mind. The river bend—snake-like. The stone face. The cat symbol engraved in a tree long ago. He knew that place. He had stood beside that tree months ago, following trails that led to the sacred chamber. He'd passed it without a second glance, never knowing what waited inside.

"Tomorrow," he said, forcing himself to breathe. The old impulse was there—the urge to leave *now*, tonight, to chase the discovery before it could slip away. But he'd learned a truth in the past year. Some things were worth waiting for. Some things were worth doing right.

"We leave tomorrow. And we bring Thomas." He looked at Clara, who had given him this gift after decades of guarding it. "The guardians should be there when we find what Hathenbruck left behind."

CHAPTER TWO

The Hollow Tree

The morning dawned clear and cold, the kind of winter day that made the mountains look like they'd been carved from crystal. Ammon stood at the trailhead with Aspen, Thomas, Robert, and Jonas—five people bundled against the cold, their breath forming clouds in the still air.

The journey took three hours. Nobody spoke much. The weight of what they might find seemed to press down on all of them, turning conversation into intrusion.

Then, as they rounded a bend in the river, Ammon saw it: the watching stone.

It rose from the riverbank, and Ammon's breath caught. The stone's surface had been carved by centuries of wind and water into something that was not quite a face but could not be mistaken for anything else— deep shadows where eyes would be, a ridge that suggested a brow, the patient set of features that had watched this river bend for longer than humans had walked these mountains.

On the far bank stood the tree. Massive. Ancient beyond imagining. A bristlecone pine split by lightning but still alive—cat symbol faded, but visible—its trunk containing a hollow cavity large enough for a person to stand inside.

"The hollow of the ancient tree," Aspen breathed. "It's real."

They crossed the frozen river in single file, testing each step, the ice groaning beneath their weight. No one spoke. The only sounds were their boots on the frozen surface and the soft rush of water moving somewhere beneath.

Ammon reached the tree first. He shone his flashlight into the cavity, his heart hammering. At first, he saw nothing but wood—the interior walls of the tree, blackened by age and weather. He ran his hands along the rough surface, feeling for seams, for hidden compartments, for anything that might suggest a secret. Nothing.

A century of waiting, and maybe there was nothing here at all.

"Hand me the tools," he said.

Jonas passed him the small pack they'd brought—a folding shovel, a hand pick, a brush. Ammon had insisted on bringing them, just in case. The others had looked at him strangely, but he'd learned from his father's journals: Hathenbruck buried things. He protected them with earth and time.

Ammon knelt at the base of the hollow and began to dig. The ground was frozen, resistant, and each strike of the pick sent shocks up his arms. The others stood without speaking as he worked, their breath forming clouds in the still air.

Six inches down. Eight. His shoulders ached. Doubt crept in—maybe the message had been metaphorical, maybe the hollow of the ancient tree meant something else entirely—

The pick struck metal.

The sound rang out sharp and clear in the winter silence. Ammon froze, then struck again. The same dull clang, unmistakable.

"There's something here," he breathed.

He switched to the folding shovel, working more carefully now, scraping frozen earth away from what lay beneath. Gradually, the outline emerged: a rectangular shape, roughly the size of a large chest. The others crowded closer as he brushed dirt from the surface, revealing tarnished brass—dulled by more than a century of burial, but intact.

The lid was engraved with symbols he recognized from the sacred chamber—the same geometric patterns, the same stylized figures that had haunted his dreams for months.

"Help me with this," Ammon said, the words unsteady.

Thomas and Robert knelt beside him. Together, they worked the edges of the lid, frozen earth crumbling away as they pried at the seal. For a long moment, nothing gave—and then, with a groan of ancient hinges, the lid came free.

Inside, wrapped in oilcloth that had somehow survived the decades, lay a stack of notebooks—dozens of them, filled with Hathenbruck's precise handwriting. Beneath the notebooks were folders of drawings, diagrams, translations. And at the bottom, sealed in a leather pouch, a collection of small objects: pottery shards, stone tools, fragments of metalwork— samples taken from the chamber itself, preserved as proof of what the larger archive contained.

Ammon sat back on his heels, his hands trembling, dirt caked under his fingernails. Twenty years of Hathenbruck's secret labor, buried in frozen ground for over a century. And now, finally, unearthed.

"My God," Robert breathed. He reached toward the notebooks but stopped himself, his hand hovering. "All these years. All these generations. And he never told us."

"So many writings. So much work," Thomas said. His voice was thick, and when Ammon looked at him, he saw an unexpected emotion in the old guardian's face—not just awe, but what might have been grief. Or perhaps recognition. The look of a man realizing that the people we revere are always more complicated than we know.

Robert pointed to an engraving on the box's lid. Ammon translated the faded German:

"*To whoever finds this: You are now the keeper of knowledge that spans ages. Guard it well, share it wisely, and remember—the sacred vein runs through all of us, connecting past to present to future.*"

Ammon felt something shift in his chest—old grief loosening, long-held questions settling. His father had spent his life searching for this. Generations of Lundquists chasing a treasure they never found. But they had kept the search alive, passed down the clues that eventually led here.

"Hathenbruck's note hidden in the locket called it a shadow archive," Ammon mused. "And that's exactly what it is." Leafing through the pages, he recognized symbols and translations from the archives in the chamber. Hathenbruck had spent twenty years creating this, and had taken extraordinary care to hide it.

The sacred vein. Not gold, not treasure. The true sacred vein was connection—the thread linking those who came before to those who would come after.

At the trailhead, they found an unexpected welcoming committee. Silas stood beside his car, looking uncertain about whether he belonged there. And next to him, wrapped in a heavy coat against the cold, stood Clara— Ammon's aunt, who had driven through the night to be part of whatever happened next.

"You found it," Silas said, reading the answer in Ammon's face.

"Everything Hathenbruck preserved. Twenty years of his life, waiting all this time."

Clara's eyes glistened. She stepped forward, stopped—her hands rising and falling as if she'd forgotten how to do this—then closed the distance and pulled Ammon into an embrace. The first she'd given him since his father's funeral, fifteen years ago.

"Brock would be so proud," she whispered. "He always believed someone in the family would finally figure it all out."

As they drove away, the metal box secure in Ammon's pack, Aspen took his hand. "Happy?"

Ammon considered. He had been through fire. But he had also found love, purpose, community. He had solved a mystery that consumed five generations.

"Yes," he said. "Finally, completely, happy."

The archive would go to the tribal cultural center, subject to the same protocols as the chamber. The slow work of understanding would begin—translating, cross-referencing, piecing together what Hathenbruck had preserved against the darkness. It would take years. Maybe decades. And Ammon would be part of it, not as a treasure hunter anymore, but as something else. Something his father had never managed to become.

A keeper. A guardian. A link in the chain.

Hathenbruck's final gift, delivered after waiting patiently for over a century.

Or so he thought.

CHAPTER THREE

Six Months Later

"I need access to the comparative database." The voice cut through the translation room's careful quiet, sharp enough to turn heads.

Ammon Lundquist identified the source before he'd fully turned from the observation window: Dr. Yuki Tanaka, the Stanford cryptolinguist who'd arrived three weeks ago, was facing down one of the guardian monitors with her arms crossed and her jaw set. Her workstation behind her was organized chaos—three monitors, overlapping printouts, cold coffee.

Six months of careful work, and here it was, threatening to crack.

The monitor—David Ouray, a young man with a patience that belied his years—spread his hands in a gesture of conciliation. "Dr. Tanaka, the protocols exist for a reason. We've had external servers probe our systems three times this month alone. Until we can verify that your analysis software doesn't create vulnerabilities—"

"Vulnerabilities?" Tanaka's laugh was sharp. "These are standard—" She stopped, took a breath. "Look, I understand caution. I just don't understand *this much* caution."

"The trust you're asking for has to be earned. Nothing personal."

From the observation window above, Ammon noted Tanaka's shoulders tighten. He'd reviewed her credentials before she arrived—Harvard undergrad, Stanford Ph.D., tenure track at thirty-one, publications in every major journal. Brilliant, her references said. Driven. Occasionally difficult. Under other circumstances, exactly the kind of person they needed.

"You're brooding again."

Ammon turned. Thomas Wopsock approached with the careful deliberation that had become his habit—left arm stiff, shoulder lower than the right. The injuries from six months ago had healed. Mostly.

"Observing," Ammon corrected.

"Trust builds slow," Thomas said, observing the confrontation below. "What you're feeling? That's the work happening."

"I should handle this."

Thomas's hand caught his arm. "Be careful. Good people can still cause harm when they feel cornered."

Ammon nodded and made his way down to the translation floor. Tanaka saw him coming and her expression shifted—not quite hostile, but wary.

"Dr. Tanaka. I couldn't help overhearing. What's the specific analysis you're trying to run?"

"Phoneme mapping." She spoke quickly, the words tumbling out. "The codex uses at least three different writing systems—see this? Syllabic. But this section?" Her finger jabbed at another cluster. "Logographic. If I can map the phonemic structures, I might determine whether they're representing one language or several. Like a Rosetta Stone but with more layers."

She grabbed a printout, thrust it toward him. "Potentially the most significant linguistic discovery since—" She stopped, reined herself in. "But I need pattern recognition software that your security people won't let me install."

Ammon considered this. He understood the guardian concerns—the Consortium's reach had extended further than anyone imagined. But he also understood Tanaka's frustration. The knowledge locked in these codices had waited centuries already.

"What if we ran the analysis on an isolated system? Air-gapped, no network connection. You'd work in the high-security annex, but you'd have full access to your tools."

Tanaka's eyes narrowed. "That would slow things down."

"But it would work."

A beat of silence. Then, grudgingly: "It would work. For now."

"For now is all any of us have."

She turned back to her workstation, then paused.

"Ammon," she said, testing the name. "You're the one who found the chamber. The one whose ancestor left the trail."

"That's right."

"Then you understand what we're looking at. This isn't just archaeology." She pulled up an image, pointed to a mathematical notation. "These people knew things that shouldn't have been possible. Mathematical concepts not formally described until the nineteenth century. Astronomical observations requiring instruments they couldn't have had."

Her voice dropped. "If I'm right about the linguistic connections—and I am right—it means contact with civilizations across the Atlantic thousands of years before Columbus. This knowledge should be shared with the world."

"I understand," he said. "But I've also learned there's a difference between sharing and dumping."

Tanaka studied him, then shook her head—not disagreement, but recognition. "You sound like my grandmother. Fire can warm or burn, depending on how you tend it." She shrugged. "I hated when she was right, too."

"Smart woman."

"She was. And she would have hated all these protocols too." A ghost of a smile. "Tomorrow morning, then. High-security annex. I'll try not to burn anything down."

Ammon returned to the observation window. Below, Tanaka was already back at her workstation, fingers flying across the keyboard. The translation room pulsed with its quiet industry, researchers bent over their work, the fragile partnership holding for another day. He should have been content. Instead, he found himself studying the horizon beyond the glass, his body still tuned to a frequency the world no longer broadcast.

He needed air. He needed Aspen.

He found Aspen on the observation deck's far end, watching the afternoon light shift across the canyon. They didn't turn when he approached, but they shifted—making room for him beside them.

"Tanaka?" they asked.

"Handled. For now."

"For now is a lot, around here." The corner of their mouth curved.

They stood in comfortable silence, the canyon stretching golden below them. Three times this week, Ammon had caught himself reaching for his great-grandmother's locket—the one that had started everything—only to remember it now lived in a museum case downstairs, where anyone could see it. Exactly where it belonged. Exactly where it seemed wrong.

Then his phone buzzed—Chen's number—and the world came rushing back.

He found Dr. Chen waiting in the corridor outside the secure translation room, her usually composed face flushed with controlled urgency.

"Ammon." She was out of breath, which was unlike her. "Thank God. I've been looking everywhere—Thomas is in a meeting, and you're the only other person who should see this first."

"See what?"

Chen glanced around, ensuring they were alone. Then she leaned in, her voice barely above a whisper.

"We've found something in the shadow archive—in one of the notebooks you brought back from the tree." Her fingers trembled. "Pages that weren't in Hathenbruck's main transcription. Pages he kept separate. Hidden."

Ammon's heartbeat accelerated. "What do they say?"

"That's just it. We've only decoded part of it." Chen took a shaky breath. "But there's one phrase that appears again and again. 'The First Temple.' We're working to decode the rest."

The words hit him like a wave of cold water.

"What first temple? He never mentioned anything like that in his testimony."

"That's what's so strange. The shadow archive was supposed to be a complete copy of everything in the chamber. But these pages—" Chen shook her head. "He removed them from his own archive. Hid them inside a false cover on one of the notebooks. We only found them because Martinez noticed the binding was too thick."

"Why would he hide something from his own backup?"

Ammon's hand went to his chest—an unconscious gesture, reaching for a locket that was no longer there.

"Because whatever the First Temple is, Hathenbruck thought it was too dangerous even for the shadow archive. Dangerous enough to keep secret from everyone—including his own family."

Ammon looked back toward the observation deck, where Aspen's silhouette still held the canyon light. He thought of the careful architecture of trust they'd built—Thomas and the guardians, the researchers and their protocols, the balance that kept everything from collapsing. One more secret. One more thing Hathenbruck had hidden.

The hunt wasn't over after all.

CHAPTER FOUR

The Testimony

The secure translation room occupied the innermost sanctum of the cultural center, a windowless space protected by three inches of reinforced concrete and security protocols that would have made the Pentagon envious. The air held a particular stillness here—filtered, temperature-controlled, stripped of the subtle currents that moved through ordinary rooms. Fluorescent panels cast an even, shadowless light that flattened everything beneath them. Banks of whirring equipment lined the walls: climate monitors, electromagnetic shielding systems, the soft pulse of servers maintaining constant surveillance. The silence wasn't absence of sound—it was presence of protection, secrets held under guard.

Ammon had been inside perhaps a dozen times in six months—only for matters of the highest sensitivity, only when the guardians deemed it necessary. This, apparently, qualified. Thomas arrived fifteen minutes after Chen's summons, having extracted himself from his administrative meeting with the kind of abrupt departure that would generate rumors for days. He paused at the threshold, one hand braced against the doorframe, and Ammon saw him gather himself before entering—a small ritual of preparation that spoke to the pain he carried in his joints, in his back, in the places where age and old injuries had accumulated. Robert Colorow followed, his lined face unreadable, his presence a reminder that whatever they were about to see touched the deepest roots of the guardian tradition.

He moved to a chair in the corner and settled into it with the patience of someone who had learned that the most important things often required waiting. Dr. Chen had the documents already arranged on the central table— high-resolution photographs of codex pages, their surfaces showing the distinctive texture of aged vellum, the ink faded to a brown that spoke of centuries. Strange symbols crowded the margins: geometric patterns that seemed almost mathematical, stylized figures that might have been human or might have been something older. Her translation notes filled neat columns, and a laptop displayed spectral analysis that revealed hidden text—layers of writing beneath what the naked eye could see.

The damaged section Martinez had stumbled upon turned out to be anything but damaged; it was camouflaged, deliberately made to look degraded while remaining perfectly legible under the right light. Hathenbruck had hidden his testimony in plain sight. For over a century, it had waited for someone with the right tools—and the right reasons—to look closer.

"Start from the beginning," Thomas said, lowering himself into a chair with the careful movements of a man managing constant pain. His hand gripped the armrest as he descended, knuckles whitening briefly before he released. A muscle jumped in his jaw—not quite a wince, but close. Dr. Chen half-rose, an instinctive offer of assistance, but Thomas's eyes stopped her.

He would accept many things, but not help sitting down. Not yet.

"Everything you've translated so far." Chen nodded and pulled up her notes. Her fingers moved with the precision of someone who had spent decades working with ancient texts, but Ammon noticed the slight tremor in her hands—excitement or anxiety, he couldn't tell.

"The testimony begins with what appears to be a formal declaration, following the same format as other guardian entries in the codex. Date, name, circumstances of guardianship." She paused, looking around the room.

"Listen." She cleared her throat and read aloud, her pronunciation of the German careful and precise: "*Ich, Friedrich Wilhelm Carl Hathenbruck, schreibe dies im Jahr des Herrn 1889, in der heiligen Kammer, die meine größte Verantwortung und mein tiefstes Geheimnis geworden ist.*"

"*I, Friedrich Wilhelm Carl Hathenbruck, write this in the year of our Lord 1889, in the sacred chamber that has become my greatest responsibility and my deepest secret,*" Ammon translated automatically, the German flowing through his mind like water through familiar channels. His great-grandmother had spoken to him in German throughout his childhood. His father had insisted on it, saying it connected them to their roots.

He'd never imagined those roots ran quite this deep. Chen continued reading, and Ammon continued translating, but now his voice seemed disconnected from his body, as if someone else were speaking the words.

"*I have kept a journal for my descendants, hoping that one day they might find this place and understand what I have done. But there are things I could not write in that journal—things that would have endangered both my family and the guardians who trusted me. Those things I record here, in the language of my birth, for those who come after.*" Chen stopped reading. The pause that followed was different from the room's usual quiet—heavier, more deliberate.

Thomas's face had gone very still.

"He kept two sets of records. One for family. One for... what? Posterity?"

"For protection," Ammon said, though he wasn't sure whose protection his ancestor had meant.

"Go on," Robert said. His voice was low, measured—the voice of a man who understood that some words, once spoken, could not be taken back.

"Let us hear what else he felt he could not share." Chen's eyes returned to her notes. When she spoke again, her academic precision had taken on a different quality—something closer to reverence.

"*When Chief Walkara first showed me this chamber, I wept. Not from the gold—the gold means nothing—but from the knowledge preserved here. Records of peoples I had never heard of, civilizations that rose and fell before Europe emerged from barbarism. I understood immediately that this knowledge could change everything we think we know about human history. And I understood, just as immediately, that the world was not ready to receive it.*"

The room fell silent again. Ammon's eyes tracked to Robert Colorow's hands, resting on his knees—saw them curl into fists, then release. The elder's face remained impassive, but emotion moved behind his eyes, what looked like grief wearing the mask of patience. When Robert finally spoke, his words came with the gravity of someone choosing each one as if it might be his last.

"He never told us any of this." A pause, long enough that Ammon thought he might not continue.

"Generations of guardians. My grandfather. My father. Me." Another pause, and now Ammon could see the cost of this measured speech—the effort it took to contain what wanted to spill out.

"We thought we knew him. We thought—" Robert stopped, pressed his lips together.

"We thought he trusted us." The betrayal in those words filled the room like a physical weight.

"He trusted you with the chamber," Ammon said, though the words seemed inadequate.

"Maybe he thought that was enough." Robert's eyes met his—dark, ancient eyes that had seen more than Ammon could imagine.

"Perhaps. Or perhaps he believed that some burdens should not be shared." He paused again.

"We will hear the rest. And then we will decide whether he was wise or merely afraid."

"Keep reading," Thomas said. His voice was flat, controlled in a way that suggested strong emotion being forcibly contained. His grip on the armrest had returned, tension running up his forearm like a cable under strain.

"There's more." Chen nodded and continued. The next section described Walkara's dying request, the passing of guardianship to a foreigner, the burden of responsibility Hathenbruck had carried for decades. But then the tone shifted.

"Aber ich war nicht zufrieden, nur zu schützen."

"*But I was not content merely to protect,*" Ammon translated, as the words landed in his stomach like stones. Chen paused, looking up from her notes. Her professional composure had cracked, and he could see a fierceness beneath it—the hunger of a scholar who had found something unprecedented.

"Here's where it gets significant."

"*Ich kopiere.*"

"*I copy.*" The two words hung in the air. The drone of the climate control seemed suddenly louder, the fluorescent light harsher.

Chen's voice steadied as she continued, her hands no longer trembling—she was fully in the grip of the discovery now.

"*Over the course of twenty years, working in secret during my visits to the chamber, I transcribed every codex, every inscription, every symbol I could find. I translated what I could understand and documented what I could not. I created a complete record of everything this chamber contains—a shadow archive that could survive even if the chamber itself were destroyed.*" No one spoke. The words seemed to require silence, a space in which to be fully understood.

"A shadow archive," Thomas repeated finally. The words seemed to cost him—Ammon could see it in the way his shoulders dropped, the way the lines around his mouth deepened.

"He copied everything."

"That's not all." Chen scrolled through her notes, fingers trembling again—but differently now, with the energy of someone who understood they were about to change the shape of the world.

"There's more. And this is the part that—" She stopped, pressed her palms flat against the table.

"Just listen." Ammon translated the next passage with a growing sense of dread: "*But I did not copy everything. There are certain pages I have removed from the archive, pages I could not in good conscience leave for any future seeker to find. They describe a place called the First Temple—a site far older than this chamber, far older than anything I believed possible. The First Temple holds knowledge that could reshape the world, but that knowledge comes with dangers I cannot fully understand.*

I have hidden these pages separately, in a place where only the most dedicated seeker might find them. May God guide whoever reads these words to wisdom rather than folly."

Silence filled the room like water filling a vessel. Ammon was aware of his own heartbeat, loud in his ears, and of the others—Thomas gripping the armrest, Chen with her hands pressed flat on the table, Robert utterly motionless in his corner chair.

"The First Temple," Thomas said finally, his voice rough.

"In all my years as guardian, all the oral histories I've learned, I've never heard that name." Robert stirred—the first movement he had made since Chen began reading the final passage.

"Nor I. And my grandfather taught me stories that went back to Walkara himself." He paused, and the pause stretched long.

"If this First Temple exists, it was hidden even from the guardians who came before Hathenbruck. Hidden from Walkara himself. Hidden from everyone who ever swore the oath we swore."

"Or," Ammon said, "it was hidden from everyone. Hathenbruck found something in the codices that nobody else had ever decoded.

Something so dangerous he couldn't even write it in his secret testimony."

"But he didn't destroy the pages," Chen pointed out, steadying.

"He says he hid them separately. Which means they're still out there somewhere, waiting to be found." Ammon thought of his father, who had spent his life chasing shadows of this mystery. Of his uncle Marcus, who had died still searching. Of generations of Lundquists consumed by a hunt they never fully understood.

Hathenbruck had given them a trail to follow—but he'd removed the most crucial pieces and hidden them somewhere else. He'd wanted his descendants to find the chamber, to take their place in its protection. But the First Temple? That, he'd kept even from his own family.

"Why would he do this?" Ammon asked.

"If the First Temple is real, if it's as significant as he suggests—why hide it? Why not trust the guardians with everything?" Thomas's answer came with care.

"Because guardianship isn't just about keeping secrets. It's about understanding what those secrets could do if they fell into the wrong hands."

He met Ammon's eyes, and there was a new light in his gaze—a wariness that hadn't been there before.

"Your ancestor trusted us with the chamber because he believed we could protect it. But the First Temple... whatever it is, he believed it was too dangerous for anyone to know. Even us."

"But now we know it exists," Chen said.

"The First Temple is real, and somewhere out there are pages that describe exactly where to find it." Robert rose from his chair—with the careful movements of age—and moved to the table.

"And if we know, others will find out soon enough. Information this significant doesn't stay secret for long. Not in the modern world." His eyes swept over the photographs, the translations.

"The question is not whether others will seek these pages. The question is who will find them first." Ammon looked around the secure room—at the reinforced walls, the monitored doors, the protocols designed to prevent exactly this kind of leak. Six months of building trust, proving that the past could be protected. And now a secret that his own ancestor had tried to bury forever was rising to the surface.

"What do we do?" he asked. Thomas didn't answer immediately. His gaze fixed on some point beyond the walls. When he spoke, his voice carried the finality of decision.

"We find those pages before anyone else does. And then we decide—together—whether the world is finally ready for what they contain." The words should have been a plan. Instead, they seemed like the first step into darkness. He thought of Hathenbruck, alone in this chamber over a century ago, making choices that would echo through generations.

Standing in the same space, facing the same impossible questions, Ammon wasn't sure his ancestor had been wrong.

CHAPTER FIVE

The Second Gift

Clara was expecting them this time.

The drive to Denver was different than it had been six months ago, when Ammon had made this journey not knowing if his aunt would even open her door. Now she had called twice to confirm they were coming, to ask if they needed anything, to say she'd been going through the attic.

"She sounds different," Aspen said.

"She is different." Ammon watched the mountains recede in the mirror. "We all are."

Clara met them at the door with what might have been a smile. The interior of the house had changed too—family photographs now lined the hallway, and the living room seemed less like a museum exhibit than a home.

"I've been thinking about what you found," Clara said, settling into her chair. "About Hathenbruck's archive and everything he preserved. And I realized—there might be more."

"More?"

"When I was young, my mother told me stories about Anna. About how she kept Friedrich's secrets after he died, passed them down through the family." Clara rose and moved toward the hallway. "She mentioned letters once. Anna's personal correspondence, stored somewhere in the house. I never looked for them—I didn't want to know. But now..."

She led them up narrow stairs to the attic, pulling a chain that brought a single bare bulb flickering to life. Boxes labeled in faded handwriting—*Christmas decorations 1987, Mother's china, DO NOT OPEN*—were stacked against sloped walls.

"If the letters exist, they'd be in here somewhere. I never had the courage to look." Clara's voice was soft. "I was afraid of what I might find. What other secrets the family had buried."

They spread out across the cramped space, opening boxes, sifting through generations of accumulated life. Ammon found old photographs, report cards from the 1940s, a collection of buttons in a rusted tin. But it was Aspen who found the letters.

The box was unmarked, shoved into a corner beneath a pile of moth-eaten quilts. Inside, wrapped in brown paper that crumbled at the touch, lay a bundle of envelopes tied with faded ribbon—and beneath them, a leather portfolio embossed with Anna Hathenbruck's initials.

"These are hers," Aspen breathed. "Anna's."

The letters were in German, written in a precise feminine hand. Ammon translated, piecing together fragments of a life lived in the shadow of an enormous secret. Most were mundane—household matters, news of children and grandchildren, the small concerns of daily existence. But near the bottom of the stack, he found something different.

A letter from Friedrich himself, dated 1926—two years before his death. The paper was fragile, threatening to crack along the fold lines, but the handwriting was unmistakably Hathenbruck's.

"*My dearest Anna,*" Ammon translated. "*I write this knowing you may never read it, but I must set down somewhere the weight I carry. I have told you of the sacred chamber, of the archive I created to preserve its knowledge. But there is something I have told no one—a discovery I made decades ago that troubles me still.*"

He paused, his hands trembling. Clara and Aspen leaned closer.

"*Among the oldest texts in the chamber, I found references to something called the First Temple—a place described as 'the source from which all knowledge flows.' The chamber we protect is not the original repository. It is merely a branch, one of many scattered across the world when some ancient catastrophe forced the keepers to divide their wisdom.*"

"The First Temple," Aspen whispered. "Just like the hidden pages said."

"*I have removed from my archive all pages relating to this First Temple. The knowledge they contain is too dangerous—not because of what it reveals about history, but because of what it could enable. The coordinates I found would lead to a place of immense power, and I have seen enough of human nature to know that such power must remain hidden until humanity proves itself worthy.*"

Ammon's voice caught. "*I have left two gifts for our descendants. One in the tree where I first met my teacher. One in the church where I first understood what I was protecting. The first gift preserves knowledge. The second preserves the key to knowledge yet hidden. May whoever finds them have the wisdom to know the difference.*"

"Two gifts," Clara said. "You found the tree. The shadow archive. But the church..."

"He was a religious man," Ammon said. "His journal mentions attending services, finding comfort in faith. But which church? There must have been dozens in the territory."

Aspen was already pulling out their phone. "His first years in America. Where did he settle before he went to the mountains?"

"Texas," Ammon remembered. "San Antonio. He mentions it in the journal—working at a German immigrant community before he traveled west."

"Then that's where we look. For a church that meant something to a German immigrant doctor in the late 1860s." Aspen's eyes met his. "For the second gift."

CHAPTER SIX

Old Sins

The visiting room of the Federal Correctional Institution at Englewood smelled of industrial disinfectant layered over something older and more human—sweat, anxiety, the desperation of people forced to conduct outside conversations under fluorescent lights. Margaux Vance had been here three times in the past eight months, and the smell never changed. Neither, unfortunately, did her father. She sat in a molded plastic chair that had been designed for neither comfort nor dignity, her hands folded on a metal table scarred with decades of fingernail scratches and desperate graffiti that the guards had tried to sand away. Around her, other families conducted their own awkward reunions—a woman bouncing a toddler who kept reaching for a father he barely knew, an elderly couple sitting in silence across from a son who wouldn't meet their eyes.

The buzz of the overhead lights competed with hushed conversations and the occasional bark of a guard's instructions. Elias Vance entered through the security door with the unhurried grace of a man attending a faculty dinner. At sixty-seven, he wore prison-issue khakis that should have diminished him, yet somehow made the uniform look like a deliberate fashion choice—casual Friday at a country club. His silver hair was neatly combed, his posture erect, his expression carrying that particular warmth he deployed like a precision instrument.

"Margaux." He settled into the chair across from her, taking a moment to arrange himself as though the plastic seat were a leather wingback. His eyes moved over her face with the clinical attention of a collector appraising an acquisition.

"You've been sleeping poorly. Those circles under your eyes—that's not jet lag, that's worry. And you've been skipping meals again. I can see it in your clavicles." A small smile.

"The Michaelmas term must be particularly demanding this year." Margaux kept her expression neutral, though her jaw tightened. Even now, even here, he couldn't resist demonstrating his perceptiveness—couldn't simply say hello like a normal person. She'd learned long ago that showing emotion around her father was a tactical error.

"You said it was important."

"Straight to business. You get that from your mother—she never had patience for the social pleasantries either." He steepled his fingers, a gesture she remembered from childhood, from board meetings she'd been allowed to observe, from the night he'd explained why the Caravaggio they'd bought needed to disappear before the Italian authorities asked uncomfortable questions.

"Tell me, have you been following the Utah situation?"

"Everyone has. Ancient chamber found in the Uintas, evidence of pre-Columbian contact, the tribal nation and academics working together." She recited the facts flatly, refusing to give him the engagement he was fishing for.

"It's been significant news in archaeological circles."

"The public news. The sanitized version." Elias leaned forward, and she saw it—that brightness in his eyes she remembered from a hundred expeditions, a thousand late-night phone calls, the look that meant he'd caught the scent of something.

"'*Qui habet aures audiendi, audiat.' He who has ears to hear, let him hear.* The translation work they're doing has begun revealing things that haven't been made public. Things that could reshape our understanding of human history." Margaux's stomach tightened.

This was the pattern she'd spent years trying to escape—her father's obsessive pursuit of discoveries that always seemed just out of reach, always requiring one more investment, one more expedition, one more compromise of principle.

"I'm not here to chase shadows from a prison cell," she said.

"Whatever the Consortium was looking for—"

"Was never about treasure." His voice sharpened, the warmth evaporating.

"It was about knowledge. About proving that human history is far more complex and interconnected than the academic establishment has been willing to admit. Plato wrote of Atlantis; Herodotus described voyages to lands beyond the pillars. We dismissed them as mythology because the evidence was inconvenient." He spread his hands.

"The Utah chamber proves the evidence exists. I was right, Margaux."

"You were right that the chamber existed." She met his eyes.

"That doesn't vindicate how you tried to find it. The intimidation. The forgeries. The people who got hurt when your 'expeditions' went wrong." The silence that followed was thick enough to touch.

Margaux studied her father's face, saw a flicker behind his eyes—anger, perhaps, or closer to grief—before his expression smoothed into careful neutrality.

"'*Errare humanum est*,'" he said softly.

"*To err is human.* I let the pursuit become more important than the methods. But the underlying goal was never wrong." He paused, and when he spoke again, his tone had shifted—less the chairman commanding a board meeting, more a father asking something of his daughter.

"I need your help." She'd been expecting this. Dreading it.

"With what?"

"The Consortium's assets. The accounts in Zurich, the Caymans, Singapore. They're still there, frozen but accessible—to someone with the right authorization." His fingers drummed once against the metal table—the only nervous gesture she'd ever seen him make.

"I gave you those codes when you were eighteen. Insurance, I called it."

"I remember." She also remembered the sick feeling when she'd realized what those codes represented—a fortune built on stolen artifacts, smuggled antiquities, academic reputations destroyed.

"I've never touched that money."

"I know. You built your career on your own merits, separate from me. I respect that more than you realize." He held her gaze, and for a moment she almost believed she saw genuine admiration there.

"But now there's something called the First Temple—a site the codices describe as predating the Utah chamber by millennia. If it exists, if it can be found..." His voice dropped to barely above a whisper.

"This is what I spent my whole life looking for. Proof of civilizations we've never imagined. Proof that humanity's past is far greater than we've been taught." The conflict rose in Margaux's chest like bile. She'd devoted her academic career to trans-oceanic contact theories—the study of possible pre-Columbian connections between hemispheres.

It was a field full of cranks and amateurs, but also legitimate questions that mainstream archaeology refused to take seriously. The Utah discovery had already validated some of her theoretical work. If the First Temple was real, it could vindicate everything she'd dedicated her professional life to. But accepting her father's help meant accepting his methods. His money.

His legacy.

"I can't become what you were," she said.

"I'm not asking you to." He leaned back, spreading his hands in a gesture of surrender that she didn't believe for a moment.

"You have something I never had—legitimate credentials, institutional access, a reputation untainted by my mistakes. Use them. Investigate. Find out what's really being discovered in Utah and whether the First Temple exists."

"And if I find something?"

"Then we decide together what to do with it." His smile was warm, paternal, and entirely calculated.

"I'm in prison, Margaux. I can't run operations or fund expeditions. All I can offer is information and resources. What you do with them is your choice." It was a lie, of course.

Her father never relinquished control willingly. But it was a lie she could almost believe—or pretend to believe, which might be close enough.

"I'll look into it," she heard herself say, the words feeling like a surrender.

"But I'm not making promises. And if I find out you're using me to restart what you built—"

"You'll walk away. I understand." He raised his head with the graciousness of a man who had already won.

"Thank you, Margaux. For giving an old man one more chance." She stood, the plastic chair scraping against concrete with a sound that made her teeth ache. At the door, she paused, her hand on the frame.

"Why me?" she asked without turning around.

"You have other contacts. Other resources. Why involve your daughter?" A long pause. When he spoke, his tone had shifted—or perhaps she only imagined it.

"Because you're the only person I trust. The only one who understands what we could find and why it matters." Another pause.

"And because I owe you a truth I should have given you years ago. The hunt was never about acquiring things, Margaux. It was about proving that the world was bigger, older, more wonderful than anyone imagined. I lost sight of that sometimes. But you never did."

Margaux walked out without responding. The security corridor stretched before her like a throat—cinder block walls painted institutional beige, doors that required buzzing through, the echo of her heels against polished concrete. She kept her spine straight, her expression composed, aware that cameras tracked her progress and guards assessed her from behind reinforced glass. The last door released her into a waiting area that smelled of vending machine coffee and resignation, and then she was through the final checkpoint, retrieving her phone and keys from a plastic bin, signing the log with a hand that didn't shake. Outside, the Colorado afternoon hit her like absolution—crisp mountain air, a sky so aggressively blue it seemed fake, the Front Range rising in the distance like broken teeth against the horizon.

She stood on the concrete steps for a long moment, breathing, letting the prison atmosphere leach out of her clothes and hair. In her rental car, she sat with her hands on the wheel, not starting the engine. Through the windshield, the prison complex squatted against the landscape—razor wire glinting, guard towers punctuating the perimeter, all of it designed to contain men like her father. Men who believed their visions justified any cost. She caught her reflection in the rearview mirror—her father's eyes looking back at her—as the familiar cold fear rose that had haunted her since childhood.

Not fear of him. Fear of becoming him. Of waking up one day to find she'd crossed lines she couldn't uncross, justified compromises she couldn't unjustify. She'd spent fifteen years building a career separate from his shadow. Fifteen years proving she could succeed on her own merits, without his money or his introductions or his name opening doors.

Now he was asking her to step back into his world—to use resources accumulated through decades of crimes she'd spent her adult life pretending she didn't know about. It wasn't a choice. It was a trap. But she could also see the possibilities. The First Temple, if it existed, would be the find of the century.

And she was uniquely positioned to pursue it—with her father's resources, her own credentials, and knowledge that whatever academic competitors might be circling didn't yet have. She started the car and pulled out of the prison parking lot, her mind already mapping next steps.

In the visiting room, Elias Vance waited until his daughter's footsteps faded before allowing his expression to shift. The warmth drained from his features like water from a sink, leaving a colder expression, more calculating beneath. He had perhaps three minutes before the guards came to escort him back to his cell.

Long enough. The phone was a small thing, barely larger than his thumb, tucked into a space he'd spent considerable resources to create and maintain. He palmed it from its hiding spot and dialed the only number stored in its memory.

"Viktor," he said when the line connected.

"It's done. She's in."

"And if she proves too soft?" The voice on the other end carried the flattened vowels of Russian filtered through years abroad—professional, unhurried, devoid of the emotional complications that made other people so tedious to manage.

"Your daughter has scruples. They could become... inconvenient."

"Then you'll compensate for them." Elias spoke low, his eyes on the door.

"Track her progress. Report to me. And be ready to step in when the time comes."

"Understood. And the resources?"

"She has the access codes. If she won't use the accounts, we'll find another way." A pause.

"The First Temple is real, Viktor. I've spent my whole life searching for it, and now we're closer than ever. I won't let sentimentality get in the way."

"Even family sentimentality?"

"Especially family sentimentality."

The line went dead. Elias tucked the phone away just as the security door buzzed—the guards, right on schedule. He walked back to his cell with the measured pace of a man who had learned to find dignity in confinement. The concrete walls that had become his world held no power over him—not really. Walls were temporary.

Bars were temporary. The First Temple had waited for millennia; it could wait a little longer. Lying on his bunk, staring at the ceiling, Elias allowed himself a moment of genuine feeling. He did love his daughter. In his way.

In the only way he'd ever learned. But some things were more important than love. Some discoveries justified any sacrifice. The First Temple would be his legacy. One way or another.

CHAPTER SEVEN

The German Church

By the following afternoon, they'd traded the thin mountain air of Colorado for the Gulf Coast. The humidity hit Ammon like a wall the moment he stepped out of the rental car. San Antonio in late autumn carried an almost tropical warmth after the cold of the Utah mountains—but it was the moisture in the air that caught him off guard. Gulf Coast humidity, thick and heavy, pressing against his skin and settling into his lungs with each breath. His shirt clung to his back within seconds.

The limestone buildings seemed to sweat alongside him, their pale surfaces darkened in patches where moisture had seeped into the stone. Aspen emerged from the passenger side, squinting against the afternoon glare.

"St. Johannes Lutheran Church," they said, consulting their phone.

"Founded 1876 by German immigrants from the Rhineland. Decommissioned in 1952, converted to a museum of Texas German heritage in 1978." They looked up, pushing a strand of dark hair from their face where it had begun to stick.

"It's about a mile from here, in the King William Historic District." They walked through streets lined with Victorian mansions, their elaborate facades softened by the Spanish moss that draped from ancient oaks like gray-green lace. The trees provided merciful shade, though the air beneath them hung just as heavy. Ammon had done his research on the flight down—the German immigration to Texas was one of the largest in American history, bringing craftsmen, farmers, and intellectuals to a frontier that welcomed their skills and enterprise. Hathenbruck would have fit right in.

A German physician with scientific training and restless ambitions, seeking something in the American wilderness that Europe couldn't provide. A white panel van sat at the corner ahead—unremarkable except for the way it faced them, its dark windshield giving nothing away. Ammon's attention snagged on it, some instinct pricking at the back of his mind. He said nothing to Aspen, but he noticed when they passed that no one sat in the driver's seat. At least, no one visible.

The church appeared around the next corner, and for a moment Ammon forgot the van entirely. The limestone facade glowed golden in the afternoon light, warm as honey, the stone seeming to hold the sun's heat and radiate it back. A modest bell tower rose from one end, topped by a copper weathervane green with age. Beside the main doors, a brass plaque announced visiting hours and listed the museum's founding members. Inside, the temperature dropped fifteen degrees.

Ammon paused just past the threshold, letting his eyes adjust to the dimness while the cool air washed over him like a benediction. The space smelled of old wood and candle wax, of hymnals and history—the familiar perfume of sacred spaces that had absorbed decades of prayer and presence. Dust drifted through colored shafts of light where the afternoon sun pierced the stained glass windows, painting the worn floorboards in fragments of ruby and sapphire and gold.

"Beautiful craftsmanship," Aspen murmured, their ranger's eye moving across the space with professional appreciation.

"Look at those ceiling beams—hand-hewn, probably from local timber. And the pews are all original. You can tell by the wear patterns." They ran their fingers along the back of the nearest bench, tracing the groove worn smooth by generations of hands. Display cases held letters in cramped German script, sepia photographs of stern-faced pioneers, agricultural tools and household implements that testified to the practical ingenuity of the immigrant community.

The altar had been preserved, its wooden surface gleaming with the patina of age, and behind it the original stained glass depicted Christ as shepherd, his robes rendered in deep blues and purples that seemed to glow with their own inner light. An elderly woman sat at a desk near the entrance, her silver hair pinned in a style that might have been fashionable in the 1950s. She looked up as they approached, her eyes bright behind thick glasses, and Ammon caught the slight lilt in her voice before she even spoke—the ghost of an accent that had been German before it was Texan.

"Welcome to St. Johannes," she said, rising with the careful deliberation of someone who had learned to negotiate with aging joints.

"I'm Helga Weber—Pastor Weber, if you like, though I haven't led a congregation in twenty years. I volunteer here now, keeping the old place company." She smiled, and the years fell away from her face.

"Are you here for the regular tour, or is there something specific I can help you with?"

"Something specific, actually." Ammon stepped forward, choosing his words carefully.

"We're researching a German immigrant who spent time in San Antonio in the late 1800s. A physician named Friedrich Wilhelm Carl Hathenbruck. Our family records suggest he had a connection to this church." Pastor Weber's face transformed, her eyes widening behind her glasses.

"Hathenbruck? *Oh, mein Gott.*" She pressed a hand to her chest.

"Please, please, sit down." She gestured toward a pair of wooden chairs near her desk, her movements suddenly animated.

"Are you family? Descendants?"

"I'm his great-great-grandson," Ammon said, feeling the familiar weight of that lineage settle onto his shoulders.

"We've recently discovered some documents that suggest he helped fund construction here, but we're looking for more details."

"Helped fund construction," Pastor Weber repeated, and something between a laugh and a sob escaped her.

"Dr. Hathenbruck didn't just help—he paid for the entire altar reconstruction. The whole thing, every *pfennig*. It was quite the scandal at the time, *ja?* A stranger appearing from nowhere with that kind of money, no congregation membership, no family ties anyone knew of."

She leaned forward conspiratorially.

"Some of the old Frauen thought he must be a criminal. Or worse—a Catholic."

"Was he?" Aspen asked, a smile playing at the corner of their mouth.

"Heavens, no. He was a healer—one of the best the community had ever seen. He spent three months here in the winter of 1889, treating typhoid victims when the regular doctors had given up. Saved dozens of lives, they say." Pastor Weber's eyes grew distant, drawing on stories handed down through generations.

"My *Großmutter* used to say he had hands blessed by God himself. That he could look at your face and know what ailed you before you spoke a word." Ammon exchanged a glance with Aspen. 1889—the same year Hathenbruck had written his testimony in the guardian codex. The same year he claimed to have completed his shadow archive.

"The altar," he said carefully.

"You said he paid for it specifically?"

"Insisted on it, according to the church records. He said every community needed a place where heaven and earth could meet—where the sacred could touch the ordinary." She tilted her head, studying Ammon with new interest.

"You have his eyes, you know. I see it now. That same... intensity." Through the stained glass window, Ammon caught movement outside—a figure passing, silhouetted against the colored light. Walking too deliberately.

He forced his attention back to Pastor Weber.

"Would it be possible to examine the altar more closely?" he asked.

"The construction details, the woodwork—anything that might tell us more about his involvement?"

"For family?" Pastor Weber was already rising, reaching for a ring of old brass keys that hung from a hook beside her desk.

"Of course. Come, come. I'll show you everything." She led them down the center aisle, her footsteps echoing in the hushed space. The altar stood on a raised platform of limestone, three steps up from the main floor.

Up close, the woodwork was even more impressive—dark oak panels carved with intricate patterns of vines and wheat, symbols of abundance and life. The craftsmanship spoke of German precision, each joint fitted with an exactness that had allowed the structure to survive more than a century.

"The original altar was much simpler," Pastor Weber explained, running her weathered hand along the carved surface with obvious affection.

"Plain pine, functional. When Dr. Hathenbruck made his donation, he brought in craftsmen from Fredericksburg—German woodworkers who knew the old ways. Took them four months to complete." She paused, her fingers tracing a carved rosette.

"There's a dedication plaque somewhere... ah, here." She pointed to a small brass plate set into the altar's side, green with age. Ammon leaned close to read the inscription: "Donated by F. W. C. Hathenbruck, 1889. 'That which is hidden shall be revealed in its proper time.' "

The words sent a jolt through him. A message, hidden in plain sight for over a century. Waiting for someone who would understand.

"That inscription," he said, keeping the words steady with effort. "Do you know why he chose those words?"

"Scripture, I always assumed. Something from Ecclesiastes, perhaps, or the Gospels." Pastor Weber shrugged.

"He was a mysterious man, Dr. Hathenbruck. Generous, brilliant, but mysterious. He left as suddenly as he came—went west, they said. Looking for something in the mountains."

Aspen had moved to the other side of the altar, their eyes scanning the carved panels with the focus Ammon had come to recognize—the look they wore when tracking something through difficult terrain.

"Ammon," they said.

"Come look at this." He circled around to join them. They were pointing to a section of carving near the altar's base, a pattern of interlocking circles that was subtly different from the surrounding decoration. Where the other carvings were purely ornamental, these circles contained small symbols—a star, a serpent, a sun.

"That's not standard Lutheran iconography," Aspen murmured.

"And the craftsmanship here is different. Finer. Like it was added separately." Ammon's heart began to pound. He knelt beside the altar, running his fingers over the carved circles.

The wood was smooth, worn by time, but as he pressed against each symbol in turn, something shifted beneath the serpent—a tiny give, barely perceptible. He pressed harder. Nothing. Tried the star. Nothing.

Then, on instinct, he pressed the serpent and the sun simultaneously. A soft click echoed in the silent church.

"Was that—" Pastor Weber started, but Ammon was already feeling along the panel's edge, his fingers trembling, searching for the seam he knew must be there. He found it—a hairline crack, invisible unless you knew to look, running along the base of the altar where wood met stone. The panel swung inward with the faintest whisper of hinges, revealing a cavity perhaps six inches deep. Ammon's breath caught in his throat. Beside him, he heard Aspen's sharp intake of air.

Pastor Weber had gone completely still, one hand pressed to her mouth. Inside the hidden compartment, wrapped in oilcloth that had gone brittle with age, lay a small metal box. Ammon's hands shook as he lifted it out. The box was brass, tarnished nearly black in places, its surface engraved with symbols he didn't recognize—circles and lines, dots and curves, a language of geometry that seemed to whisper of older things than German churches and Texas towns. He held the box for a long moment, feeling its weight—heavier than it looked, dense with secrets.

The brass was cold against his palms despite the warmth of the day. This was it. Whatever Hathenbruck had left behind, whatever message he'd encoded in an altar paid for with mysterious funds, it rested in Ammon's hands. Slowly, carefully, he worked the lid open. The hinges resisted, then gave with a soft groan of metal that hadn't moved in over a century.

Inside, cushioned by what might once have been velvet—now faded to gray and crumbling at the edges—lay a single page of paper covered in dense handwriting. Hathenbruck's handwriting. Ammon recognized it immediately from the journal that had started his quest six months ago—the same precise Germanic script, the same confident strokes. But the text was different. Where the journal had used a cipher based on German medical terminology, this page was covered in symbols—circles and lines, dots and curves, a writing system that looked nothing like any alphabet Ammon had ever seen.

It matched the engravings on the box itself, as if box and message were two parts of a single puzzle.

"It's coded," he said, barely above a whisper. The disappointment mixed with a strange, fierce excitement.

"Different from the journal cipher. Different from anything in the codex."

"Can you read any of it?" Pastor Weber had moved closer, her earlier shock transforming into bright-eyed curiosity.

"What does it say?"

"Not yet." Ammon studied the page, his scholar's mind already cataloging patterns, looking for repetitions that might suggest vowels, clusters that might indicate common words. Near the bottom, below the main body of symbols, there was a line of text in German—the only readable portion of the document. He translated it aloud, his voice hushed in the sacred space: "'The physician's library holds the key.

Seek where the healer and the hunter meet.' "

"The physician's library," Aspen repeated.

"Another clue?"

"Another trail to follow." Ammon carefully photographed the page from multiple angles before wrapping it back in its protective cloth. He would need time to study this, consult experts, try to break the cipher. But the German text gave them a starting point.

The healer and the hunter. Asklepios and Orion. Something about the phrasing tickled at the edge of his memory—a reference he couldn't quite place, hovering just beyond reach.

"Thank you," he said to Pastor Weber, closing the hidden compartment with a soft click.

"You've been incredibly helpful. More than you know."

"Anything for family," she said, beaming despite the wonder still evident in her face.

"Anything that helps understand Dr. Hathenbruck. He was—he is—a mystery. Appeared from nowhere, saved our community, then vanished just as suddenly. My grandmother wondered about him until the day she died."

"He went to Utah," Ammon said, rising and brushing dust from his knees.

"Spent the rest of his life protecting something he'd found in the mountains."

"Protecting?" Her voice sharpened with interest.

"That's an unusual word choice for a scholar."

"It's the right one, I think. He was a guardian more than anything else. Even when no one knew what he was guarding." They said their goodbyes and stepped out into the afternoon glare.

After the cool dimness of the church, the heat struck Ammon like opening an oven door, the humidity instantly beading on his skin. The light seemed too bright, too exposed, after the sheltered intimacy of the discovery. The white panel van was gone from the corner. Somehow, that was worse than if it had still been there. Ammon's mind was already racing ahead, cataloging research possibilities, experts to consult, databases to search.

The physician's library. There had to be a connection—a medical school, a hospital archive, something Hathenbruck had known about in the 1880s that still existed today— He was so absorbed in his thoughts that he almost missed it. A man stood across the street, leaning against a lamppost with studied casualness. Average height, athletic build, wearing clothes that were deliberately unremarkable—the kind of outfit designed to blend into any crowd. He held a smartphone, apparently checking messages, but his eyes flicked up at regular intervals.

Watching the church entrance. Watching Ammon and Aspen emerge. For a moment, their gazes met. The man's expression didn't change—didn't acknowledge the contact at all. But his posture shifted, a subtle straightening, a readiness that spoke of professional training.

Military, perhaps, or intelligence. Someone who had been taught to watch without being seen, and who didn't particularly care that he'd been spotted. Then he looked back at his phone and began walking away, disappearing into the flow of tourists and locals with a practiced ease that made Ammon's skin prickle.

"Ammon?" Aspen had noticed his pause, the sudden tension in his shoulders.

"What is it?"

"Someone was watching us." He spoke low, resisting the urge to turn and search for the man in the crowd.

"Professional, from the look of him. Not an amateur treasure hunter—something more serious." Aspen's expression hardened, their ranger's instincts snapping into focus.

"How long?"

"I don't know. There was a van parked on the corner when we walked up—white panel van, dark windows. It's gone now." He thought about the figure silhouetted against the stained glass, the one walking too deliberately past the church windows.

"If he was there when we arrived..."

"Then he knows about the church. About Pastor Weber." Aspen's voice went flat.

"About whatever we found in that altar." The warmth of the Texas afternoon turned oppressive. Six months of building a careful, protected research operation at the cultural center—and now, within days of discovering the First Temple's existence, they were already being watched.

"We need to be more careful," Ammon said.

"This isn't just academic anymore. Someone else knows we're looking."

"Someone else knows there's something worth looking for." Aspen pulled out their phone, already dialing.

"I'm calling Thomas. This changes everything." As they stepped away to make the call, Ammon stood in the shadow of the church where Hathenbruck had hidden his secrets and thought about his ancestor—a man who had spent decades protecting knowledge that others would kill to possess. Who had built hidden compartments and coded messages, leaving trails that only the dedicated could follow. Hathenbruck had known this day would come.

Had planned for it, prepared for it, tried to ensure that when the secrets finally emerged, they would fall into the right hands. But he couldn't have predicted everything. Couldn't have known who else might be hunting the same secrets, or what lengths they might go to find them. The brass box was heavy in Ammon's pocket. Heavy with possibility.

Heavy with danger. The hunt had begun in earnest. And Ammon was no longer sure he was the only one hunting.

CHAPTER EIGHT

Ghosts of the Network

Jonas West was three hours into decrypting Hathenbruck's new cipher when his past came knocking. He'd colonized half his apartment with the work. Three monitors formed a loose semicircle on the dining table he never used for dining, their blue glow the only light in the room. Empty Red Bull cans stood like sentinels along the windowsill. His pattern recognition software churned through substitution matrices while he hunched over a fourth screen—his laptop, balanced on the arm of a couch that had seen better decades—cross-referencing the new cipher against Hathenbruck's journal entries.

The cipher was elegant. He'd give the old German bastard that much. Not a simple substitution, not a transposition—something layered, probably keyed to a text Hathenbruck assumed his descendants would know. The Bible was the obvious candidate, but which version? Which book?

Jonas had been running Luther's German translation against the King James for two hours and getting nowhere. He loved it. The puzzle, the chase, the way his brain lit up when he caught the faintest whiff of a pattern. This was why he'd gotten into hacking in the first place—not the money or the thrill of trespass, but the pure intellectual joy of cracking something that didn't want to be cracked. Of course, these days he tried not to mention that to journalists.

The reformed hacker narrative played better without the part where he admitted he'd loved every minute of his criminal career. The chamber discovery had made him famous in ways he'd never anticipated, and the fame sat on him like a borrowed coat—wrong size, wrong cut, impossible to get comfortable in. Media outlets had latched onto his story: former black-hat turns hero, uses his skills to expose criminal conspiracy and protect ancient knowledge. There had been interviews, profiles, even a book deal he kept forgetting to respond to. The attention was flattering in the way a stranger's intense eye contact was flattering—nice for about three seconds, then deeply uncomfortable.

He was reaching for his fourth Red Bull—caffeine was a tool, not a vice, he told himself—when his secondary monitor flickered. Not a crash. The software kept running, the algorithms kept churning. But in the corner of the screen, a small notification had appeared. An encrypted message, routed through relay channels that officially no longer existed, using protocols he hadn't touched in six years.

His hand froze over the Red Bull can. His stomach dropped before his brain caught up. The message was two lines: Been watching the Utah story. We should talk. — Phantom

He stared at the name, and six years of careful reconstruction—the legitimate consulting business, the clean record, the fragile new life—seemed suddenly as thin as the screen displaying them.

Phantom. Real name David Reznick—a detail Jonas had learned only after the Collective scattered, when court documents from a case Phantom narrowly escaped became briefly public. They'd never met in person. Back in his black-hat days, they'd been part of a loose network that called itself the Ghost Collective—a rotating cast of hackers who specialized in the kind of infiltration that governments and corporations pretended was impossible. Phantom had been the best of them. Better than Jonas, which was saying something.

When the Collective had scattered—some imprisoned, some vanished, Jonas himself barely escaping prosecution through a combination of luck and a very expensive lawyer—Phantom had disappeared so completely that Jonas sometimes wondered if he'd imagined him. Apparently not. Jonas knew he should delete the message. Pretend he'd never seen it. The FBI had never fully bought his reformation story; any whiff of contact with his old associates could torch everything he'd built.

He thought about Ammon, about Dr. Tanaka, about the translation work that actually mattered. Then he thought about the phrase "watching the Utah story," and his fingers were typing before he'd made a conscious decision: Where and when? The response came in under three seconds: Liberty Park. Pavilion by the pond.

One hour. Come alone.

The pavilion was one of those faux-rustic structures that parks committees loved—thick wooden beams, a peaked roof that provided shade without walls, benches that faced the pond where ducks congregated like they were being paid to look picturesque. Jonas sat on the eastern bench, watching the water and trying to look like a man who'd come to enjoy nature rather than meet a ghost from his criminal past. He spotted the man approaching from the north path before he was consciously looking for him—something about the fluid, economical stride that suggested constant awareness of everything within a fifty-foot radius. Jonas had never met Phantom in person, but he'd seen the one photograph that existed: a blurry conference shot from a DEF CON afterparty, circa 2015.

The man approaching was older now, mid-forties probably, with gray touching his temples and the kind of lines around his eyes that came from too many late nights staring at screens. But the way he moved—that was unmistakable. Hackers who'd survived as long as Phantom had developed certain instincts, and those instincts showed in the body.

"Jonas West." Phantom settled onto the far end of the bench, leaving three feet of deliberate space between them.

"The media darling. The reformed hacker who saved the sacred chamber."

"David. You look like you've actually seen sunlight. I'm impressed."

"Mediterranean sabbatical. Three years in Portugal before I got bored." Phantom's smile was thin, more reflex than warmth.

"Most of the old Collective is dead or in prison. We're the lucky ones who found exits."

"Lucky." Jonas let the word sit there for a moment, tasting its inadequacy.

"Why are you here?"

"Because interesting things are happening, and you're standing in the middle of them without knowing it." Phantom pulled out a phone, held it casually, the way someone might check messages. Jonas recognized the gesture—a prop, something to do with his hands while his eyes stayed on the environment.

"Someone's hiring. Reaching out to what's left of our community, offering real money for specific work."

"What kind of work?"

"Full penetration of the tribal cultural center's systems. Email, documents, internal communications—everything the translation team is touching."

Phantom's eyes never quite met Jonas's, staying instead on the pond, the paths, the other park visitors. Professional paranoia, burned deep.

"They want to know what you're finding before you know you've found it." Jonas's hands went still on his knees—the same stillness that used to come over him when a hack was about to go wrong.

"Who?"

"First buyer, I don't have a name. Money trail's buried under enough shells to stock an aquarium. But the methods they specified—the approach, the tools, the operational security—that's intelligence community training. Not government, though.

Private sector. Someone who learned the craft on Uncle Sam's dime and then went freelance."

"Consortium remnants."

"Maybe." Phantom turned the phone over in his hands, a nervous habit that didn't match his controlled voice.

"But there's a second buyer. That's what got my attention." Phantom looked at him, and Jonas saw a shift in those eyes that surprised him: genuine worry. Not the calculated concern of someone angling for advantage, but the real thing.

"Same targets, different methods. Older methods. More patient. They pay through channels that trace back to European foundations with histories measured in centuries, not decades. One of my contacts called them 'the Church,' though whether that's literal or code, I couldn't tell you."

Jonas's mind raced. The Vatican's long history with archaeological controversies. The Galileo affair.

Rumors about hidden archives, suppressed discoveries, quiet interventions whenever something surfaced that challenged established narratives.

"You're saying the actual Vatican might be interested in Utah?"

"I'm saying someone with very deep pockets and very long memories is paying attention to what your friends are digging up." Phantom stood, tucking the phone away.

"The work you're doing, the people you're helping—they're swimming in waters that have sharks they can't see."

"Why tell me?" Jonas stood too, suddenly unwilling to let Phantom have the height advantage. "What's your angle?"

Phantom was quiet for a moment.

When he spoke, his voice had dropped the professional flatness, something more human bleeding through.

"We did bad things back in the day. Both of us. I've spent years trying to make peace with that, finding ways to use what I know without making the world worse." He smiled faintly.

"You found something worth protecting. That's more than most of us managed. I'd hate to see it burned because you didn't know what you were walking into." He turned to leave, then paused.

"One more thing. The first buyer—the one with the intelligence training—they've already received preliminary data. Intercepted communications, schedules, personnel files. They know about your translation progress. They know about the new researcher who showed up last month.

They know about your security upgrades." His expression hardened.

"They know enough to hurt you."

"How do you know what they received?" Phantom's smile went crooked, self-mocking.

"Because I sold it to them. Before I understood what they were really after." He shrugged, the gesture carrying more weight than the casual movement suggested.

"The money was good. I didn't ask questions. That's how I used to operate."

Anger hit Jonas like a system crash—total, immediate, and completely unproductive.

Phantom had compromised them.

Had sold their communications, their schedules, their people, and was standing here pretending to be helpful.

"And the second buyer? The Church?"

"Them too." Phantom met his eyes now, unflinching.

"Like I said—good money, no questions. But I've learned more since then. What's in that chamber, what it means—that's bigger than profit. That's why I'm giving you this warning free of charge." He paused, something shifting in his expression.

"After this conversation, I'm gone. Really gone this time. I've burned too many bridges trying to play both sides. Whatever happens next, you won't see me again." He walked away before Jonas could respond, disappearing into the park's wandering crowds with the ease of long practice.

Jonas stood by the pavilion for a long time, following the ducks as they drifted across the pond like nothing in the world had changed. Two buyers. At minimum, two separate factions with access to their communications, their schedules, their people. One with intelligence training and deep pockets—Consortium remnants seemed likely. One with the patience and resources of an institution that measured its history in millennia.

And somewhere in the data Phantom had sold them, information about Dr. Tanaka. About the translation work. Maybe about the new codex discoveries. Jonas pulled out his phone and called Ammon.

"We need to talk," he said when the line connected.

"In person. Somewhere you're sure is clean." He paused, following a family of four walk past—mother, father, two kids throwing bread at the ducks—and wondered how many of the other park visitors were actually as innocent as they looked.

"There are people watching. More than we thought. And they've already been inside our systems." Silence on the line. Then Ammon's voice, stripped of its usual academic warmth: "How bad?"

"Bad enough that they know about Tanaka. About the translation progress. Maybe about the new codex material." Jonas leaned closer, though no one was close enough to hear.

"And that's just the buyers I know about. There might be others." A long pause. Then: "Get to the cultural center. Tonight. We need everyone together for this."

Jonas ended the call and pocketed the phone. The afternoon sun was warm on his face, the park beautiful in that manicured way that municipal parks always managed, and none of it touched the cold settling into his chest. He'd thought going legitimate meant leaving the shadows behind. Building something clean on top of the wreckage of who he used to be.

But shadows didn't work that way. They followed. They waited. And the ones gathering around the Utah discovery were darker than anything he'd encountered in his black-hat days. He started walking toward his car, scanning the park with new eyes.

Every jogger, every dog-walker, every person sitting alone on a bench—any of them could be watching. Any of them could be reporting back. The game had changed. And Jonas wasn't sure any of them were ready for what was coming.

CHAPTER NINE

The Physician's Library

The University of Texas at Austin sprawled across forty acres of Texas hill country, its red-roofed buildings rising from manicured lawns. Ammon had visited the campus once before, years ago, for an academic conference on frontier history. The scale of it had impressed him then. Now, walking toward the Perry-Castañeda Library with Aspen and Dr. Tanaka, all he could think about was how many places there were to hide.

Jonas's warning had changed everything. Two factions, at minimum, with unknown resources and unknown goals. Professional surveillance already in place. And somewhere in the background, something Phantom had called "the Church"—a presence that suggested stakes far beyond treasure hunting or academic rivalry.

They'd debated whether to continue the investigation at all. Thomas had argued for pulling back, consolidating their security, waiting until they better understood what they were facing. But Ammon had pushed back. Every day they waited was a day their competitors could be getting closer to the First Temple. The only way out was through.

Still, they'd taken precautions. Jonas was monitoring communications, looking for signs of interception. Thomas had increased security at the cultural center. And they'd chosen to approach the next clue—the physician's library—without advance publicity or official channels.

Dr. Tanaka had been the one to make the connection. "Hathenbruck was a physician," she'd said when Ammon showed her the coded page from the church altar. "If he donated medical texts anywhere, the most likely repository would be a major research library. Texas had some of the best medical collections in the country during that era."

A few hours of research had confirmed her hypothesis. The University of Texas medical archives held a collection of nineteenth-century German medical texts, several of which had been donated by one "Dr. F. W. C. Hathenbruck" in 1891. The collection had been catalogued but never thoroughly examined—just another set of historical documents in a library that held millions.

The archivist who met them in the rare books room was a thin woman in her fifties named Dr. Rosario, whose eyes lit up when they explained their research interest.

"The Hathenbruck donation? Oh, that's wonderful. No one's looked at those volumes in decades." She led them through climate-controlled corridors where the air held a particular stillness—not just quiet, but the dense, thrumming silence of carefully regulated temperature and humidity. The faint mechanical breath of HVAC systems provided the only soundtrack.

"We have the original donation register, if you'd like to see it. Dr. Hathenbruck specified very particular conditions for the gift—insisted that the books be kept together, preserved in their original condition, available to any 'qualified seeker' who asked for them by name."

"Qualified seeker," Ammon repeated. "He used that specific phrase?"

"According to the register, yes. Somewhat unusual language for an academic donation, but we've honored his wishes."

Dr. Rosario gestured toward a table where a dozen volumes had been arranged, their leather bindings cracked with age. "Here they are. Mostly German medical treatises—anatomy, pathology, pharmacology. Standard references for a nineteenth-century physician."

Tanaka was already moving toward the books, her professional interest overriding any pretense of casual curiosity. She pulled on the white cotton gloves Dr. Rosario provided—the fabric impossibly thin, almost ceremonial—and lifted the first volume carefully, examining its spine and cover.

"This binding is exquisite," she murmured. "Hand-tooled leather, gold leaf embossing. These weren't ordinary medical texts—these were investments. Someone meant them to last."

While Tanaka examined the books, Ammon found himself drifting toward the room's tall windows. Austin spread out below them, a city that had grown from frontier town to tech hub in barely a century. So much change, so much transformation—and yet here they were, chasing secrets left by a man who had walked these same Texas lands before automobiles or airplanes or the internet existed.

"You're quiet," Aspen said, appearing at his elbow. They'd been tracking the room's entrances, he noticed—always alert, always aware of potential threats. The surveillance training they'd received after becoming security lead for the chamber project had changed them in subtle ways.

"Thinking about time," he said. "About how the past keeps reaching into the present, no matter how much we try to move forward."

"That's what archaeology is, isn't it? The past reaching into the present."

"I suppose. But usually the past just wants to be understood. This past—Hathenbruck's past—it's different. It wants something from us. Wants us to act, to choose, to take on responsibilities we never asked for."

Aspen was quiet for a moment. When they spoke, their voice was softer than usual.

"Is that really so different from any inheritance? My family passed down the guardian tradition without asking whether I wanted it. Your family passed down the search for the chamber. We both ended up here because of choices other people made, generations ago."

"And that doesn't bother you?"

"Sometimes. But then I think about what they were protecting, and why, and I realize..." They trailed off, searching for words. "They didn't just pass down responsibility. They passed down meaning. Purpose. Something to believe in that's bigger than any individual life." They met his eyes. "That's worth something, isn't it?"

Before Ammon could answer, Tanaka's voice cut through the quiet.

"I found something."

They crossed to where she sat hunched over one of the medical texts, a thick volume on surgical techniques that had fallen open to its middle pages. In the margins, barely visible against the yellowed paper, was writing—but not ordinary writing. The symbols were rendered in iron gall ink that had aged to a rusty sepia, the strokes precise and deliberate despite their miniature scale. Some characters resembled Greek letters; others looked almost like musical notation; still others were entirely unfamiliar, geometric shapes nested within curves.

"It's the same cipher," Tanaka breathed. "Look—the symbol patterns, the spacing, the way certain characters repeat. Whoever wrote the church document also annotated this book." Her finger hovered above the page, trembling with excitement. "The handwriting—see how the descenders curve? Identical to the San Antonio page. Same hand, same ink formula, same deliberate spacing."

"Can you read it?" Ammon asked.

"Not directly. But I can analyze it, look for patterns, try to break the code." Her eyes were bright, almost feverish, with the focused intensity of an academic confronting a genuine puzzle. "It's definitely a substitution cipher of some kind, but more complex than the one in Hathenbruck's journal. Multiple symbol sets, possibly representing different concepts or categories. God, this is beautiful. The complexity—whoever designed this was a genius."

She pulled out her phone and began photographing the marginalia, page by page, her movements quick and almost frantic. "There's a lot here. Annotations on almost every page, some just a few symbols, others entire paragraphs. Whatever Hathenbruck wanted to communicate, he distributed it across the entire book. This could take weeks to decode. Maybe months. I might have to develop entirely new analytical frameworks—"

"A security measure," Aspen said, gently interrupting. "Anyone who found just one page would only get a fragment. You'd need the whole collection to assemble the complete message."

"Clever," Tanaka agreed, barely slowing down. "And it means this isn't just a clue pointing somewhere else. This might be the actual information— whatever Hathenbruck considered important enough to hide. I need better equipment. Spectral analysis. Pattern recognition software. My lab at Stanford—"

"Utah first," Ammon said. "We need secure facilities."

They spent the next two hours documenting everything. Dr. Rosario hovered nearby, fascinated by their interest in a collection she'd always considered minor. By the time they finished, Tanaka had photographed over three hundred pages of marginalia, enough raw material to keep her analysis algorithms busy for days.

"I can work on this back in Utah," she said as they prepared to leave. "Cross-reference the symbol patterns, look for frequency distributions, try to identify anchor points that might unlock the rest. If I'm lucky, I'll have preliminary results within a week."

"If we have a week," Ammon said. The surveillance incident in San Antonio weighed on his mind—the knowledge that their movements were being tracked, their discoveries observed.

They were walking through the library's main corridor, heading for the exit, when Tanaka suddenly stopped.

"The marginalia," she said. "I just realized—one section was different from the others. Clearer, more deliberate, like it was meant to be the key to everything else."

She pulled up the photograph on her phone, enlarging the image until a particular annotation filled the screen. Unlike the other symbols, this one included German text—a phrase that Ammon translated immediately:

"Der Treffpunkt von Asklepios und Orion—wo der Heiler und der Jäger sich begegnen."

"The meeting place of Asklepios and Orion—where the healer and the hunter meet," he said aloud.

"The same phrase from the church document," Aspen said. "He's repeating himself."

"Or emphasizing." Tanaka's brow furrowed in concentration. "Asklepios is the Greek god of medicine—the healer. Orion is the hunter. In astronomical terms..." Her eyes widened. "They're constellations. Asklepios is another name for Ophiuchus, the serpent-bearer. And on certain nights of the year, Ophiuchus and Orion are visible together in the sky, aligned in specific ways depending on your location."

"So the meeting place isn't a physical location," Ammon said. "It's an astronomical event. A specific alignment visible from somewhere."

"Which means the location is determined by where you need to stand to see that alignment correctly." Tanaka was already typing on her phone, pulling up star charts and astronomical databases. "This is going to take some calculation. The positions of constellations change over time—precession of the equinoxes—so I'll need to figure out what the sky looked like in Hathenbruck's era, then work backward to find the viewing coordinates."

"Can you do that?"

"Given enough time and processing power? Absolutely." She looked up with a fierce grin. "This is exactly the kind of puzzle I specialize in."

They emerged from the library into the fading afternoon light. The campus was quieting as the day wound toward evening, long shadows stretching across the limestone paths as students drifted toward dormitories and off-campus apartments. The air had cooled, carrying the faint scent of freshly cut grass and something else—the electric anticipation of a Texas evening about to unfold.

Ammon was already thinking about next steps—getting Tanaka secure transport back to Utah, coordinating with Jonas on communications security, updating Thomas on their progress—when Aspen's hand closed on his forearm.

A warning grip. They went still beside him, their body shifting into a stance he recognized from their time together: weight balanced, center low, ready.

"Ten o'clock," they murmured. "Doorway. He's been there since we came out."

Ammon spotted him—a figure in the shadowed alcove of a side entrance, unremarkable clothes, casual posture that somehow communicated anything but relaxation. The man didn't move. He was observing them observe him.

Then he stepped forward into the dying light, and Ammon recognized him. The same man from San Antonio. The one who had been watching them outside the church.

Viktor Semenov moved like water flowing around stones—economical, unhurried, each step placed with the precision of someone who had learned long ago that rushed movement was wasted movement. He was shorter than average but broad through the shoulders, with the compact muscularity of someone who trained for efficiency rather than show. His silver-streaked hair was cropped close, and his gray eyes held the patient calculation of a predator assessing whether prey was worth the effort.

He crossed the fifteen feet between them in what seemed both an instant and an eternity, and when he stopped, he positioned himself exactly where he could watch all three of them while keeping the library's main entrance at his back. Cutting off their retreat.

Ammon catalogued exit routes automatically—a habit he'd developed in the months since the chamber discovery. The main path behind Viktor. A side route through the architecture quad to their left. Emergency exits somewhere in the building behind them, but they'd have to turn their backs to reach them.

"Dr. Lundquist." Viktor's voice was accented—Russian, refined, the consonants softened by what sounded like years in Western Europe. The voice of a man who had learned to be charming in multiple languages. "Dr. Tanaka. Ranger Rhoades. A productive afternoon, I hope."

Aspen moved immediately, positioning themself between Viktor and the others. Their right hand drifted toward their hip—where their service weapon would be if they were on duty. They weren't armed today. Ammon saw them register that fact, saw them recalculate.

"Who are you?" they demanded.

"No one of consequence." Viktor's smile was thin and cultured, the expression of a man who found genuine amusement in his own private jokes. "An observer, merely. A student of human nature, you might say. I find it fascinating, the lengths people will go to for knowledge. The sacrifices they're willing to make."

His eyes swept across all three of them, assessing, cataloguing. Ammon had the uncomfortable sensation of being inventoried.

"You've been very diligent in your research. Very thorough. But you're not the only ones who understand what Hathenbruck left behind. And my employers are growing impatient."

Tanaka had gone pale, her phone still clutched in her hand. Ammon saw her thumb move across the screen—texting Jonas, he hoped. Calling for help they couldn't expect to arrive in time.

"Who are your employers?" Ammon asked, keeping steady.

"For now? That's not your concern." Viktor spread his hands—a gesture of openness more threatening than a clenched fist. "What matters is that you understand you're being watched. That every move you make, every discovery you uncover, is being noted and analyzed. Every conversation. Every phone call. Every moment you believe you're alone."

He paused, letting the words settle.

"Consider this a professional courtesy. We're not enemies yet. Whether we become enemies depends entirely on the choices you make next."

"And if we refuse to be intimidated?"

Viktor's smile widened—the expression of a teacher pleased by a student's predictable response.

"Intimidation. Such an ugly word. I prefer to think of this as... education. You're intelligent people. Surely you understand that there are forces in this world larger than academic curiosity. Older than your universities, your governments, your comfortable assumptions about how power operates."

He took one step closer. Aspen tensed.

"The Consortium has resources you can barely imagine, Dr. Lundquist. Expertise. Manpower. Influence in places that would keep you awake at night if you understood what I'm telling you."

Ammon said nothing. There was nothing to say that wouldn't sound like bravado or weakness.

"They've been in this business far longer than your family has been searching," Viktor continued. "Longer than America has been a country."

He stepped aside then, clearing the path with an almost courtly gesture.

"Continue your research. By all means. Find what Hathenbruck hid. You're doing excellent work, and my employers appreciate efficiency." His voice dropped, losing its pleasant veneer. "But understand this: when you find it—and you will find it, because they've decided to let you—there will be a reckoning. Others have claims to this knowledge. Older claims, some would say, than yours. The question is whether you'll be wise enough to recognize that when the moment comes."

Without waiting for a response, he turned and walked away. Not hurried. Not looking back. The walk of a man who had absolute confidence that no one would be foolish enough to follow him.

He disappeared around the corner of the library building, and the evening seemed to exhale.

For a long moment, none of them moved. Then Tanaka exhaled, and Ammon realized his hands were shaking. The adrenaline dump hit him all at once—heart pounding, mouth dry, every nerve ending suddenly screaming that they needed to move, to run, to get somewhere safe.

"That was—" Tanaka's voice cracked. She tried again. "That was terrifying."

"That was a warning," Aspen said grimly. They were scanning the area now, checking windows, doorways, the paths between buildings. Looking for backup. For other watchers. "He wanted us scared. Wanted us to know they're watching every move. And he wanted us to know they could have done more than talk."

"Well, he succeeded." Tanaka's voice was shaky, but her jaw was set. Her hands trembled as she pocketed her phone. "I'm terrified. But I'm also angry. Who does he think he is, threatening scholars on a university campus? We should call campus security. The police. Someone."

"And tell them what?" Ammon asked. "A man spoke to us? Made vague threats? He didn't break any laws. Didn't touch us. Didn't even raise his voice."

He looked at the path Viktor had taken, empty now in the evening light.

"That's the point. That's why they sent someone like him. He's a message, not a weapon. The weapon comes later, if we don't listen."

"We need to move," Aspen said. "Now. Assume we're still being watched. Don't go back to the hotel—they'll have that covered. There's a car rental place two miles from here. We get a new vehicle, we take a route nobody's expecting, and we don't stop until we're somewhere secure."

They were already walking, not waiting for agreement. Ammon and Tanaka fell in beside them, moving quickly across the darkening campus.

"Someone who represents people willing to kill for what we're looking for," Ammon said, his mind processing what had just happened. "The First Temple—whatever it is, whatever it contains—it's important enough to draw this kind of attention. Important enough to risk open confrontation."

Tanaka clutched her phone tighter, her knuckles white. "What do we do?"

"We keep going," Ammon said. The words surprised him even as he spoke them. An hour ago, he'd been a historian chasing a family mystery. Now he was something else. Something he hadn't asked to become.

"We find what Hathenbruck hid before they do. We figure out what's worth threatening people over." He met Aspen's eyes, then Tanaka's. "And we make damn sure we're ready for whatever comes next."

The game had changed. And there was no going back now—only through.

CHAPTER TEN

Convergence

San Antonio — 8:47 PM

The hotel room looked exactly as they'd left it. That was the first sign something was wrong.

Ammon stood in the doorway, scanning the space with new awareness. The beds were made with military precision. Their laptops sat on the desk, closed but positioned at subtly different angles than he remembered. The curtains hung straight and even, though Aspen had left them partially open that morning.

"Don't touch anything," Aspen said. They'd noticed the same details, their training kicking in automatically. "Someone's been here."

They searched the room methodically, looking for what had been taken—and what had been left behind. Their clothes were undisturbed. Their documents remained in the hotel safe, untouched. The electronics showed no signs of tampering, though Jonas would need to examine them properly to be sure.

The message was clear: We can reach you whenever we want. We chose not to. This time.

"Viktor's people," Tanaka said. She was pale but composed, her scientist's mind processing the violation analytically. "They wanted us to know they're watching. That nowhere is safe."

Jonas had arrived an hour earlier. He'd driven through the night from Utah after Ammon's call about Viktor's confrontation at the library. His presence was a small comfort—another set of trained eyes, another mind working the problem.

"I should check the electronics first," Jonas said, already reaching for the laptops.

"Don't." Tanaka's voice cracked on the word. Her hands were shaking— she'd shoved them into the pockets of her cardigan, but Jonas could see the tremor in her shoulders. "Isolate the devices first. Standard protocol."

She wasn't looking at him. She was looking at the laptops like they might explode.

"Yuki." He used her first name deliberately. "I've done this before."

"So have I." Finally she met his eyes, and he saw something there he recognized: the particular terror of someone who had built their life on logic and procedure, seeing it all come apart. "That's how I know what happens when you skip steps."

Jonas's irritation collapsed into recognition. She wasn't being pedantic. She was holding herself together with procedure, the way he'd once held himself together with code.

"Okay," he said softly. "We do it by the book."

"Pack your things," Ammon said. "We're not staying here tonight."

They found a different hotel across the city, paying cash and using false names that Aspen provided from a kit they'd prepared for exactly this kind of emergency. Even then, Ammon couldn't shake the feeling of exposure—of invisible eyes tracking their every movement, noting every decision.

Standing in the new hotel's corridor, Ammon found himself staring at the fire exit sign—the red glow promising escape, anonymity, the simple life he'd had before the chamber. He could walk through that door. Get in the car. Drive until the mountains were behind him and the treasure hunt was someone else's problem.

Aspen would understand. Eventually. Thomas would find another way. The guardians had protected these secrets for generations without him—they would manage for generations more.

The temptation was so strong it had a taste: copper and exhaustion, the flavor of surrender.

Then he thought of his father. Of the generations of Lundquists who had searched and failed and died searching. Of Hathenbruck, alone in the wilderness, making choices that would echo through centuries.

He wasn't running. Not now. Not when they were finally close.

Later, in the new room, Ammon sat in an uncomfortable chair by the window while Jonas worked on the isolated electronics at the desk. Tanaka had retreated to the adjoining room, claiming she needed to review her notes.

Aspen emerged from the bathroom, their hair still damp from the shower. They crossed to where Ammon sat and settled onto the arm of his chair, their hip warm against his shoulder.

"You're brooding," they said.

"I'm thinking."

"Same thing, with you." They ran their fingers through his hair, a gesture so casual and intimate that it made something ache in his chest. Six months ago, they'd barely known each other. Now their touch was home.

"Talk to me."

He leaned into their hand. "Twelve hours ago, we were researchers following an academic puzzle. Now we're targets in a game whose rules we don't understand."

"We've been targets before."

"This feels different. More... professional. Viktor's people didn't take anything because they didn't need to. They already know everything we know. They're just letting us know they're watching."

Aspen was quiet for a moment. Their hand stilled in his hair, then resumed its gentle motion.

"When I was a ranger, we had a saying about mountain lions. If you see one, there's a good chance it's been watching you for miles. The visibility is the message."

"So what do you do when you spot the lion?"

"You don't run. You make yourself bigger. You show it you're not easy prey." They tilted his chin up so he was looking at them. In the dim light from the window, their eyes were dark and steady. "We're not easy prey, Ammon. We survived the chamber. We'll survive this too."

He reached up and covered their hand with his own. "I don't know what I'd do without you."

"You'd brood more and accomplish less." But they smiled as they said it, and bent to kiss him softly. "Get some sleep. Tomorrow we figure out our next move."

They slid off the chair arm and moved toward the bed. Ammon followed their movement, feeling the warmth of the moment fade into the cold reality of their situation.

His phone buzzed with an incoming email. He almost ignored it—another notification in an endless stream. But something about the sender's name caught his attention.

Dr. Margaux Vance, Oxford University — Subject: Proposed Collaboration — Hathenbruck Translation Project

He opened it with a mixture of curiosity and wariness.

Dear Dr. Lundquist,

I hope you'll forgive the unsolicited contact. Your recent work on the Uinta chamber discovery has attracted considerable attention in academic circles, and I believe we may have overlapping research interests. My specialty is pre-Columbian trans-oceanic contact theory—

specifically, the possibility of cultural exchanges between Old and New World civilizations prior to Columbus. I've been following the chamber translation project with great interest, and I've come across certain references in my own research that may be relevant to your work.

I'm currently in the United States attending a conference, and I wonder if we might meet to discuss potential collaboration. I believe I can offer expertise that would be valuable to your team, and in return, I would greatly appreciate the opportunity to contribute to what is clearly a breakthrough discovery. Please let me know if this would be possible. I'm flexible with timing and happy to travel to wherever is convenient for you.

Best regards,
Dr. Margaux Vance Professor of Archaeological Theory
St. Catherine's College, Oxford

Ammon read the message twice, his mind racing. On its face, it was exactly the kind of inquiry they'd been receiving since the chamber discovery went public—legitimate academics wanting to contribute to a significant project. The credentials seemed solid; he'd heard of St. Catherine's, remembered reading about trans-oceanic contact theories in graduate school.

But the timing seemed too convenient. Hours after Viktor's warning, after their hotel room was searched, an unknown academic reaches out wanting access to their research?

He couldn't shake the suspicion, even as he acknowledged it might be paranoia. After everything that had happened today, every stranger seemed a potential threat.

"What is it?" Aspen asked, noticing his expression from across the room.

"Maybe nothing. Maybe just bad timing." He forwarded the email to their phone. "An academic from Oxford wants to collaborate. Claims expertise in trans-oceanic contact theory."

Aspen crossed the room and took his phone, reading the message with narrowed eyes. "The day we get threatened and our room gets searched, someone new wants access to the project. That's a lot of coincidence."

"Could be exactly that—coincidence. These inquiries have been coming in for months."

"Could be." Aspen handed the phone back, their expression skeptical. "Or could be someone trying a softer approach after the hard one didn't scare us off."

"We'll need to research her thoroughly before responding," Ammon said. "Check the credentials, look for any connections that raise flags. No more assumptions about who's friendly."

He set the phone aside, but his mind kept returning to the email. Dr. Margaux Vance. The name meant nothing to him—no recognition, no warning bells beyond the timing. Just another academic, or something more?

In the morning, he'd have Jonas run a background check. For now, he needed sleep.

But sleep was a long time coming.

Over the Atlantic — Night

Margaux Vance stood in the aircraft's small lavatory, staring at her reflection in the mirror. The woman looking back at her had her mother's cheekbones and her father's eyes. She'd spent years trying to escape that combination—building an academic career under her own merits, publishing papers that stood on their research rather than family connections.

For a while, she'd almost convinced herself she was her own person.

Then her father went to prison, and the name Vance became synonymous with criminal conspiracy rather than archaeological innovation.

She pulled out her phone and scrolled to a saved voicemail—a message her father had left her three days before his arrest, when she'd still believed he was just an eccentric collector with unconventional methods.

"Margaux, darling. I know we don't speak as often as we should. But I want you to know—everything I've done, everything I've sought, it was never just for acquisition. There are truths buried in this world that deserve to be found. Truths that could change everything. I hope someday you'll understand that the pursuit of knowledge sometimes requires... flexibility."

Flexibility. Such a gentle word for bribery, theft, and—she now knew—worse.

She deleted the voicemail. Her thumb hovered over the trash folder for three seconds before she retrieved it.

She always retrieved it.

Back in her seat, she opened her tablet to Viktor's surveillance report. Photographs of Ammon Lundquist entering the University of Texas library. Images of the research team examining old medical texts. Notes on their conversation topics, gleaned from long-range directional microphones.

And the confirmation that they'd changed hotels—spooked by the search of their room.

She'd told Viktor to make the search obvious. Not threatening, exactly, but unmistakable. She wanted Lundquist and his team to know they weren't alone in this hunt. Wanted them nervous, off-balance, more likely to make mistakes.

The approach was her father's—she recognized that, even as she implemented it.

She closed the tablet and stared out the window at the darkness of the Atlantic below. The collaboration email had been sent an hour ago, carefully crafted to appeal to Lundquist's academic sensibilities. If he accepted, she'd have direct access to the translation project. If he refused, she'd at least know that he was suspicious—and suspicion could be worked with.

Her phone buzzed. A text from Viktor:

Team relocated. New location identified. Awaiting instructions.

Her thumb hovered over the keyboard. She could tell him to maintain surveillance only. To keep distance. To let her academic approach work before escalating.

Or she could tell him to apply more pressure. Her father's way. The way that got results.

She typed: *Surveillance only. I'll handle the approach.*

Then she deleted it and typed instead: *Maintain position. Be ready to move if academic approach fails.*

She stared at the message for a long moment. It wasn't her father's way. But it wasn't entirely her own way either. It was a compromise—a compromise she told herself was necessary.

She hit send before she could change her mind again.

I'm not him, she told herself. *I won't become him.*

But sitting in a chartered jet, reviewing surveillance reports, planning infiltration strategies—how different was she, really?

Different enough, she told herself. *I won't hurt anyone. Won't threaten violence. I'll compete fairly, even if the competition is hidden.*

The justification was thin. But she clung to it like a lifeline over dark water.

◆ ◆ ◆

Vatican City — 3:12 AM

Father Tomás Adão sat in his study, surrounded by shadows and centuries of accumulated silence.

The room was small—a monk's cell, really, though Tomás had not been a monk for decades. Shelves lined every wall, filled with books and documents that traced the long, complicated history of the Church's engagement with inconvenient truths. The Galileo files. The suppressed archaeological reports from South America. Correspondence with researchers who had been persuaded, one way or another, to revise their findings.

The burden of protecting faith was not a light one. Tomás had carried it for thirty years.

Tonight, the burden was heavier than usual.

The report from his American contacts lay open on his desk. *First Temple. Pre-Columbian contact. Evidence of civilizations that the historical record said couldn't have existed.*

If the translations from Utah were accurate—and his sources suggested they were—then the discovery could challenge fundamental assumptions about human history. Challenge assumptions about biblical chronology. About the uniqueness of Middle Eastern civilization. About the authority of Scripture as historical record.

Tomás knew what the hardliners in his faction would say: destroy it. Seal the site, discredit the researchers, ensure that whatever the First Temple contained never reached public awareness. They'd done it before. The techniques were well-established.

But Tomás was tired of destruction. Tired of suppression. Tired of the endless war against knowledge that the Church had been fighting since Alexandria burned.

Perhaps there was another way. Perhaps the First Temple, whatever it contained, could be managed rather than destroyed. Framed in a context that supported faith rather than undermining it. Used as evidence of God's providence across all civilizations rather than proof against biblical literalism.

It was a hope. A thin one. But hope was what faith was built on.

He reached for his phone and dialed a number from memory. It rang twice before connecting.

"Konstantin." The voice on the other end was calm, professional—the voice of a man who handled problems that required moral flexibility. "It's late, Father. Or early, depending on your perspective."

"I have a task for you. In the United States."

"The Utah situation?"

"You've heard?"

"I hear many things." Konstantin's tone carried a slight edge of amusement. "The First Temple has attracted considerable attention. Multiple parties are now actively seeking its location."

"I need you to monitor the situation. Position yourself to act when the location is discovered." Tomás paused, choosing his words carefully. "I don't want destruction, Konstantin. Not yet. I want options."

"Options." The word carried weight. "That's more complicated than simple elimination."

"I know. That's why I'm calling you rather than someone else."

A long pause. Then: "What kind of options are we talking about?"

"I want to be there when they find it. Want to see what it contains before any decisions are made. The hardliners will push for immediate action, but I believe there may be a better path—a way to preserve rather than destroy, to control rather than eliminate."

"And if the contents prove as dangerous as the intelligence suggests?"

Tomás looked at the shadows filling his study—shadows that had witnessed so many similar conversations over the centuries. So many compromises. So many calculations of lesser evils.

"Then we do what we've always done," he said softly. "We protect the faithful from truths they're not ready to receive. But let's not make that decision until we know what we're deciding about."

"Understood." Konstantin's voice turned businesslike. "I'll need resources. Travel, surveillance, operational support."

"You'll have them. And Konstantin?"

"Yes?"

"There are others involved. The Consortium remnants—they have people in the field. And the Lundquist team, of course. I don't want anyone hurt unless it becomes absolutely necessary."

Another pause, longer than the last. "You've gone soft, Father."

"Perhaps. Or perhaps I've learned that methods shape outcomes more than intentions do."

Konstantin's laugh was soft, without humor. "That's a new operational parameter for me."

"Consider it professional development."

The call ended. Tomás sat in the darkness, listening to the silence of the Vatican at night.

Somewhere in America, forces were converging on a secret that had been hidden for millennia. A secret that could transform human understanding—or tear it apart.

He had sent Konstantin to shape that convergence. To ensure that whatever happened, the Church would have a voice in the outcome.

It was the best he could do. The most he could offer.

He hoped it would be enough.

Salt Lake City — 10:15 PM

In a hotel room in Salt Lake City, Konstantin ended the call and stood at the window, watching the city lights glitter against the darkness of the mountains beyond.

Father Tomás was a good man—one of the few genuine believers Konstantin had encountered in thirty years of service to the Church. But good men made poor decisions when their faith conflicted with necessity.

Options. Tomás wanted options. As if truth were a negotiation.

Konstantin had learned otherwise in Belgrade, in 1994. He'd been twenty-three years old, newly recruited from Serbian military intelligence, when the Vatican's secretive archaeology division had sent him to retrieve documents from a monastery that Serbian forces were about to shell.

The monks had discovered something in their archives—correspondence from the fifteenth century that suggested certain foundational Church documents had been... edited. Amended. Improved.

He'd gotten the documents out. He'd also gotten the senior archivist out—a seventy-year-old monk named Brother Mihail who had spent forty years studying those letters and who believed the world deserved to know what they contained.

Konstantin still remembered the old man's eyes when he'd understood what was about to happen. Not fear. Something worse. Pity.

You think you're protecting faith, Brother Mihail had said. *But faith that requires ignorance is not faith. It's fear wearing a mask.*

The shell had landed three minutes later. The monastery, Brother Mihail, and the dangerous knowledge he carried—all of it erased in a single thunderclap of convenient timing that Konstantin had arranged with a Serbian artillery captain who owed him a favor.

He'd told himself it was necessary. Told himself for thirty years.

And he still believed it—believed that some truths were too dangerous for a world that could barely handle the truths it already had. The faithful needed their certainties. They needed to believe that Scripture was eternal, that the Church's authority was unbroken, that the foundations beneath their feet were solid stone rather than carefully maintained illusion.

Brother Mihail had been wrong. Faith didn't require ignorance—it required protection. Someone had to stand between the faithful and the chaos that would consume them if every buried truth were suddenly exhumed.

That someone was Konstantin.

He turned from the window and began planning. Father Tomás wanted options. Very well—Konstantin would provide them. And when Tomás inevitably chose wrong, when his conscience led him toward some soft compromise that endangered everything, Konstantin would do what he'd always done.

The First Temple would not see the light of day.

◆ ◆ ◆

San Antonio — 10:23 PM

Ammon couldn't sleep.

He lay in the unfamiliar hotel bed, staring at the ceiling, running through the day's events in his mind. The marginalia in Hathenbruck's books. The astronomical reference. Viktor's warning. The searched room.

And now this email from an Oxford professor whose timing was suspiciously convenient.

Beside him, Aspen's breathing was slow and even, the sleep of someone who had learned to rest when rest was available. He envied that ability—the soldier's skill of grabbing peace in the gaps between crises.

His phone buzzed softly. A message from Jonas:

Ran background on Margaux Vance. Credentials check out—Harvard undergrad, Oxford doctorate, tenure at St. Catherine's. Published work is legit, cited in peer-reviewed journals. No obvious red flags.

But here's the thing: her father is Elias Vance. Former head of the Whitmore Foundation. Currently in federal prison for the Consortium stuff. She's kept her distance publicly—different career path, no involvement in his organizations—but she's still his daughter.

Ammon's stomach tightened.

Margaux Vance wasn't just an academic seeking collaboration. She was the daughter of the man who had funded the mercenaries, the surveillance, the violence that had nearly killed them all last year.

But was that her fault? She'd built her own career, her own reputation. Jonas said there were no obvious red flags—no involvement in her father's crimes, no connections to Consortium operations.

Still. The timing. The convenience. The fact that she reached out the same day Viktor delivered his warning.

He typed a quick response: *Don't reply to her yet. We need to discuss this with Thomas. Could be legitimate, could be something else. Need more information before we decide.*

Then he lay back, staring at the ceiling, processing the implications.

Three factions now, at minimum. Viktor and whoever he worked for—Consortium remnants seemed likely. The mysterious "Church" that Phantom had mentioned. And now possibly Margaux Vance, with her academic credentials and her complicated family history.

All of them hunting the same thing. All of them converging on secrets that Hathenbruck had spent his life protecting.

The game had become a race. And Ammon was no longer sure who he could trust.

Beside him, Aspen stirred in their sleep, their hand finding his in the darkness. He held it, drawing what comfort he could from the warmth of their skin.

Tomorrow, the hunt would continue. Tonight, at least, he wasn't alone.

PART TWO

THE HUNT

CHAPTER ELEVEN

The Wolf in the Fold

Two weeks later—after background checks, encrypted debates, and a compromise that satisfied no one—Dr. Margaux Vance stood in the secure wing of the tribal cultural center. Ammon found himself impressed despite his suspicions.

She was smaller than he'd expected from her academic reputation—compact and precise in her movements, with dark hair cut short in a practical style that suggested fieldwork experience. Her eyes were sharp and assessing, taking in every detail of the translation room with the focused attention of someone cataloguing resources.

"The climate control is impressive," she said, her accent carrying the clipped vowels of Oxford common rooms.

"Museum-grade, if I'm not mistaken. One doesn't often see such investment outside the major institutions."

"The artifacts deserve proper protection." Thomas stood near the entrance, arms crossed, carrying the measured formality he reserved for outsiders.

"The guardian tradition has learned, through bitter experience, what happens when sacred knowledge falls into careless hands." If the implied accusation landed, Margaux gave no sign.

"Quite right. The history of archaeology is rather littered with examples of extraction without regard for indigenous sovereignty. What you've built here—this partnership model—it's precisely what the field ought to have done decades ago." She turned to Ammon with a smile that seemed genuine.

"I've read your published papers on the collaboration framework. Groundbreaking work, truly."

"Thank you." Ammon kept neutral, trying to reconcile his wariness with the evidence before him. The background check Jonas had run showed legitimate credentials: Harvard undergraduate, Oxford doctorate, tenure track at one of the world's most prestigious universities.

Her published work on trans-oceanic contact theories was respected if controversial, pushing boundaries without crossing into pseudoscience. And then there was her father. Elias Vance had tried to kill them. Had funded mercenaries, orchestrated surveillance, threatened everything they'd worked to protect. The man was serving federal time for conspiracy and cultural heritage crimes—and here was his daughter, offering to help with the very project he'd tried to steal.

"Your specialty is pre-Columbian contact theory," Aspen said. They stood apart from the group, their posture deceptively casual.

"What exactly do you think you can contribute here?"

"Several things, actually." Margaux pulled a tablet from her bag and swiped to a document.

"I've been studying the linguistic structures reported in your published translations. The symbol patterns show striking similarities to Old World writing systems—Phoenician, proto-Sinaitic, possibly Mediterranean Bronze Age scripts. If I'm right about the connections, it would provide evidence for my trans-oceanic contact theories while helping you understand the codex origins."

"We have linguists," Thomas said.

"You do. Excellent ones, from what I understand—Dr. Tanaka's work on cipher analysis is particularly impressive." Margaux's composure didn't waver.

"But I'm offering something rather different. Context. The broader theoretical framework that could help interpret what you're finding. The codices don't exist in isolation, do they? They're part of a larger story of human migration and cultural exchange spanning continents and millennia."

She spoke with passion—the kind of fervent conviction Ammon recognized from his own academic career, when ideas had consumed him completely. It was hard to fake that kind of intellectual fire. But then again, she'd had a lifetime to practice.

"Could we speak privately?" Ammon said to Thomas and Aspen.

"Give us a moment, Dr. Vance?" Margaux nodded graciously and stepped toward the observation window, giving them space while appearing to study the translation floor below. The conversation that followed was tense and whispered.

"No." Aspen didn't wait for him to speak.

"Absolutely not."

"Just—"

"She's Vance's daughter, Ammon. His daughter. The man who burned Jonas's apartment and tried to kill us for the chamber. The timing alone—"

"I know who her father is." He spoke low.

"But we can't just assume—"

"The Consortium planned in generations." Thomas's interruption was soft but final.

"Who is to say this was not always their strategy? Build the daughter's credentials over decades, position her as the reasonable alternative after the father's methods fail." Ammon glanced toward Margaux's silhouette against the observation window.

"Then wouldn't we rather have her where we can watch her? If she's working against us, better here than—"

"Better nowhere near us at all." Aspen stepped closer, dropping their voice further.

"We don't need her expertise badly enough to—"

"Don't we?" The frustration escaped before he could contain it.

"The First Temple is out there. We're not the only ones looking. If we reject everyone who might pose a risk, we'll be working alone against people with resources we can barely imagine." Thomas considered the question. When he spoke, his voice carried a weight that made Ammon's chest tighten.

"Your ancestor spent his life protecting these secrets. He understood that some knowledge is too dangerous to share carelessly."

"My ancestor also left a trail. He wanted someone to find it eventually— he just wanted it to be the right someone." Ammon met the older man's eyes.

"I'm not saying we trust her completely. Limited access. Supervised sessions. If she proves dangerous, we remove her immediately." The silence stretched.

Aspen's jaw was tight. Thomas had gone still in the way he did when deeply troubled.

"You've already decided." Thomas's voice was heavy.

"I can see that." He turned and walked toward the translation floor, his careful gait heavy with unspoken disappointment. The gesture said everything: This is your choice. You'll bear the consequences. Aspen lingered.

"He's right to be worried."

"I know."

"But you're doing this anyway."

"I don't see another option that doesn't leave us more exposed." He reached for their hand, found it cool and tense.

"I need you to trust me." They were quiet. Then they squeezed his hand once and let go.

"I trust you. But I'm keeping an eye on her. And if I see anything—"

"Then we act. Immediately." They nodded and followed Thomas toward the translation floor.

Ammon turned back to Margaux, who had been studying their reflection in the window with carefully concealed interest. She turned as he approached, her expression professionally curious.

"Decision made?"

"Welcome to the project, Dr. Vance. Limited access—supervised sessions, no removal of materials, regular check-ins with our security team. If that arrangement works for you, we can discuss expanded involvement as trust develops."

"That's more than fair." Margaux extended her hand, and Ammon shook it. Her grip was firm, her smile warm.

"Thank you for the opportunity. I know my background raises questions. I appreciate your willingness to judge me on my own merits."

"Everyone deserves that chance." He meant it, even as warning bells continued in the back of his mind.

"Let me show you to your workstation." He led her down to the translation floor, introducing her to Dr. Chen and the other researchers, explaining protocols and security measures. Margaux absorbed everything with visible enthusiasm, asking intelligent questions, demonstrating exactly the expertise she'd claimed. She was good.

Very good. If this was an act, it was a masterful one.

The cultural center emptied in stages. First the researchers departed—Dr. Chen gathering her notes, the graduate assistants chatting about dinner plans as they filed toward the parking lot.

Then the administrative staff, the security guard making his initial rounds, the cleaning crew working through the public galleries. Margaux waited in her temporary office, laptop open to a journal article she wasn't reading, until the building settled into the hollow silence of empty institutional spaces. 11:47 PM. The security guard would be in the east wing for another twenty minutes. She moved through the darkened hallways with practiced care, her soft-soled shoes silent on the polished concrete. The building's HVAC system clicked and whirred around her—mechanical breathing that masked whatever small sounds she couldn't avoid.

The translation room's keypad glowed faintly in the darkness—she'd memorized the code during her orientation, watching Dr. Chen's fingers from the corner of her eye while asking a question about humidity controls. The door clicked open. Inside, the climate control breathed its constant whisper, and the emergency lighting cast everything in dim red—the color of developing darkrooms, of secrets kept from the light. Her hands were steady as she retrieved the pen from her jacket pocket.

It looked ordinary—matte black, silver clip, the kind academics carried by the dozen. The camera concealed in its barrel could capture documents in low light with remarkable clarity. She started with the astronomical references, the pages Dr. Tanaka had been analyzing that morning. Click.

The cipher analysis worksheets. Click. The preliminary notes on the First Temple—coordinates, speculation, cross-references to symbols she didn't yet understand. Click. Click.

The work was mechanical, methodical. She'd done this before—not often, not proudly, but when her father's requests had seemed reasonable and the targets had seemed legitimate. Academic rivals hoarding data. Museums sitting on unpublished finds.

It had been easy to justify then: knowledge belonged to everyone, and those who tried to control it deserved to have it taken. This was different. These weren't institutional bureaucrats protecting their publication records. These were people who had nearly died to protect something sacred, something they believed in with the kind of conviction she'd only ever seen in her father's eyes. She photographed the next document anyway.

The lies she told herself were comfortable, well-worn: the knowledge in these codices belonged to the world, not to a single tribe or a single team of researchers. Her father's methods had been wrong, but his goals had been right. The ends justified the means, and she was the reasonable Vance, the one who would do this properly. Somewhere beneath those justifications, a smaller voice whispered that she was simply her father's daughter after all— that the apple hadn't fallen far, only rolled into different shadows. She ignored it.

She was good at that. Nineteen minutes. She slipped back through the service entrance the security briefing had mentioned in passing, out into night air that was cold and clean and carried the scent of mountain pine. Her breath fogged in the darkness. Her pulse was slowing.

Her phone buzzed. Viktor, checking in. Package secured. Full documentation of current translation progress. Awaiting further instructions.

She typed the response quickly, then deleted the thread. In the morning, she would return to the cultural center as Dr. Margaux Vance, legitimate academic and collaborative researcher. She would smile at Ammon and ask thoughtful questions and pretend not to notice Aspen tracking her every move. The wolf had entered the fold.

And the sheep had no idea how sharp her teeth really were.

CHAPTER TWELVE

The First Temple

The breakthrough came at 3:13 AM, and Dr. Yuki Tanaka was alone when it happened. She'd been staring at the same symbol cluster for forty minutes. Her eyes burned. Her lower back had graduated from aching to screaming somewhere around midnight, and she'd stopped noticing it an hour ago—which probably wasn't a good sign.

The high-security annex thrummed with the white noise of air filtration and the soft whir of the air-gapped system Ammon had arranged for her, processing data in digital isolation from the outside world. Seven coffee cups stood in formation across her desk like soldiers who'd given their lives for the cause. The eighth was clutched in her hands, gone cold an hour ago. She drank it anyway. Cold caffeine was still caffeine.

The cipher had been beating her for weeks. Not just resisting—mocking her. Every time she thought she'd found the pattern, it slipped away like water through her fingers. Unlike Hathenbruck's journal code, which used a German phrase as a substitution key—clever but ultimately conventional— the marginalia cipher was something else entirely. Something that seemed to shift between encoding schemes depending on context, as if the person who created it had anticipated exactly the kind of systematic attack she'd been mounting.

She'd tried frequency analysis—dead end. Symbol mapping to Phoenician, Proto-Sinaitic, Linear B—fragments of similarity, nothing conclusive. Statistical modeling, neural network pattern recognition, every computational tool in her considerable arsenal.

Nothing. Nothing. Nothing.

She rubbed her eyes hard enough to see stars and considered, not for the first time, that she might be chasing a ghost. That the marginalia might be decorative rather than meaningful.

That she'd spent three weeks of her life trying to decode what amounted to ancient doodling. Except she didn't believe that. Couldn't believe it. The symbol placement was too deliberate, the frequency distributions too structured. There was meaning here.

She could feel it, the way she'd felt it with the Voynich manuscript before that project had broken her heart. The way she'd felt it with Linear A before admitting defeat. Third time's the charm, she thought bitterly. Or third time proves I'm a masochist who should have gone into dentistry like Mom wanted. She was about to surrender to exhaustion when her gaze snagged on something she'd seen a hundred times before—but hadn't truly seen.

The astronomical passages. She'd noticed weeks ago that certain symbol combinations appeared with unusual regularity in sections that seemed to describe celestial events. She'd noted it, filed it, moved on. But now, her exhausted brain made a connection her conscious mind had missed. The combinations bore similarities to Phoenician numerals.

Not exact matches—close enough to suggest common ancestry, different enough to indicate independent evolution. As if two branches of the same linguistic tree had grown in isolation for millennia. Her hands trembled as she pulled up her comparison database. Wait. Wait.

What if the cipher wasn't encoding text at all? What if it was encoding multiple types of information simultaneously—linguistic content in one layer, numerical data in another, perhaps even something else in a third? The thought hit her like ice water to the face. Suddenly she wasn't tired anymore. She began separating the layers, using statistical analysis to identify which symbols carried which type of information.

The work was painstaking—each step building on the last, each assumption requiring verification—but slowly, agonizingly slowly, meaning began to emerge from chaos. The numerical layer came first. Coordinates, she realized. Astronomical coordinates describing star positions with a precision that made her breath catch. Then the linguistic layer started yielding to her attack, fragments of meaning coalescing like fog condensing into rain.

And when the first complete sentence resolved itself on her screen, Yuki Tanaka forgot she had a body at all. *Templum Primum.* The First Temple. Not metaphor. Not symbol.

The codex described a physical structure, built in a specific location, by a specific civilization. A civilization that shouldn't have existed. According to the decoded text, the First Temple had been constructed approximately seven thousand years ago—millennia before the earliest known American civilizations, millennia before the pyramids rose from Egyptian sands or the ziggurats of Mesopotamia reached toward heaven. Its builders had crossed the ocean following routes mapped by stars and currents, carrying accumulated knowledge spanning countless generations. They had not come alone.

The codex described ongoing contact between the First Temple and sites across the Atlantic—regular voyages, exchanges of knowledge, a network of learning that spanned continents in an age when conventional history insisted the Americas were utterly isolated. Tanaka's coffee cup slipped from nerveless fingers and shattered on the floor. Ceramic shards scattered across the concrete, coffee pooling in the dim light.

She didn't notice. This would rewrite human history.

Migration patterns, technological development, the entire framework of civilization itself—all of it would need to be reconsidered.

Everything she'd been taught, everything she'd taught others, every assumption underlying her entire academic career. She forced herself to breathe. To continue decoding. The next section was harder, the language shifting into something more archaic and formal—the voice of priests or scribes recording what they considered sacred history. The Temple holds the accumulated wisdom of ages.

The words appeared on her screen like a voice from seven thousand years ago. Knowledge of the stars and their movements. Knowledge of metals and their working. Knowledge of medicine and the healing of wounds. Knowledge of the mathematical arts and the measurement of time. Knowledge of the inner workings of the soul and the manipulation of the spirit. Knowledge of forces that move unseen through the world.

All gathered, preserved, protected against the darkness that consumes. Tanaka paused over that last phrase. Knowledge of forces that move unseen through the world. Her academic instincts wanted to interpret it as metaphor—religious language describing natural phenomena the ancients didn't understand. But something in the careful phrasing, the deliberate word choice, suggested otherwise.

The next passage made her skin prickle with unease: But knowledge is fire. It can warm or destroy. The ancestors understood this truth, for they witnessed what became of those who wielded knowledge without wisdom— civilizations that rose and fell like breath, consumed by their own discoveries. The proud ones who thought to command forces beyond their comprehension. The seekers who opened doors that should have remained sealed.

The builders who raised towers to touch the heavens and were cast down into ash. We have seen the marks they left upon the world. We have read the warnings etched in stone. We know the price of hubris. The Temple was built not merely to preserve, but to protect.

To ensure that the fire would not spread until those who received it were ready to bear its heat. Its location was hidden from all but the chosen guardians. For the world was not ready. Perhaps it would never be ready. But hope endures, and the guardians wait, and someday—the ancestors believed—someone worthy would come to carry the flame forward.

Tanaka sat back, her heart hammering against her ribs. The academic in her wanted to focus on the historical implications. Ancient transoceanic contact. A network of civilizations predating everything in the archaeological record. This alone was earth-shattering.

But the warnings... the warnings were something else entirely. The builders of the First Temple had sealed it deliberately. Not because they'd abandoned their knowledge—they'd painstakingly preserved it. Not because they feared invasion—the temple's concealment suggested they feared something far more fundamental. They'd looked at what they'd gathered and decided the world wasn't ready to receive it.

What had they seen? What kind of knowledge scared people badly enough to hide it for millennia? The text mentioned civilizations consumed by their own discoveries, forces beyond comprehension, doors that should have remained sealed... A chill ran down her spine that had nothing to do with the air conditioning. She thought about the guardians she'd been working alongside—Thomas with his quiet authority, Robert Colorow with his careful watchfulness. She'd assumed their tradition was about the sacred chamber, about protecting indigenous heritage from exploitation.

But if what she was reading was accurate... they were inheritors of something far older. A duty passed down through seven thousand years of human history, across civilizations that had risen and fallen, protected by guardians who understood that some fires were too dangerous to spread unchecked. No wonder Hathenbruck had hidden the pages describing the temple's location separately. He'd understood—perhaps more clearly than anyone in generations—what discovery of the First Temple would mean. The knowledge it contained could transform human understanding.

It could also, if the warnings were accurate, cause devastation that defied imagination. She needed to tell Ammon. Needed to tell Thomas. Needed to— Her phone buzzed with a message. She glanced at the screen automatically, still half-lost in the revelation.

It was from Dr. Margaux Vance. Working late too? I saw the light under your door. Coffee break?

I'd love to discuss the trans-oceanic parallels you mentioned yesterday. Tanaka stared at the message, her exhaustion-fogged brain processing its implications. Margaux had been observing her. Had noticed her late-night work sessions. Had waited until this moment—until 4 AM—to reach out.

Coincidence? Or something else? She thought about the new researcher's credentials, her convenient expertise, the way she'd arrived just as the investigation was heating up. Ammon had vouched for her, but Aspen's suspicions hadn't been subtle. And Jonas had mentioned something about background checks that raised questions he couldn't articulate.

The First Temple had been hidden for seven thousand years because its guardians understood that some knowledge required protection. Tanaka was beginning to understand that too. She closed her translation files, encrypted them with a password she'd never shared with anyone, and shut down her workstation. The breakthrough could wait until morning. Until she could share it with people she trusted completely.

She typed a quick response to Margaux: Heading home. Early meeting tomorrow. Rain check? Then she gathered her things and slipped out through the back entrance, taking a different route than her usual one. Probably paranoid.

Probably unnecessary. But she thought about the ancient scribes who'd encoded their knowledge in layers of cipher, hiding truth within truth within truth. They'd been paranoid too. And they'd been right.

She slept for three hours—not enough, but all her racing mind would allow. By 9 AM, she'd gathered the people she trusted in the secure translation room: Ammon, Aspen, Thomas, Robert Colorow, Jonas, and Dr. Chen.

She'd deliberately not invited Margaux, claiming the meeting was about internal protocols rather than research progress. The lie sat uneasily in her stomach. But the revelation she carried was too important, too dangerous, to share with someone she wasn't certain about.

"The First Temple is real," she said without preamble.

"Not metaphorical, not symbolic—an actual physical location where an ancient civilization preserved knowledge that predates everything we think we know about human history." She walked them through the decoded sections, reading their faces as the implications sank in. Thomas grew increasingly pale. Robert's eyes widened with something that looked like recognition—as if pieces of oral tradition he'd known his whole life were suddenly clicking into place. Ammon leaned forward with the intensity she'd come to associate with his most driven moments.

"Seven thousand years," Dr. Chen breathed.

"That would make it older than the Pyramids. Older than anything we thought possible in the Americas."

"If the dating is accurate, yes." Tanaka pulled up her analysis on the room's main display.

"The astronomical references correspond to star positions from approximately 5000 BCE, give or take a few centuries. That's when the temple was built—or at least when the records we're translating were first created."

"And the location?" Ammon asked.

"That's where it gets complicated." She switched to a map display.

"The codex describes the temple's position using astronomical coordinates—the alignment of specific stars as seen from the site on the winter solstice. Between stellar drift and the precession of equinoxes, those coordinates have shifted significantly over seven millennia."

"Can you calculate where they point now?"

"I'm working on it. But there's something else."

She hesitated, weighing how much to reveal.

"The codex contains warnings. Extensive warnings about what the temple holds and why it was sealed." She read them the passage about civilizations consumed by their own discoveries, about forces beyond comprehension and doors that should have remained sealed. The room fell into a deeper silence.

"That sounds familiar," Robert said.

"The guardian tradition has always emphasized protection over sharing. We thought it was about the sacred chamber, but if what you're saying is true..."

"Then the tradition predates the chamber by thousands of years," Thomas finished.

"We're not the originators. We're inheritors—carrying forward a duty that began long before our people came to these mountains." The weight of that settled over the room. Tanaka read their faces, seeing the magnitude of realization hit each of them differently. The sacred trust they'd accepted wasn't centuries old.

It was ancient beyond measure—a responsibility passed down through countless generations, protected by guardians who understood something about the nature of knowledge that modern civilization had forgotten.

"Hathenbruck knew," Ammon said finally.

"That's why he removed those pages. He found the temple's location and realized what it meant."

"So he hid it separately," Tanaka agreed.

"Created a trail that only someone who truly understood the responsibility would be able to follow."

"A trail we're now following." Aspen's voice was tight.

"And we're not the only ones." The reminder cut through the wonder of discovery. They weren't just academics unraveling a historical mystery. They were participants in a race—against forces that might use whatever the First Temple contained for purposes its ancient builders had never intended.

"We need to move faster," Ammon said.

"Find those pages before anyone else does."

"Agreed." Thomas rose from his chair, his injured body moving with renewed purpose.

"But we also need to be more careful. If what Dr. Tanaka has found is accurate, the stakes are higher than we ever imagined. This isn't about family legacy or academic discovery anymore." He met each of their eyes in turn.

"The ancients sealed that temple because they believed its contents could destroy as easily as enlighten. We'd be fools to assume they were wrong."

"Then let's make sure we're the ones who control the match," Ammon said.

"Starting with finding where Hathenbruck hid those pages." He didn't notice that outside the translation room, in the corridor that led to the main research area, a shadow had been listening. Margaux Vance stepped back from the door, her face carefully blank. She'd heard enough.

The First Temple was real. Its location was hidden in pages that Hathenbruck had concealed separately. And the team was racing to find those pages before their competitors did. She pulled out her phone and typed a quick message to Viktor: First Temple confirmed. Location unknown but parameters established.

Recommend immediate escalation. Time is critical. The response came within seconds: Understood. Activating secondary assets. Be ready to move within 48 hours.

Margaux deleted the message thread and returned to her assigned workstation, her face composed into an expression of studious concentration. Phase Two was beginning. And by the time the team realized what was happening, it would already be too late.

CHAPTER THIRTEEN

The Convert

Ammon had never visited a prison before.

He'd imagined it would feel oppressive—walls closing in, the weight of incarceration pressing down on visitors and inmates alike. Instead, walking through Englewood's processing checkpoints, what struck him was the bureaucratic mundanity of it all. Forms in triplicate. A metal detector that beeped at his belt buckle. A corrections officer who examined his ID with the enthusiasm of someone counting down to retirement.

Evil, apparently, was processed through the same tedious machinery as everything else.

The visitation room was smaller than he'd expected—pale green walls, fluorescent lights buzzing at a frequency just below conscious hearing. A handful of other visitors sat scattered around the room, carefully not looking at each other. Prison etiquette meant minding your own business.

He chose a table near the back and waited, trying to reconcile what he was about to do with everything he believed about second chances. Six months ago, Jeremiah Stone had tried to steal the chamber's secrets. Had held a gun on Thomas. Had nearly died on a cliff face before Ammon pulled him back from the edge.

Now Ammon was here to ask for his help.

The man the guard escorted through the far door unsettled him more than the facility itself. Six months ago, Jeremiah had carried himself like a weapon—coiled, ready, dangerous even when standing still. The man who sat down across from Ammon had shed that aggressive energy, but what replaced it wasn't weakness. It was deliberation. He lowered himself into the chair like someone who'd learned to measure every movement, every gesture.

His eyes were what struck Ammon most. The calculating gleam was gone—that look that had made every interaction feel like a chess match. In its place was patience. The look of someone who'd stopped racing toward destinations and started paying attention to where he actually was.

"Dr. Lundquist." Jeremiah's voice had changed too—each word chosen rather than deployed. "I didn't expect to see you again."

"Neither did I." Ammon sat, the metal chair cold even through his jacket. The table between them was scratched with years of nervous fingernails and carved initials. "But I need your help."

A flicker of surprise crossed Jeremiah's careful composure. Not the dark amusement Ammon might have expected from the man he'd known before—a complicated mix of emotions. Surprise, and underneath it, a flicker of what might have been hope.

"The last time we faced each other, you were pulling me off a cliff." Jeremiah's hands rested flat on the table, deliberately visible—another learned behavior, Ammon suspected. Nothing hidden. "Before that, I was trying to steal everything you'd worked to protect. And now you need my help."

"Things change."

"Do they?" The question wasn't rhetorical. Jeremiah seemed genuinely uncertain, as if he was still testing the proposition against his own experience. "I've had six months to sit with what happened in that chamber. Six months of four walls and my own thoughts, trying to understand what broke open in me when I stood in that sacred space." He paused, and Ammon realized he was waiting—not for permission to continue, but to see if Ammon actually wanted to hear the answer. The old Jeremiah would have kept talking, would have filled silence with strategy. This version understood that silence had its own weight.

"What did you find?" Ammon asked.

"That I was wrong. About everything." The words came out without self-pity, without the theatrical gravity of performed confession. Just fact. "The Consortium told me I was pursuing knowledge. Preserving history. Serving something greater than profit or ego. And I believed it because believing it made me feel like more than what I was." His gaze dropped to his hands on the table. "But standing in that chamber, feeling what the guardians built there, what they protected for centuries—I understood what real service looks like. What it costs to protect something sacred instead of just taking from it."

Ammon remembered that moment. Jeremiah on his knees, tears cutting through the dust on his face, his whole body shaking as the guardian tradition crashed over him. It had seemed genuine then. Sitting here now, noting the way Jeremiah held himself, the way he spoke like someone who'd learned to hear his own words before they left his mouth—it seemed genuine still. But he hadn't come to discuss redemption.

"I need information," Ammon said. "About the Consortium. About what's left of their network."

Jeremiah nodded, as if he'd expected this. "The FBI was thorough after your revelations. Vance is locked up, the Whitmore Foundation is being picked apart by forensic accountants, most of the operational structure is gone." He shifted in his chair, and for a moment a harder edge surfaced in his expression. "But organizations like that don't die clean. There are always pieces that survive. People who kept their heads down. Money that was hidden well enough."

"What about personnel? People who might still be operational?"

The question hung in the air. Jeremiah didn't answer. Ammon saw a complicated expression work behind his eyes—not reluctance, exactly, but the discomfort of a man about to use knowledge he wished he didn't have.

"Viktor Semenov." The name came out flat. "Former Russian military intelligence, then private security, then whatever Vance needed him to be. He was never officially Consortium—kept everything at arm's length, payment through cutouts, deniability built into every arrangement. The FBI never connected him directly."

"Tell me about him."

Jeremiah's jaw tightened. "Viktor doesn't believe in anything except competence. No ideology, no loyalty beyond the current contract. He's a pure mercenary. If someone offered him more money tomorrow, he'd switch sides without blinking. That makes him more dangerous than the true believers— you can't predict him through his convictions because he doesn't have any." He paused, and when he continued, his voice carried an edge of shame. "I watched him work. Twice. The first time, a researcher in Munich was getting too close to something the Consortium wanted kept quiet. Viktor didn't threaten him directly—he mapped the man's entire life first. Knew where his daughter went to school, what time his wife left for work, which route his elderly mother took to church on Sundays."

Ammon's stomach tightened.

"He never touched any of them," Jeremiah continued. "Didn't have to. He just let the researcher know that he could. That was Viktor's method— he'd show you exactly how vulnerable you were, then give you a choice. Most people made the smart choice." His hands had curled on the table, no longer quite so carefully relaxed. "I told myself it was just business. Just pressure, not violence. But watching that researcher's face when he understood what

Viktor was showing him—" He stopped. Swallowed. "I should have walked away then. I didn't."

"Viktor is working for someone now," Ammon said. "He searched my hotel in San Antonio and sent me a message outside UT Austin. I learned first-hand that he is calculating. Professional. Controlled."

"Then someone with deep pockets activated him." Jeremiah leaned forward. "What exactly are you pursuing? The chamber project was supposed to be translation work, not field operations."

Ammon weighed how much to share. But he'd come here for help, and half-truths wouldn't get him what he needed.

"The codices revealed something. A site called the First Temple—ancient, older than anything in the archaeological record. Hathenbruck found references to its location and hid them separately because he believed the knowledge was too dangerous to preserve with the rest."

"And now people are hunting for those pages." Jeremiah nodded, recognition clicking into place behind his eyes. "That explains Viktor. If what's left of the Consortium is involved, they'd want a discovery like that for the same reasons Vance always wanted such things—vindication that his methods were justified, profit, control over something powerful."

"There's more." Ammon forced himself to continue. "Three weeks ago, an academic approached us. Oxford doctorate, published research, genuine expertise in trans-oceanic contact theory. Her name is Margaux Vance, daughter of Elias."

Jeremiah went still—not the controlled stillness he'd shown since sitting down, but something visceral. His careful composure cracked.

"Vance has a daughter?"

"You didn't know?"

"I knew the name. Heard it mentioned once or twice in contexts that made clear she was off-limits for discussion." Jeremiah's voice had quickened, losing some of its measured quality. "She was supposed to be separate. Legitimate career, no operational involvement, complete deniability. Vance was protective of her in a way he wasn't protective of anything else."

"She presented herself as exactly that—an academic who wanted to study the codices on their own merits. I argued for giving her a chance."

"Of course you did." There was no accusation in Jeremiah's tone, just weary recognition. "That's who you are—you believe in giving people the opportunity to be better than their circumstances. It's why you pulled me off that cliff."

"Was I wrong? About her?"

Jeremiah fell silent. When he spoke, each word seemed to cost him.

"I don't know. And that's the honest answer—I don't know if Margaux is what she claims or what she's been positioned to be. Vance was a planner. He thought in decades, not months. It's possible he kept her separate precisely so she could be deployed later, when the family name was compromised but her credentials were clean."

"Or?"

"Or she genuinely built a life apart from her father's crimes, and now she's being pulled back in—willingly or not." Jeremiah met Ammon's eyes. "But if she's there, if Viktor is operational, if someone is funding this—then the pieces are in place. That's how Vance built the Consortium. Legitimate cover, academic access, patient cultivation of trust. Then, when the moment is right, the knives come out."

The words settled into Ammon's chest like stones. He thought of the arguments he'd made to Thomas and Aspen. His insistence that Margaux deserved judgment on her own merits. His blindness to warning signs that should have been obvious.

"She's had access for three weeks. The translation room, research notes, team discussions—"

"Then assume she knows everything you know. Assume she's been reporting to whoever's running this operation." Jeremiah's voice had hardened, but not with the old aggression—with urgency. "This is standard procedure. Someone like Viktor handles external pressure, an inside asset handles internal access. Classic structure."

"Her father's in prison. He couldn't be coordinating this."

"Prison doesn't stop Elias Vance. The man built redundancies into everything. Contacts, resources, leverage—all of it designed to survive exactly this situation." Jeremiah shook his head. "I underestimated him when I worked for him. Made the mistake of thinking I understood the full scope of his operations. Don't make the same error."

Ammon's mind raced. If Margaux had been reporting for three weeks, they knew about the First Temple. Knew about the astronomical coordinates. Knew that Hathenbruck's pages were the key. They'd been ahead since the moment she walked through the cultural center's doors. Every conversation, every breakthrough, every debate about next steps—all of it observed and transmitted.

"What do I do?" The question came out rawer than he'd intended. The voice of someone whose careful plans had crumbled.

The question hung between them. When Jeremiah spoke, his voice carried a weight that Ammon recognized as hard-won—the wisdom of someone who'd learned through failure.

"You expose her. Carefully—you don't want Viktor escalating to more direct action. Remove her access, lock down communications, and assume everything she's seen is compromised." He paused. "And then you move faster. If they know about the First Temple, they're already accelerating. You need to reach those pages before they do."

"How? We don't even know where to look."

"Hathenbruck hid them separately, but he left a trail. He wanted them found eventually, by the right person—that's clear from everything you've told me." Jeremiah leaned back, his expression thoughtful. "Think about what mattered to him. What he trusted. Where he would have hidden something precious that he still wanted his descendants to find."

Family. The word surfaced in Ammon's mind immediately. Hathenbruck had trusted family—his wife, his descendants. People who shared his blood and, he'd hoped, his values.

"What about Consortium records?" Ammon asked. "You tracked Hathenbruck's movements for years. Is there anything in that research that could help?"

A complicated expression crossed Jeremiah's face. He reached into his pocket—visibly, still performing the nothing-hidden gesture that prison had taught him—and withdrew a folded piece of paper.

"Names," he said, sliding it across the table. "People who might still be active. Locations that mattered to operations. Financial institutions the Consortium used." His voice dropped. "And three sites that Vance flagged as high-priority for Hathenbruck research. We never understood why they mattered. Maybe you will."

Ammon took the paper. It weighed almost nothing, but he felt its importance in his fingers.

"Why are you doing this?"

"Because you saved my life when every rational calculation said you should let me fall." Jeremiah's voice was quiet, stripped of everything except honesty. "I've spent six months trying to understand why. The only answer that makes sense is that you believed I could be more than what I'd been." A pause. "Maybe it's time I tried to prove you right."

Ammon stood, tucking the paper into his jacket. "Thank you."

"Don't thank me yet." Jeremiah's eyes were grave. "If Margaux is Consortium, if Viktor is operational, if Vance is still pulling strings from inside—you're walking into something that's been planned for a long time. Be careful. These people don't believe in mercy."

"Neither did you. Once."

"No." A ghost of a smile crossed Jeremiah's face. "But I stood in a place where mercy was built into the walls. Maybe that changes a person. Maybe some people are beyond changing." He met Ammon's eyes one final time. "Watch your back, Dr. Lundquist. And the backs of everyone you care about."

Ammon left through the series of checkpoints, collecting his belongings, signing forms, walking back out into the January wind. The mountains were sharper now against the late afternoon sky, and the parking lot seemed impossibly open after the close corridors of the facility.

Margaux was Consortium—or close enough that the distinction didn't matter. Viktor was operational. The race for the First Temple had just become infinitely more dangerous.

And somewhere behind him, in a cell with pale green walls and buzzing fluorescent lights, Jeremiah Stone sat with his thoughts and hoped—perhaps for the first time in his life—that the right side would win.

CHAPTER FOURTEEN

Alliance

Aspen knew something was wrong three seconds before the call came through.

The surveillance feeds had been quiet all morning—the usual pattern of researchers arriving, the slow dance of scholarship that had become routine over six months. Nothing flagged by the automated systems. Nothing that should have triggered the prickle at the base of their skull.

But the prickle was there. The forest ranger's instinct that had kept them alive through bear encounters and flash floods, the guardian's inheritance that recognized threat before threat announced itself. They'd learned to trust that instinct years ago, back when ignoring it had nearly cost them a hand to frostbite on a winter rescue gone wrong.

They were already reaching for their phone when it buzzed with Ammon's name.

"Margaux is Consortium." His voice was tight, controlled in a way that meant he was fighting not to panic. "I just confirmed it with Jeremiah Stone. We need to—"

"Slow down." They were moving even as they spoke, pulling up internal camera feeds on their workstation. The monitors cast blue light across their face in the dim security office. "Where is she now?"

"I don't know. I'm still two hours out from the center. But if she's been reporting to them this whole time—"

"Then she knows everything we know." The words tasted like ash.

Aspen found Margaux's assigned workstation on the feeds. Empty. The screen dark, the chair pushed back at an angle that suggested hurried departure—not the careful tidiness Margaux usually displayed.

"She's not at her station. Let me check the building."

Their fingers flew across the keyboard, cycling through cameras with the efficiency of someone who'd memorized every angle, every blind spot, every potential threat vector. Six months of security work had burned the building's layout into their muscle memory.

Camera 3: the translation room, where Dr. Chen bent over a codex fragment, oblivious, her reading glasses perched on the end of her nose.

Camera 7: the break room, two researchers they didn't recognize eating lunch with the casual body language of people who didn't know their world was about to shatter. Camera 12: the main corridor, empty except for the afternoon light slanting through the skylights. Camera 15: the high-security annex.

Aspen's stomach dropped.

The door was open. Not ajar—open, propped with something that caught the fluorescent light. Inside, they could see scattered papers, overturned equipment, a mug still steaming on Tanaka's workstation like a ghost of normalcy. The secure storage cabinet hung open, its steel door swung wide.

And on the floor, a dark shape that could only be a body.

"Oh no," they breathed.

"What? What is it?"

"The secure storage. Someone's been in it." They were running now, phone pressed to their ear, feet pounding against the corridor floors. The climate control droned its ceaseless note; the skylights cast their eternal shadows. Everything looked normal except everything was wrong.

"I need to get there. I need to—"

They burst through the annex doors and the chaos hit them like a freight train. Papers everywhere—scattered across every surface as if a wind had blown through, except there was no wind, only the aftermath of hurried search. File drawers hung open, their contents rifled with method behind the apparent madness. Someone had known what they were looking for. Someone had found it.

The smell of something sharp in the air—the acrid scent of fear, of adrenaline, still hanging in the air. The secure storage cabinet's lock had been picked—professionally, without visible damage, the kind of work that took training and practice. Inside, empty spaces marked where the most sensitive documents had been, dark rectangles in the dust where folders had sat for months.

And on the floor, David Ouray lay unconscious, blood trickling from a wound at his temple.

"David!" Aspen dropped to their knees beside him, their fingers finding his pulse. Steady. Breathing normal. They tilted his head gently, examining the wound—a bruise already forming where he'd been struck from behind, the skin split but not deeply. Professional. Someone who knew exactly how much force was needed to incapacitate without killing.

David's eyes flickered beneath closed lids, consciousness trying to swim back to the surface.

"Aspen? Aspen, what's happening?"

"They're gone." The words came out flat, distant, as if someone else were speaking them. "Margaux is gone. She knocked out David, took what she could from secure storage, and ran."

They heard Ammon curse softly on the other end of the line. In all the time working together, they'd rarely heard him swear.

"How bad?"

Aspen surveyed the damage, their trained eye cataloging what was missing. "Bad. The astronomical coordinate analyses. Tanaka's decryption notes—I can see the empty folders. Whatever she could carry." They paused, a new horror dawning. "She's had three weeks, Ammon. Three weeks of access. She could have been photographing documents, copying files, building a complete picture of everything we've discovered."

Three weeks of patient betrayal. Three weeks of smiling collaboration while she systematically stole everything they'd worked to protect.

"I'm turning around," Ammon said. "I'll be there as fast as I can."

"No." Aspen's voice sharpened. "Stay on the road. If she has people watching the center, they'll know you're coming. Find somewhere safe and wait for my call."

"Aspen—"

"Trust me. I need to handle this."

They ended the call and turned their attention to David, who was groaning now, one hand rising weakly toward his head.

"Easy," they said, keeping calm despite the adrenaline screaming through their veins. "You took a hit. Don't try to move yet."

"Dr. Vance," David managed. "She... I didn't see..."

"I know. It's not your fault."

But even as they said it, Aspen's own failure pressed down. They'd had suspicions about Margaux. Small things—the way her questions sometimes probed a little too deep, the careful interest she showed in security protocols, the occasional glance that seemed to be measuring rather than observing. Aspen had mentioned it to Ammon once, early on, and he'd assured them that Margaux's credentials were impeccable, that her academic reputation was beyond reproach.

They should have pushed harder. Should have trusted their instincts over his optimism.

The next two hours were a blur of damage assessment and recrimination. By the time Ammon arrived—ignoring their instructions, as they'd known he would—the full scope of the breach had become clear. Margaux had taken photographs of the astronomical coordinate analyses, copies of Tanaka's decryption notes, duplicates of every codex translation they'd completed in the past month. The security protocols had prevented her from copying digital files directly, but she'd photographed screens, printed documents, accumulated paper copies with the patience of a spider spinning its web.

The tribal council convened an emergency session in the main conference room. Late afternoon light slanted through the windows, casting long shadows across the table where elders and advisors sat with expressions ranging from anger to grief. Aspen stood against the back wall, arms crossed, observing Ammon face the consequences of his decision.

"You vouched for her." Robert Colorow's voice was heavy with disappointment, each word landing like a brick. "You argued against our caution, insisted she deserved a chance to prove herself."

"I did." Ammon didn't flinch from the accusation. His face was pale but composed, accepting judgment without deflection. "I was wrong."

"Wrong doesn't begin to cover it." Thomas spoke from his seat near the council's center, his injured body lending his words authority. The wounds from six months ago had healed, but he moved carefully now, a man who had learned the cost of violence firsthand. "You wanted so badly to believe in partnership that you forgot our enemies wear many faces. The Consortium tried to kill us, and you invited the daughter of their leader into our most sacred spaces."

The words hung in the air, sharp as broken glass.

"I take full responsibility," Ammon said.

"Responsibility doesn't recover what was lost." Thomas's eyes were cold in a way Aspen had never seen before—not angry, but disappointed. "She knows about the First Temple. Knows about the astronomical coordinates. Knows that Hathenbruck's pages are the key to finding the location. Everything we've discovered, everything we've worked to protect—she's carrying it straight to the people who will use it to destroy what we're trying to build."

Aspen wanted to defend Ammon—wanted to point out that they'd had suspicions too, that they'd all failed to act on the warning signs, that blame shared was blame diminished. But Thomas was right. They'd been too trusting, too eager to believe that academic credentials meant pure intentions, too willing to see what they wanted to see.

And now they were paying the price.

"What do we do?" they asked, breaking the heavy silence. "Damage assessment is important, but we need to move forward. What's our next step?"

"Our next step is containment." Dr. Chen spoke for the first time, her usually calm voice tight with stress. "Lock down everything Margaux didn't get access to. Change all security protocols, passwords, encryption keys. Assume everything she touched is compromised."

"And then?"

"Then we beat her to the pages." Ammon's voice was quiet but determined, steel beneath the surface. "She doesn't have everything. The location of Hathenbruck's hidden pages—that trail leads through family connections she doesn't know about. Through documents that were never at the cultural center. Through Clara."

"You hope," Thomas said darkly.

"I know. Clara has papers that Margaux never saw. Letters from Anna Hathenbruck's sister in Germany, references to a family property that Friedrich insisted must never be sold. The trail continues—we need to follow it before they do."

The council deliberated in low voices, the sound washing over Aspen like distant water. They saw Ammon standing alone in the center of the room, bearing their judgment with a stoicism that made their throat tighten. He'd made a mistake—a serious one—but he was still the same man who'd risked everything to protect the chamber six months ago. Still the man they'd chosen to trust, to follow, to love.

They moved to stand beside him. Not defending, exactly. But present. Supportive in the face of condemnation.

Thomas noticed the gesture. Something shifted in his expression—not forgiveness, but perhaps acknowledgment that loyalty had its own kind of honor.

"We continue," Thomas said finally. "Dr. Lundquist will pursue the family leads. The rest of us will implement containment protocols and prepare for whatever comes next." He paused, his next words heavy with foreboding. "Because something is coming. Margaux and her handlers—they won't stop with what they've stolen. They'll want the pages themselves. And when they realize we're still pursuing them..."

He didn't need to finish the sentence.

The attack came three hours later.

"Viktor must have had teams staged nearby," Aspen said grimly when they saw the feeds. "Waiting for her signal that she'd extracted what she could."

They were in the security office, coordinating the protocol changes with IT, when the first anomaly registered on Camera 7. A glint of sunlight where there shouldn't be any—a vehicle moving too deliberately down the access road, its speed controlled, purposeful.

They leaned closer to the monitor, their ranger's instincts prickling.

"David, bring up the northern approach. Full magnification."

David—back at his post despite medical advice, a bandage wrapped around his head—complied without question. The image resolved, pixels sharpening into clarity.

Three SUVs, matte black, riding low on reinforced suspension—the heft of armor plating and extra personnel evident in how they handled the curves. No plates. Tinted windows that revealed nothing. Moving in formation: lead vehicle ahead, flanking vehicles staggered to prevent a single obstruction from stopping all three.

Professional. Military-grade professional.

Aspen was reaching for the emergency broadcast before conscious thought caught up with instinct. Their voice came out steady—years of wilderness emergencies had trained the panic out of their vocal cords—but their hands trembled as they keyed the building-wide intercom.

"Contact! Multiple hostiles approaching the main entrance! All personnel evacuate immediately! This is not a drill!"

The next minutes were chaos. They found Ammon in the translation room, grabbing hard drives and encrypted storage devices—anything that could be carried, anything that hadn't already been compromised. Tanaka was with him, stuffing papers into a fireproof bag with shaking hands, her face pale but focused. Dr. Chen was already gone, evacuated through the east exit with the other researchers.

"Out the back," Aspen commanded. "Service corridor to the parking structure. My truck is there."

"The codices—" Ammon started.

"Are in the vault, which is rated to survive anything short of a direct missile strike. We can't carry them, and we can't protect them better than the vault can." They grabbed his arm, pulling him toward the door. "But we're no good to anyone dead. Move!"

They ran. The service corridor was narrow and poorly lit, designed for maintenance access rather than emergency evacuation. Pipes ran along the ceiling; electrical conduits snaked along the walls. The air smelled of dust and old concrete. Aspen led the way, their security training taking over—checking corners, listening for pursuit, keeping the civilians behind them and out of the line of fire.

Behind them, they heard the crash of the main doors being breached. Shouted commands in Russian-accented English—Viktor's people, had to be. The sound of boots on tile, moving fast and professional. The attackers weren't trying to be subtle anymore.

"Left here," Aspen hissed, guiding them around a corner. The corridor branched—right toward the loading dock, left toward the parking structure. They'd almost taken the right turn out of habit before their mental map reasserted itself. The loading dock had no vehicles. The parking structure had their truck.

They burst into the parking structure just as the first of the attackers reached the service corridor entrance. Fluorescent lights buzzed overhead, casting everything in harsh white light. Aspen's truck was where they'd left it—a lifted 4x4 with off-road tires and reinforced bumpers. They'd bought it for mountain rescues, for reaching backcountry locations that standard vehicles couldn't handle.

Right now it was an escape vehicle.

"Get in!" They slid behind the wheel, keys already in their hand, engine roaring to life as Ammon and Tanaka piled into the back seat. "Hold on to something!"

They floored it. The truck lurched forward, tires screaming against concrete as they took the parking structure's ramps at speeds they were never designed for. The engine howled; the suspension groaned. Behind them, they heard gunfire—bullets pinging off metal, sparking against concrete pillars, close but not close enough.

Then they were out—bursting through the parking structure's exit barrier in an explosion of wood and plastic, splinters showering the windshield as they aimed for the access road that led up into the mountains.

"They're following!" Tanaka shouted, twisted around in the back seat to stare through the rear window. Her voice cracked with fear. "Two vehicles— no, three! They're right behind us!"

"I see them." Aspen's hands were steady on the wheel, their focus narrowed to the immediate necessities of speed and direction. The access road climbed sharply ahead, switchbacking up the mountain face in a series of tight curves. Curves they knew like they knew their own heartbeat.

They'd driven this road a thousand times—summer hikes, winter supply runs, the occasional search-and-rescue that required reaching the high backcountry before daylight. They knew every curve, every grade, every patch of gravel that tended to wash out after heavy rain.

Tonight, that knowledge was the only thing keeping them alive.

The first switchback came up fast—a hairpin turn with a sheer drop on the outside edge, nothing but darkness and a hundred feet of empty air. Aspen downshifted hard. The transmission protested, and threw the wheel over. The truck's back end slid on loose gravel, tires fighting for traction. For one heart-stopping moment they were sliding toward the edge, toward oblivion.

Then the tires caught. The truck straightened. The switchback fell behind them.

"Jesus Christ," Ammon breathed from the back seat.

"Don't talk," Aspen said through gritted teeth. "Don't distract me."

In the rearview mirror, they tracked the pursuing vehicles take the same turn—slower, more cautious, their drivers unfamiliar with the road. Good. That gave them seconds. Seconds mattered.

The next stretch was straight, climbing steeply between walls of pine. They pushed the accelerator to the floor, feeling the engine's power surge through the chassis. The speedometer climbed—fifty, sixty, seventy on a road designed for thirty. The headlights cut white tunnels through the gathering darkness.

"They're gaining!" Tanaka's voice was rising toward panic. "They're faster than us!"

"On the straights," Aspen acknowledged. The SUVs behind them were built for speed—lower, more aerodynamic, probably tuned for pursuit. On a highway, they'd catch their truck in minutes.

But they weren't on a highway.

"Not on the curves."

The second switchback approached—tighter than the first, a true hairpin that doubled back on itself. Aspen held their speed until the last possible second, then braked hard and yanked the wheel. The truck pivoted, rear end swinging wide, gravel spraying into the darkness like shrapnel. G-forces pressed them against the door.

Through it. Accelerating again. The pursuing headlights disappeared around the turn behind them, reappeared, fell back.

"There's a fire road about two miles ahead," they said, strained with concentration. "Unmarked, nothing on GPS. If we can reach it before they see us turn off—"

"You want to go off-road?" Ammon's voice was incredulous. "In the dark?"

"I want to survive. This is how we survive."

Another switchback. Another controlled slide, tires screaming, the smell of hot rubber filling the cab. Tanaka whimpered in the back seat, her knuckles white where she gripped the door handle. Aspen blocked out the sound, blocked out everything except the road and the pursuit and the narrowing calculus of escape.

A bullet shattered the back window. Tanaka screamed. Glass exploded inward, showering the back seat with glittering fragments. Cold mountain air rushed through the opening, carrying with it the sound of pursuit—engines roaring, men shouting, the crack of another shot that went wide and sparked off a rock face to their right.

"Stay down!" Aspen shouted. "Both of you, get down!"

Ammon pulled Tanaka below the level of the seats, shielding her with his body. In the rearview mirror, Aspen could see the lead SUV closing—close enough now that they could make out the shape of a man leaning from the passenger window, the dark outline of a weapon in his hands.

Professional killers. Viktor's team. The attackers weren't trying to capture anymore—they were trying to end this.

The road ahead curved sharply to the right, skirting the edge of a ravine. Aspen made a decision in the space between heartbeats. Instead of slowing for the curve, they accelerated—pushing the truck to its limits, feeling the wheels fight for grip on the loose surface.

The pursuing SUV tried to match their speed. It couldn't.

They saw it happen in the mirror—the black vehicle taking the curve too fast, its driver unfamiliar with the road's particular treachery. The rear end swung wide. Overcorrection. The SUV clipped the guardrail with a shriek of metal, spun, and came to rest sideways across the road, blocking the vehicles behind it.

A precious gift of time. Maybe a minute, maybe two, while they cleared the obstruction.

The fire road was close now. Aspen could feel it more than see it—a gap in the tree line on the left, a slight widening in the shoulder where forest service vehicles turned off during fire season. In daylight it was obvious. In darkness it was nearly invisible.

Nearly.

The pursuing headlights disappeared behind a curve, buying them seconds of invisibility. Aspen killed their own headlights, plunging them into darkness lit only by moonlight and memory. The world reduced to silver shapes and black shadows, to the ghost of the road ahead.

"What are you doing?" Tanaka's voice was barely a whisper, terrified.

"Trust me."

The fire road materialized on the left—a gap in the tree line that looked like nothing, that was nothing unless you knew exactly what to look for. Aspen took it without braking, the suspension bottomed out as they dropped onto the unpaved surface, heard branches scraping against the doors as the forest closed around them like a living thing.

Behind them, the pursuing headlights swept past on the main road and continued climbing—chasing a truck that was no longer there.

The tension drained from Aspen's shoulders. They drove another mile on the fire road, navigating by moonlight and instinct, before pulling into a clearing and killing the engine.

Silence fell—heavy, absolute, broken only by the tick of cooling metal and the sound of three people trying to remember how to breathe.

"Is everyone okay?" Aspen asked, hoarser than they'd expected.

"Define okay." Ammon's voice was shaken but intact. "We just escaped a paramilitary assault on a tribal cultural center. We're fugitives in our own country. And everything we've worked to protect is—"

"Still protected," Aspen cut in. "The codices are in the vault. The cultural center's staff evacuated—I saw them heading for the emergency exits. The knowledge isn't lost."

"But the advantage is." Ammon's voice was heavy with self-recrimination, each word laden with the weight of his failure. "Margaux has everything she needs to find the First Temple. And now Viktor's people know we're running, know we have something they want. We're targets."

"We were always targets." Aspen turned in their seat to face him, their expression fierce despite their exhaustion. Moonlight caught their face, illuminating the determination beneath the fear. "Since the moment we found the chamber, we were targets. The only difference now is that we know it."

"What do we do?"

"We go to ground. Find somewhere safe to regroup, assess what we have, plan our next move." They pulled out their phone, the screen's glow harsh in the darkness, and considered options. "Clara's house in Denver. It's the one place that's not connected to the cultural center, not in any of Margaux's intelligence."

"You think they don't know about Clara?"

"I think they might not have had time to track all your family connections. And right now, 'might not' is the best we've got."

Ammon didn't respond. Through the trees, Aspen could see a sliver of the main road far below—headlights still moving, still searching, not yet ready to give up. They'd figure out eventually that their prey had vanished. They'd come back with dogs, maybe, or thermal imaging. They had time, but not much.

"Thank you," Ammon said. He reached forward and squeezed their shoulder—a gesture of gratitude, of partnership, of something deeper than either of them had words for. "For getting us out."

"Thank me when we've won." Aspen started the engine again, keeping the headlights off until they were well away from the main road. "Until then, we've got work to do."

The truck crept through the darkness, navigating by moonlight toward a network of back roads that would take them away from the mountains, away from the cultural center, away from everything they'd built over six months. Toward Denver. Toward Clara. Toward whatever came next in a race that had just become far more deadly.

In the back seat, Tanaka had stopped shaking. Ammon stared out the window at the silver-and-shadow landscape sliding past, his face unreadable in the darkness. And Aspen drove, their hands steady on the wheel, their mind already racing ahead to the challenges that waited.

They'd escaped. They'd survived.

But the relief was hollow, edged with guilt. They glanced at Ammon in the rearview mirror and saw the same haunted awareness in his eyes—how close they'd come, how easily it could have ended differently. The adrenaline was fading now, leaving behind a bone-deep exhaustion and the trembling aftermath of fear allowed to surface.

Now they had to figure out how to fight back.

CHAPTER FIFTEEN

The Vatican's Interest

The archive occupied a wing of the Apostolic Palace that appeared on no official maps.

Father Tomás Adão walked its corridors with the familiarity of thirty years, his footsteps echoing against marble worn smooth by centuries of careful feet. The air carried traces of old incense and older paper—that particular mustiness of documents that had survived wars, plagues, and the rise and fall of empires. Climate control whispered behind the ancient walls, a modern intrusion that kept humidity at precisely forty-five percent, temperature at a constant eighteen degrees Celsius. The technology was invisible, as all the best secrets were.

Somewhere above, tourists drifted through the public galleries, marveling at Michelangelo's ceiling. They had no idea what lay beneath their feet.

He paused at a particular shelf, running his fingers along the spines of leather-bound volumes. Each one represented a chapter in the Church's long engagement with inconvenient truths. The Galileo papers, now partially declassified but still incomplete. Suppressed accounts of archaeological discoveries in South America that predated orthodox chronology. Correspondence with researchers who had been persuaded—through various means—to revise their conclusions. A file on the Cathars that remained sealed after eight hundred years. Letters between popes and kings, discussing artifacts that officially did not exist.

His hand trembled as he withdrew it. He noticed, and pressed his palm flat against his cassock until the tremor stopped.

"You look troubled, Tomás."

Father Pietro Benedetti stood in the doorway, his round face creased with concern. The corridor's electric light framed him from behind, softening his features, making him look younger than his sixty-two years. Pietro was one of the few colleagues Tomás trusted completely—a fellow Jesuit who understood the necessity of their work even when he questioned its methods.

"The American situation." Tomás kept even, professional. "It's escalating faster than we—" He stopped. Swallowed. Started again. "There's a secondary site. Something called the First Temple."

"Beyond Utah?"

"If our intelligence is accurate, it predates the chamber by millennia. Predates everything we thought we knew about human civilization in the Americas." Tomás turned to face his colleague, and something in his expression made Pietro step closer. "The translation team has decoded references to transoceanic contact with Old World civilizations. Ongoing cultural exchange. A network of knowledge-keepers spanning continents."

"The implications for biblical chronology—"

"Would be devastating. Yes."

Pietro was quiet for a moment. "Or liberating."

Tomás didn't answer. He found himself studying the archive's vaulted ceiling, the frescoes depicting saints who had died for truth. Sebastian bristling with arrows. Lawrence on his gridiron. Catherine broken on her wheel. What would they make of a priest who spent his life managing truth rather than proclaiming it?

"Tomás." Pietro moved into the archive, his footsteps echoing in the quiet space. "I've known you for twenty years. You're a man of genuine faith. But sometimes I wonder if you confuse protecting God's truth with protecting the Church's interpretation of it."

"There's no difference."

"Isn't there?" Pietro's hand swept toward the shelves surrounding them. "If God's truth is true, it can withstand any challenge. Every discovery, every revelation, every piece of evidence that contradicts our current understanding—it all serves to deepen faith, not destroy it. The universe is far stranger and more wonderful than our ancestors imagined. That's not a threat to faith. It's an invitation to expanded understanding."

"You sound like a progressive."

"I sound like a scientist who happens to believe." Pietro almost smiled. "The Jesuits were founded to pursue truth wherever it led. Ignatius himself wrote that we must be ready to change our minds if reason and evidence demand it. When did we become guardians of comfortable lies?"

The words touched wounds that Tomás had carried for decades. He remembered his own faith journey—the passionate seminary student in Lisbon who had believed that truth and doctrine were the same thing. The young priest who had first learned about the archive's existence, standing in this very room while his mentor explained the burden he was inheriting. The way his hands had shaken then, too, when he understood what he was being asked to protect. What he was being asked to become.

"It's not God's truth I worry about," he said. "It's man's faith. The billions of people who find meaning and purpose in the Church's teachings. Who structure their lives around beliefs we've spent centuries defending." He paused, searching for words that kept slipping away like water through fingers. "Faith is fragile, Pietro. It can survive intellectual challenge, yes—but only if that challenge is managed. Contextualized. Presented in ways that strengthen rather than—"

He stopped. The sentence was incomplete, even to him. Especially to him.

"And you believe you have the wisdom to manage truth for all of humanity?"

Tomás opened his mouth. Closed it. His fingers found the rosary in his pocket, worn smooth from decades of prayers he wasn't sure anyone heard anymore. The beads were warm from his body heat, familiar as his own heartbeat.

"I believe I have the responsibility to try."

Pietro considered this. The archive's climate system held its constant note. Somewhere in the distance, a door closed softly.

"I pray you're right, my friend. I pray the burden you've chosen doesn't crush you." His grip tightened on Tomás's shoulder. "But more than that—I pray that somewhere along the way, you remember that faith is not our possession to protect. It's God's gift to share."

He left without waiting for a response. Tomás stood alone in the archive, surrounded by centuries of secrets, feeling every choice that had led him to this moment.

A soft footstep behind him. He didn't turn.

"You heard all of that, I assume."

"Most of it." The voice was cultured, precise—German vowels smoothed by years of international work, each syllable placed with the care of a man who understood that language was merely another tool. Konstantin emerged from the shadows between shelving units, his movements economical and silent despite the hard marble floor. He wore a beautifully tailored charcoal suit, the fabric catching what little light reached this deep into the archive.

His silver hair was swept back from a face that might have belonged to a distinguished professor or a concert pianist—high cheekbones, a strong jaw, eyes the pale gray of winter ice. Only those eyes betrayed something harder beneath the polish. Something patient and very, very cold.

"Father Benedetti makes compelling arguments," Konstantin continued, adjusting his cufflinks with the casual precision of a man who noticed every detail and forgot none of them. "He would have made an excellent defense attorney in another life. Or perhaps a Jesuit himself—he certainly has the rhetorical training."

"He makes me question things I thought I'd settled long ago."

"Questions are luxuries, Father." Konstantin moved to stand beside Tomás, surveying the archive shelves with the appreciative eye of a connoisseur examining a wine cellar. "In my experience, men who question too long find themselves overtaken by men who act. The world does not pause for philosophical contemplation."

He pulled a slim phone from his jacket pocket, its screen glowing blue in the archive's dim light. The illumination carved harsh shadows across his features.

"The Consortium assault on the Utah facility succeeded. The targets escaped but are running. My sources indicate they're heading for a secondary location in Denver. The First Temple references are confirmed—location unknown but actively pursued by multiple parties."

"Multiple parties." Tomás turned the phrase over, tasting its implications. "Who else?"

"The Consortium remnants under Vance's daughter. The American team, obviously." Konstantin's smile was thin. "And now us. Three factions, all converging on secrets that have waited millennia to be found." He tucked the phone away. "The next few weeks will determine who writes this chapter of history."

Tomás processed the implications. Multiple factions converging on secrets the Church had monitored for centuries. Secrets that could transform or destroy everything they had built.

He thought about Pietro's words. About faith as gift rather than possession. About the arrogance of believing himself wise enough to manage truth for humanity.

And then he thought about the billions of people whose lives were built on beliefs that the First Temple could undermine. The families who found comfort in Scripture. The communities bound together by shared faith. The moral framework that Christianity provided for cultures across the world. The grandmother in São Paulo who lit candles every Sunday for her dead husband. The father in Manila who taught his children to pray. The countless millions who had built their entire understanding of existence on foundations that a single archaeological discovery could shatter.

Could he risk all of that for the sake of abstract truth?

"Continue monitoring," he said. The words were bitter on his tongue. "Position yourself to act when the location is discovered. Primary objective: secure the site before any information can be released. Secondary objective: assess whether controlled disclosure is possible." He paused, his hand tightening around the rosary until the beads pressed painful impressions into his palm. "Avoid violence unless absolutely necessary."

Konstantin lifted his head—a gesture that managed to convey acknowledgment without agreement, obedience without submission. "And if the American team reaches the site first?"

Tomás stared at the shelves—the accumulated record of centuries spent managing knowledge, controlling narratives, ensuring that faith remained unchallenged by inconvenient facts. The Galileo files were within arm's reach. Four centuries from condemnation to rehabilitation—and the admission had come on the Church's terms, at the Church's pace. That was the difference.

"Then we do what we've always done." His voice sounded unfamiliar to his own ears—distant, like someone else speaking through him. A stranger wearing his face. "We protect the faithful from truths they're not ready to receive."

"Whatever that requires?"

The silence stretched between them, heavy with implications neither man chose to name. Above them, the frescoed martyrs gazed down with painted eyes.

"Yes," Tomás said. The word struggling to roll off his tongue.

Konstantin smiled—a thin expression that didn't reach his winter-gray eyes. "I'll be in touch." He moved toward the archive's exit with the fluid grace of a man who had learned long ago how to enter and leave rooms without being remembered, then paused at the threshold.

"For what it's worth, Father—I find it refreshing to work with a man of conviction. So many of my clients are motivated by greed or fear. Base instincts, easily predicted, easily manipulated. You genuinely believe you're serving something greater." The smile sharpened, became something almost like respect. "Whether that makes what comes next easier or harder for you, I couldn't say. But I suspect you'll find out soon enough."

He disappeared into the corridor, his footsteps fading into silence with unnatural speed.

Tomás stood alone in the archive. Above him, the frescoed saints gazed down with expressions that might have been compassion or judgment—impossible to tell in the uncertain light. Saint Lawrence seemed to stare directly at him, flames licking at painted flesh, mouth open in either agony or ecstasy. The Church had made him a saint for his suffering.

What did the Church make of those who caused suffering in its name?

He pulled the rosary from his pocket and began to pray, but the familiar words rang hollow in his mouth—sounds without meaning, ritual without faith. Somewhere in the palace above, a bell tolled vespers. The sound drifted down through stone and centuries, calling the faithful to evening prayer.

Tomás didn't move. He had decisions to make. Choices that would affect millions of lives.

But first—first he needed to remember what it was to believe without doubt. To pray without calculation. To trust that truth and faith were the same thing, as he had once believed with all his young and foolish heart, standing in a Lisbon chapel with his whole life ahead of him and God's love burning like a fire in his chest.

The memory wouldn't come. It had been too long. He had become something else entirely.

After a long moment, he returned the rosary to his pocket and walked toward the chapel where he prayed every evening—going through motions that had become ritual without meaning, duty without joy, faith without fire.

Behind him, the archive held its secrets in patient silence, waiting—as it had always waited—to see what men would do in the name of protecting other men from truth.

CHAPTER SIXTEEN

Safe House

Clara's house was dark when they arrived, the bungalow's tidy silhouette barely visible beneath the shadows of mature trees.

Six months ago, the place had seemed like a museum. Now, even in darkness, something about it seemed more alive.

Ammon sat in the truck's passenger seat, watching the quiet street for signs of surveillance while Aspen killed the engine. His hands were still trembling from the adrenaline that had sustained him through their mountain escape—now, in the sudden stillness, his body was beginning to register the cost.

"This is the one place they shouldn't know about," Aspen said, echoing his thoughts. "No connection to the cultural center, no mention in any of the project documents."

"Unless they've been tracking our personal lives longer than we thought."

"Then we'll deal with that when we have to." Aspen's voice was tired but determined. "Right now, it's the best option we've got."

They approached the house carefully, Aspen leading with their hand on the holstered weapon at their hip. The front door opened before they reached it, revealing Clara's worried face in the gap.

"I saw the news," she said, ushering them inside. "Armed assault on a tribal cultural center. Multiple casualties, suspects at large. They're calling it domestic terrorism."

The interior had continued its transformation since his last visit. The family photographs Clara had hung six months ago still lined the hallway, but now the living room showed signs of hurried preparation—a card table set up near the window, a pot of tea steeping in the kitchen, the careful order disrupted by the urgency of their arrival. Clara had been waiting for them.

It was still a house built for hiding in plain sight, Ammon realized. But now it was hiding them.

"That's probably Viktor's people planting a narrative." Ammon collapsed onto Clara's worn sofa, exhaustion catching up with him. A spring pressed against his back, but he was too drained to shift. "Make the victims look like threats, create confusion about who the real aggressors were."

"Is anyone hurt? The people at the center—"

"They evacuated before the assault team breached. As far as we know, everyone got out." Aspen did a quick sweep of the house, checking windows and exits with professional efficiency. "But we can't go back there. Not until we understand the full scope of what we're dealing with."

Clara disappeared into the kitchen and returned with mugs of tea, pressing one into Ammon's hands before he could refuse. The ceramic was chipped at the rim, clearly a favorite she'd had for years. It was such a normal gesture—hospitality amid crisis—that Ammon felt the knot behind his sternum begin to unravel.

Tanaka had been quiet since they arrived, her hands still trembling from the mountain escape. She'd claimed a corner of Clara's living room almost immediately, pulling out her laptop like a shield against everything that had happened. The translation work was her anchor—the one thing she could control when everything else had spiraled into chaos.

Jonas arrived an hour later, having taken a circuitous route from Salt Lake City that included three vehicle changes and a brief stint on foot through a shopping mall. He looked haggard but focused, his laptop bag clutched like a lifeline, dark circles under his eyes speaking to the toll of the past twenty-four hours.

"I'm probably being paranoid," Jonas said as he set up his equipment, "but I'd rather be paranoid than dead."

"I've been tracking their communications," Jonas said, pushing aside a stack of gardening magazines and a half-finished crossword puzzle to make room for his laptop. "Margaux's been using encrypted channels, but there are patterns—timestamps, routing signatures, things that tell me more than she probably wants me to know."

"And?" Aspen had taken up position by the window, where they could watch the street while still participating in the conversation.

"She's not just reporting to Viktor. There's a second chain of communication—different encryption, different routing, different schedule. Someone else is getting her intelligence, independent of the Consortium remnants."

"The Church," Ammon said grimly. "Phantom mentioned them—an institutional buyer with deep pockets and old connections."

"That's my guess too. Which means we're not just racing the Consortium anymore. We're caught between at least two factions, maybe more, all of them converging on the same target."

Tanaka remained in a corner of the living room, her laptop balanced on a stack of Clara's old travel books. She sat cross-legged on the floor, shoes kicked off, working through astronomical calculations with fierce concentration. Jonas glanced over at her occasionally, and Ammon noticed something in those glances—a kind of grudging admiration for the way she could wall off fear and focus on the work.

"The meeting place of Asklepios and Orion," she murmured, more to herself than to the room. "The alignment Hathenbruck described—it would have been visible from a specific location during the winter solstice in the late nineteenth century. If I can calculate the stellar positions from that era and account for precession..."

"How long will that take?" Ammon asked.

"Another few hours. Maybe less if I can find the right reference data." She looked up, her eyes bright with the particular fever of someone close to breakthrough. "But there's something else. The codex passages I decoded—they mention 'painted walls where ancestors speak.' Rock art. The location must be near significant petroglyphs."

"That narrows it down to half of Utah and most of the Southwest," Aspen said dryly.

"Optimist," Jonas muttered, and Tanaka actually laughed—a short, surprised sound that seemed to catch them both off guard.

"Combined with the astronomical coordinates, it should give us a much smaller target area. Maybe small enough to search."

Clara had been moving through the conversation like a hostess at a very unusual dinner party—refilling coffee cups, bringing out crackers and cheese when she noticed no one had eaten, quietly adjusting the thermostat when she saw Tanaka shiver. Now she stepped forward, her voice hesitant but steady.

"I might be able to help. With the immediate problems, I mean—not the astronomical calculations."

"What kind of help?" Ammon asked.

"I spent decades running from the family legacy. Hiding from anything connected to the treasure hunt, the obsession that killed your father and uncle." Clara's jaw tightened, but she didn't look away. "I got very good at disappearing. At setting up communications that couldn't be traced, finances that couldn't be tracked. At knowing when eyes were watching and how to slip away from them."

"You were that paranoid?"

"I was that afraid. Of ending up like them—consumed by a search that destroyed everyone it touched." She met Ammon's eyes. "I never thought I'd use those skills to help the search. But if you need to go underground, to operate without being found—I can show you how."

The offer was unexpected and precisely what they needed. Over the next few hours, Clara proved herself invaluable—helping Jonas establish secure communication channels, providing cash from a safety deposit box that she'd maintained for exactly this kind of emergency, teaching Aspen tricks for spotting surveillance that even professional training hadn't covered.

"Your grandmother's rainy day fund," Clara said, handing Ammon a thick envelope of bills. "She always said the family would need it someday. I never thought I'd be the one handing it over."

"Thank you." The words were inadequate for everything Clara was offering—not just money, but the transformation of years of avoidance into active assistance. "I know this isn't what you wanted."

"What I wanted was for the search to end. For the family to be free of this obsession." Clara's smile was sad but genuine. "Maybe this is how that happens. Maybe you find what Hathenbruck hid and finally—finally—the mystery is solved. The circle is closed."

"Or maybe we just add another chapter to the obsession."

"Maybe. But at least this chapter will be written by someone who cares about more than treasure." She touched his face, a gesture of maternal affection that made him yearn for something he never really had. "Your father would be proud of you, Ammon. He got lost in the search, but he never forgot what he was really looking for—answers, understanding, meaning. You've found what he couldn't. Don't let anyone take that from you."

Later, after Clara had gone to bed and the others were absorbed in their work—Jonas typing with quiet intensity, Tanaka muttering coordinates under her breath—Ammon found Aspen on the back porch, staring at the Denver skyline in the distance. The city lights blurred in the autumn haze, millions of people going about their lives with no idea what was converging in the shadows.

"You should sleep," he said, joining them. The porch swing creaked as he sat down, and they shifted to make room for him without quite touching.

"Can't. Too wired." They didn't look at him, their eyes fixed on the city lights. "I keep replaying the escape, wondering what I could have done differently. If I'd caught Margaux sooner, if I'd trusted my instincts instead of deferring to your judgment..."

"This isn't your fault."

"It's not yours either. Not entirely." Now they turned to face him, their expression complicated in the dim light that spilled from the kitchen window. "You made a mistake, Ammon. A serious one. But you made it for good reasons—wanting to believe the best about people, wanting to build the partnerships you've been working toward. Those aren't bad impulses."

"They nearly got us killed."

"They also built something worth protecting. The collaboration at the cultural center, the trust you've earned from Thomas and Robert and the tribal council—that's real. One betrayal doesn't erase it."

Ammon leaned back against the porch swing, feeling the cool night air against his face and the warmth of Aspen beside him. "Thomas was right. I wanted so badly to believe in partnership that I forgot our enemies wear many faces."

"Thomas was speaking from pain. He's been fighting to protect the guardian tradition his whole life, and he just watched it get violated by someone you invited in." Aspen's voice softened. "That doesn't mean he's given up on you. It means he's reminding you what's at stake."

"And you? Have you given up on me?"

The question hung in the air between them. Aspen didn't answer, and when they moved, it wasn't to speak—they reached out and took his hand, their fingers cold from the night air, their grip fierce.

"I haven't given up on you," they said, their voice rough. "But I need you to understand something. My loyalty isn't just to you. It's to the guardians, to the knowledge we're protecting, to the responsibility my family has carried for generations. If there comes a point where those loyalties conflict..."

"You'll choose the guardians."

"I'll choose what I believe is right. And I hope—I need—for you to understand that." They squeezed his hand harder, and the tremor in their grip that exhaustion and adrenaline had left behind. "We're partners, Ammon. In everything. But partnership means being honest about where we stand, even when it's complicated."

"I understand." He squeezed their hand back, then did something he hadn't allowed himself to do in the chaos of the past days—he pulled them close, felt them stiffen briefly before relaxing against him, their head finding· the hollow of his shoulder like it belonged there.

They sat like that for a long moment, breathing together, letting the silence hold what words couldn't.

"And for what it's worth—I hope I never put you in a position where you have to make that choice."

"So do I," they whispered against his neck, and they exhaled—long and slow, releasing something they'd been holding since the mountain roads.

They stayed there until the cold became uncomfortable, until the sounds from inside reminded them they weren't alone, until the world's demands began to reassert themselves. Tomorrow they would resume the hunt, chase leads across the country and maybe across the world, race against forces that would kill to possess what they were seeking.

But tonight, in this moment of quiet between storms, they had each other.

And that would have to be enough.

CHAPTER SEVENTEEN

The Healing Stars

The numbers weren't cooperating, and Dr. Yuki Tanaka was starting to take it personally.

She'd been staring at star charts for six hours straight, her eyes burning from the laptop's glow in the otherwise dark dining room. Clara's house had become a war room of sorts—papers spread across every surface, mugs multiplying like evidence of a caffeine-fueled siege, the blinds drawn against prying eyes that might or might not be watching from the street outside.

The problem was that she'd been approaching this all wrong. She'd been treating Hathenbruck's clue like a cipher, breaking it into component parts and analyzing each one with the systematic precision that had served her so well in her academic career. But Hathenbruck hadn't been a cryptographer. He'd been a physician with an amateur's interest in astronomy and a desperate need to hide something important.

He wouldn't have created an elaborate cipher. He would have hidden meaning in plain sight.

"The healer and the hunter," she murmured, rubbing her temples. "Where the healer and the hunter meet."

"You've said that about forty times in the last hour." Jonas's voice came from the couch, where he'd set up his own laptop station. Dark circles under his eyes testified to a night without sleep, but there was an alertness to him that suggested his mind was still churning. "Not that I'm counting."

"Forty-three, actually. I've been keeping track." She shot him a look that might have been irritation if she'd had the energy for it. "And I've been overthinking it. That's the problem."

"How so?"

"Asklepios is the Greek god of medicine—the healer. But that's his mythological role." She pulled up a new search window, her fingers moving with renewed purpose. "His astronomical role is different. The constellation Ophiuchus—the serpent-bearer. It was named after Asklepios because the god was often depicted holding snakes, symbols of healing and regeneration."

Jonas set his laptop aside and moved to the dining table, genuinely curious now. "I didn't know Asklepios had a constellation."

"Most people don't. Ophiuchus isn't part of the standard zodiac—it sits between Scorpius and Sagittarius, overlooked by most astronomical traditions. The thirteenth constellation that nobody talks about." She couldn't help the small smile that crossed her face. "A hidden healer. Hathenbruck would have appreciated the symbolism."

"And Orion is the hunter." Jonas was leaning over her shoulder now, close enough that she could smell sandalwood and worn leather. She shifted away—old habit, maintaining professional distance. "One of the most recognizable constellations in the sky."

"Exactly. Bright stars, distinctive shape, visible from almost anywhere on Earth." She pulled up celestial mapping software, her excitement building despite her exhaustion. "Most of the year, Ophiuchus and Orion aren't visible together. They occupy different parts of the sky, rise at different times. But during the winter months, in the right location, at the right time..."

She entered coordinates, adjusting for latitude and time period. The star chart shifted, showing the sky as it would have appeared in late December 1889.

"There." Her voice dropped to barely a whisper. "The winter solstice, approximately two hours after sunset. From certain locations in the American Southwest, both Ophiuchus and Orion would be visible simultaneously—Ophiuchus setting in the west, Orion rising in the east."

"And at the exact moment of alignment?" Jonas asked.

"Their positions would form an axis. A line." She traced it on the screen with her finger. "If you drew a straight line from the heart of Ophiuchus to the belt of Orion, it would point toward a specific location on the horizon—different depending on where you were standing."

Jonas was quiet for a moment, processing. "He wasn't just hiding a location. He was providing instructions for how to find it."

"Stand in a certain place at a certain time," Tanaka confirmed, "watch the alignment of the healer and the hunter, and follow where they point."

She turned to look at him, and for the first time since they'd met, she saw something other than irritating confidence in his expression. She saw genuine intellectual engagement—the same spark she knew when a puzzle started yielding its secrets.

"Can you help me calculate the location?"

"What parameters do you need?"

"Precise stellar positions for December 21, 1889. Atmospheric refraction tables for elevations between 5,000 and 8,000 feet. Topographical data for the

American Southwest." She gestured at the cluttered table. "I've been working with what I can access through academic databases, but the processing power to calculate all the variables—"

"I can help with that." His fingers were already dancing across his laptop. "There are astronomical calculation tools that can handle precession and parallax. Give me the base parameters, and I can run the numbers faster than your standard software."

"You know astronomical software?"

"I know algorithms." He flashed her a grin that was less annoying than usual. "The domain doesn't matter much once you understand the math."

They worked together for the next hour, their laptops side by side, feeding data into Jonas's modified algorithms and refining the results with each iteration. Tanaka found herself explaining stellar mechanics while Jonas translated her requirements into code, their different expertise dovetailing in ways she hadn't expected.

He asked smart questions—not the kind designed to show off, but the kind that came from actually trying to understand. And when she made a calculation error that would have sent them down the wrong path for hours, he caught it without making her feel stupid about it.

During a pause while the algorithm processed, Jonas looked at her sideways. "Can I ask you something? You seem more invested in this than just professional interest. Most cryptolinguists would kill for this kind of discovery, sure, but with you it feels... personal."

Tanaka was quiet for a moment, watching the progress bar crawl across her screen. "My grandmother was Okinawan. During World War II, the Japanese government suppressed Okinawan language and culture—called it primitive, tried to erase it. My grandmother's mother knew songs, stories, traditions that had been passed down for generations. She was forbidden to teach them to her children."

She paused. "My grandmother spent her whole life trying to reconstruct what was lost. Fragments of songs. Half-remembered stories. She died still searching for pieces of her own heritage that someone had decided the world was better off without."

"I'm sorry," Jonas said.

"Don't be. It's why I do what I do." Tanaka met his eyes. "Every time someone suppresses knowledge—burns books, buries discoveries, decides that some truth is too dangerous for ordinary people to know—they're doing what was done to my grandmother. They're stealing pieces of humanity's inheritance."

She turned back to her screen. "If this temple exists, if it really contains what the codex suggests, then it's proof that suppression doesn't work forever. That truth has a way of surviving, no matter how hard people try to bury it."

The algorithm finished. Jonas was looking at her differently now—not with the casual flirtation she'd been deflecting, but with something closer to respect.

"Precession," she muttered at one point, staring at a particularly stubborn variable. "The Earth's axis wobbles over time. What Hathenbruck saw in 1889 isn't exactly what we'd see today."

"So we calculate backward," Jonas said. "Figure out what the alignment looked like in his era, then determine where he must have been standing to see it."

"Exactly." She caught his eye and held it for a moment longer than strictly necessary. "You're not as insufferable as I thought you were."

"High praise from the woman who called me a 'techno-dilettante' yesterday."

"I stand by that assessment in general. But you're proving useful in this specific instance."

The others woke to find them still huddled over laptops, empty mugs forming a protective perimeter around their workspace. Ammon appeared first, bleary-eyed but alert, with fresh tea that Clara had prepared.

"Any progress?" he asked.

"Getting close." Tanaka didn't look up from her screen. "The alignment Hathenbruck described would have been visible from a narrow band across southern Utah and northern Arizona. But the specific angle—the exact direction the line would have pointed—that depends on the precise location."

"How narrow is the band?"

"Maybe fifty miles wide. Still a huge area, but combined with the other reference—"

"The painted walls," Ammon said.

"Exactly." Tanaka looked up, her face alight with the particular joy of intellectual discovery despite her exhaustion. "The codex mentions 'painted walls where ancestors speak'—rock art. There aren't that many locations in southern Utah with significant petroglyphs. If we can narrow the astronomical data to match one of those sites—"

Jonas made a sound—not quite a shout, but something close to it. His whole body went rigid, eyes fixed on his screen.

"Wait." Tanaka grabbed his arm. "Run it again. Different parameters."

Jonas did. The same coordinates resolved on the screen.

"That's not a calculation error," he said. "That's confirmation."

Tanaka was at his side in an instant, her heart hammering against her ribs. The numbers on his screen swam before her eyes for a moment before resolving into coordinates, topographical data, satellite imagery. And there it was—a remote canyon system in the Grand Staircase-Escalante area, virtually inaccessible, the astronomical alignment pointing directly to it like a finger indicating the way.

"Oh my God." The words came out as a breath. She reached for Jonas's shoulder without consciously deciding to reach for him, gripping hard. "Oh my God, that's it. That's really it."

Jonas turned to look at her, and his grin was incandescent—pure, unguarded joy that transformed his face into something almost boyish. "We did it."

"We did it," she echoed, and was grinning back just as wide.

The others gathered around as Jonas turned the laptop to show them. The satellite imagery revealed a maze of narrow slots and towering walls, sandstone formations carved by millennia of wind and water. Cliff faces that, according to the archaeological databases Tanaka had cross-referenced, were covered in ancient rock art.

"The Butler Wash area," Tanaka said, steadier now as she shifted into explanation mode. "I've read about it—archaeologists have documented thousands of petroglyphs there, some dating back millennia. It's one of the most pristine sites in the entire Southwest."

"And one of the hardest to reach," Aspen added, studying the map over their shoulders. "No roads, minimal trails, terrain that would challenge even experienced backcountry travelers. The kind of place that would have remained hidden even as the rest of the region was explored and developed."

"The perfect place to hide something," Ammon said. "Something you wanted to stay hidden for a very long time."

Tanaka stared at the canyon walls on the screen, and a chill ran through her that had nothing to do with the early morning cold. The codices she'd been translating described a civilization that shouldn't exist—a culture with astronomical knowledge rivaling anything the ancient Greeks possessed, with transoceanic capabilities that defied conventional history. If the First Temple was real, if it contained what the codices suggested...

"Do you understand what we might find down there?" she heard herself say. "If even half of what the codices describe is accurate, we're talking about evidence of a civilization that maintained contact between hemispheres thousands of years before Columbus. Astronomical observatories. Metallurgical techniques. Writing systems that predate anything we've documented in the Americas." She shook her head. "This isn't just a historical footnote. This is the kind of discovery that rewrites textbooks. Collapses paradigms. Makes careers—and ruins them."

"And attracts attention," Aspen said grimly.

"The area is massive," Tanaka continued, forcing herself back to practicalities. "Even with the astronomical coordinates narrowing things down, we're still looking at hundreds of square miles. It could take weeks to search thoroughly."

"We don't have weeks." Jonas had switched to monitoring his communication intercepts, his earlier joy fading into focused concern. "Margaux is working the same problem with the same data she stole. If she has access to astronomical expertise—and she probably does, given her father's resources—she could reach the same conclusions we have."

"Then we need more information." Ammon's jaw was tight with determination. "The astronomical reference gets us to the region. But Hathenbruck's removed pages—those would contain the specific location. The exact coordinates of whatever he buried."

"And we still don't know where those pages are," Aspen said. "We know they're not with the main archive. We know Hathenbruck hid them separately, wanting them found only by someone who truly understood what they protected." Ammon paced the small space between the dining table and the kitchen doorway, thinking aloud. "The trail doesn't end with the astronomical reference. That was just another waypoint. There has to be something more—another clue that points to the pages themselves."

"But we've followed every lead," Tanaka said. "The church, the library, the marginalia in the medical texts. What else is there?"

"Family." Clara's voice came from the kitchen doorway. She'd been listening quietly, but now she stepped forward. "I've been thinking about this since you left with the locket. Hathenbruck trusted family above all else. His wife, his descendants, the bloodline that carried his legacy forward. You've followed the trail he left in documents and hidden messages. But some things can't be written down. Some secrets have to be passed person to person, generation to generation."

"The German relatives," Ammon breathed. "Anna's letter mentioned a family property near Freiburg that Friedrich insisted must never be sold. We never followed up on that."

"Because we found the astronomical clue first," Aspen said. "We thought we had what we needed."

"But we didn't. The astronomical clue is only half the puzzle." Ammon's eyes were distant, working through the logic. "Hathenbruck built redundancy into his system. Multiple paths to the same destination, each revealing part of the truth. The American trail through the church and the library leads to the region. The European trail through the family property leads to the exact location."

"You're going to Germany," Clara said. It wasn't a question.

"Someone has to." Ammon looked at the team—exhausted, hunted, working from a safe house with borrowed resources and borrowed time. "The Consortium knows about the American trail. They'll be watching every airport, every connection to our known movements. But a trip to Germany, to visit distant relatives no one's contacted in decades—that might slip under their radar."

"I'll go with you," Jonas said. "If there are documents at the family property, you'll need someone to analyze them quickly. And I can monitor our communications, make sure we're not being tracked."

Tanaka felt something twist in her chest—concern, she realized with some surprise. "Be careful," she said, and was embarrassed by how much she meant it.

Jonas met her eyes, and his expression softened into something that wasn't quite a smile. "Keep working on the location data. If we find those pages, we're going to need your brain to make sense of them."

"What about us?" Tanaka asked, looking to Aspen.

"Stay here. Keep refining the location data." Ammon looked at Aspen. "And watch our backs. If Viktor's people figure out where we are..."

"They won't." Aspen's voice was steel. "Clara's been off-grid for thirty years. If anyone can help us stay hidden, it's her."

Clara nodded, her expression resolute. "I've been running from this family's secrets my whole life. Maybe it's time I helped uncover them instead."

The decision was made. Tomorrow, Ammon and Jonas would fly to Germany, following the trail that Anna's letters had revealed. Meanwhile, Tanaka would continue her astronomical analysis, and Aspen would coordinate security from the Denver safe house.

They were splitting up—a risk, given the forces arrayed against them. But it was also their best chance of winning a race they couldn't afford to lose.

Tanaka turned back to the satellite imagery, to the canyon that had swallowed so many secrets over so many millennia. Whatever waited down there in the darkness, it had been patient. It could wait a little longer.

But not much longer.

The First Temple was waiting. And one way or another, they were going to find it first.

CHAPTER EIGHTEEN

Family Secrets

Three days had passed since their escape from the mountains. Clara's dining room had become an archive.

She had spent the morning pulling boxes from closets and crawl spaces, containers Ammon hadn't known existed. Now they covered the oak table in uneven stacks—cardboard boxes gone soft with age, a leather valise with a broken clasp, manila envelopes thick with documents that exhaled dust when touched. The smell of old paper filled the room, the odor of secrets kept too long in darkness.

"I kept everything," Clara said, lifting the lid from a hatbox filled with photographs. "After your grandmother passed, I couldn't bring myself to sort through it. Seemed like disturbing the dead." Her hands trembled as she set the lid aside—whether from age or emotion, Ammon couldn't tell.

Ammon picked up a photograph from the top of the pile—sepia-toned, mounted on thick cardboard stock with gilt edges that had flaked away in places. A family posed before a wooden farmhouse, the women in high-collared dresses, the men in dark suits despite what must have been summer heat. The image had the formal stiffness of the era, everyone holding unnaturally still for the long exposure. Someone had written on the back in faded pencil: Hathenbruck Familie, Freiburg, 1867.

"That's Friedrich," Clara said, pointing to a bearded man standing apart from the others. "And that's Anna beside him. This was taken the year before they emigrated."

Ammon studied his ancestor's face—stern, guarded, the eyes of a man already carrying secrets. Even in the frozen stillness of the photograph, there was something watchful about him, alert to dangers others couldn't see. Anna looked younger than Ammon had imagined, her hand resting on Friedrich's arm with a possessiveness that spoke of deep attachment. She would follow him across an ocean, leaving everyone else in this photograph behind.

"There's more." Clara slid a bundle of letters across the table, bound with a ribbon that had once been blue but had faded to gray. The ribbon left marks on her fingers—dye that had waited decades to transfer. "These are from Anna's sister, Margarethe. She stayed in Germany when Anna left."

The paper was fragile, threatening to crack along the fold lines that had been pressed and repressed over a century of reading and rereading. Ammon handled the first letter carefully, unfolding it to reveal dense German script, the handwriting ornate and difficult to parse. The ink had faded to brown, the color of dried blood.

"Can you read it?" Aspen asked, looking over his shoulder. Their breath was warm against his neck, grounding him in the present even as the past pressed close.

"My German's not good enough for this. The old script—Kurrent, I think it's called—I can barely make out individual letters. Clara?"

Clara pulled reading glasses from her cardigan pocket—thick lenses, the frames held together at one hinge with tape—and took the letter. Her lips moved silently as she worked through the text, occasionally pausing to trace a word with her finger. The silence stretched, broken only by the tick of an old clock in the hallway and the distant sound of traffic on the street outside.

"It's dated April 1912," she said. "Margarethe writes: *'Meine liebste Schwester—'* That's *'My dearest sister.'* She goes on about family matters for a bit, health concerns, a nephew's wedding. Then here—let me read this part directly:"

"*'Ich schreibe dir mit Neuigkeiten über das Anwesen in Freiburg. Friedrichs Anweisungen wurden genau befolgt. Das Haus bleibt in der Familie, und das Gewölbe unter dem alten Arbeitszimmer ist unberührt. Meine Söhne verstehen ihre Pflicht, so wie ich die meine issenen.'*"

Clara looked up, translating: "*'I write to you with news of the property at Freiburg. Friedrich's instructions have been followed precisely. The house remains in the family, and the vault beneath the old study is undisturbed. My sons understand their duty, as I understand mine.'*"

"Vault," Jonas said from his position by the window, where he'd been watching the street. "There's actually a vault."

"It gets more specific." Clara's finger traced further down the page: "*'Sie werden diese Verantwortung an ihre Kinder weitergeben, wie unsere Eltern sie an uns weitergegeben haben. Die Kiste ist versiegelt, und Friedrich ließ uns versprechen, sie niemals zu öffnen—nur zu bewachen, bis jemand aus deiner amerikanischen Linie kommt, um sie zu beanspruchen. Er sagte, die Zeit würde kommen, wenn die Welt bereit ist für das, was sie enthält.'*"

"*'They will pass this responsibility to their children, as our parents passed it to us. The box is sealed, and Friedrich made us promise never to open it—only to guard it until someone from your American line comes to claim it. He said the time would come when the world is ready for what it contains.'"*

"Wait—there's an earlier letter here." Clara carefully extracted a more brittle page from near the bottom of the bundle. "Dated March 1891."

Ammon leaned forward. 1891 would have been twenty-three years after Friedrich emigrated. What could Margarethe have been writing about then?

Clara translated, her voice hushed: "*'Friedrich came home. After all these years, he stood in our doorway like a ghost—older, weathered by the American sun, but with the same fire in his eyes that I remembered from our youth. He stayed only four days. He would not speak of why he had come, only that he carried something that must be protected. Something his enemies could never be allowed to find.'"*

"He went back to Germany," Jonas said. "After discovering whatever he discovered in America, he made the journey home."

Clara nodded and continued reading: "*'He worked through the nights in Father's old study. I heard him beneath the floor, building something—metal against metal, the sound of machinery I did not understand. When he finished, he made me swear an oath. Guard what he has hidden, he said. Never open it. Never speak of it. Wait for the one who will come from my American line, carrying the knowledge to unlock what I have sealed. Only together—the German branch and the American—can the truth be revealed.'"*

"Two halves of a puzzle," Tanaka murmured. "Separated by an ocean."

"'He left before dawn on the fifth day,'" Clara finished. "*'I never saw my brother again. But I have kept my promise, as I know you keep yours, dear sister. The vault remains sealed. The secret remains safe. And we wait, as Friedrich asked us to wait, for the future he believed would come.'"*

The room had gone still. Tanaka leaned forward from her seat at the far end of the table, her analytical mind visibly working behind her eyes.

"He split his archive. The American trail leads to the region—the astronomical references, the petroglyphs, the general location. But the specific coordinates..."

"Are in Germany," Ammon finished. "Hidden with family who had no idea what they were protecting. Just like the American branch. Two halves of a map, separated by an ocean."

Clara set down the first letter with the care of a museum curator and picked up another, this one dated years later. The paper was less fragile— newer—but the handwriting had grown shakier with age.

"There's more. Margarethe writes again in 1923:"

"'Manchmal frage ich mich, was Friedrich uns zur Bewahrung anvertraut hat. Die Kiste ist schwer für ihre Größe, als enthielte sie Metall oder Stein. Mein ältester Sohn fragte einmal, ob wir sie öffnen sollten, nur um zu issen. Ich sagte ihm, was Friedrich mir sagte, bevor er nach Amerika aufbrach: dass es nicht uns zusteht zu entscheiden. Wir sind Hüter, nicht Richter. Er glaubte an eine Zukunft, die wir nicht sehen können.'"

Clara's voice was hushed as she translated. *"'Sometimes I wonder what Friedrich entrusted to our keeping. The box is heavy for its size, as if it contains metal or stone. My eldest son once asked if we should open it, just to know. I told him what Friedrich told me before he left for America: that it is not for us to decide. We are guardians, not judges. He believed in a future we cannot see.'"*

Guardians, not judges. Ammon turned the phrase over in his mind. Friedrich had used that word deliberately—the same word the Ute tradition used for those who protected the sacred chamber. Had he learned it from them? Or had he arrived already understanding what guardianship meant?

He thought of Marcus—his uncle who had traveled to Germany in 2011, who had come back changed, obsessed, frightened. Had he found the property? Had he seen the vault? The family had long assumed his "hunting accident" three months later was simple misfortune. Ammon had since learned it was murder. Now he wondered if Marcus had gotten closer to this secret than anyone realized—and paid for that proximity with his life.

"We need to find out if the property still exists," he said. "If the German branch of the family is still there, still guarding whatever Friedrich left behind."

"Marcus's papers might help." Clara rose and crossed to a box she hadn't yet opened—newer than the others, the cardboard still crisp, a strip of packing tape across the top that had never been cut. "These are his. Everything he brought back from Germany, plus his research notes. Marcus had become paranoid. Thought your grandfather's place was being watched. Felt he couldn't keep them there, or with Silas. He hid them here with me. I couldn't look at them after he died. It felt like..."

She trailed off, her hand resting on the box as if drawing warmth from it.

"Like opening a wound," Aspen said gently.

"Yes. Exactly like that."

Ammon lifted the lid, the tape separating with a sound like a held breath finally released. Inside, Marcus's handwriting covered dozens of legal pads—cramped, urgent, the script of a man racing against something only he could see. There were photocopies of old documents, maps with locations circled in red pen, genealogical charts tracing family branches across two continents and five generations.

And there, tucked into a folder marked FREIBURG—CONTACTS in Marcus's blocky capitals, a list of names and addresses. German relatives Marcus had found and visited. Some names had check marks beside them. Others had question marks. One had been circled multiple times, the pen pressing hard enough to nearly tear the paper: Hoffmann, Greta—Hathenbruck house. Property still in family.

"Hoffmann," Clara said, reading over his shoulder. "That must be through marriage. The German line would have changed names over the generations, daughters marrying out, the Hathenbruck name passed along through different families."

Beneath the contact list, a handwritten note in Marcus's script, dated August 2011: *Property now operates as B&B. Greta (78) remembers stories from grandmother about 'the American box.' Says no one has opened the vault in living memory. Knows it exists beneath the study but has never seen inside. Willing to show me—said it was finally time for the American line to claim what was left. Return visit scheduled for October.*

Marcus had died in September. Three weeks before his scheduled return.

"He was so close," Ammon said, rough. "Weeks away from seeing what Friedrich had hidden. And then the gunshot that changed everything—"

"Now you're going to follow the same trail, and I need you to promise me something." Clara gripped his arm with surprising strength. "Be careful. Whatever's in that vault, it's been waiting over a century. It can wait a little longer. Don't let it cost you what it cost Marcus."

Ammon covered her hand with his. "I promise."

"And you'll come back. Whatever you find, you'll come back and tell me. I'm done with not knowing."

"I will."

He turned to the others—Aspen with their guarded expression, Jonas already reaching for his laptop, Tanaka watching with the intensity of someone who had staked her academic career on this mystery.

"So we're set," he said, looking at the others. "Jonas and I leave for Germany tomorrow. We'll make contact with the Hoffmann family, find out if the vault is still intact. Tanaka, keep refining the target area based on the astronomical data. Once we have the specific coordinates from Germany, we'll know exactly where to look in Utah."

"I'll hold the fort here," Aspen said. "Coordinate communications, watch for any sign that Margaux or her people have picked up our trail. If they trace us to Denver—"

Ammon shuddered at the thought. He met their eyes, hoping they could read what he couldn't say aloud: that splitting up terrified him, that every hour apart would feel like a held breath, that he needed to know they were safe even if safe meant separated.

Something in their expression softened. "Just don't do anything stupid over there."

"I'll do my best."

"One more problem," Ammon continued. "How do we fly without them tracking us? If Viktor's people are sophisticated enough to stage that assault, they'll be watching airports, monitoring flight manifests."

Clara crossed to a desk drawer and pulled out a manila envelope. "I told you I got good at disappearing." Inside: two passports with photos that matched Ammon and Jonas but names that didn't. The documents looked authentic—worn enough to seem used, the stamps and visas telling a plausible story of ordinary travel. "A contact in Colorado Springs. Retired now, but he still does work for people who need to move quietly. The documents won't survive a deep background check, but for tourists visiting German relatives, they'll hold."

"You just had these ready?"

"I've had escape routes planned for twenty years. Alternate identities, cash reserves, contacts who don't ask questions." Clara's expression was unreadable. "I never thought I'd use them for this. But the family obsession has a way of pulling you back in, one way or another." She handed the envelope to Ammon. "Cash only from here on. No credit cards, no phones that connect to your real identities. Jonas—you can set up secure communications?"

"Already working on it. Encrypted channels, burner devices, the works."

"It's still a risk," Aspen said. "If they're running facial recognition at major hubs—"

"Then we're two faces in ten thousand," Jonas replied. "Denver to London to Frankfurt—one of the busiest routes in the world. By the time anything flags, we're already on the ground in Freiburg."

Aspen didn't look convinced, but they nodded. "Just move fast. And check in every six hours. If I don't hear from you, I'm assuming the worst."

Jonas was already typing. "I can have us on a flight tomorrow morning. Routing through London, then Frankfurt, then train to Freiburg. Longer but harder to track—and with these documents, we're just two Americans on vacation."

"Do it."

Clara began carefully repacking the oldest documents, handling each piece like the artifact it was. Outside, the Denver sky had gone dark, winter clouds pressing low over the city, and the first flakes of snow were beginning to fall.

Somewhere across the Atlantic, in a house that had guarded secrets for over a century, a vault waited to be opened.

Ammon gathered Marcus's notes, the contact information, the photographs of ancestors he had never known. Tomorrow he would fly to Germany and follow the trail his uncle had blazed three decades ago.

This time, he intended to survive what waited at its end.

CHAPTER NINETEEN

Competing Intelligence

Margaux Vance sat in the chartered jet's leather seat, watching the clouds pass below and wondering if she'd made a terrible mistake. The Gulfstream's cabin was obscenely comfortable—hand-stitched Italian leather, burled walnut trim, crystal decanters secured in their velvet cradles. Her father had always insisted on traveling well, even when the Consortium's funds would have been better spent elsewhere. The trappings of legitimacy, he'd called it. People trust those who appear successful.

Tonight, the luxury felt like mockery. The documents spread across the table in front of her represented weeks of careful infiltration—photographs, notes, translations, the accumulated intelligence of her time inside the cultural center. She'd applied the same methodological rigor to espionage that she'd once applied to her doctoral research: systematic observation, careful documentation, triangulation of sources. It should have been enough. Should have given her everything she needed to find the First Temple before anyone else.

Instead, it left her with more questions than answers. She pressed her fingertips against her temples, trying to relieve the pressure that had been building since San Antonio. When had she last slept properly? The skin beneath her eyes felt papery and thin. Her neck ached from hours hunched over stolen documents, and her jaw was sore from clenching it while pretending to be someone she wasn't.

The astronomical reference was clear enough—that much, at least, her Oxford training could parse. The meeting place of Asklepios and Orion, visible from a specific location during the winter solstice. Her father's contacts had connected her with an astronomer who'd calculated the same parameters that Tanaka was probably working through right now—a broad swath of southern Utah and northern Arizona where the alignment would have been visible in Hathenbruck's era. But "broad swath" wasn't useful. The target area covered hundreds of square miles of some of the most rugged, inaccessible terrain in the American West.

Without more specific coordinates, finding the First Temple would require a search that could take months—months she didn't have, not with the Consortium's resources dwindling and Viktor's patience wearing thin. She needed the removed pages. The ones Hathenbruck had hidden separately, the ones that would pinpoint the exact location. And those pages were somewhere she couldn't reach. Her phone buzzed with Viktor's latest report.

She read it quickly, her frustration deepening with each line. Targets fled cultural center during assault. Current location unknown—they've gone completely dark. Surveillance of known contacts has detected nothing. Either they're extremely careful or they're receiving professional assistance.

Additional concern: third party also active in the area. Methods suggest intelligence community connections, possibly European. Could be governmental or private. Recommend caution.

Margaux had suspected as much from Phantom's warnings to Jonas—someone else was in the game, someone with resources that dwarfed even her father's remaining network. The Church, Phantom had called them. An institutional buyer with centuries of experience in managing inconvenient truths. She was outmatched. The realization settled over her like a cold blanket, forcing her to confront possibilities she'd been avoiding since this began.

In graduate school, she'd written a paper on institutional memory—how organizations like the Vatican accumulated not just archives but methodologies, refined over centuries, for controlling the flow of dangerous information. She'd treated it as an academic exercise. Now she was living it. Her father had always believed that determination and resources could overcome any obstacle. That the key to success was pushing harder, taking risks others wouldn't take, doing whatever was necessary to reach the goal.

It was a philosophy that had built the Consortium's power—and ultimately destroyed it when his methods crossed lines that couldn't be uncrossed. Was she making the same mistakes? Following the same path toward the same destruction? The documents on the table blurred as her eyes lost focus. She'd told herself this was different.

That she was pursuing knowledge, not profit. That her methods were cleaner, her motives purer than her father's had been. She'd even constructed an ethical framework to justify it—the utilitarian calculus of a greater good, the democratization of knowledge that belonged to all humanity rather than a single tribe. But she'd infiltrated the cultural center under false pretenses. Had photographed sacred documents without permission.

Had stolen intelligence from people who'd trusted her with their work.

She flagged down the flight attendant and ordered a whiskey she didn't want, just to have something to do with her hands. The ice clinked against the plastic cup. She watched the bubbles rise and pop without lifting it to her lips.

Her father would have laughed. *Sentiment is a luxury*, he liked to say. *The successful learn to afford it only after they've won.*

She wasn't winning. She wasn't even sure anymore what winning would look like.

And when Viktor's assault team had attacked, she'd been safely on a jet heading toward Europe, leaving the researchers to face the violence she'd helped orchestrate. How was that different from her father? How was any of this different? The ice in her untouched whiskey had melted, diluting it to amber water.

She couldn't remember when the flight attendant had brought it, or how long ago. Hours, maybe. The jet vibrated around her, a cocoon of recycled air and muffled engine noise, insulating her from the consequences waiting below. Her phone buzzed again. A message from her father's prison account, routed through layers of encryption that made it effectively untraceable.

Progress report requested. Consortium assets require deployment decisions. Time is critical. Even now—diminished, incarcerated, dependent on her for everything—he couldn't simply ask. Couldn't say how are you or be careful or any of the things a father might say to a daughter carrying his legacy into danger.

Just demands dressed in the passive voice. Assets require deployment. As if she were one of those assets. As if she'd ever been anything else. Time was critical.

Resources were limited. Competitors were closing in. All the pressures that had pushed her father toward increasingly desperate measures, now pushing her in the same direction. She could see the path ahead clearly. More surveillance, more infiltration, more violence if necessary.

Viktor had resources—men with skills and no scruples, ready to do whatever was required to secure the First Temple's location. All she had to do was authorize their deployment.

The message from Viktor arrived as the plane began its descent.

Phase Two approved. Target: Denver safe house. Extraction of Ranger Rhoades and Dr. Tanaka. 0300 local time.

Margaux read it twice. Then a third time, as if the words might rearrange themselves into something less damning.

They were going to take Aspen. Tanaka. People she'd worked beside, shared meals with, argued with about translation protocols. People who had trusted her.

Her thumb hovered over the keyboard. She could send a warning. Two words—*Get out*—and they would know. They would run. Viktor's team would find an empty house, and Margaux's cover would be destroyed, and her father's network would collapse, and—

And what? She would have saved two people who would never forgive her anyway. Who would testify against her at trial. Who would tell the world that Elias Vance's daughter was exactly what everyone had always assumed.

The plane touched down. The seatbelt sign chimed. Passengers began to stir.

Margaux deleted the draft message she hadn't realized she was composing and typed a response to Viktor:

Understood. Standing by.

She pressed send before she could change her mind.

It felt like jumping off a cliff—the moment after your feet leave the edge, when you realize gravity is a force you can't negotiate with. What she'd done could not be undone. The people who would be hurt tonight would be hurt because she had chosen not to stop it.

She told herself there was still time. Still options. Still some future where she could make this right.

But the whiskey she'd ordered sat untouched, the ice melted, and Margaux watched the lights rise from the darkness below like accusations she wasn't ready to answer.

CHAPTER TWENTY

The Freiburg House

The flight from Denver to Frankfurt had been eleven hours of turbulent sleep and recycled air, followed by a rental car journey through increasingly dense forest.

By the time the GPS guided them off the main road onto a track that wound between ancient pines, Ammon's body had lost all sense of time. The Black Forest earned its name in these deeper stretches—evergreens pressing so close that the world took on a greenish twilight quality even at midday.

"It's like driving through a fairy tale," Jonas said from the passenger seat, his face pressed close to the window.

"Or a horror movie."

The Black Forest town of Freiburg im Breisgau rose from the Rhine valley like something out of the stories that had been born in these woods. Medieval spires pierced the afternoon mist, cobblestone streets wound between half-timbered buildings, and the Münster cathedral's tower dominated the skyline with the same quiet authority it had maintained for seven centuries. Ammon's exhaustion temporarily lifted in the face of such preserved beauty—the kind of continuity that made American history feel like a brief footnote.

"The Hathenbruck property is on the outskirts," Jonas said, consulting his phone. "About fifteen minutes from the old town. Listed as a bed and breakfast now. Family-run."

"Family-run by descendants of Anna's sister Margarethe." Ammon felt the weight of that connection—a branch of his family he'd never known, guarding secrets across an ocean for over a century.

Jonas navigated the narrow streets with the careful attention of someone driving in an unfamiliar country where everything felt off-kilter. "According to the genealogy records I pulled, the current owner is Gerhard Hoffmann. His mother was Greta Hoffmann—the woman Marcus met in 2011."

"Was?"

"She passed away about five years ago, according to the records. Gerhard inherited the property."

The property appeared around a curve in the road—a substantial house in the traditional Black Forest style, with a steep roof designed to shed heavy snow and dark timber framing against white walls. Flower boxes adorned every window despite the season, filled with hardy winter pansies in deep purple and gold. A hand-painted sign announced "Gasthaus Hoffmann" in Gothic script, the letters faded by decades of sun and rain.

Behind the house, the forest pressed close, evergreens standing sentinel like they'd been guarding this spot since before the house existed.

A man emerged as they parked, tall and deliberate in his movements, with large hands that suggested decades of practical work. He had sharp eyes that Ammon recognized from photographs of Friedrich—the same strong jaw, the same watchful quality. He studied the rental car with the assessing gaze of someone who didn't often receive unexpected visitors.

"Americans," he said in accented but fluent English. "Not many tourists this time of year. You are the ones who called ahead?"

"I'm Ammon Lundquist." He stepped forward, offering his hand. "Friedrich Hathenbruck was my great-great-grandfather. I believe we're related."

The man's expression transformed. The guarded wariness fell away, replaced by something warmer—the particular recognition of long-awaited arrival.

"You must be Marcus's nephew. I am Gerhard Hoffmann. My mother spoke of your uncle often, in her final years. She always hoped someone from the American line would return." He clasped Ammon's hand in both of his, his grip surprisingly strong. "Please—come inside. We have much to discuss."

The next hour dissolved into the particular warmth of German hospitality. Gerhard's wife Elke—a woman with silver hair pulled back in a practical bun and the efficient movements of someone who had spent decades running a household—refused to let them discuss anything of substance until they had been fed.

"You look half-starved, both of you, and frozen besides," she declared, ushering them into a kitchen that smelled of fresh bread and something savory simmering on the stove.

They ate Käsespätzle—soft egg noodles baked with cheese and topped with crispy onions—while Gerhard shared stories that bridged generations and an ocean. A grandfather clock ticked steadily in the corner, its pendulum catching the light. The walls were covered with framed photographs spanning what looked like a century: stern-faced ancestors in formal poses, wedding portraits, children at various ages, the guesthouse itself in different eras.

"Your uncle Marcus visited in 2011," Gerhard said, refilling Ammon's coffee cup. The coffee was stronger than American brew, dark and bitter in a way that felt appropriate for this conversation. "My mother was still alive then—she was seventy-eight, sharp as ever, the keeper of all the family secrets. She liked Marcus very much. Said he had Friedrich's intensity."

"What did he want to know?"

"Everything." Gerhard's voice carried the weight of old memory. "Where Friedrich came from, what he did before emigrating, why he went to America. He was particularly interested in what Friedrich left behind. In the vault."

Ammon's heart rate quickened. "The vault beneath the study."

"You know of it." Gerhard nodded. "My mother showed Marcus where it was. She told him she would grant him access—that after all these years, it was time for the American line to claim what Friedrich had left. But Marcus said he needed to return home first, to gather certain information. He believed the vault required something to open it, something only the American descendants would have." Gerhard's expression darkened. "He was supposed to return in October. Instead, we received word of his death."

"A hunting accident," Ammon said. "That's what the family was told."

Gerhard studied him for a long moment. "You say that as if you no longer believe it."

"I've learned things since then. Things that suggest his death wasn't an accident at all."

Elke made a small sound of distress. Gerhard reached for her hand.

"My mother suspected as much," he said. "She believed Marcus had gotten too close to something dangerous. She carried that guilt with her until she died—wondering if she should have warned him more strongly, if showing him the vault had somehow led to his death."

"It wasn't her fault. There are people who have been hunting Friedrich's secrets for a very long time. They would have found Marcus eventually, whether your mother helped him or not."

Gerhard absorbed this in silence. Then: "These people who hunt secrets—they came here once. Long before Marcus."

Ammon leaned forward. "When?"

"The 1970s. A priest from Rome, very scholarly, very polite. He said he was researching German immigrant families who had settled in America. He offered to purchase any documents related to Friedrich—letters, journals, photographs. A generous sum, enough to repair the roof and modernize the kitchen." Gerhard's jaw tightened. "My mother was young then, newly married, struggling to keep this place running. She was tempted."

"But she didn't sell."

"She was cleverer than that." A ghost of a smile crossed Gerhard's face. "My mother understood that a priest from Rome doesn't travel to the Black Forest to buy old letters unless those letters contain something valuable. So she gave him what he wanted—but not everything."

"What do you mean?"

"There was a hiding place in the wall of the study—a false panel that my grandmother had used to store family papers. My mother filled it with documents that seemed important but weren't. Copies of letters, old photographs, medical records from Friedrich's practice. She let the priest 'discover' this cache during his visit, acted surprised and reluctant, negotiated a good price." Gerhard's smile sharpened. "He left believing he had found everything. He never thought to look for the vault."

"Because he didn't know it existed."

"The vault has been a secret passed from mother to daughter—and in my generation, mother to son—since Margarethe herself. Friedrich made his sister promise: never speak of it to outsiders. Never open it. Guard it until someone from the American line comes to claim what's inside." Gerhard met Ammon's eyes. "My mother waited her whole life for that person. So did I. And now, finally, you are here."

The kitchen had grown darker while they talked, the winter afternoon fading toward evening. Ammon was aware of the clock ticking, of generations pressing down on this room where his ancestors had lived and worked and kept their secrets.

"Will you show us?" he asked.

Gerhard rose without a word and gestured for them to follow.

They walked through a corridor lined with framed photographs—generations of Hathenbrucks, their faces echoing across the decades like variations on a theme—and into a room that had clearly once been a study. Bookshelves lined the walls, filled with volumes in German and English, their spines cracked with age. A window looked out onto the darkening forest, and the smell of old paper and wood polish hung in the air.

"This was Friedrich's room," Gerhard said. "Where he worked before he left for America. Where he wrote the letters that Margarethe kept until her death."

He crossed to a worn rug in the center of the room and rolled it back, revealing wide oak floorboards darkened by a century of foot traffic. Four of the boards were subtly different from the others—the same wood, the same finish, but the nails were set at different angles, invisible unless you knew to look.

"Help me," Gerhard said.

Together, they pried up the boards—each one requiring careful manipulation, a specific sequence that Gerhard performed from memory. Beneath them lay not empty space but a metal plate set into the floor, its surface covered with an intricate mechanism unlike anything Ammon had ever seen.

"Friedrich was a physician," Gerhard said, "but his true passion was engineering. Friedrich built this when he returned to Germany in 1891— twenty-three years after he first emigrated. My mother said he came back with secrets from America, secrets he needed to protect on both sides of the ocean. He spent four days here, working through the nights, and then disappeared before dawn. No one in the family ever saw him again." Gerhard ran his fingers along the edge of the mechanism. "A lock that cannot be picked, cannot be forced. It requires knowledge to open—specific knowledge that he divided between the two branches of the family."

Ammon studied the mechanism. It consisted of four rotating cylinders, each inscribed with letters and numbers. Above them, engraved into the metal plate, was an inscription in German:

"*'Der Heiler und der Jäger treffen sich, wo das heilige Blut fließt,'*" he read aloud. "*'The healer and the hunter meet where the sacred blood flows.'*"

"My mother could never solve it," Gerhard said. "Nor could her mother, nor any of us. We understood it must be a riddle—something that required information only the American descendants would have. That's why we've waited. That's why we guard but never open."

But Ammon was smiling. The exhaustion of the journey fell away as the pieces clicked into place.

"The healer and the hunter," he said. "Asklepios and Orion—the constellations Friedrich used to mark the location in America. And 'where the sacred blood flows'—" He looked at Jonas. "Die heilige Ader. The Sacred

Vein. It's what Friedrich found inside chamber—a gold vein, yes—and so much more."

"You know the answer?" Gerhard's voice was hushed.

"Part of it. The healer is Asklepios—Ophiuchus in astronomical terms. The hunter is Orion." Ammon knelt beside the mechanism, his mind racing. "But I need the German half. What did Friedrich tell Margarethe? What knowledge did he leave with your family?"

Gerhard was quiet for a moment, reaching into memory. "There was a phrase my mother taught me. She said it came from Margarethe, who had it from Friedrich himself. 'The year of departure, the month of meeting, the day of promise, the hour of stars.'"

"Dates," Jonas said, catching on. "Four numbers. The cylinders need four inputs."

"The year of departure—1868, when Friedrich left for America." Ammon counted on his fingers. "The month of meeting—that would be when he first encountered the guardians. His journal mentions July."

"The day of promise?" Gerhard asked.

Ammon thought of the locket, of Anna's portrait, of the vows Friedrich had made. "His wedding day. Anna's letters mention it—the fifteenth."

"And the hour of stars," Jonas said. "The winter solstice alignment. When Asklepios and Orion are both visible. That happens around—"

"Twenty-one hundred hours," Ammon finished. "Nine p.m. The time Friedrich recorded in his journal as the moment of revelation."

He looked at Gerhard. "1868. July—the seventh month. The fifteenth day. Twenty-one hours."

"Sixty-eight, seven, fifteen, twenty-one," Gerhard breathed.

Together, they rotated the cylinders. The mechanism was stiff with age, each number requiring careful pressure to align. Ammon's hands trembled as he set the final cylinder into place.

For a moment, nothing happened.

Then, with a click that seemed impossibly loud in the silent room, the metal plate shifted. A seam appeared where none had been visible, and the plate lifted—just enough for fingers to find purchase.

Gerhard helped him lift it aside, revealing a shallow compartment lined with oilcloth that had protected its contents from moisture for over a century. Inside lay a leather satchel, its surface cracked with age but still intact.

Ammon reached in with hands that no longer trembled. Whatever fear or uncertainty he'd carried across the ocean had burned away, leaving only the steady certainty of purpose. This was what he'd come for. This was what five generations had protected.

The satchel contained two items.

The first was a letter in Friedrich's distinctive handwriting, the German text covering both sides of the paper in neat, precise script. The second was a folded map—hand-drawn with the careful attention of a trained surveyor, showing canyon systems and geographical features that Ammon recognized immediately as southern Utah.

"Can you read it?" Jonas asked, barely whispering.

Ammon's German was adequate but not fluent. He translated haltingly, feeling each phrase, letting the words settle into English:

"'Wer auch immer dies findet—To whoever finds this—'" He paused, his throat tight. "'I am Friedrich Wilhelm Hathenbruck, and I have carried a burden that no man should bear alone.'"

Elke had followed them into the study. She made a small sound, her hand finding her husband's arm.

"'What I have hidden in the American wilderness is too dangerous for the world to know, yet too important to destroy. I have sealed the truth in a place where only those worthy to find it will think to look.'"

Ammon turned the letter over, his hands steady now, as if Friedrich's words had given him purpose:

"'The map shows where I buried the final truth. The location marked with my initials contains documents that will lead the finder to what I have called the First Temple—a site that predates all known American civilizations, holding knowledge that could transform or destroy the world as we understand it.'"

Jonas was already photographing the map, his phone clicking rapidly in the silence. But Ammon barely noticed. He was focused on the final paragraph, the words that had survived across more than a century, waiting for this moment:

"'Möge Gott mir vergeben, wenn ich Unrecht tat, dies zu verbergen.'" His voice caught. "'May God forgive me if I was wrong to hide this. May whoever finds these words have the wisdom to know what should be revealed and what should remain buried.'"

He looked up at Gerhard and Elke, who were watching him with expressions of wonder and relief—the relief of guardians whose long watch had finally ended.

"There's more," he said, and read the final lines:

"'Die heilige Ader durchzieht uns alle—The sacred vein runs through all of us—connecting us to the past and obligating us to the future. I have done what I believed was right. Now the choice passes to you.'"

The room was silent except for the ticking of the grandfather clock somewhere deeper in the house. Outside, the Black Forest had settled into evening darkness, the same darkness that had surrounded Friedrich when he was a young man dreaming of distant mountains and ancient secrets.

Gerhard and Elke looked stunned—they had guarded this secret their whole lives without understanding its magnitude. And Ammon held his ancestor's final message, feeling the full weight of inheritance settle onto his shoulders like a mantle that had been waiting five generations to be claimed.

The map was clear. The location was specific. A spot in the canyons of southern Utah, marked with Friedrich William Claude Hathenbruck's initials: FWCH.

After more than a century, Hathenbruck's greatest secret was finally ready to be found.

They stayed for dinner—Elke insisted, and neither Ammon nor Jonas had the heart to refuse.

Over Sauerbraten and red cabbage, they promised to stay in touch, to share whatever they discovered, to bridge the gap that had separated the family for too long. Gerhard pressed a bottle of local wine into Ammon's hands as they left. Elke hugged him like a long-lost son.

"Your uncle would be proud," Gerhard said at the door, gripping Ammon's shoulder. "My mother always said he had Friedrich's determination. Now I see you have it too."

But as they drove away into the darkness of the Black Forest, the satchel tucked safely in Ammon's jacket, he couldn't shake the feeling that they weren't the only ones interested in what they'd discovered.

The Vatican had sent a priest to this house fifty years ago. The Consortium had been tracking Hathenbruck's trail for decades. And somewhere out there, forces he couldn't see were converging on the same destination.

The race was no longer theoretical. It was real, immediate, and potentially deadly.

And it had just entered its final phase.

CHAPTER TWENTY-ONE

Konstantin

The cobblestones of Freiburg's old town were slick with morning dew as Ammon and Jonas stepped out of the Hathenbruck guesthouse.

Church bells from the Münster Cathedral tolled the hour—eleven chimes rolling across the medieval rooftops, each note hanging in the crisp autumn air before fading into the murmur of the city. Ammon paused on the threshold, letting his eyes adjust to the brightness after the dim interior of Friedrich's old study.

The envelope felt heavy in his jacket pocket—heavier than paper and ink should feel. A map to the First Temple. Coordinates that had waited over a century to be found. His ancestor's final secret, hidden in a vault beneath the study floor that even the Vatican's agents had missed.

The street opened onto a small plaza where students from the university clustered around café tables, laptops open, coffee cups steaming. A bakery on the corner exhaled the warm scent of fresh Brötchen, and somewhere nearby, a street musician played something melancholy on a violin. It was the kind of scene that belonged on a postcard—the picturesque heart of the Black Forest region, unchanged in its essential character for centuries.

Jonas fell into step beside him. "That was almost too easy."

"Nothing about this has been easy."

"You know what I mean. The cousins just... let us poke around Friedrich's study? Didn't ask questions when we found a hidden vault?"

"They're family. They trust us." Ammon navigated around a group of tourists photographing the half-timbered buildings. "Besides, to them it's just old papers. They don't know what we're really looking for."

They walked in silence for a block, passing a bookshop with a display of local histories in the window, a pharmacy with its green cross glowing, a narrow alley where someone had strung fairy lights between the buildings despite it being full daylight. Ammon found himself cataloging details the way he had learned to do over the past months—exits, sight lines, faces that appeared more than once.

It was Jonas who first noticed something wrong.

"Gray Audi," he said, carefully casual. "Behind us. I saw it when we left the guesthouse. Then again on Bertoldstraße. Now it's circling the block."

Ammon resisted the urge to look back. "You're sure it's the same car?"

"Dented rear bumper. German plates but rental sticker in the window." Jonas had spent years evading authorities in the digital world; the skills translated surprisingly well to physical surveillance. "And there's a guy at the café we just passed. Gray jacket, silver hair. He was reading a newspaper, but he hasn't turned a page in ten minutes."

"Viktor's people?"

"Different energy." Jonas shook his head. "Viktor's team are operators— military bearing, tactical awareness. This guy is something else. More... refined. Like a professor who moonlights as an assassin."

They turned onto a narrower street, one that would lead them toward where they had parked their rental car. The crowds thinned here, the tourist traffic funneling toward the Münsterplatz and its famous market. Ammon's hand drifted toward the envelope in his pocket, an unconscious protective gesture.

That was when the man in the gray jacket stepped out of a side alley, blocking their path.

He moved with the easy confidence of someone accustomed to controlling spaces—a single smooth motion that transformed him from part of the scenery into an obstacle that could not be ignored. Up close, Ammon could see that his first impression had been accurate: cultured, prosperous, dangerous. The man's gray eyes held the patient calculation of a chess player who had already seen the endgame.

"Dr. Lundquist. Mr. West." His voice carried a faint accent—something Slavic, Ammon thought, perhaps Eastern European, though softened by years of cosmopolitan polish. "A moment of your time, if you please."

Ammon stopped, acutely aware of the alley to their left, the solid wall of a medieval building to their right. The street ahead was empty except for the man in gray. Behind them, the café and its crowds suddenly seemed very far away.

"Who are you?"

"My name is Konstantin." The man inclined his head, an old-world courtesy that made the threat more immediate. "I represent certain institutional interests that have been monitoring your activities with considerable attention. You have been very diligent in your research, Dr.

Lundquist. More diligent than most who have sought what Hathenbruck hid."

"Vatican interests," Jonas said.

Konstantin's eyes flickered with something that might have been approval. "Your intelligence network is impressive, Mr. West. Yes, I serve the Church—though not in any capacity you would find in an organizational chart. There are... quieter offices within the Vatican. Older ones. We have been guardians of certain truths since before your country existed."

He took a step closer, and Ammon felt Jonas tense beside him. The street was still empty. The violin music from the plaza had faded to silence.

"I believe you have just left the Hathenbruck family home with something my employers would very much like to acquire." Konstantin's smile was patient, almost gentle. "A map, perhaps? Coordinates that have been waiting a century to be found? Your ancestor was clever—more clever than the priest we sent in the seventies. Father Heinrich was too direct, too eager. He missed what you found. But that oversight can now be corrected."

Ammon's mind raced. The envelope in his pocket. The photograph Jonas had taken as backup—still on his phone, unsent. If Konstantin took both, the map would be lost. Everything they had discovered in Friedrich's study would vanish into the Vatican's archives, buried alongside whatever other inconvenient truths the Church had collected over two millennia.

"What do you want?" he asked, keeping steady.

"I want you to give me the map and walk away. Peacefully, quietly, without anyone getting hurt." Konstantin spread his hands—a gesture of reasonableness that did nothing to soften his eyes. "The Church is not interested in the First Temple for profit or exploitation. We are not treasure hunters, Dr. Lundquist. We are shepherds. And sometimes shepherds must protect their flock from knowledge that would harm them."

"Harm them how?"

"Do you know the story of the Tower of Babel?" Konstantin's voice took on a contemplative quality, as if they were discussing theology over wine rather than standing in a confrontation on a medieval street. "God scattered humanity and confused their tongues because they sought to build a tower to heaven. Not because the tower was impossible—but because the ambition itself was dangerous. Some forms of knowledge are like that tower. They do not elevate humanity; they shatter it."

"And you've decided the First Temple is one of those forms of knowledge."

"I have seen the preliminary translations from your Dr. Tanaka's work." Konstantin's admission sent a chill down Ammon's spine—how deep did their surveillance go? "A civilization that predates all known history. Transoceanic contact millennia before Columbus. Knowledge of astronomy, metallurgy, medicine that suggests a sophistication we can barely imagine. Do you understand what that would mean, Dr. Lundquist? Not just for archaeology, but for faith?"

"I understand it would mean rewriting history."

"History is words on paper. It can survive revision." Konstantin shook his head. "But faith—faith is the architecture of billions of souls. The Church has spent two thousand years building a structure that gives meaning to human existence. Birth, death, suffering, joy—all of it comprehensible within the framework of divine providence. What happens when you tell those billions that their framework is built on incomplete foundations? That their sacred texts are not the beginning of the story but merely a chapter in a much longer book?"

He paused, letting the question settle.

"Some doors are closed for good reasons, Dr. Lundquist. The civilizations that built the First Temple understood this—which is why they sealed it. The guardians who have protected it for millennia understood this. Your own ancestor understood this, which is why he went to such lengths to hide what he found rather than publish it to the world."

"He also left a trail for us to follow."

"Yes—a trail for his family. For people he trusted to make the right choice when the time came." Konstantin's expression hardened, the philosophical veneer cracking to reveal something colder beneath. "But the time for that choice is now, Dr. Lundquist. And I am here to ensure the right decision is made."

While Konstantin spoke, Jonas had been calculating. His phone was in his jacket pocket—left side, easily accessible if he turned to face Ammon. The photograph of the map was still queued from when he had taken it as backup in Friedrich's study. All he needed was to unlock the screen, select the image, choose Aspen's contact, and send. Four actions. Maybe six seconds if he was fast.

But Konstantin was watching them both with the attentive stillness of a predator, and six seconds might as well be an hour. He needed a distraction.

"And if we refuse?" Ammon was asking, carrying the stubborn edge that Jonas had come to recognize. "If we believe the First Temple's knowledge should be studied, understood, shared with the world?"

"Then things become more complicated." Konstantin's smile faded entirely. "I have resources at my disposal, Dr. Lundquist. People who can make problems disappear with remarkable efficiency. I have been doing this work for thirty years—longer than you have been studying history. I would prefer not to use the more... direct methods. Violence is inelegant. It leaves traces, creates martyrs, invites scrutiny. But I will use them if necessary. The stakes are too high for squeamishness."

Jonas made his move.

His hand slid into his pocket with a casualness that he hoped read as nervous fidgeting. His thumb found the power button—one press to wake the screen. The familiar haptic buzz of the phone coming to life. He angled his body, as if shifting his weight, using Ammon's bulk to shield the movement from Konstantin's line of sight.

Face ID. The phone recognized him, unlocked. His thumb found the photos app by muscle memory—he had practiced this exact sequence a hundred times during his hacking days, when being able to send information quickly could mean the difference between freedom and a prison cell.

The map photograph was still the most recent image. One tap to select it. The share button in the corner. Aspen's contact was in his favorites—thank God for small efficiencies.

Konstantin's eyes narrowed. He had noticed something—a tension in Jonas's posture, perhaps, or the subtle glow of the phone screen reflecting off his jacket.

"Mr. West—"

Jonas hit send.

The notification chimed—a small, cheerful sound that seemed obscenely loud in the silent street. Message sent. Delivered. The blue checkmark appeared almost instantly; Aspen's phone was connected, the image already on its way across the Atlantic.

Jonas pulled the phone from his pocket and held it up, showing Konstantin the confirmation screen. His hand was shaking—adrenaline, fear, the aftermath of a risk that could not be taken back.

"The map is now in the hands of our colleagues in America," he said, steadier than he felt. "Even if you take it from us, the information is out of your control."

For a long moment, Konstantin simply stared at him. The urbane mask had cracked completely now, revealing something raw beneath—not anger, exactly, but a cold reassessment, the rapid recalculation of a man whose carefully constructed plans had been disrupted.

Then, unexpectedly, he laughed.

It was a genuine sound, holding notes of respect and frustration in equal measure. "Resourceful. I can see why your former associates spoke highly of your skills, Mr. West. The Collective always did produce capable hacking operatives."

The mention of his old hacking network sent a fresh wave of unease through Jonas. How much did they know? How long had they been watching?

Konstantin stepped back, the immediate threat receding like a tide withdrawing from a beach—leaving behind the knowledge that it would return.

"Very well. You have changed the parameters of our negotiation. The physical map is now redundant; I won't waste time trying to retrieve it." He adjusted his jacket, the gesture restoring his earlier composure. "You may leave this street. Leave this country. Return to America and continue your search."

"So we're free to go?"

"Free is a strong word." Konstantin's eyes swept across both of them, memorizing details with the practiced attention of someone who planned for all contingencies. "Saint Augustine wrote that we are free to choose, but not free to choose the consequences of our choices. You have chosen to spread this knowledge rather than contain it. The consequences of that choice are now in motion."

He paused, letting the words sink in.

"The Church has protected certain truths for two thousand years. We will protect this one too. I hope we don't meet again, gentlemen." His voice dropped, losing its philosophical edge and becoming something simpler, harder. "For your sake. Because if we do, it will mean all other options have been exhausted, and I will no longer feel obligated to be civil."

He turned and walked toward the alley from which he had emerged, his pace unhurried, his posture relaxed. At the mouth of the alley, he paused and looked back over his shoulder.

"Your ancestor understood something that you have not yet learned, Dr. Lundquist. Some knowledge is too heavy for the world to bear. Friedrich

Hathenbruck spent the last years of his life protecting humanity from what he had found. I wonder if you will have the same wisdom—or if you will force us to protect them from you."

Then he stepped into the shadows of the alley and was gone. Not vanished—Ammon could track his movement for a few seconds, the gray jacket visible between the medieval walls—but absorbed into the fabric of the city with the ease of someone who had spent a lifetime learning how to disappear.

Jonas released a shaky breath. His hands were still shaking; he shoved them into his pockets to hide the tremor.

"That was too close," he said.

"But you got the map out." Ammon was already moving toward the car, his pace quickened with urgency. "We need to leave. Now. Before Konstantin decides that civility is overrated."

They drove in tense silence, constantly checking mirrors for the gray Audi or any other signs of pursuit.

Jonas monitored his phone, confirming that Aspen had received the image and was forwarding it to Tanaka for analysis. The information was secure now—spread across multiple locations, impossible for any single party to suppress.

But the encounter had revealed something disturbing. The Vatican wasn't just monitoring the First Temple situation from afar. They had operational assets in the field, people willing and able to use force if persuasion failed. And they had been doing this for a very long time.

"He mentioned a priest in the seventies," Jonas said as they approached the airport. "Father Heinrich. That's over fifty years of the Church watching this family. Watching this secret."

"Which means they probably knew about Marcus too." Ammon's jaw was tight. "My uncle spent years researching our family's European roots. He came back from Germany changed, obsessed. What if he encountered Konstantin or someone like him? What if they warned him off—or worse?"

The question hung in the air, unanswerable.

"Konstantin talked about protecting faith," Jonas said. "About the architecture of billions of souls. He wasn't lying—I mean, he believes it. He really thinks he's doing the right thing."

"That's what makes him dangerous." Ammon stared out the window at the German countryside passing by—green hills, ancient forests, villages that had stood for centuries. "A man who knows he's doing wrong can be reasoned with. A man who believes he's righteous? He'll do anything."

"You think he might be right?"

"I think the question of what to do with dangerous knowledge is more complicated than anyone wants to admit." Ammon's voice was tired. "Konstantin believes sealing the truth away is protection. Margaux believes sharing it is liberation. The guardians believe controlling the narrative is wisdom. Hathenbruck believed hiding it from everyone—even the people who trusted him—was the only safe choice."

He paused.

"And I'm starting to wonder if any of us really knows what we're doing."

"So what do we do?"

"We find the First Temple first. We see what it actually contains. And then—" Ammon took a deep breath— "then we make a decision based on what we know, not what we assume."

It wasn't a satisfying answer. But it was the only one that made sense.

The flight back to America was long and tense, filled with discussions of security protocols and contingency plans.

Somewhere over the Atlantic, Jonas voiced the question that had been gnawing at him since they left Freiburg.

"Konstantin knew we were in Germany. Knew we'd visited the Hathenbruck house. Knew about Phantom and my hacking days. How deep does their surveillance go?"

"Deep enough." Ammon's voice was grim. "Which means they probably know about our safe house in Denver. About Tanaka and Aspen. About everything we've been doing since we went underground."

"So nowhere is safe."

"Nowhere was ever safe." Ammon closed his eyes, exhaustion catching up with him. "We just didn't know it."

Jonas tried to rest, but his mind kept circling back to Konstantin's warning: I hope we don't meet again. Because if we do, I will no longer feel obligated to be civil.

The plane carried them toward home. Whatever came next would be unlike anything they had faced before.

CHAPTER TWENTY-TWO

The Physician's Heir

The safe house was supposed to be exactly that—safe.

Aspen had been so careful. Rotating watch schedules with military precision. Checking the perimeter every few hours, scanning the street for unfamiliar vehicles, faces that appeared twice, anything that triggered their ranger's instinct for things out of place. Clara had been helping, using her decades of experience living off-grid to spot the subtle signs of observation—the same car parked too long, the neighbor who walked his dog at irregular hours, the delivery van that never seemed to deliver anything.

None of it mattered when Viktor's people came.

They woke to a sound that didn't belong—a whisper of displaced air, the softest creak of a floorboard under weight it wasn't expecting. The bedside clock read 3:07 AM, that dead hour when the body's defenses were lowest, when even trained soldiers struggled to shake off sleep's grip.

Aspen's hand was already moving toward the Glock on their nightstand when the bedroom door exploded inward.

Two shapes, black-clad and fluid, poured through the opening. The first one hit them before they could bring the weapon to bear, driving them back onto the mattress with a forearm across their throat. The second grabbed their gun hand, twisting with practiced efficiency until the Glock clattered to the floor.

Somewhere in the house, glass shattered. A muffled cry—Clara's voice, cut short. Tanaka screaming from the guest room down the hall.

"Don't fight." The voice came from the doorway, accented and calm, like a surgeon explaining a routine procedure. "Unnecessary violence benefits no one."

Aspen fought anyway. Instinct and years of training took over, their body moving through defensive patterns before their conscious mind could calculate the odds. They bucked their hips, throwing the man on top of them off-balance, then drove their elbow into his throat. He gagged, grip loosening for just a moment—and that moment was enough.

They rolled off the bed, came up in a crouch. The second attacker swung at their head with something that glinted in the darkness. They ducked under it, felt it whisper past their ear, and countered with a palm strike to his solar plexus that doubled him over.

The window. Three steps away. If they could reach it, get out onto the roof—

They made it two steps before the first attacker tackled them from behind, driving them into the wall hard enough to crack the drywall. Stars exploded across their vision. They twisted in his grip, got a hand free, raked their nails across his face. He swore in Russian and threw them to the floor.

Aspen scrambled toward the window on hands and knees, fingers finding the cold metal of the radiator beneath the sill. Almost there. Almost—

The taser caught them between the shoulder blades.

Every muscle in their body seized at once. Their jaw clamped shut so hard they tasted blood. The world became a white-hot wire of agony running from their spine to the tips of their fingers and toes. They collapsed to the floor, their body no longer their own, twitching and helpless as a fish on a riverbank.

"I said don't fight." Viktor Semenov stepped over their prone form, his face professionally neutral in the thin light bleeding through the curtains. He was shorter than they'd expected, compact and economical in his movements, with the kind of stillness that came from absolute confidence in one's capabilities. "Now we do this the hard way."

Hands grabbed their wrists, zip-tied them behind their back. Someone patted them down—professional, thorough, finding their service knife in its belt sheath.

Someone pulled a hood over their head, plunging them into darkness that smelled of canvas and old sweat. They tried to speak, to demand answers, but their muscles still weren't responding properly, their tongue thick and uncooperative in their mouth.

The last thing they heard before being dragged from the room was Viktor's voice, calm and businesslike: "The old woman escaped through the basement. Send a team, but don't chase too far. We have what we need."

Clara had gotten away. Aspen held onto that thought as darkness swallowed them whole.

The next hours were a blur of darkness and motion.

They forced Aspen into a vehicle—a van, they thought, from the way the engine rumbled through the floor beneath them. The metal was cold against their cheek where they'd laid them on their side. Their wrists ached from the zip ties, their shoulders screaming from the awkward angle.

Somewhere nearby, they could hear Tanaka's ragged breathing, the occasional whimper that told Aspen the cryptolinguist was trying to be brave, *trying* being the operative word.

Aspen tried to track the journey the way they'd been trained—counting turns, estimating speed from the pressure of acceleration, noting the texture of the road beneath the tires. Left turn, then straight for what felt like ten minutes. A stop, probably a light. Right turn, rougher road now, maybe gravel.

But the disorientation was too complete. The taser had scrambled their internal compass, left them swimming in a darkness that had no up or down. After a while, they stopped trying to track the route and focused instead on slowing their breathing, conserving their strength. Whatever came next, they would need every advantage they could muster.

When the hood came off, harsh fluorescent light stabbed into their eyes like needles. Aspen blinked, tears streaming down their face as their vision adjusted.

Concrete walls, unpainted and sweating with condensation. A floor stained with oil and rust and things they didn't want to identify. The air was cold and stale, carrying the industrial ghost of machinery that had long since been removed—an abandoned factory or warehouse, somewhere far from anyone who might hear a scream.

Tanaka sat in a metal chair across from them, hands bound in front of her, eyes wide and glazed with fear. A bruise was already darkening on her cheek—evidence that she'd tried to resist too, despite having none of Aspen's training. Brave person. Foolish, maybe, but brave.

Their captors had positioned them to face each other, close enough to see every expression, every flinch. Aspen understood immediately what that arrangement meant. This wasn't about hurting them. This was about making them watch.

The door opened with a screech of metal on metal, and Margaux Vance walked in.

She looked different from the last time Aspen had seen her—harder, the veneer of academic enthusiasm stripped away to reveal something colder beneath. She'd flown through the night to be here, redirecting mid-flight the moment Viktor confirmed the capture. Gone were the tortoiseshell glasses and the cardigan that had made her look like everyone's favorite graduate student. She wore practical clothes now, dark and functional, and moved with the efficient purpose of someone who had stopped pretending.

"Ranger Rhoades." Margaux's voice was flat, businesslike. She pulled a metal chair across the concrete floor with a screech that set Aspen's teeth on edge, then sat, positioning herself at eye level. "I wish we could have met again under better circumstances."

"You're wishing for a lot of things that aren't going to happen."

"Perhaps." Margaux studied them for a moment, something flickering behind her eyes—was that regret? Or just exhaustion? "But here's what I know: your friends just sent you a photograph from Germany. A map showing the exact location of what Hathenbruck hid in the Utah canyons."

So Viktor's people had been monitoring their communications. The encryption Jonas had set up, the secure channels Clara had established—all of it compromised. Aspen kept their face neutral, giving nothing away.

"I don't know what you're talking about."

"Please don't insult my intelligence." Margaux's voice hardened, but there was something brittle in it, like ice too thin to bear weight. "We intercepted the transmission. We know the map exists. What we need is the decryption key to open the image file. Your people were careful—the photograph is encrypted with a one-time pad that only someone with the proper key can decode."

Small mercies. Jonas had insisted on that additional layer of security, paranoid even by his standards. The image was useless without the key, and the key was divided between multiple people in multiple locations. Even if Aspen talked, they could only give them part of what they needed.

But they wouldn't tell them that.

"I can't help you," they said.

"Can't? Or won't?"

"Both."

Margaux held their gaze. Then she stood and walked toward the door, her footsteps echoing off the concrete walls.

"Viktor. Come in, please."

The Russian entered like smoke filling a room—quiet, inexorable, impossible to ignore. His face was still professionally neutral, but Aspen had seen men like him before. Men who treated violence as a tool, neither enjoying nor avoiding it, simply using it when the situation required. There was nothing personal in his eyes. That made him more dangerous than any fanatic.

"I don't want to do this," Margaux said, and Aspen heard what might have been genuine reluctance in her voice. "I've spent my entire career trying to be different from my father. Trying to pursue knowledge through legitimate means, without the methods he used."

She paused at the doorway, her hand resting on the frame as if she needed it for support.

"But some knowledge is worth any price. And the First Temple... that's knowledge that could change everything we think we understand about human history."

"So you'll torture us for it?"

"I'll do what I have to do." Margaux's eyes went to Tanaka, who had begun trembling visibly, her breath coming in short, sharp gasps. "Dr. Tanaka has valuable expertise, but she's not essential to finding the temple once we have the location. She's simply... leverage."

The implication was clear. Viktor wasn't here to question Aspen. He was here to hurt Tanaka until Aspen gave up the decryption key.

"Don't." Aspen's voice came out sharper than they intended. "She doesn't know anything. She's a cryptolinguist, not a spy. She joined this project because she believed in the power of knowledge, because she wanted to translate texts no one else could read. Hurting her won't get you what you want."

"Perhaps not." Margaux's voice was cold now, the reluctance buried beneath something harder. "But watching her hurt might convince you to cooperate."

She stepped closer, and for a moment Aspen saw the war playing out behind her eyes—the academic who had wanted to do this differently fighting against the daughter who had been raised in her father's shadow, who had learned his lessons despite herself.

"I'm giving you a chance, Ranger Rhoades. One chance to avoid unnecessary suffering. Give me the decryption key, tell me where your friends are heading, and Dr. Tanaka goes free. You both go free. No one has to get hurt."

Aspen looked at Tanaka—brilliant, passionate Tanaka, who had walked into danger because she believed in the power of understanding, who had never signed up for violence or betrayal. Tanaka, whose eyes were pleading with Aspen to make this stop, to say the words that would end the nightmare before it began.

And they thought about the First Temple. About the knowledge it contained, knowledge that had been protected for millennia by people who understood its weight. About Ammon and Jonas, flying across the ocean right now, trusting that Aspen would keep their secrets safe. About Thomas, plotting from a secure location, trusting that the guardian tradition he'd devoted his life to wouldn't be betrayed by someone he'd chosen to trust.

About what it meant to be a guardian. Not just of places or secrets, but of the trust people placed in you.

"No," they said.

The word came out steadier than they expected. Steadier than they felt. The cold of the concrete was seeping through their clothes, into their bones, but they didn't waver.

Margaux's expression flickered—disappointment? Or something closer to respect? Perhaps she understood, on some level, what it cost to make that choice.

"Very well." She nodded to Viktor. "Begin with Dr. Tanaka. Start with questions about her work, her translation methods. Nothing permanent." A pause. "Not yet."

Viktor moved toward Tanaka with the unhurried patience of a man who had all the time in the world.

Aspen watched, helpless. They couldn't save Tanaka. Couldn't fight their way free, couldn't negotiate better terms, couldn't do anything except watch and endure and pray that somehow, somewhere, help was coming before this broke them both.

But they also couldn't betray the people who trusted them. Couldn't give up the location that would let the Consortium—or anyone else—beat them to the First Temple.

Some choices had no good options. Only terrible ones, and more terrible ones.

As Tanaka's first scream echoed off the concrete walls, Aspen closed their eyes and held on to the only thing they had left.

Hope that the nightmare would end before they broke.

CHAPTER TWENTY-THREE

Unholy Alliance

The flight from Germany landed at Salt Lake City International just after midnight, local time.

Ammon was already on the phone before the wheels touched the runway, trying to reach Aspen at the safe house. No answer. His calls went straight to voicemail—not the normal busy signal of someone unavailable, but the immediate disconnect that suggested a phone deliberately disabled.

"Something's wrong," he said to Jonas as they hurried through the terminal. "I can't reach anyone. Aspen, Tanaka, Clara—all of them are dark."

Jonas pulled out his own phone, running through alternative channels. His fingers moved across the screen with practiced urgency. "The secure line is dead. The backup server isn't responding. It's like the whole Denver operation just... stopped."

They found a quiet corner near an empty gate, and Jonas began working his digital magic, tracing connections and checking surveillance feeds they'd set up around Clara's house. What he found made his face go pale.

"Police were called to Clara's address four hours ago. Neighbors reported sounds of a disturbance." He scrolled through the reports, his expression growing more strained. "There's an ambulance record—someone was transported to Denver General with non-life-threatening injuries."

"Clara?"

"Could be. But there's no record of anyone else being taken anywhere. Either the police didn't find them..."

"Or someone else got there first."

The terminal buzzed with late-night travelers, oblivious to the dread settling into Ammon's gut. Four hours. Viktor's people had a four-hour head start.

They rented a car and drove through the night, pushing the speed limit on empty highways while Jonas worked the phone, trying to piece together what had happened. The mountains loomed dark against the horizon, indifferent witnesses to their desperation.

Dawn was breaking over Denver when they arrived. The safe house was a crime scene now—yellow tape across the doors, a patrol car parked outside.

But the officers were gone, called away to other emergencies, leaving the house empty and violated. The front door hung ajar, a silent testament to the violence that had occurred.

Clara was at Denver General, recovering from a concussion and a broken wrist. She looked small in the hospital bed, her silver hair matted with dried blood that the nurses hadn't fully cleaned away. But her eyes were sharp, alert despite the pain.

"They came in force," she said, weak but determined. "Professional, organized. Not the kind of assault you improvise—they'd been watching, planning. Waiting for the right moment."

"Viktor's people."

"Had to be. And..." Clara paused, pain flickering across her face as she shifted position. "There was someone giving orders. A woman. I didn't get a good look, but she was speaking English with a British accent. Educated. Cold."

"How did you get away?" Ammon asked.

Clara's smile was grim. "The basement exit I prepared years ago. Hidden door behind the furnace, leads to the neighbor's yard through an old storm drain. All those years of paranoid preparations paid off." Her smile faded. "I just wish I'd saved everyone, not just myself."

Margaux. Of course. She'd played them perfectly—used her academic cover to get close, gathered what intelligence she could, and when the opportunity presented itself, she'd struck.

Ammon sat in the hospital waiting room, head in his hands, trying to think through options that seemed to narrow with every passing minute. The fluorescent lights buzzed overhead, casting everything in a harsh, unforgiving glow. Other families occupied nearby chairs, lost in their own private agonies, unaware that his crisis involved ancient temples and international conspiracies.

Aspen was captured. Tanaka was captured. The map's location was known to their enemies, and the only thing preventing its use was a decryption key that Aspen would never willingly reveal. But Viktor's people had methods that didn't require willingness. Ammon had read the files Jeremiah had provided about the Consortium's interrogation techniques. The thought of those methods being used on Aspen made his stomach twist.

He needed help. The kind of help that went beyond his small team, beyond the guardians' traditional networks. He needed resources, manpower, authority—things he'd never had access to. Things he'd actively avoided seeking, believing that small and nimble was better than large and bureaucratic.

That belief felt like hubris now.

He made a decision that would have seemed unthinkable twenty-four hours ago.

"I need to make some calls," he told Jonas. "Stay with Clara. Make sure she's safe."

"What are you going to do?"

Ammon stood, feeling exhaustion and fear pressing down on him. "Something I'm probably going to regret."

Special Agent Diana Reyes looked exactly like her FBI file photo—professional, skeptical, and utterly unimpressed by academic credentials.

Mid-forties, with short-cropped hair and the kind of posture that suggested years of fieldwork rather than desk duty. She'd agreed to meet Ammon at a coffee shop near the Denver field office, her expression making clear that this was a courtesy she could withdraw at any moment.

"Dr. Lundquist." She sat across from him, coffee untouched. "Your message said you had information about the cultural center attack. Information you could only share in person."

"That's correct."

"You understand that withholding information about a terrorist incident is a federal crime."

"I understand. That's why I'm here."

Ammon took a breath, steadying himself. "Agent Reyes, what I'm about to tell you is going to sound insane. But I can prove every word of it, and if you don't help me, people are going to die."

He told her. Not everything—he held back the full scope of the First Temple, the transoceanic implications, the deeper history that would rewrite textbooks. But he gave her enough: the chamber, the codices, the competing factions. The Consortium's remnants and their assault on the cultural center. Margaux Vance's infiltration and betrayal. The abduction of Aspen and Tanaka.

Reyes listened without interrupting, her pen moving occasionally across a small notebook. Her face remained impassive, professionally neutral, giving nothing away.

When he finished, she flipped back through her notes, taking her time.

"So you're telling me this wasn't domestic terrorism."

"It was made to look that way. The narrative was planted to create confusion, buy time."

"By a dead antiquities trafficker's daughter who's running a paramilitary operation with—" she checked her notes "—former Russian military intelligence?"

"Not quite. Elias Vance isn't dead. He's in federal prison. And his daughter inherited his network, his resources, and apparently his obsession."

"I know who Elias Vance is." Reyes set down her pen. "I also know that his operation was dismantled. We made sure of that."

"You got the pieces you could see. The pieces he wanted you to find. The offshore accounts, the hidden personnel—those were always kept separate, compartmentalized."

Reyes studied him. "You know an awful lot about the internal structure of a criminal organization, Dr. Lundquist. That makes me wonder how you came by that knowledge."

"I have a source. Someone who was inside the Consortium before he decided to cooperate."

"Ah, yes—Jeremiah Stone. We know about your prison visits. My colleagues found that... interesting."

Ammon felt a chill. The FBI had been watching him too. Of course they had.

"Stone provided actionable intelligence. Everything he's told me has checked out."

"And you trust a convicted criminal's word because...?"

"Because he has nothing to gain by lying. His cooperation won't reduce his sentence. He's not angling for a deal." Ammon leaned forward. "He's helping because something changed in him. I was there when it happened."

Reyes's expression flickered—skepticism mixed with something else. Curiosity, perhaps.

"You're a strange man, Dr. Lundquist. Most people who get tangled up with criminals don't come out believing in redemption."

"I have evidence." Ammon pulled out his phone, steering the conversation back to safer ground. He showed her photographs of maps, translations from the codex, communications Jonas had intercepted between Viktor's people and Margaux. "The attack on the cultural center wasn't random—it was a targeted operation to capture specific individuals and intelligence."

Reyes studied the evidence, scrolling through images. Her skepticism was eroding, but reluctantly, like a cliff face resisting the tide.

"Even if I believe you—and I'm not saying I do—this is way beyond a routine field office investigation. We're talking about international actors, potential involvement of foreign governments, multiple jurisdictions."

"That's why I need you. You have resources I don't have. Authority I don't have."

"And what do you offer in return?"

"The biggest archaeological discovery in human history. A story that—"

"Stop." Reyes held up a hand. "I don't care about stories. I don't care about discoveries. I care about two things: evidence that holds up in court, and operations that don't get my people killed."

She leaned forward, and for the first time, her professional mask slipped, revealing the hard-edged pragmatist beneath.

"You want my help? Then you play by my rules. Warrants, proper procedures, chain of custody. No vigilante nonsense, no running off half-cocked because you think you know better than people who've actually done this before."

"That's exactly what I want."

"Is it?" Her eyes were hard. "Because professors tend to think they're the smartest person in every room. And that kind of thinking gets people killed in the field."

Ammon met her gaze without flinching. "My partner is being held by people who will hurt them to get what they want. I'm not here because I think I'm smart. I'm here because I know I'm not smart enough to save them alone."

Something shifted in Reyes's expression—not softening, but a recalculation. The hard pragmatism remained, but now it was directed at a different problem: assessing whether this desperate academic could actually be useful.

"I'll make some calls," she said. "No promises. But if your evidence holds up, and if my superiors don't laugh me out of the building, we might be able to put together a task force. Small, discreet. Off the books until we know what we're dealing with."

"That's all I'm asking."

"No, it isn't. You're asking me to stake my career on the word of a history professor I just met." She stood, tucking her notebook away. "I'll be in touch. Don't leave town. Don't do anything stupid. And Dr. Lundquist?"

She paused at the door.

"If you're lying to me—about any of this—I will personally ensure you spend the next decade explaining yourself to federal prosecutors."

The second call was harder. Much harder.

Ammon sat in his hotel room as evening settled over Denver, staring at the phone number Jonas had traced through half a dozen Vatican communication channels. The room was anonymous, forgettable—a king bed, a desk, a window overlooking the highway. The kind of place where important decisions felt absurd.

Father Tomás Adão. The man who had sent Konstantin to intercept them in Germany, who believed the First Temple should remain sealed forever. A man who had spent thirty years quietly suppressing discoveries that challenged orthodox history.

The enemy. But also, perhaps, an ally against a greater threat.

He dialed before he could talk himself out of it.

The phone rang three times before an unfamiliar voice answered—not Konstantin, but Tomás himself. His voice was measured, calm, utterly unsurprised.

"Dr. Lundquist. I wondered how long it would take you to reach out."

"You know what's happening. Your people have been monitoring everything."

"We try to stay informed." A pause, weighted with unspoken knowledge. "I understand you've had a difficult few days. My condolences on the capture of your colleagues."

"Don't." The word came out sharper than Ammon intended. "Don't give me condolences while your man is still out there with explosives and a mission to bury what we're looking for."

The silence that followed was weighted, considering. Ammon could almost hear the priest calculating, assessing, weighing options.

"You're proposing an alliance," Tomás said. "Between the institution you believe is your enemy and the man who's been trying to stop you at every turn."

"I'm proposing a conversation about shared interests."

"We have no shared interests, Dr. Lundquist. You want to reveal. I want to protect. These are fundamentally incompatible goals."

"Are they?" Ammon held steady despite the rage burning in his chest. "The Consortium has Aspen and Tanaka. They have the map's location, even if they can't decrypt it yet. Margaux Vance isn't interested in your kind of protection—she wants to exploit what's in that temple. Sell it, publicize it, use it to rehabilitate her father's reputation. If she reaches it first, you get the worst possible outcome. Uncontrolled revelation with no consultation, no context, no consideration for impact."

Another pause. When Tomás spoke again, his voice had shifted—less certain, more tired. The voice of a man who had been fighting shadows for too long.

"You understand that even if we work together temporarily, our fundamental disagreement remains. I cannot allow knowledge that threatens the faith of billions to spread without... measures."

"Measures." Ammon's jaw tightened. "You mean suppression. Destruction. The same tactics your predecessors have used for centuries."

"You speak as though preservation of faith is a crime."

"I speak as someone whose partner is in the hands of people who will hurt them. I don't have time for theological debates." Ammon forced himself to breathe, to think past the fear and the anger. "Here's what I'm offering: help me rescue Aspen and Tanaka. Help me stop the Consortium from reaching the temple first. And in return, I'll share what we find. The Church gets a voice in how the discovery is handled, how it's revealed to the world."

"A voice. Not a veto."

"A voice at the table. That's more than you'd have if Margaux Vance reaches it first."

Tomás laughed—a short, humorless sound that carried decades of weariness. "You're asking me to trust a man I've spent months trying to stop. A man who represents everything I've worked against."

"I'm asking you to distrust me less than you distrust the alternative."

The pause that followed seemed to stretch forever. Ammon could feel them weighing the offer, calculating risks, trying to predict outcomes that were inherently unpredictable.

"Konstantin answers to Rome directly now, not to me," Tomás said. "After Germany, certain parties decided I was too accommodating. They've taken a harder line. But I have... influence. I can ensure he doesn't interfere with your rescue operation."

"That's not enough."

"It's what I can offer."

"Then we have nothing to discuss." Ammon moved to end the call.

"Wait." The word came quickly, almost involuntarily. Another silence, longer this time. When Tomás spoke again, something had cracked in his voice—the first genuine emotion Ammon had heard from him.

"I'm tired, Dr. Lundquist. Tired of the shadow war. Tired of fighting people who should be allies against greater threats." His voice hardened, regaining some of its earlier edge, but the weariness remained beneath it. "I'll call off Konstantin. More than that—I'll provide intelligence on the Consortium's operations. We've been monitoring them longer than you have. We have substantial resources—men with training for exactly this kind of situation. Former military, now serving the Church in... unofficial capacities. They can support your rescue operation."

"And in return?"

"I want to be present when the temple is found. Not to control what happens—to witness it. To see with my own eyes what we've been protecting the world from, or..." He paused, and Ammon heard something unexpected in the silence. Doubt. "Or what we've been protecting from the world. There's a difference, and I'm no longer certain which applies."

"You want a seat at the table."

"I want to be able to report to my superiors—the ones who still listen to me—that the discovery was handled responsibly. That engagement was the right path, not suppression. If I can demonstrate that, perhaps the hardliners lose some of their influence. Perhaps the next discovery doesn't require shadow wars and explosives."

"And the temple?"

"If what's in that temple challenges the foundations of Christian faith— truly challenges them, not merely complicates or contextualizes—I will not allow it to spread without extraordinary measures to manage its impact." His voice softened, almost pleading. "But I give you my word: I will not act unilaterally. We will discuss. We will decide together. Even if that decision tears me apart."

It wasn't everything Ammon wanted. It wasn't even close. But it was more than he'd expected—and more than he had any right to demand from a man whose entire worldview he was threatening to destroy.

"I'll send coordinates for a rendezvous point," Tomás continued, his voice steadying. "Bring your FBI contact. Bring whatever resources you've assembled. We plan the rescue together."

"Together," Ammon repeated, testing the word. It felt strange in his mouth, applied to this context.

"A temporary, fragile, probably doomed arrangement," Tomás said. "But an arrangement nonetheless."

The call ended, and Ammon sat staring at his phone, the screen fading to black. Outside, the Denver skyline glittered against the darkening sky, oblivious to the strange alliances being forged in anonymous hotel rooms.

He thought about Thomas, who would be furious when he learned Ammon had made a deal with the Vatican. About Aspen, who was counting on him to find them, to save them. About his ancestor F.W.C. Hathenbruck, who had spent his life navigating between worlds, building bridges that others thought impossible.

Had Hathenbruck ever felt this way? This mixture of desperation and doubt, this sense of reaching for something that might crumble the moment he grasped it?

Either way, there was no going back now. The unholy alliance was formed. The rescue was planned.

And somewhere in the approaching darkness, the First Temple waited to reveal its secrets—to whoever reached it first.

CHAPTER TWENTY-FOUR

The Race Begins

The conference room on Englewood's administrative level felt like a different world from the cell block where Jeremiah Stone had spent his federal prison time until now.

Cleaner—fresh industrial disinfectant instead of the stale funk that permeated the housing units. The fluorescent lights whined at a slightly higher frequency, and the people waiting for him wore suits instead of corrections uniforms. Small mercies, Jeremiah thought as the guards led him through the door.

His wrists ached where the handcuffs had rubbed during the long walk from his unit. He'd lost weight since his arrest—the prison food sat poorly with him, and sleep came in fragments between the noise and the nightmares. His reflection in the one-way glass showed a man who looked a decade older than his forty-two years.

Two marshals positioned themselves near the door. Jeremiah sat in the metal chair they indicated and waited.

He didn't have to wait long.

When Ammon Lundquist walked through the door, Jeremiah felt something shift in his chest—a complicated mixture of shame, gratitude, and something that might have been hope. The professor looked exhausted, dark circles under his eyes and tension in every line of his body. But he moved with purpose, and when their eyes met, Jeremiah saw the same thing he'd seen six months ago in this same facility's visitation room: someone who believed redemption was possible.

"Dr. Lundquist." Jeremiah's voice came out rougher than he'd intended—months of mostly silence would do that. "I had a feeling you'd come back eventually. Though I didn't expect it under these circumstances."

"The circumstances have changed." Ammon pulled out the chair across from him and sat, his movements deliberate. Up close, the exhaustion was even more apparent. "Aspen and Dr. Tanaka have been taken. Viktor's people, working with Margaux Vance."

Jeremiah's hands clenched into fists beneath the table. He forced them to relax, finger by finger. "I warned you about her."

"You did." Ammon's jaw tightened. "I should have listened sooner. But we're past recriminations now. I need your help."

"My help—again." Jeremiah allowed himself a thin smile, though it didn't reach his eyes. "The information I gave you last time wasn't enough?"

"It was valuable. But this is different." Ammon leaned forward, and Jeremiah could see the desperate hope beneath the professor's controlled exterior. "I don't just need information this time. I need you in the field. Your knowledge of Viktor's operational patterns, his security protocols, the way he thinks—I need that in real-time, not filtered through prison visitation."

Jeremiah sat back, processing what Ammon was actually asking. Not intelligence passed across a metal table. Active participation. A chance to step outside these walls and put his skills toward something that mattered.

"And in exchange?"

"Agent Reyes has agreed to hear what you have to offer. If your intelligence checks out, she's open to discussing modified terms—possibly supervised release for the operation." Ammon paused, and something in his expression softened. "Nothing's guaranteed until she sees what you're bringing to the table. But it's more than that, Jeremiah. It's a chance. A chance to prove that what happened in the sacred chamber wasn't just a moment—that you've really changed."

Jeremiah sat very still, processing the offer and everything it implied. He'd spent the months since his arrest replaying that moment in the chamber—the overwhelming wave of understanding that had crashed over him when he touched those ancient walls, generations pressing down on his consciousness. He'd clung to the memory through the darkest hours, told himself it was real even when doubt crept in during the endless gray nights.

But he'd also wondered. When the cell walls closed in and the future stretched out like a corridor with no end. He'd wondered if the transformation was genuine, or just something he'd convinced himself of because the alternative was unbearable.

Now Ammon was offering him a chance to find out.

"You saved my life," he said, the words coming before he could stop them. His hands were trembling; he flattened them against his thighs to still them. "When I was hanging off that cliff, ready to let go, you held on. You wouldn't let me fall."

Ammon was silent, waiting.

"I've wondered why, every day since. Why you bothered. Why you thought I was worth saving when I didn't think it myself."

"Because you were worth saving." Ammon's voice was quiet but carried weight—conviction tested and held. "Because everyone deserves a chance to be better than their worst moments. Because the chamber showed me that redemption isn't just possible—it's necessary. For all of us."

Jeremiah felt his eyes burn. He blinked rapidly, looking down at his scarred hands—hands that had done terrible things in service of greed and ambition.

"Then let me prove you right," he said, rough. "Let me show you that what happened in that chamber was real. That I'm not the person I used to be."

He took a breath, steadying himself, and when he spoke again his voice was more controlled, professional—the operative surfacing beneath the penitent.

"Viktor operates from fixed locations. He doesn't improvise—he plans, prepares, establishes secure sites in advance. When I worked with the Consortium, we maintained a network of safe houses across the western states. Most were compromised after Vance's arrest, but there was one location we kept completely off the books."

"Where?"

"An abandoned mining complex in Nevada. Remote, defensible, with infrastructure for operations that needed to stay hidden." Jeremiah's voice grew more certain as the details sharpened. "The main shaft goes down three levels. Viktor would use the second level—it has reinforced rooms that were originally built for storing explosives. If he needed to hold prisoners without anyone finding them, that's exactly where he'd go."

"Can you confirm that? Show us on a map?"

"I can do better than that." Jeremiah met Ammon's eyes directly. "I know the facility's complete layout—every entrance, every security point, every vulnerability in their defensive perimeter. I spent three years helping Elias Vance plan operations. I know how they think, how they deploy, how they react to threats." He paused. "If you're planning a rescue, that knowledge could be the difference between getting everyone out alive and walking into a trap."

The door opened, and a woman entered—late forties, sharp eyes, the watchful stillness of someone who'd spent years in law enforcement. Agent Reyes, Jeremiah assumed.

"Mr. Stone." Her expression gave nothing away. "I understand you're offering cooperation in exchange for modified terms of incarceration."

"I'm offering cooperation because it's the right thing to do." Jeremiah held steady, though his heart was pounding. "The terms are your department. I just want to help fix what I broke."

Reyes studied him, and Jeremiah had the uncomfortable sensation of being assessed, catalogued, and filed.

"The facility you're describing—we've had reports of suspicious activity in that area. Nothing concrete enough to warrant investigation, but consistent with the kind of operations you're suggesting."

"Viktor is careful. He wouldn't leave obvious traces."

"No, he wouldn't." Reyes turned to Ammon. "If Stone's intelligence is accurate, we can assemble a tactical response. But it would require coordination—Bureau, local law enforcement, possibly federal marshals."

"And Father Tomás's resources," Ammon added.

Reyes's expression shifted toward something resembling disbelief. "You're seriously proposing we work with Vatican operatives on a domestic law enforcement action?"

"I'm proposing we use every advantage available." Ammon remembered the call he'd made from his Denver hotel room—Tomás's weariness, the unexpected crack in the priest's decades-old certainty, the fragile agreement they'd reached.

"The Church has people on the ground, assets we can't match. Tomás has agreed to cooperate—he's broken with the hardline faction that sent Konstantin. He wants to be present when the temple is found, to have a voice in how it's handled. In exchange, he's offering intelligence on Viktor's operations and men trained for exactly this kind of extraction."

"You trust him?" Reyes asked.

"I trust that he distrusts the Consortium more than he distrusts me. Right now, that's enough."

Reyes weighed the fragile alliance Ammon was describing.

"For now," she said, her tone making clear how provisional she considered that trust. "It's better than fighting on multiple fronts."

Jeremiah watched the exchange, recognizing the tension between pragmatism and principle. He'd navigated that tension for years, always choosing the expedient path. It had led him here, to this room, to this moment of desperate hope.

"Let me help," he said. "Not just with intelligence—with the operation itself. I know Viktor, know how he thinks. I can anticipate his responses in ways your tactical teams can't."

"Absolutely not." Reyes's voice was sharp. "You're an incarcerated federal prisoner. Having you participate in an active operation would create more legal complications than I can count."

"There's something else." Jeremiah played his last card, leaning forward despite the clink of his chains. "When I worked for Vance, I helped him set up insurance—documents, records, financial trails that would expose the Consortium's entire network if anything happened to him. He kept copies in that Nevada facility, in a secure location that only three people knew about. Vance is locked away in federal prison, and even if he weren't, he'd never cooperate with authorities. His lawyer is dead. That leaves me."

Reyes's eyes narrowed. "Insurance?"

"Names, dates, transaction records. Everything you'd need to bring down what's left of the Consortium permanently." Jeremiah kept his gaze steady. "Let me help with the rescue, and I'll show you where those documents are. It's the final piece—the thing that could end this once and for all."

The silence stretched. Jeremiah could feel them weighing the offer, calculating risks, trying to predict outcomes that were inherently unpredictable.

"I spent years serving the wrong masters," he said, his voice dropping to barely above a whisper. "Following orders I knew were wrong because it was easier than standing up for what was right. The chamber showed me what that cost—not just to the people I hurt, but to myself." He looked up, meeting both their eyes in turn. "Something died in me during those years. Something I thought was gone forever."

He paused, running a hand over his face—feeling the stubble, the hollow of his cheeks, the physical evidence of what he'd become.

"I don't know if I can make up for what I did. Don't know if redemption is really possible for someone like me." His voice steadied. "But I know I have to try. And this—helping save people who are in danger because of the organization I served—this is where that trying starts."

The silence that followed was heavy with consequence. Finally, Reyes spoke.

"Supervised participation. Limited tactical role. You stay behind the main assault team and you follow every order without question." She held up a warning finger. "One deviation, one hint that you're playing us, and you spend the rest of your sentence in maximum security. Understood?"

"Understood."

"Then we have a deal." Reyes stood. "We move tonight. I'll coordinate with local law enforcement and our... Vatican allies. Mr. Stone, you'll provide detailed briefings on facility layout and security protocols. We have less than twelve hours to plan an assault on a fortified position."

It wasn't enough time. It would have to be.

She left to make arrangements. Ammon remained, studying Jeremiah with an expression that mixed hope with caution.

"You know this could go wrong," Ammon said. "Viktor is dangerous. His people are professionals. There's a real chance some of us don't walk away from this."

"I know."

"And you're still willing to help?"

Jeremiah thought about the chamber. About the history that had pressed down on him, showing him all the harm he'd caused, all the lives he'd damaged. About the overwhelming sense of purpose that had followed—the conviction that he'd been given a second chance, if he had the courage to take it.

"More than willing," he said. "This is what I've been waiting for. A chance to prove—to myself as much as anyone—that the change was real."

Ammon hesitated. Then he extended his hand across the table.

Jeremiah looked at it—this simple gesture that meant everything. An offer of trust from a man he'd once tried to destroy. A bridge across the gulf between who he'd been and who he was trying to become.

He took it. The grip was firm, genuine—two men acknowledging a shared purpose that transcended their complicated history. Ammon's hand was warm, steady, and Jeremiah felt a fist he hadn't known he was clenching finally open somewhere behind his ribs. Not forgiveness—he hadn't earned that, might never earn it. But something adjacent. What felt like the beginning of hope.

"Prove me right," Ammon said. "Prove that what happened in the chamber was real."

"I intend to."

In the concrete room beneath Nevada, Aspen counted heartbeats to stay sane.

The fluorescent lights never dimmed. The air tasted of dust and old machinery. Tanaka had stopped responding to their coded taps, and Aspen didn't know if that meant she was sleeping or something worse.

Their mind never stopped working. Eyes never stopped scanning. Against the far wall, an old electrical junction box hung open, its cover missing. Exposed wiring and a jagged metal edge where the cover had been pried off. Aspen noted it automatically—years of wilderness survival had taught them to see potential tools everywhere. They filed it away.

Aspen's wrists ached from the binding, arms uncomfortable behind their back. They pressed their palm against the back of the chair and told themself help was coming.

It had to be coming.

Jonas found Clara in the safe house's back room, staring out the window at stars she probably couldn't name.

Astrophysics had always been someone else's department. She sat wrapped in a blanket in a worn armchair they'd positioned away from the windows—proper protocol, even now—her broken wrist in its cast resting on her lap, her silver hair still bearing traces of the hospital's hasty cleaning.

"Trouble sleeping?" he asked.

She didn't startle—she'd heard him coming, then. Good situational awareness, even now. He was starting to appreciate that about her.

"Trouble stopping my brain." She gestured to a second chair nearby. "Tomorrow we're attempting a paramilitary extraction from a hostile facility. It's not exactly conducive to rest."

"Want company, or solitude?"

"Company." The word came quickly—quickly enough that it surprised them both. "I mean. If you're offering."

He sat. The room was cold despite the heating, the kind of chill that seeped through old walls and settled in your bones.

"For what it's worth," Jonas said after a while, "the assault plan is solid. Jeremiah knows that facility inside and out. The FBI team is experienced. We have numbers and surprise on our side."

"Is this supposed to be reassuring?"

"Is it working?"

She laughed—a small sound, more exhale than anything. "Actually, yes. A little." She pulled the blanket tighter around her shoulders, looking older than her years in the dim light. "I'm not good at this. The waiting part. I spent decades preparing for emergencies that never came. Now one finally has, and all I can do is sit here while younger people risk their lives."

"You've done more than you know." Jonas spoke gently. "The escape routes you built, the documents you preserved, the connections you maintained—none of this would be possible without you. Tomorrow's rescue wouldn't be happening if you hadn't gotten away, hadn't been able to tell us what happened."

"Small comfort when Aspen and Tanaka are in that place because I couldn't protect them."

"That's not on you. Viktor's people are professionals. They would have found a way in regardless."

Clara considered him. Then, tentatively, she reached out and patted his hand—a grandmother's gesture, warm despite the cold.

"You're a good young man," she said. "Ammon chose well when he brought you into this."

"I'm not sure 'chose' is the right word. More like 'stumbled into' and 'couldn't get rid of.'"

"Same thing, in my experience." She smiled. "The family has always attracted strays. Friedrich did. My grandmother did. Now Ammon does. It's how we've survived this long—by recognizing the people who belong, even when they don't recognize it themselves."

Jonas didn't know what to say to that. So he said nothing, and they sat together in the darkness, two unlikely allies waiting for dawn.

The rescue was planned for midnight. By morning, one way or another, the second act of this story would be complete.

What came after was up to them.

PART THREE

THE CHOICE

CHAPTER TWENTY-FIVE
Extraction

The Nevada desert held its breath. Ammon lay prone on the ridge, the cold seeping through his tactical vest and into his bones. The temperature had dropped thirty degrees since sunset, and now the high desert air carried the sharp bite of a winter that never quite arrived at lower elevations. Sage and creosote perfumed the darkness—ancient smells, unchanged since this land had been home to peoples whose names were lost to history. Two hundred yards ahead, the abandoned mining complex rose from the flat expanse like a wound that had never healed.

Rusting industrial structures. Collapsed tunnels. The skeletal remains of equipment that hadn't moved in decades, their silhouettes sharp against a sky heavy with more stars than seemed possible. The Milky Way stretched overhead, a river of light that reminded Ammon how small he was—how small all of this was, against the scale of time and space. The facility had been built in the 1950s, during the uranium boom that had briefly transformed this stretch of Nevada into a landscape of hope and desperation.

Men had come here seeking fortune, digging deep into the earth in search of the element that would power the atomic age. They'd found it, too—for a while. Then the veins had run dry, the money had moved on, and the desert had begun the slow process of reclaiming what had been taken from it. Now the Consortium had found a different use for these abandoned tunnels. A place to hide. A place to interrogate. A place where screams wouldn't carry beyond the empty hills.

Somewhere inside that ruin, Aspen was waiting.

He pressed the binoculars tighter against his eyes, scanning the facility's perimeter for the hundredth time. Guard positions. Patrol patterns. The faint glow of monitors behind grimy windows. Twelve FBI tactical agents were moving into position around the compound, their dark shapes barely visible against the darker landscape. Local law enforcement maintained a wider cordon, ready to catch anyone who slipped through. And Father Tomás had contributed four of his people—men whose bearing was unmistakably military, whatever their current employment might claim.

"Viktor will have motion sensors on the approach roads." Jeremiah Stone's voice was barely above a whisper, his breath forming pale clouds in the cold air. "Cameras at every entrance. Pressure plates near the main doors—he's paranoid about frontal assaults."

"But?"

"The old ventilation shafts on the north side." Jeremiah pointed toward a section of the complex that had partially collapsed. "They were never properly secured. The original mine operators used them for air circulation in the lower levels, but when the Consortium converted the facility, they focused all their attention on the obvious entry points. The shafts are the blind spot."

Ammon lowered the binoculars and studied the man beside him. Jeremiah wore a tactical vest over civilian clothes, an ankle monitor hidden beneath his jeans—the FBI's insurance policy against flight. His face was gaunt from months of prison food and sleepless nights, but his eyes held something that hadn't been there during their last confrontation: clarity. Purpose.

The transformation still unsettled Ammon. In the sacred chamber, he'd watched Jeremiah break down—watched the man who had hunted them confront the emptiness at the center of his life. But change like that didn't happen in a moment. It happened day by day, choice by choice, and tonight was Jeremiah's chance to prove that his change was real.

"How sure are you about those shafts?"

"Sure enough to bet my freedom on it." Jeremiah met his gaze without flinching. "I helped Vance design the security protocols for this place, three years ago. I know what they missed because I'm the one who missed it."

The radio in Ammon's ear crackled with Agent Reyes's voice: "All teams, report status."

A chorus of responses followed—Alpha team in position at the main entrance, Bravo team covering the vehicle bay, the Vatican contingent holding at the secondary access point. Voices calm despite the tension, professional despite the stakes.

"Civilian assets?" Reyes asked.

Ammon keyed his radio. "In position. Ready on your mark."

A pause. Then: "On my mark. Three... two... one... execute."

The night split apart.

Flash-bang grenades detonated at three entry points simultaneously— brilliant white flashes that painted the desert in stark shadows, followed by concussive booms that echoed off the surrounding hills like thunder. Even from two hundred yards away, Ammon felt the pressure wave in his chest.

Then the shooting started.

The FBI teams moved with choreographed precision—dark shapes flowing through the chaos like water through broken rock. Radio chatter filled Ammon's ear: "Alpha team breaching main entrance—contact, two hostiles down—moving to secondary positions—"

"Now," Jeremiah said, and they were running.

The ventilation shaft entrance was exactly where Jeremiah had said it would be—a rusted grate half-hidden by collapsed debris, sized for industrial airflow rather than human passage. Ammon helped Jeremiah pry it open, the metal groaning in protest, and then they were crawling into darkness.

The shaft was worse than he'd imagined. Decades of accumulated dust coated every surface, rising in clouds with each movement and coating his tongue with the taste of abandonment. The metal walls pressed close on all sides, cold against his shoulders and knees as he crawled forward. Somewhere ahead, Jeremiah's flashlight bobbed and weaved, casting wild shadows.

Something scuttled away from the light—a spider, maybe, or a scorpion. Ammon forced himself to keep moving.

The shaft groaned with each shift of his weight, the old metal protesting the intrusion after decades of silence. Rust flaked off under his hands, sharp-edged and iron-smelling. He tried not to think about how deep they were going. Tried not to imagine the tons of concrete and earth pressing down from above. Tried not to remember the stories he'd heard about abandoned mines—collapses, cave-ins, men buried alive in the darkness.

"Left junction coming up," Jeremiah whispered, the words echoing strangely in the confined space. "That leads to the kitchen—original building, before the conversion. We want straight ahead, second junction, then down."

The sounds of combat filtered through the metal walls—muffled gunfire, shouts, the crash of doors being breached. Ammon tried to interpret what he was hearing, tried to gauge which direction the fighting had moved, but the acoustics turned everything into an incomprehensible roar.

"How far?" he asked.

"Maybe fifty more yards. The shaft opens into a storage area on the lower level." Jeremiah paused at a junction, shining his light down a side passage before continuing forward. "From there, it's maybe a hundred feet to the command center. That's where Viktor will be."

"Where the prisoners will be."

"Where the prisoners will be," Jeremiah confirmed. "Maximum control. Maximum leverage."

The shaft angled downward, and Ammon had to brace himself against the sides to keep from sliding. His elbows scraped against rusted metal. Sweat trickled down his back despite the cold. The darkness pressed in, broken only by Jeremiah's flashlight beam, and for a long moment Ammon felt all the earth above him, all the concrete and steel and decades of secrets.

Then the shaft opened into empty air, and they were through.

Aspen heard the assault begin with something that felt like hope.

They'd lost track of time during their captivity—hours blending into days, marked only by the rhythm of Viktor's interrogations and the thin meals that arrived at irregular intervals. The room where they were held was windowless, lit by a single bulb that never turned off, and the constant illumination had eroded their sense of reality until they weren't sure if they'd been here for days or weeks.

But they hadn't broken. That was the important thing.

Viktor had tried pressure, then pain, then the threat of pain to Tanaka. And still they hadn't given him the map's location, hadn't revealed what they knew about the First Temple. There had been moments—dark moments, in the small hours of whatever passed for night in this place—when they'd wondered if holding out was worth it. When the pain had been bad enough to blur their thinking, when Viktor's voice had seemed almost reasonable. Just tell us what we want to know. End this. Go home.

But then they'd thought of Ammon. Of Thomas. Of the sacred chamber and everything it represented. They'd thought of the generations of guardians who had suffered more than this to protect what was precious, and they'd summoned strength again.

Some things were worth suffering for.

The first explosion shook the building, sending dust raining from the ceiling. Aspen lifted their head, suddenly alert. Across the room, Tanaka met their eyes—the cryptolinguist looked terrible, her face bruised and one eye swollen nearly shut, but there was fierce intelligence in her expression.

"Rescue," Tanaka whispered. "Or at least that's what I'm hoping."

Viktor appeared in the doorway, his face tight with controlled fury. In the corridor behind him, Aspen could hear guards scrambling—shouts in Russian, the clatter of weapons being readied.

"Get them up," Viktor ordered. "We're moving to the secondary location."

Two guards entered the room, moving toward the prisoners with the casual confidence of men who had done this many times before. But as the men reached for them, another explosion rocked the facility—closer this time, the lights flickering, and for a moment everything was chaos.

Aspen made their move.

They'd been planning this since they first catalogued the room—the broken bracket on the wall, its edge jagged where the metal had sheared. During one of Viktor's absences, they'd worked their chair closer, inch by careful inch, until they could reach it with their bound hands.

Now, with the guards distracted by the explosion, they pressed the zip ties against that sharp edge and sawed. The angle was awkward, painful, but desperation gave them strength.

Three quick motions and the zip ties parted. They kept their hands behind their back, waiting, watching the guard who was reaching for Tanaka—

Now.

They came up from the chair like a coiled spring releasing, driving their shoulder into the nearest guard's midsection. He folded with a grunt of surprise, and then their knee was coming up into his chin and he was falling backward, his weapon clattering to the floor.

The second guard was turning, his hand going for his sidearm, but Aspen was faster. They grabbed the fallen weapon—a compact submachine gun, heavier than they expected—and brought it up just as he cleared his holster.

"Don't," they said.

He froze. Smart man.

Viktor was already gone—they could hear him shouting orders somewhere down the corridor, organizing his response to the assault. They had seconds, maybe less, before more guards arrived.

"Tanaka. Come on."

They pulled the cryptolinguist free of her restraints, noting how Tanaka winced at the movement—ribs, probably cracked. But the woman was moving under her own power, and that was what mattered.

"Can you run?"

"I can do whatever I have to do." Tanaka's voice was hoarse but steady. "Where are we going?"

Not the main corridor—Viktor was there, and God knew how many of his men. But during their brief glimpses of the facility, Aspen had spotted a service entrance that led to the tunnels below. It was a guess, but it was better than staying here.

"Follow me. Stay close."

They ran.

The corridors were lit only by emergency lighting—red-tinted and dim, casting everything in shades of blood. Aspen moved by instinct, choosing turns based on the sound of fighting and the feel of the air currents. Behind them, Tanaka kept pace despite her injuries, her breathing harsh but controlled.

The first guard appeared around a corner without warning. He was young—maybe twenty-five, with the look of ex-military that Viktor seemed to favor. His weapon was already raised, and for a frozen instant Aspen saw death in his eyes.

But he hesitated. Just for a heartbeat, he hesitated—surprised to see the prisoners free, trying to process the change in situation—and that heartbeat was all Aspen needed.

They fired twice.

The shots were louder than they expected in the confined space, the recoil jarring against their injured wrists. The guard went down without a sound.

Aspen stood over him for a moment, watching the blood pool on the concrete floor, feeling something cold settle in their chest. They'd killed men before—in the sacred chamber, defending the people they loved—but it never got easier. Never should get easier.

"Aspen." Tanaka's hand on their shoulder. "We have to keep moving."

They nodded and stepped over the body.

The second encounter came three corridors later—two guards this time, moving toward the sound of the first gunshots. But Tanaka saw them first.

"Left," the cryptolinguist hissed, and Aspen was already moving, pulling Tanaka into a side room just as the guards rounded the corner.

They counted their footsteps. Waited until they were almost past the doorway. Then they stepped out behind them.

Two more shots. Two more bodies.

They were a forest ranger, they reminded themself as they continued down the corridor. They'd become a ranger to protect the wilderness, to preserve what was beautiful and sacred. Not to kill. But they'd been taught by guardians who understood that protection sometimes required violence. And tonight, they were protecting something more important than trees.

The service entrance was exactly where Aspen remembered. Beyond it, a stairwell led down into darkness.

"Where does this go?" Tanaka asked.

"Away from Viktor. That's enough for now."

They descended into the tunnels below.

Ammon and Jeremiah found Vance's cache exactly where Jeremiah had said it would be.

The storage area they'd entered from the ventilation shaft was a maze of crates and abandoned equipment, half of it bearing Cyrillic markings from whatever Russian investors had funded this operation. Jeremiah navigated confidently, leading Ammon through corridors he'd walked years before in service of a different cause.

"Here." Jeremiah stopped at a section of wall that looked identical to every other section of wall. "Third panel from the left, fourth row from the bottom."

He pressed, and the panel swung inward to reveal a hidden compartment.

Inside, stacked in waterproof containers that gleamed in the flashlight beam, were the documents that represented the Consortium's complete history. Financial records going back decades. Communication logs between Vance and his network of collectors and smugglers. Names—hundreds of names—of members and associates reaching across continents. Photographs. Coordinates. Account numbers in a dozen offshore jurisdictions.

Ammon stared at it, understanding what they'd found. This wasn't just evidence. This was the skeleton key that would unlock the entire organization, expose every crime, prosecute every criminal. Years of work, decades of secrecy, all of it compressed into these waterproof containers.

"This is everything," Jeremiah breathed. "The whole network, exposed."

"We need to—" Ammon began.

"To die," said a voice from the shadows, "is what you need to do."

Viktor Semenov stepped into the light.

He looked worse than the last time Ammon had seen him—blood on his face from a cut above his eye, his tactical gear torn, one arm held stiffly at his side. The fighting had clearly caught up with him. But the gun in his hand was steady, and his eyes held the desperate clarity of a man who had nothing left to lose.

Behind Viktor, Ammon could hear more gunfire—distant now, the battle moving through other parts of the facility. No one was coming. No one knew they were here. Whatever happened in this room, they would have to handle themselves.

"Dr. Lundquist." Viktor's voice was calm despite everything. "You've been impressively persistent. I almost respect it."

"It's over, Viktor." Ammon kept his hands visible, away from the weapon at his hip. "The facility is compromised. Your people are scattered or captured. The FBI is securing the perimeter. There's nowhere to run."

"Perhaps." Viktor's gaze flicked to the documents behind them. "But I can still complete my primary objective. Destroy the evidence, eliminate the witnesses. It won't save the operation, but it will protect my employers from the consequences."

"You'd die too."

"I've made peace with that possibility." He raised the gun, sighting down the barrel at Ammon's chest. "Have you?"

Jeremiah stepped forward. "You don't have to do this."

"Ah, the traitor speaks." Viktor's expression hardened. "You know what we do to traitors, Stone. The chamber transformation you claim to have experienced—it won't protect you from what's coming."

"I'm not afraid of dying," Jeremiah said quietly. "Not anymore. But I don't think you want to die either. I think you want to survive this, to find another employer, to keep doing what you're good at. That's who you are—a professional. So act like one. Put down the weapon and walk away."

For a moment, Ammon thought it might work. Viktor's expression flickered, something uncertain passing behind his eyes.

Then his jaw set. "Some prices are worth paying."

He raised the gun—

And Aspen hit him from behind like a freight train.

The tackle drove both of them to the ground, Viktor's gun discharging wildly as he fell. The bullet ricocheted off concrete somewhere in the darkness, the sound shockingly loud in the confined space. Then they were struggling on the floor—Viktor's greater size against Aspen's training, his desperation against their fury.

They rolled across the cold concrete, grappling for position. Viktor's injured arm gave him a disadvantage, but he was still strong—still dangerous—and his free hand closed on Aspen's throat and squeezed.

Black spots danced at the edges of their vision. They could feel their airway closing, their lungs burning for oxygen that wouldn't come. In the dim light, Viktor's face was a mask of determination, all humanity stripped away by the simple imperative to survive.

Viktor got a hand free and swung at their face. Aspen blocked with their forearm, feeling the impact reverberate through their bones, then drove their elbow into his throat. He gagged, his grip loosening, and they used the moment to roll him onto his stomach.

"Ammon!" they shouted. "Jeremiah! Now!"

They moved together, pinning Viktor's arms while Aspen secured his hands with plastic ties like the ones that had bound them. He struggled against them, cursing in Russian, but three against one was too many.

Viktor sagged against the floor, the fight going out of him.

"It's over," Ammon said, helping Aspen to their feet. "It's over."

They looked at him—really looked at him—and he saw the exhaustion in their eyes, the pain, the relief. Then they were in his arms, holding on like they'd never let go.

"You came for me," they whispered.

"Always," he said. "I will always come for you."

The cleanup took hours.

FBI agents swept the facility room by room, securing prisoners and cataloging evidence. Medical teams treated the wounded—remarkably few casualties on either side, thanks to the precision of the assault and the confusion it had sown among Viktor's forces. Father Tomás's men melted away before anyone could question their presence too closely, having fulfilled their part of the fragile arrangement.

Outside, the Nevada dawn was painting the sky in shades of rose and gold. Ammon sat on an overturned crate near the FBI's mobile command center, watching the sun rise over the desert. After the violence of the night, the world seemed impossibly peaceful—birds calling in the distance, the wind carrying the scent of sage, the stars fading into memory as the sky grew bright.

Aspen was with the medics, getting their injuries treated. Their wrists were raw from the restraints, their face marked by Viktor's interrogation techniques, but they were alive. They were safe. That was what mattered.

Tanaka was there too, being examined for the ordeal she'd endured. The cryptolinguist had held up remarkably well—her spirit unbroken even when her body had been battered. Ammon had seen that strength before, in the guardians who protected the sacred chamber. Some people had a core that couldn't be touched, no matter what was done to them.

Jonas had arrived with the support team an hour earlier, having coordinated communications from the staging area throughout the assault. Now he hovered near the medical tent like a man afraid to go in but unable to leave.

"She's asking for you," Ammon said.

Jonas looked at him, startled. "She is?"

"Go. I'll keep an eye on the evidence processing."

He watched Jonas disappear into the tent, and the tightness he'd been carrying between his shoulders finally eased. After everything—the danger, the fear, the violence—there were still moments of connection. Moments of humanity that made all of it worthwhile.

Inside the tent, he knew Jonas was finding Tanaka, their awkwardness giving way to something more genuine. They'd been circling each other for weeks now—the former hacker and the brilliant linguist, both prickly, both guarded, both recognizing something in the other that felt like home.

Some good things could still emerge from the darkness.

But the most surprising development came from Margaux Vance.

She could have run. When the facility's security collapsed, she'd had a clear path to an exit, a vehicle waiting, resources sufficient to disappear into the wilderness of international jurisdictions that still protected people with enough money. The smart move—the Consortium move—would have been to escape and regroup, to fight another day.

Instead, she walked toward the FBI command post with her hands raised, moving deliberately so no one would mistake her intentions. She asked to speak with Agent Reyes, and when the agent arrived—suspicious, hand near her weapon—Margaux said simply: "I'm done. I'm not my father. I won't die for his dream."

What followed was hours of debriefing. Locations. Contacts. Financial pathways that would take forensic accountants years to unravel. Everything the Bureau would need to dismantle what remained of the Consortium network, laid out in meticulous detail by the woman who should have been its heir.

In exchange, she asked for only one thing: the chance to see the First Temple when it was finally discovered.

"Why?" Ammon asked later, when the initial chaos had subsided and they found themselves standing outside the command post, watching the sun climb higher over the desert. "You had everything you needed to disappear."

Margaux didn't respond immediately. In the harsh morning light, she looked older than her years—not just tired, but worn, as if some essential part of her had been ground away by the events of the past months. Her hands, Ammon noticed, were trembling—the only outward sign of what this confession was costing her.

"I spent my whole life trying to prove I wasn't my father's daughter," she said. "Trying to build something legitimate apart from his shadow. But every step I took brought me closer to becoming exactly what he was."

She turned to face him. "In the facility, watching Viktor work on Dr. Tanaka, I saw myself. Saw what I was becoming. And I decided I'd rather face justice as Margaux Vance than keep running as a shadow of Elias."

"That's not redemption," Ammon said.

"No." She almost smiled, but her eyes were bright with what might have been grief for the life she was surrendering. "But it's a start."

Inside the medical tent, Jonas found Tanaka sitting on the edge of a cot, a medic finishing up the last of her bandages. She looked up when he entered, and something shifted in her expression—some wall coming down that he'd never seen her lower before.

"You came for us." Her voice was hoarse, rough from the ordeal she'd endured. "You actually came."

"Of course we came." Jonas's hands were shaking as the medic finished and stepped away, leaving them alone. "Did you think we wouldn't?"

"I thought..." She stopped, swallowed. "I thought we were assets. Useful specialists. I didn't think—"

"You're not an asset." The words came out fiercer than he intended. "You're not a resource to be recovered. You're—"

He stopped, suddenly aware of how close they were, of how her eyes were searching his face.

"I'm what?"

"You're Yuki." It felt strange to use her first name, strange and right. "You're brilliant and difficult and you snore when you're exhausted and you make terrible coffee and you argue with everyone about everything and—"

He was babbling now, the adrenaline finding outlet in words.

"And I was terrified. When we lost contact. When we didn't know if you were alive. I was more scared than I've ever been in my life."

"Jonas—"

"I'm not good at this. At saying things. At feeling things. I spent so many years behind screens because screens are safe, they can't hurt you, they can't—"

She kissed him.

It was awkward—wrong angle, wrong timing, both of them exhausted and battered and running on the last fumes of adrenaline. Her lip was split and his hands were still shaking and nothing about it should have worked.

It was also perfect.

"I'm not good at this either," she said when they separated. "At people. At needing people. But I'm very good at learning, and I think..."

She touched his face, gentle despite her bruised fingers.

"I think I want to learn this. With you. If you're interested."

"I'm interested." He laughed, unhinged with relief. "I'm very, very interested."

Outside the medical tent, Ammon found Aspen.

They were standing apart from the bustle of the command post, their back to him, arms wrapped around themself despite the warmth of the morning sun. He'd been searching for them since the assault ended—needing to see them, touch them, confirm that they were real and whole and here.

"Aspen."

They turned, and he saw it all in their face—the exhaustion, the bruises Viktor's people had left, the fierce determination that had carried them through. But beneath all of that, something raw and vulnerable that they rarely let anyone see.

He crossed the distance between them in three steps and pulled them close. They stiffened for just a moment—the ranger's instinct, the guardian's wariness—and then they were holding him back just as fiercely, their fingers digging into his shoulders like they were afraid he might disappear.

"I thought—" His voice broke. He tried again. "When we lost contact, when I didn't know if you were—"

"I know." Their voice was rough against his neck. "I know."

They stood like that for a long moment, breathing together, letting the simple fact of each other's presence wash away some of the terror of the past days. There would be time later for words, for processing, for the thousand things that needed to be said. Right now, this was enough.

The map. That was the problem that remained.

Margaux had turned over the encrypted image file as part of her cooperation. But the decryption key—the one-time pad that would unlock its contents—had been divided among multiple people. Jonas had his piece. Aspen had theirs. Tanaka had memorized her portion.

"Even with cooperation, this will take time to reconstruct," Jonas said, working at a laptop in the FBI's mobile command center. His fingers flew across the keyboard, but his expression was frustrated. "The encryption was designed to prevent exactly this situation."

"We don't have time." Ammon stared at the satellite imagery of the Utah canyon system that Tanaka had identified. "Konstantin was tracking this assault. By now, the Vatican knows exactly where we're heading—and Tomás can't control what the hardliners do with that information."

"Tomás is supposed to be an ally," Aspen pointed out.

"For now. Until we find something that threatens his version of faith." Ammon shook his head. "The alliance was always temporary. We need to move before it expires."

The decryption key was reconstructed within the hour—fragments assembled, algorithms run, the map revealing its secrets. Hathenbruck's handwriting showed a specific location within the canyon system, marked with coordinates and annotations in German that Tanaka translated with steady precision despite her exhaustion.

"Porta Veritatis," she read aloud. "The Door of Truth."

Ammon looked at the map, at the X that marked a location in some of the most remote and unforgiving terrain in the American West. His ancestor had hidden something there, more than a century ago—something so important that he'd created an entirely separate archive to protect it.

And somewhere out there, Konstantin was watching. Waiting. The Vatican operative who answered to Father Tomás—or perhaps to forces within the Church that even Tomás didn't fully control. The alliance they'd forged was fragile, temporary, built on mutual convenience rather than trust. When they reached the First Temple, that alliance would be tested. And Ammon wasn't sure it would survive.

But that was a problem for tomorrow. Today, they had won. Today, Aspen was safe. Today, the Consortium had been broken.

The race's final leg had begun.

CHAPTER TWENTY-SIX

The Canyon

The Grand Staircase-Escalante National Monument spread across 1.9 million acres of southern Utah—a landscape so vast and rugged that significant portions remained unexplored even in the age of satellite imagery. Slot canyons carved through sandstone over millions of years, creating a maze of narrow passages and towering walls that defied conventional navigation. Somewhere in that maze, the First Temple waited.

The helicopter dropped them at a staging area on the monument's eastern edge, where Agent Reyes had established a perimeter under the guise of a federal crime scene investigation. Local law enforcement had been told only that evidence related to the Consortium arrests might be found in the area—enough justification to keep civilians away without revealing the true nature of what they were seeking.

Thomas was waiting for them. The elder guardian had insisted on being present despite the physical toll the journey would demand. His face was drawn with pain, but his eyes blazed with the intensity of someone approaching the culmination of a lifelong purpose. Beside him stood Robert Colorow, another guardian elder whose weathered features and quiet bearing spoke of decades spent protecting sacred knowledge.

"The last time I saw this landscape," Thomas said as they gathered their gear, "I was a young man learning the guardian traditions from my grandfather. He told me stories about places even deeper in the canyons— places the guardians had protected for generations without fully understanding why."

"You think he knew about the First Temple?"

"I think he knew there were secrets beyond the sacred chamber. Secrets passed down through oral tradition, fragmentary and incomplete." Thomas gazed at the red rock formations rising around them. "What we're about to find—it's what they were all protecting. The original source."

Father Tomás approached from the communications tent, his presence at the staging area a surprise to some but not to Ammon. The priest had insisted on joining the expedition when he'd heard about the temple's discovery, flying in the night before.

"I need to see this for myself," Tomás had explained during their call. "If I'm going to argue for engagement rather than suppression, I need to witness what we're dealing with. I need to be able to tell my superiors exactly what's at stake."

It was a risk—having the Vatican's representative present when they uncovered knowledge that might challenge Church doctrine. But Ammon had decided the risk of excluding him was greater. Better to have Tomás as a witness than as an adversary imagining the worst.

The staging area buzzed with controlled activity. FBI agents checked equipment and reviewed maps, their tactical gear incongruous against the ancient landscape. Aspen supervised the distribution of supplies—water, first aid kits, emergency beacons—with the practiced efficiency of someone who understood that the desert forgave no mistakes.

Jeremiah Stone stood apart from the federal agents, his presence a condition of his continued cooperation—Reyes had argued against it, but Ammon had insisted. If Konstantin was tracking them, as intelligence suggested, they needed someone who understood how the Vatican's fixer thought.

Ammon found himself standing apart, staring at the canyon entrance where Hathenbruck's map indicated they should begin. The red rock walls rose like sentinels, their striated layers recording epochs of geological time. Somewhere beyond those walls, his ancestor had walked this same path over a century ago. Had Friedrich felt this same mixture of anticipation and dread?

"You're doing that thing again," Jonas said, appearing at his elbow with a satellite phone. "The thousand-yard stare. Very dramatic, very unhelpful."

"I'm thinking."

"About?"

Ammon gestured toward the canyon. "Everyone who came before us. Hathenbruck. The original guardians. The builders themselves, whoever they were. They all made this journey, and most of them never came back to tell the world what they found."

"We're coming back," Jonas said firmly. "We've got FBI backup, satellite communications, and—" he patted his pack "—enough protein bars to survive a month. This isn't the nineteenth century."

"No. But the canyon is still the canyon. It doesn't care what century we're from."

Tanaka joined them, her camera already out, documenting everything. The bruises from her captivity had faded to yellow shadows, but something harder remained in her eyes—a determination that hadn't been there before Nevada.

"The weather window looks good. Clear skies for the next forty-eight hours. If we're going to do this, we should move."

"She's right," Aspen said, approaching with Agent Reyes beside them. "Desert weather can turn fast. We need to be in position before sunset."

Reyes studied the canyon entrance, her expression carefully neutral. "My team will hold the perimeter. Radio check every hour. Me and a small team will join you. If we're not back by tomorrow noon, they'll come looking."

"And if we find something that requires... discretion?" Ammon asked.

The agent's jaw tightened. "Then we'll have a very interesting conversation with my supervisors. Let's hope it doesn't come to that."

They gathered their packs and moved toward the canyon mouth. The temperature dropped as they entered the shadows between the walls, the air taking on the dry, mineral scent of ancient stone. Their footsteps echoed in ways that made the space feel simultaneously vast and claustrophobic.

The hike demanded everything they had.

Hathenbruck's map guided them through terrain that would have challenged even experienced backcountry travelers. The first mile was deceptively easy—a sandy wash between towering walls, wide enough to walk two abreast. Then the canyon narrowed, and narrowed again, until they were turning sideways to squeeze through gaps barely wider than their shoulders.

"How did Hathenbruck manage this terrain, limited with one arm missing below the elbow?" Jonas gasped, scraping through a particularly tight passage. His pack caught on a protrusion and he had to back up, remove it, and pass it through separately.

"He was tougher than us," Ammon said. "Or more desperate."

Thomas moved with surprising grace despite his injuries, his body remembering rhythms learned decades ago. He paused at intervals to study the rock walls, tracing patterns invisible to the others.

"The guardians marked this route," he said softly. "Subtle signs. A chip here, a scratch there. Hathenbruck wasn't the first."

Robert Colorow nodded, pointing to a small petroglyph nearly invisible in the rock's natural striations. "My grandfather showed me marks like these when I was a boy. Said they were older than our people's memory. Now I understand what he meant."

The slot canyons gave way to sandstone ledges requiring careful climbing. Ammon's hands found holds worn smooth by countless predecessors, grooves cut into the rock at just the right intervals. Ancient steps, he realized. Someone had made this path accessible, long before Hathenbruck, long before the guardian tradition as they knew it.

"Water break," Aspen called, and they stopped on a ledge overlooking a vast panorama of red rock formations. The sun had moved past its zenith, casting long shadows that transformed the landscape into something alien and beautiful.

Ammon drank deeply, feeling the water ease the tightness in his throat. His muscles ached, his lungs burned from the altitude, and they still had miles to go. But the landscape itself seemed to be pulling him forward, as if the canyon recognized that he belonged here.

"Look," Tanaka said softly, pointing at the cliff face beside them.

Petroglyphs covered the stone—faded images of bighorn sheep and human figures, geometric patterns that might have been maps or calendars or something entirely beyond modern understanding. They had entered sacred ground.

"This place has been sacred for millennia," Aspen said quietly, their ranger's eye taking in the signs of human presence scattered throughout the landscape. "Look—fire rings, evidence of seasonal camps. People have been coming here for thousands of years."

"Pilgrims," Tanaka suggested. "Coming to visit a holy site the same way people visit temples and cathedrals."

They pressed on. The afternoon heat was brutal, the sun reflecting off the sandstone until the canyon felt like an oven. They picked their way carefully around dry washes—the kind that could become death traps if the rains came. Pinyon pines clung to impossible ledges, their roots finding purchase in cracks that seemed too small to sustain life. Ravens called from the heights, their voices echoing through the canyons like the pronouncements of ancient gods.

Ammon found himself walking beside Thomas during a relatively easy stretch. The elder guardian's breathing was labored, but he refused offers of rest.

"Tell me about your grandfather's stories," Ammon said. "The ones about deeper places."

Thomas was quiet for a long moment. "He spoke of a time before the sacred chamber. Before the codices, before the guardians as we know them. He said there was an older tradition—one that came from a people who sailed across the great water. They brought knowledge that changed everything."

"And the First Temple?"

"He never used that name. But he described a place where the old ones kept their greatest secrets. A library of stone and bronze, sealed against time itself." Thomas's voice dropped. "I thought they were just stories. The kind elders tell children to make them feel connected to something larger. I never imagined..."

"That they were true."

"That I would live to see them proven."

The petroglyphs grew denser as they penetrated deeper into the canyon system. At first they were familiar—the common iconography of the Southwest, images that might have been carved by Fremont or Anasazi peoples millennia ago. But gradually, other images appeared. Symbols that matched the codex. Ships with square sails crossing wavy lines that could only represent ocean. Star charts showing constellations in configurations that had shifted over millennia. Figures holding tools and instruments that looked more Mediterranean than American.

"They recorded everything," Tanaka breathed, running her fingers along a panel covered in intricate carvings. "Their voyages, their astronomical observations, their trading relationships. This canyon wall is like a library— thousands of years of history preserved in stone."

Ammon studied the images, feeling time pressing down on him. The people who had carved these symbols were long dead, their civilization forgotten by mainstream history. But their knowledge had survived— preserved in codices, protected by guardians, waiting for someone to decode it.

Aspen crouched beside a particularly elaborate panel, their expression troubled. "These aren't like any petroglyphs I've catalogued. The style, the precision—they're almost like technical drawings."

"Because that's what they are," Tanaka said. "Instructions. Records. This wasn't casual marking of territory or spiritual expression. Someone was deliberately preserving information for future generations."

Jonas was photographing everything, his camera clicking steadily. "If this is just the approach route, what the hell is waiting at the end?"

No one answered. No one had to.

They hiked in silence for the last hour, words having run out somewhere around the seventh mile. The canyon walls rose around them—red and orange stone layered like pages in a book that recorded millions of years rather than words. Ammon found himself thinking about all the others who had made this journey. Hathenbruck, over a century ago, following clues from the chamber codices. The original guardians, whoever they were, carrying whatever they thought worth preserving. And before them—the builders themselves, choosing this place for reasons that perhaps made sense only in their vanished context.

"We're close," Ammon said, consulting Hathenbruck's map. The sun was lower now, the light taking on the golden quality of late afternoon. "The entrance should be just ahead."

They rounded a bend in the canyon and stopped.

The walls here had been worked—carved and smoothed in ways that transcended natural erosion. Massive blocks of sandstone had been fitted together with impossible precision, forming an archway that framed a narrow passage leading deeper into the rock. The craftsmanship was evident even after millennia of weathering; these stones had been shaped by masters.

Above the archway, carved in letters that combined Latin and an unknown script, were the words Hathenbruck had recorded on his map:

PORTA VERITATIS

"The Door of Truth," Tanaka translated, barely above a whisper. "We found it."

For a long moment, no one moved. The weight of the discovery pressed down on them—not just the archaeological significance, but the personal meaning. Generations of guardians had protected this secret. Hathenbruck had hidden the location at the cost of his own peace. Marcus had died without ever seeing his research validated.

And now, finally, they stood before the door that had haunted Ammon's family for over a century.

Thomas moved forward, the aches of his old body forgotten in the presence of what they were seeing. He reached out to touch the carved stones, and Ammon saw tears forming in the old guardian's eyes.

"My grandfather's stories were true," Thomas said, his voice cracking. "The First Temple. The original source of the guardian tradition. It's real. It was always real."

"Just waiting for someone to follow the trail," Ammon said softly.

Aspen stood beside him, their hand finding his. "Are you ready for this?"

Ammon looked at the archway, at the darkness beyond, at the truth that awaited. He thought of his father, who had died in search of the lost Rhoades mine. Of Marcus, who discovered something deeper, something pointing to this place where Ammon now stood. Of F.W.C. Hathenbruck, who had found this place and chosen to hide it, hoping that someday someone would be worthy of what lay within.

"No," he admitted. "But I don't think anyone could be. That's not the point."

"What is the point?"

"That we're here anyway. That we came because it matters, not because we were ready."

They gathered at the threshold, seven people from different backgrounds and motivations—guardians and academics, rangers and hackers, priests and agents—united by the discovery that lay ahead. The setting sun painted the canyon walls in shades of amber and crimson, as if the landscape itself was marking this moment.

"Whatever we find in there," Jonas said quietly, "nothing is going to be the same."

"That's what we came for," Ammon replied. "To find the truth, whatever it costs."

He stepped through the archway, and the others followed him into the dark.

None of them noticed the figure watching from the shadow of a sandstone outcropping, two hundred yards back along the canyon. Konstantin had tracked them for three days, maintaining distance, using the terrain the way only someone with decades of fieldcraft could. He had watched them make camp, watched them study their maps, watched the old guardian speak words that carried on the wind without quite reaching his ears.

Now he watched them disappear into the mountain.

He checked his pack—the specialized equipment he'd assembled over weeks of preparation, the contingencies for scenarios exactly like this one. Then he began his approach, patient as stone, silent as the shadows that pooled between the canyon walls.

CHAPTER TWENTY-SEVEN

The Antechamber

The passage beyond the *PORTA VERITATIS* did not welcome them.

Ammon had expected the archway to open into darkness—the close press of stone that he remembered from the Uinta chamber six months ago. Instead, he found himself facing a wall of fitted stone blocks, each carved with symbols that seemed to pulse in the dying light of the winter sun.

"It's sealed," Jonas said, disappointment raw. "After everything—it's still sealed."

But Thomas was already moving forward, his weathered hands reaching toward the stone with the certainty of someone who had spent a lifetime learning to read what others couldn't see. The injuries from years of guardianship still showed in the careful way he moved—a slight hitch in his stride, one arm held close to his body—but his eyes held something that transcended pain.

"Not sealed," he said softly. "Waiting."

He traced a pattern on the central block—three symbols arranged in a triangle that Ammon recognized from the codex translations. Sun, earth, and water. The three elements the ancient builders had considered fundamental to life.

"The guardian traditions speak of doors that know their visitors," Thomas continued. "I always thought it was metaphor. Sacred language for simple mechanisms."

"What kind of mechanism?" Agent Reyes asked. Her hand rested near her weapon—professional caution that seemed almost absurd in this context, but Ammon understood. When you didn't know what you were facing, you prepared for everything.

"The kind that requires understanding, not force." Thomas turned to face the group. "The oral traditions describe a test. Not of strength or cleverness, but of intention. The builders wanted to ensure that whoever entered this place came with the right purpose."

"And what's the right purpose?" Tanaka asked.

Thomas's smile was sad. "That's what we're about to find out."

He positioned himself before the sealed entrance and began to speak—not in English, but in a language Ammon had never heard. The words were guttural and flowing at once, rising and falling in patterns that seemed to follow the symbol arrangements on the stone. Behind him, Robert Colorow joined in, their voices weaving together in harmonies that felt older than memory.

The winter sun had been setting as they passed through the archway, its light angling through the canyon rim in a golden shaft that painted the sealed door in amber and rose. Now that light seemed to intensify, focusing on the three central symbols Thomas had touched. The stone began to warm beneath their feet—not dangerously, but noticeably, as if the mountain itself were awakening.

"The solstice alignment," Tanaka breathed. "Of course. They built this entrance to catch the winter solstice sunset. The light is the key."

As she spoke, the golden shaft narrowed further, becoming a concentrated beam that struck the sun symbol dead center. For a heartbeat, nothing happened.

Then the symbols began to glow.

Not reflected light—something deeper, as if the stone itself remembered fire. The glow spread from symbol to symbol in a pattern that matched Thomas's chanted words, each element illuminating in sequence: sun, earth, water, sun, earth, water. The rhythm built, the light intensified, and Ammon felt the hair rise on his arms as something vast and ancient stirred in the rock around them.

The grinding sound came from everywhere and nowhere—stone moving against stone after seven thousand years of silence. The sealed wall didn't swing open like a door or slide aside like a gate. Instead, the blocks began to rotate, each one turning independently in a sequence so complex it would have taken modern engineers months to program. In seconds, what had been an impenetrable barrier became a passageway, the blocks reconfigured into an archway that framed a corridor stretching into darkness.

No—not darkness. As Ammon's eyes adjusted, he realized the corridor beyond was lit by the same method as the entrance: shafts of illumination descending from narrow openings carved into the canyon rim far above, positioned with mathematical precision to catch the dying sun. The effect was deliberate, architectural. Someone had engineered this space to be navigable without torches, to draw visitors deeper through pools of radiance separated by corridors of shadow.

Thomas lowered his hands, his voice trailing into silence. When he turned to face them, tears streamed down his weathered cheeks.

"My grandfather taught me those words when I was seven years old," he said. "He made me repeat them until I could say them in my sleep. He told me that someday, they might matter. That someday, I might need them to open a door that had been closed since before our people came to these mountains."

He looked at the passageway before them.

"I thought he was telling stories. Teaching traditions. I never imagined..."

"That the door was real," Ammon finished softly.

"That any of it was real."

Agent Reyes studied the reconfigured stone blocks, her tactical mind already assessing vulnerabilities. "How long will it stay open?"

Thomas shook his head. "The traditions don't say. The mechanism is designed to welcome seekers, not trap them. It may stay open until the solstice light fades, or until someone speaks the closing words."

"Do you know the closing words?"

"I know words that might work. But I'd rather not test them until we're ready to leave."

Reyes frowned but nodded. "Then we move quickly. I don't like having an unsecured entrance at our backs."

None of them saw the shadow that slipped through the archway ten minutes later, moving with the practiced silence of a man who had spent thirty years learning to be invisible.

They moved through the entrance corridor in reverent silence, their footsteps echoing against walls that weren't rough-hewn cave rock but dressed stone, fitted together without mortar in a technique that reminded Ammon of Incan masonry. Blocks so precisely cut that a knife blade couldn't slip between them, yet somehow more refined—as if the Incan builders had been students working from a master's template.

Petroglyphs covered every surface: spirals and handprints and figures that seemed to dance in the shifting light. Some Ammon recognized from the codex translations—symbols for water, for stars, for the cardinal directions. Others were entirely new, vocabulary from a language they hadn't yet learned to read.

"The construction alone," Tanaka breathed, running her fingers along a seam between blocks that she couldn't feel despite knowing it was there. "This would have taken generations. And the precision—we couldn't replicate this today without laser measurement."

"Maybe not," Jonas said, "but we could get close. What we couldn't do is maintain it for seven thousand years without degradation. These joints are as tight as the day they were made. That's not just precision—that's material science we don't understand."

Aspen had taken point, their instincts mapping the space even as something deeper responded to what they were seeing. They stopped at an intersection where the corridor branched—left into deeper shadow, right toward a source of warmer light.

"This way," they said, gesturing right. "I don't know how I know, but— this way."

Thomas nodded. "The guardian heritage. Your ancestors walked these corridors. Something in you remembers."

They followed the light. The corridor widened gradually, the ceiling rising until it disappeared into shadows that the shafts of illumination couldn't reach. The temperature dropped, the air taking on the dry, mineral scent of deep stone—ancient and clean, untouched by the contaminations of the modern world.

And then the corridor opened, and Ammon forgot how to breathe.

The antechamber was vast—a cathedral carved from living rock, its ceiling soaring thirty feet overhead. Columns shaped like stylized trees rose from floor to ceiling, their stone trunks branching into geometric canopies that seemed to hold the mountain above them. The last light of the winter solstice fell through an oculus at the chamber's apex, a perfect circle of fading gold that struck the floor in a beam so defined it seemed solid.

Where the light touched the stone, symbols had been inlaid in bronze that still gleamed after millennia. A map, Ammon realized. A map of the world, but wrong—continents connected by lines that crossed oceans, routes that shouldn't exist, destinations that mainstream archaeology said were impossible.

"God in heaven," Tanaka whispered.

But it wasn't the map that held Ammon's attention. It was what surrounded them.

Display alcoves lined the walls of the antechamber, carved into the stone at regular intervals, each one illuminated by its own shaft of captured light. And in those alcoves...

Artifacts. Thousands of them.

Ammon moved toward the nearest alcove as if drawn by a mystical force. His legs felt disconnected from his body, his heart hammering against his ribs with a thump that seemed likely to crack them. Inside the alcove, resting on a pedestal of polished granite, sat a mirror of bronze. He could see his reflection in its surface—clear, undistorted, as if the metal had been cast yesterday rather than before the pyramids rose.

Seven thousand years, and it still worked. His hands began to tremble.

"That's Egyptian faience." Jonas's voice came from somewhere to his left, cracking with the effort of processing what he was seeing. "That is definitely Egyptian faience. Middle Kingdom style, maybe older. Ammon— that pottery over there. The glaze technique. That's Chinese. That's Han Dynasty Chinese, except it can't be because the Han Dynasty was four thousand years after this place was built."

Tanaka had stopped in front of an alcove containing textiles—fabrics that should have crumbled to dust millennia ago, somehow preserved in the dry mountain air. Her hand hovered over the glass-smooth surface of a protective covering that Ammon couldn't identify, afraid to touch, afraid that contact would shatter the impossible reality before her.

"Mesopotamian weaving patterns," she said, her voice barely audible. "But the dye work—I've only seen that technique in pre-Columbian Andean textiles. They're both. They're—"

She couldn't finish the sentence.

Ammon moved through the alcoves in a daze, each step revealing new impossibilities. Obsidian blades laid out in careful rows, their edges still sharp enough to cut, sourced from volcanic glass that chemical analysis would later prove came from at least four different continents. Ceramic vessels painted with scenes of ships crossing stylized waves, their square sails filled with winds that had blown seven millennia ago. Gold jewelry of astonishing delicacy, crafted using techniques that wouldn't be "invented" for another five thousand years.

And everywhere, the same symbol repeated: a circle bisected by a wavy line, surrounded by twelve points arranged like numbers on a clock face. The symbol from Hathenbruck's map. The symbol that had led them here.

"They were talking to everyone," Jonas said. He had stopped moving, was simply turning in place, his technical mind trying to catalog what his rational brain insisted couldn't exist. "Ammon, these people were in contact with civilizations on every continent. Before the Bronze Age. Before writing. Before we thought anyone could cross an ocean."

"Not just contact," Thomas said. His voice came from the far side of the antechamber, where he stood before a section of wall covered in carved symbols. "Exchange. Look at this."

They gathered around him. The wall showed a stylized scene: ships arriving at a shore, figures unloading cargo, other figures greeting them with raised hands. Above the scene, a line of symbols that Tanaka began translating before Ammon could ask.

"'The vessels of the sun-followers, bearing the fruit of their knowing, welcomed by the star-readers of the western shore.'" She paused, her voice catching. "'Knowledge given, knowledge received, the circle unbroken.'"

"Sun-followers," Ammon repeated. "That's—"

"A term for Egyptian priests," Tanaka confirmed. "Solar worship was central to their religious practice. And star-readers—that could be any number of cultures, but in this context..." She gestured at the astronomical symbols scattered throughout the scene. "I think it means the people who built this place. A civilization that tracked the stars with precision we're only beginning to appreciate."

Aspen had moved away from the group, drawn toward a section of the antechamber that the others hadn't yet explored. Their voice echoed strangely when they spoke, carrying harmonics that the space's acoustics seemed designed to amplify.

"There's more over here. A lot more."

The alcoves on the eastern wall contained something different from the artifacts they'd been examining. Not trade goods or artistic objects, but tools. Instruments. Devices whose purposes Ammon couldn't begin to guess.

One alcove held what appeared to be an astrolabe, but far more complex than any he'd studied—nested rings of bronze and crystal, calibrated to track movements that modern astronomy might not even recognize. Another contained a series of graduated cylinders, their surfaces marked with measurements so fine they were barely visible, accompanied by tablets covered in mathematical notation.

"This is a laboratory," Jonas said, awe giving way to professional recognition. "Or a museum of laboratory equipment. These are scientific instruments."

"Seven thousand years ago," Agent Reyes said flatly. She had been silent since entering the antechamber, her trained skepticism warring with the evidence of her own eyes. "You're telling me that seven thousand years ago, before writing, before cities, someone built scientific instruments that we can barely understand today."

"I'm telling you what I see." Jonas picked up one of the graduated cylinders, handling it with the care of a man touching a holy relic. "And what I see is a civilization that was asking the same questions we ask. How does the world work? What can we measure? What can we know?"

"The difference," Thomas said quietly, "is what they did with the answers."

They explored the antechamber for what felt like hours, though later Ammon would learn only forty minutes had passed. Each alcove revealed new wonders, new impossibilities, new questions that multiplied faster than answers could form.

Tanaka found a collection of tablets in a language she almost recognized—"It's like finding a Rosetta Stone," she said, "except the stone is in three languages I've never seen before, and somehow I can almost understand one of them"—and immediately began photographing everything her camera could capture.

Jonas discovered a section of wall covered in mathematical equations, the symbols unfamiliar but the structure unmistakable. "This is calculus," he said, his voice cracking. "Or something that functions like calculus. They derived calculus five thousand years before Newton."

Aspen found the records. Carved tablets lining an entire alcove, each one covered in dense script that documented—what? Arrivals? Transactions? The records of a trading post that had served visitors from across the ancient world?

"These are names," Aspen said. "Lists of names. And dates—I think these are dates. But the system is unlike anything I've seen."

Thomas had been studying the central map, the bronze inlay that showed the world as the builders had known it. Now he turned to face the group, and his expression stopped Ammon's breath.

"There's a door," Thomas said. "Behind the map. Sealed."

They gathered around him. The map, Ammon now saw, wasn't simply decorative. It was functional—a key, perhaps, or a lock. The lines connecting continents weren't just trade routes. They were channels cut into the bronze, designed to guide something. Light, perhaps. Or water. Or something else entirely.

And at the center of the map, where all the lines converged, was a symbol they all recognized: a door, stylized but unmistakable, with a sun rising behind it.

"The inner chamber," Ammon said. "The archive itself. This is just—"

"The entrance hall," Thomas confirmed. "The place where visitors were received. Where they proved their worth before being granted access to what the builders actually wanted to protect."

"Proved their worth how?" Tanaka asked.

Thomas pointed to the symbols surrounding the door icon. "That's what we need to find out."

The symbols were arranged in three concentric rings, each ring containing a different script. The outer ring Tanaka recognized from the codex—the language they'd been translating for months. The middle ring was similar but more archaic, the symbols more angular and stylized. The inner ring was something else entirely: curves and spirals that seemed to move in the peripheral vision, refusing to resolve into fixed shapes.

"Three languages," Jonas said. "Like the warnings on the doorway we haven't found yet."

"Or three tests," Ammon said. The pattern was familiar—something nagged at the edge of his memory. "Three challenges. One for each kind of knowledge."

He closed his eyes, letting his mind drift back through months of research, years of study, generations of family obsession. Hathenbruck's journals. The codex translations. The oral traditions Thomas had shared.

"The outer ring is the physical test," he said, opening his eyes. "The language of trade and measurement—proving you understand the material world. The middle ring is the intellectual test. Demonstrating comprehension of the builders' philosophy and history. But the inner ring..."

"The spiritual test," Thomas said. "Proving you understand why the knowledge must be protected. Not just what it is, but what it means."

"Can we pass these tests?" Aspen asked.

Thomas looked at the group assembled in the antechamber—the academic, the hacker, the agent, the guardians, the man whose ancestor had found this place over a century ago. Seven people from different worlds, united by a trail of clues that had led them here.

"I don't know," he admitted. "But I think we have to try."

They began with the outer ring.

The symbols, Tanaka determined after careful study, described a series of mathematical relationships. Ratios and proportions, astronomical cycles, the dimensions of physical structures described in units that required translation.

"It's asking us to demonstrate understanding of their measurement system," she said. "If I'm reading this right, they want us to prove we can think the way they thought. Calculate the way they calculated."

"What do we need to calculate?" Jonas asked.

"The positions of the stars." Tanaka pointed to a sequence of symbols. "Specifically, the position of a particular constellation on a particular date. If we can work out their calendar system and their astronomical notation, we should be able to identify the date they're describing and calculate where the stars would have been."

"Should be able to," Ammon repeated.

"It's been seven thousand years. Stellar drift, precession of the equinoxes—the sky doesn't look the same as it did when this was built. We'd need to calculate backwards to find the configuration they're describing."

"Can you do that?"

Tanaka was already pulling out her tablet, calling up astronomical software. "I can try."

It took an hour. The mathematics were straightforward once they'd cracked the measurement system—the builders had used a base-12 counting system that Jonas recognized from ancient Mesopotamian influences—but the calendar conversion was agonizing. They argued about leap year equivalents, about whether the builders had accounted for the same orbital irregularities modern astronomers tracked, about whether certain symbols represented specific stars or general regions of the sky.

Finally, Tanaka looked up from her calculations, exhaustion and triumph warring in her expression.

"Winter solstice," she said. "Seven thousand one hundred and forty-three years ago. The date when this temple was consecrated. They want us to recreate the sky as it appeared on the night this place was born."

"How do we do that?" Reyes asked.

Ammon was studying the bronze map, the channels that connected continents. "The map is an orrery," he said. "A mechanical model of the heavens. If we align the channels correctly—match the stellar positions from that date—"

"We activate whatever mechanism opens the middle ring," Jonas finished.

The channels in the map, they discovered, contained small bronze spheres—spheres that had sat motionless for millennia, waiting for someone to understand their purpose. There were twelve of them, corresponding to the twelve points around the central symbol. By careful manipulation— following the positions Tanaka had calculated—they moved the spheres through the channels until each one rested in its designated position.

When the last sphere clicked into place, the outer ring began to glow.

Not with reflected light, but with the same deep radiance they'd seen when the entrance opened. The symbols brightened in sequence, each one illuminating as the pattern completed, until the entire outer ring shone like a halo of captured starlight.

And the middle ring, which had been static and unchanging, began to move. Symbols rotated past each other, rearranging into new configurations that resolved into legible script.

"It's a question," Tanaka said, translating rapidly. "Or a series of questions. About the builders' history. About why they created this place. About what they were trying to protect."

The questions were harder than the mathematics. They required not just knowledge but understanding—the ability to articulate the builders' philosophy in terms they would have recognized. Why did they gather knowledge from across the world? What did they fear would happen if that knowledge was lost? What did they hope would happen when someone finally came to claim it?

The group debated each answer, drawing on months of translation work, on guardian oral traditions, on Ammon's deep familiarity with Hathenbruck's journals. Sometimes they disagreed; sometimes the disagreement sharpened their understanding; sometimes they simply had to guess, trusting that their intentions would carry weight even if their words fell short.

When they'd formulated their final answer—spoken aloud in the antechamber, translated by Tanaka into the symbols of the middle script— the second ring began to glow.

And the inner ring revealed itself at last.

The spiraling symbols resolved into something that wasn't quite language and wasn't quite image—a flowing script that seemed to communicate directly with something below conscious thought. Ammon stared at it, feeling his mind stretch toward comprehension without quite reaching it.

"I don't—" Tanaka began, then stopped. "I don't know how to read this. It's not language. It's not even symbols in the normal sense. It's more like—"

"Music," Aspen said quietly.

Everyone turned to look at them. Aspen's face had gone pale, their eyes fixed on the inner ring with an intensity that bordered on trance.

"It's music," they repeated. "Or something that works like music. Patterns that bypass the thinking mind and speak directly to..." They trailed off, shaking their head. "I don't know how I know this. But the guardian traditions—my grandmother used to sing to me when I was small. Songs that didn't have words, just sounds. She said they were older than memory. She said they were the songs the First People used to speak to the spirits of the land."

"Can you read them?" Ammon asked. "The symbols?"

Aspen studied the inner ring, their expression shifting through uncertainty, concentration, and finally a kind of resigned acceptance. "I think—I think they're asking us to sing. To prove that we carry the tradition inside us. That the knowledge isn't just intellectual. It's—"

"Embodied," Thomas said. "The physical test proves you understand the world. The intellectual test proves you understand why. But the spiritual test proves that understanding lives in you. That you don't just know the tradition—you are the tradition."

Aspen looked at Thomas. Something passed between them— recognition, perhaps, or permission.

Then Aspen began to sing.

The sound that emerged from their throat was unlike anything Ammon had ever heard. Not quite melody, not quite chant—something older, something that seemed to resonate with the stone itself. The acoustics of the antechamber caught the sound and amplified it, harmonics building on harmonics until the air itself seemed to vibrate with meaning.

Thomas joined in. His voice wove around Aspen's, adding depth and complexity, two streams of sound becoming a river that filled the space with something that felt less like music than like memory made audible.

The inner ring began to glow.

The light built at first, then accelerated, the spiraling symbols brightening until they blazed with radiance that seemed to come from somewhere beyond the physical. The sound and the light merged, became one thing, became something that transcended both.

And the door behind the map began to open.

Stone ground against stone, the same sound they'd heard at the entrance, but deeper now, more profound. The bronze map split down the center, its two halves swinging outward to reveal what they had concealed for seven thousand years.

A passage, leading deeper into the mountain.

A passage leading to the archive itself.

Aspen's song faded into silence. For a long moment, no one moved.

Then Ammon stepped forward, toward the door his ancestor had found and sealed, toward the knowledge that had waited seven millennia for someone worthy to claim it.

"Whatever we find in there," he said, "nothing is going to be the same."

"That's what we came for," Thomas replied. "To find the truth, whatever it costs."

Together, they stepped through the door of truth.

And the shadows swallowed them whole.

CHAPTER TWENTY-EIGHT

The Price of Fire

The passage beyond the door plunged them into absolute darkness—a darkness so complete that Ammon could feel it pressing against his eyes like a physical weight.

Then, as if responding to their presence, light began to bloom.

It started as a faint luminescence in the stone itself, phosphorescent minerals waking after millennia of dormancy. The glow spread in waves, racing along the walls of the passage, illuminating carved surfaces that showed scenes of ancient life: scholars bent over tablets, astronomers studying the sky through instruments Ammon couldn't identify, healers tending to patients with tools that looked disturbingly advanced.

"Bioluminescent bacteria," Jonas said, his voice hushed. "Or something like it. They engineered the stone to respond to carbon dioxide—human breath. When people enter, the bacteria wake up and produce light."

"Seven thousand years," Tanaka whispered. "Seven thousand years, and they're still alive."

"Bacteria are hard to kill. Given the right conditions—stable temperature, proper nutrients embedded in the rock—there's no theoretical limit to how long they could survive." Jonas ran his fingers along the glowing surface, watching the light intensify at his touch. "These people understood microbiology. They understood it well enough to engineer a living lighting system that would outlast every civilization that came after them."

The implications settled over the group like a shroud. They weren't just dealing with a culture that had mastered astronomy and mathematics. They were dealing with a culture that had manipulated life itself.

The passage descended at a gentle angle, the glow brightening as they went deeper, until they emerged into a space that stopped every one of them in their tracks.

The archive chamber was vast beyond comprehension.

Ammon had explored cathedrals, palaces, ancient ruins across three continents. None of them had prepared him for this. The space swallowed sound, swallowed light, swallowed the sense of scale that usually anchored him to reality. A hundred people could have moved through this chamber without seeing each other, lost among the forest of pedestals and the shadows that pooled between them. The chamber stretched before them like an underground amphitheater, its ceiling lost in shadows that even the bioluminescent glow couldn't reach. Stone pedestals rose from the floor in concentric rings, thousands of them, each one bearing its burden of bronze tablets that gleamed in the living light. The arrangement was deliberate, mathematical—the pedestals positioned according to some organizing principle that Ammon's mind reached for without grasping.

At the chamber's center, raised on a dais of polished obsidian, stood something that made his heart stutter.

The device was perhaps ten feet tall, a construction of interlocking rings and spheres that seemed to move even as he watched—bronze and crystal and something that looked like silver but probably wasn't, calibrated to track movements that spanned scales from planetary to microscopic. An orrery, he thought at first, but that word was woefully inadequate. This was a model of the cosmos as the builders had understood it: not just planets and stars, but forces and relationships, the hidden architecture of reality rendered in metal and stone.

"Mother of God," Agent Reyes breathed. She was not, as far as Ammon knew, a religious woman. But some responses transcended belief.

"It's a calendar," Jonas said, circling the device with the reverence of an engineer confronting divinity. "But it's also predictive. Look—these smaller dials track cycles within cycles. If I'm reading this right, you could use this to predict eclipses, planetary conjunctions, maybe even..."

He stopped, staring at one particular dial whose markings were unfamiliar.

"I don't know what this tracks. But they thought it was important enough to build a dedicated mechanism for it."

Thomas stood at the edge of the dais, his expression shifting through emotions Ammon couldn't name. The guardian traditions, he now understood, had been fragments—stories passed down through generations, degraded by time and repetition until only echoes remained. Now Thomas was seeing the source. The original. The truth that his ancestors had spent millennia protecting without fully understanding.

"The star-readers," Thomas said quietly. "That's what the old stories call them. My grandfather used to say they could know the seasons before they came, could tell when the earth would shake and the waters rise. We thought it was spiritual knowledge. Intuition refined over generations."

He gestured at the device.

"It was science. They just called it something else."

The tablets surrounding the central device proved to be its documentation—mathematical tables, astronomical observations, instructions for calibration and use. Tanaka began photographing everything her camera could capture, her earlier caution giving way to scholarly compulsion.

"We'll need years to translate all of this," she said, and there was both joy and despair in her voice. "A lifetime. Multiple lifetimes."

But it was Aspen who found the key to understanding.

They had been moving through the tablet arrays while the others examined the central device, their guardian instincts drawing them toward a section that felt somehow different. When they stopped before a particular pedestal, their voice carried a weight that silenced the chamber.

"Over here. This explains everything."

The tablets on that pedestal were larger than the others, their bronze surfaces covered in both text and images—a visual dictionary, Ammon realized as he approached. The builders had created a guide for future discoverers, a key that would unlock understanding regardless of what languages those discoverers spoke.

Tanaka's breath caught. She moved toward the tablets with the reverence of someone approaching a holy relic, her hands hovering over the bronze without quite touching it.

"This changes everything," she whispered. "Do you understand what this means? With this, we can decode all of it. Every tablet in this archive. Every inscription on every wall." Her voice cracked with emotion. "They didn't just preserve knowledge—they preserved the ability to understand it. They built a teaching tool into the archive itself, knowing that whoever found this place might not share their language. This is... this is the most important archaeological discovery in human history."

She finally looked up, tears streaming down her face. "We can learn what they knew. All of it. Because they wanted us to."

The visual dictionary began with basics: numbers, represented by dots arranged in patterns; the elements, symbolized by geometric shapes that corresponded to physical properties; directions, shown as arrows radiating from a central point. From there, it grew more complex: astronomical phenomena rendered as sequences of changing symbols, biological processes depicted in stages, abstract concepts illuminated through careful analogy.

"This is designed to teach," Ammon said. "Not just to record. They wanted whoever found this place to be able to learn from it. To understand what they knew."

"The question is what they knew," Tanaka replied. She had moved to another section of tablets, these ones covered in what appeared to be historical narrative. "And whether we're ready to understand it."

The group had scattered through the archive without conscious decision, each drawn to different mysteries. Thomas and Robert moved among the tablets describing guardian traditions. Jonas circled the astronomical device, muttering calculations. Tanaka worked methodically through the visual dictionary, building her translation framework symbol by symbol. Aspen drifted toward sections that seemed to call to something in their blood.

Even Agent Reyes had been pulled in, examining tablets that appeared to describe defensive fortifications and military strategies.

In a space this vast, with attention this fragmented, no one noticed the soft scrape of boots on stone from the chamber's far reaches. No one saw the figure moving through the shadows between pedestals, pausing at structural points, working with quiet efficiency.

Father Tomás felt something—a prickle at the back of his neck, the instinct of a man who had spent decades in Vatican politics learning to sense when he was being watched. He turned, scanning the darkness beyond the bioluminescent glow.

Nothing. Just shadows and stone and the weight of seven thousand years.

He turned back to his examination of the philosophical tablets, but the unease remained, a splinter beneath his skin that he couldn't quite name.

The historical tablets told a story that rewrote everything.

Tanaka translated haltingly at first, cross-referencing each symbol with the visual dictionary, building vocabulary word by painstaking word. But as patterns emerged and understanding deepened, her pace increased, her voice growing more certain even as the implications grew more staggering.

"They called themselves the 'net-weavers,'" she said. "Not a single culture—a network. A confederation of civilizations connected by maritime routes across the Atlantic and Pacific."

She traced a symbol that appeared repeatedly throughout the texts.

"This represents their alliance. Trade relationships, cultural exchanges, shared knowledge systems. It functioned for centuries—maybe millennia—before 3000 BCE. They weren't just in contact with each other. They were building something together."

"Building what?" Jonas asked.

"This." Tanaka gestured at the chamber around them. "Not just this temple—a whole network of temples. Repositories like this one, scattered across the world, each preserving specialized knowledge while contributing to the whole."

Thomas had found the tablets that described the network itself. His weathered finger traced a map etched in bronze, showing twelve points connected by lines that crossed oceans.

"Twelve," he said softly. "There were twelve of them."

Twelve temples. Twelve repositories. Each one marked with a symbol that indicated its specialty: the sun for astronomy, the wave for oceanography, the leaf for agriculture, the heart for medicine. This temple—their temple, the one beneath the Utah desert—bore the symbol of the mountain. Earth sciences. Geology, metallurgy, the properties of stone and metal.

"They divided knowledge by domain," Tanaka explained. "Each temple preserved certain categories while maintaining connections to the others. Information could flow between them—what one temple discovered, the others could access."

"How?" Reyes asked. "We're talking about facilities spread across the globe. Even with ships, communication would take months."

"The 'net of voices.'" Tanaka pointed to a section of dense notation. "A system of messenger ships that connected the temples. Standardized protocols, scheduled routes, redundant pathways. Information could travel from Southeast Asia to here in a matter of months. They were sharing astronomical data, agricultural techniques, medical knowledge—everything."

She looked up, her face pale in the bioluminescent glow.

"They were building a global civilization. Seven thousand years before we thought it was possible."

The tablets describing the collapse were harder to read—not because of language barriers, but because of the weight of what they contained.

Around 2800 BCE, something had gone catastrophically wrong. The tablets spoke of "the great breaking"—a cascade of disasters that severed the connections between temples. Cities fell. Trade routes collapsed. The net of voices went silent.

"Natural disaster?" Reyes asked.

"Partly," Tanaka said. "There's reference to volcanic eruptions, earthquakes, floods. The text uses terms I'm not entirely sure how to translate—something about 'the earth's wrath awakened.'"

She paused, her expression troubled.

"But it wasn't just natural disaster. There are references to war. To weapons. To knowledge being 'turned against its keepers.'"

"They destroyed themselves," Aspen said. They stood apart from the group, their guardian instincts processing what the others were still struggling to absorb. "They built something beautiful and then they broke it."

The final tablets in the historical section described what came after—the creation of the guardian tradition, the sealing of the temples, the transformation of global knowledge-sharing into local protection. The survivors had made a choice: preserve what they could, hide what was too dangerous, and wait for a time when humanity might be ready to receive what they'd learned.

"Seven thousand years," Ammon said. "They've been waiting seven thousand years for someone to find this."

"Not just find it," Thomas corrected. "Understand it. The guardian tradition wasn't just about protection. It was about preparation. Each generation was supposed to be more ready than the last."

He looked around the chamber, at the accumulated wisdom of a vanished world.

"The question is: are we ready now?"

Tanaka found the answer to Thomas's question in the eastern alcove, and it wasn't reassuring.

The tablets there were set apart from the others, enclosed in a secondary chamber whose entrance bore the most severe warnings they'd yet encountered. Images of destruction carved in careful detail: cities crumbling, bodies in rows, waters turned to poison, skies filled with ash. Whatever knowledge lay inside, the builders had wanted future generations to approach it with extreme caution.

"Should we..." Reyes began.

"We need to know," Ammon said. "If we're going to decide how to handle this discovery, we need to understand what we're really dealing with."

They entered the restricted section together.

The first set of tablets made Ammon's blood run cold.

"Resonance mapping," Tanaka translated, barely above a whisper. "They're describing how to find the natural frequencies of geological formations. Fault lines. Volcanic systems."

"We do seismic surveys now," Jonas offered, though his voice was uncertain.

"We survey to predict." Tanaka's finger traced the mathematical notation. "They surveyed to influence. Look—this section describes amplification techniques. If you generate vibrations at precisely the right frequency, at precisely the right point on a fault line..."

"You could trigger an earthquake," Ammon finished. He felt the blood drain from his face.

"Or prevent one, theoretically. The inscription here talks about 'calming the earth-breath' and 'redirecting stone pressure.' But the same knowledge..."

She didn't finish the sentence. They all understood. The same techniques that could stabilize a fault could destabilize one. Technology that could save a city could destroy one.

And the mathematics were all here, carved in bronze, waiting for anyone who could read them.

The medical tablets were worse.

The treatments made sense—herbal compounds that modern pharmacology would eventually rediscover, surgical techniques that anticipated developments by millennia. But interspersed with the healing knowledge was something else.

"'The breath-stealers,'" Tanaka translated, her voice cracking. "'Invisible spirits that pass from body to body, that flourish in crowded places, that die in sunlight and heat.'"

"They understood disease transmission," Jonas said.

"They understood more than that." Tanaka pointed to a section of dense notation, her hand trembling. "This is cultivation protocol. How to grow the breath-stealers, how to keep them alive outside the body, how to... how to make them stronger. More resilient. The inscription talks about 'strengthening against the sun' and 'teaching to flourish in the dry times.'"

She stopped, her face ashen.

"For what purpose?" Aspen asked, though their voice suggested they already knew.

"The text here is damaged. But there's a reference to 'the last war' and 'weapons that killed without being seen.'"

Tanaka looked at Ammon with haunted eyes.

"I think they invented biological warfare. And then they recorded exactly how to recreate it."

Thomas had found the energy tablets—diagrams showing what the builders called "earth-fire channeling." The drawings depicted volcanic vents being controlled, directed.

"Geothermal energy?" Jonas asked, hope in his voice that this at least might be benign.

"We tap what's already there," Thomas replied, his weathered finger tracing the diagram. "They describe creating what they need. These channels don't just capture existing heat. They're designed to wake it. To reach deeper than natural vents and pull fire from places where fire doesn't normally rise."

"Induced volcanism?"

"More than that." Thomas's voice was heavy with a weight that seemed to age him years in seconds. "The mathematical section describes focusing techniques. Lenses of carved stone that could concentrate earth-fire the way glass concentrates sunlight."

He paused, letting the implication settle.

"They built weapons that could set cities on fire from beneath. No army could defend against it. No walls, no distance, no warning. Just fire, erupting from the ground without explanation."

"Did they use them?" Reyes asked.

"The historical tablets suggest yes. There's a reference to 'the great burning'—multiple cities destroyed simultaneously. Not by lava, but by focused heat that burst up through the earth without warning."

Thomas stepped back from the tablet, as if proximity itself was dangerous.

"The civilization didn't just fall because of natural disaster. They used this technology against each other. And once they started, they couldn't stop."

They moved through the remaining alcoves with a different kind of attention now—no longer the wonder of discovery but the sobered assessment of people who understood they were handling fire.

More tablets revealed themselves: engineering principles that could reshape landscapes, agricultural techniques that could feed millions or create dependent populations, astronomical predictions that could be used for navigation or for timing military campaigns. Psychological techniques for influencing crowds, methods for water purification or contamination, metallurgical secrets that could arm a nation or cripple one.

Every piece of knowledge had its shadow. Every truth could be turned to destruction.

"I understand now," Tanaka said quietly. She had stopped before a tablet that seemed to catalog the archive's contents—a master index of everything preserved within these walls. "I understand why Hathenbruck sealed this place. Why the guardians have spent seven millennia making sure no one found it until the world was ready."

"Because of the weapons?" Jonas asked.

"Because of all of it." She gestured at the chamber around them. "Every single piece of knowledge in this archive can be used to harm. The medicine can create plagues. The astronomy can time attacks. The engineering can destroy as easily as build. Even the philosophy—" she pointed to a section of tablets they hadn't yet explored "—even the philosophical texts describe techniques for manipulating belief, for controlling populations through carefully constructed narratives."

She turned to face the group, her expression haunted.

"This isn't a library. It's an arsenal. And the builders knew it. That's why they created the guardian tradition. Not to protect the knowledge from the world—to protect the world from the knowledge."

The silence that followed was absolute.

Ammon stood in the center of the archive, surrounded by the accumulated wisdom and weaponized knowledge of a vanished world. His team gathered around him—Robert, Thomas and Aspen, the guardians who had devoted their lives to protection; Tanaka, the scholar overwhelmed by what she'd found; Jonas, the technical mind trying to process implications; Agent Reyes, the representative of a government that would have its own ideas about what to do with this discovery.

And Father Tomás, who had been silent since they entered the restricted section. The priest's face had gone gray, his eyes fixed on the tablets with an expression Ammon couldn't read.

Aspen straightened suddenly, their head turning toward the passage they'd entered through.

"Did you hear something?"

Everyone froze. The chamber held its breath.

Silence. Just the faint whisper of the bioluminescent bacteria and the distant drip of water somewhere in the depths.

"Sound carries strangely in here," Jonas said after a moment. "The acoustics are designed for it—remember how Thomas's voice echoed during the tests? Probably just settling stone."

Aspen nodded, but their hand had drifted to the knife at their belt, guardian instincts whispering warnings they couldn't articulate.

"The final inscription," Thomas said quietly. He had moved to the far wall of the chamber, where a section of stone had been polished smooth and covered with carved text larger than any they'd yet seen. "This is what they wanted us to read. This is their message to whoever found this place."

They gathered before the inscription—the temple's ultimate communication to future generations. The text was written in all three languages from the tests they'd passed: the physical script, the intellectual script, and the spiritual script whose spirals Aspen had sung to life.

Tanaka translated, her voice gaining strength as the words took shape:

"Knowledge is fire. It can warm a house or burn it down.

We who built this place understood this truth. We watched our own civilization tear itself apart when the fire spread beyond the hands that could control it. We saw cities burn, peoples vanish, the accumulated wisdom of millennia turned to ash and silence.

We sealed our wisdom here not to hide it but to protect it—to wait for those worthy to carry the flame forward.

If you have found this chamber, you have proven your dedication. You have passed the tests of understanding. You have shown that you possess the knowledge of the physical world, the comprehension of why such knowledge matters, and the spiritual connection to the tradition that preserves it. But dedication alone is not enough.

Wisdom must temper knowledge. Compassion must guide power. Only those who understand why the fire was banked can be trusted to release it.

The world was not ready when we sealed these doors. Perhaps it is not ready now. Perhaps it will never be ready.

But we believed—we had to believe—that someday, someone would come who could carry the flame forward without being consumed by it. Someone who understood that the goal is not to possess knowledge but to serve it. Not to wield power but to guide it. Not to illuminate the world but to help the world illuminate itself.

Choose wisely who receives this flame. The world's future depends on those who carry it.

We leave this final warning: what sleeps here can transform or destroy. The difference lies not in the knowledge itself but in the hearts of those who wield it.

May you prove worthy of the trust we place in you. May you succeed where we failed. May the fire warm without burning, illuminate without blinding, transform without destroying.

The flame passes to you now. Guard it well."

The silence that followed was profound.

Hathenbruck had read these same words over a century ago and chosen to reseal the temple. The original guardians had chosen to create traditions of protection that spanned generations. Every person who had stood in this chamber before them had faced the same impossible choice: what to do with fire that could warm or consume.

Now the choice was Ammon's.

"What do we do?" Jonas asked, voicing what they'd all been thinking.

Ammon looked at the tablets—the astronomical wonders and the weaponized horrors, the healing knowledge and the techniques for mass destruction. He looked at the inscription, at the hope and warning encoded in its ancient message. He looked at the people who had risked everything to reach this moment.

"We do what the builders intended," he said finally. "We carry the flame forward. Carefully. Wisely. With full understanding of what it could mean."

He paused, looking at each of them in turn.

"But we carry it forward—because that's what guardians do."

Thomas nodded, something ancient and heavy shifting in his expression. "Not everything at once. Not everything to everyone. But forward."

"There's another way to read that inscription," Aspen said quietly.

The others turned to look at them. Aspen gestured at the warnings carved throughout the chamber, at the weapons alcove they'd explored, at the devastation the builders had documented.

"They didn't just seal this place to protect the world from the knowledge. They sealed it to protect the knowledge from the world. They believed someone would come who was worthy. They believed in a future that could handle the truth."

"Do you think we're that future?" Reyes asked.

Aspen looked at Ammon—at the man who had followed his ancestor's trail across continents, who had united guardians and scholars and law enforcement in common purpose, who had shown mercy to enemies and built alliances with adversaries.

"I think we have a chance to be," they said. "That's more than any generation before us could say."

Thomas nodded, and Ammon could see the guardian wrestling with generations of tradition that said protect, hide, wait.

"Not everything at once," the elder finally said. "Not everything to everyone. Some of this—" he gestured at the weapons alcove "—needs to stay sealed. Perhaps forever. But the astronomy, the medicine, the history..."

"Can be shared," Tanaka finished. "Carefully. With context. With safeguards." Her scholarly passion was returning, tempered now by what she'd learned. "We don't have to release everything to release something. We can be selective."

Agent Reyes spoke for the first time since the dangerous knowledge had been revealed.

"My agency will need to be involved. The implications for national security..."

She held up a hand as several faces turned hostile.

"I'm not saying we bury it. I'm saying we need protocols. Oversight. A framework for deciding what gets released and when."

"Governments have their own agenda," Aspen said carefully.

"So do churches. So do academics." She looked around at the assembled group. "Everyone here has interests that could corrupt this process. Including me. Including Ammon."

"Which is why none of us can do this alone," Ammon said.

The shape of something was forming in his mind—not a solution but the beginning of one.

"The ancient builders created a network. A system of checks and balances across cultures, across continents. Maybe that's what we need too. Not one guardian. Not one government. A coalition."

The decision settled over them—not a solution, but a direction. They would carry the flame forward. They would choose carefully who received it. They would try, as the builders had tried, to ensure that the fire warmed more than it burned.

The work of revelation had begun.

CHAPTER TWENTY-NINE

Revelation

The peace lasted less than an hour.

They had moved from the astronomical chamber to the tablet archive, Tanaka's excitement building with each new discovery. The smallest tablet collection sat in an alcove near the chamber's eastern wall—bronze plates no larger than playing cards, inscribed with text so fine it required magnification to read.

"'The shaping of minds,'" Tanaka translated, her voice dropping to barely above a whisper. "'Techniques for the alignment of many into one.'"

She looked up from the tablet, her face pale in the lantern light.

"This is... this is propaganda theory. Social engineering. Two thousand years before Bernays, seven thousand before mass media."

Ammon moved closer, reading over her shoulder as she continued translating. The tablets described methods that felt chillingly modern: the use of repetition to bypass critical thinking, the exploitation of tribal loyalties, the creation of common enemies to unify fractured populations. But they also described techniques that went beyond anything contemporary psychology had codified.

"'Harmonic suggestion,'" Tanaka read, her finger tracing the ancient script. "'When many voices speak as one, at frequencies that bypass the thinking-self, resistance dissolves.'"

She paused, struggling with the next passage.

"They developed audio-based mind control. Chants or songs or something that could actually suppress independent thought."

"That sounds like pseudoscience," Jonas said, but his voice lacked conviction.

"It probably is. Except..." Tanaka pointed to another section of the tablet. "They describe experiments. Results. Populations that were 'aligned' and populations that 'resisted the harmony.' The resistant populations all met the same fate."

She swallowed.

"They were destroyed by the aligned ones."

"Cult psychology," Aspen said quietly. "But at industrial scale."

"Yes. And they recorded exactly how it worked. How to create the harmonic frequency. How to train speakers who could transmit the pattern. How to identify and eliminate individuals who couldn't be aligned."

Tanaka's voice was barely audible.

"If someone could actually replicate this... could prove it worked..."

She didn't need to finish. They all understood what such knowledge could mean in the wrong hands.

Thomas stood motionless, his weathered face reflecting what they'd uncovered. This was why the temple had been sealed. This was the fire the inscription warned about.

The explosion shook the chamber before anyone could respond.

Dust rained from the ceiling in thick curtains. The sound of collapsing rock thundered through the passages behind them, a grinding roar that seemed to go on forever. Bronze tablets rattled on their shelves. The astronomical device in the main chamber groaned as ancient gears shifted under the vibration.

"The entrance," Aspen said, their hand already on their weapon. "Someone's brought down part of the main passage."

Agent Reyes was on her radio instantly, trying to reach the FBI teams stationed outside. Static. She adjusted frequencies, tried again. More static.

"Communications are down. Whatever happened has cut us off from support."

"Not whatever." Father Tomás's voice was hollow. "Whoever."

He turned toward the main archive entrance, and Ammon saw something in his expression that wasn't surprise. Tomás had warned them that the hardliners wouldn't accept his defection quietly—but knowing intellectually that retaliation would come was different from facing it in the flesh.

Konstantin emerged from the shadows near the main archive entrance— the same passage they had all used to enter. His tactical gear was dusty but intact, his movements precise and unhurried. The confidence of a man who had planned for every contingency.

"He must have followed us in," Ammon realized aloud, his mind racing. "Waited until we were deep in the archive, distracted by the discoveries. Used the time to prepare."

Konstantin's thin smile confirmed it. "You were so absorbed in your translations, you didn't notice me moving through the outer chambers. Planting charges at key structural points. Ensuring that whatever happened here today, this temple would never threaten the faith again."

But it was what he wore strapped to his vest that made Ammon's blood turn to ice.

Explosives. Not improvised devices cobbled together from available materials—military-grade charges, professionally wired, with redundant detonation systems visible even from across the chamber. The kind of ordnance designed to bring down reinforced bunkers. The kind that could turn this entire complex into a tomb.

"You had your chance," Konstantin said, his voice flat as slate. "Father Tomás made his choice. The institution noted it. But the mission doesn't change because one priest has a crisis of conscience."

"How did you get in?" Ammon demanded. "The entrance requires the guardian chant, the solstice alignment—"

"The entrance requires someone else to open it." Konstantin's thin smile held no warmth. "I've been following you for three days, Dr. Lundquist. Watching. Waiting. When your guardian spoke his words and the stones moved, I simply... followed. Ten minutes behind you, through the same door you opened."

His eyes swept the chamber with professional assessment.

"You were so absorbed in your discoveries, you never thought to watch your backs. The old man—" he nodded toward Thomas "—led you straight to the antechamber, and you spent hours there, marveling at artifacts, solving puzzles. Hours I used to study the temple's structure. To identify load-bearing points. To position charges where they would do the most damage."

"The shadows," Aspen breathed. "I heard you. I felt something wrong."

"Guardian instincts." Konstantin acknowledged it with something that might have been respect. "You came closer to catching me than the FBI agent did. But close isn't enough. Not against someone who's been doing this for thirty years."

"The entrance is already blocked," Tomás said, stepping forward. His voice shook, but he forced himself to meet Konstantin's eyes. "Your men are outside. There's no tactical advantage in destroying—"

"The point isn't escape." Konstantin's hand rested on the detonator attached to his vest—a dead man's switch, Ammon realized with growing horror. "The point is completion. These explosives are positioned throughout the temple complex. Every major chamber. Every passage. When they detonate, the entire structure will collapse. Thousands of tons of sandstone burying everything under hundreds of feet of rock."

"Including yourself."

"If necessary." Konstantin's eyes swept across the chamber—the bronze tablets, the astronomical device visible through the archway, the accumulated wisdom of millennia arrayed before him like evidence at a trial. "Some things are worth dying for. This knowledge has been sealed for thousands of years. It can remain sealed for thousands more."

Ammon's mind raced through options. Konstantin was too far away to rush. The dead man's switch meant any attack could trigger immediate detonation. And the explosives distributed throughout the complex meant even if they stopped him here, the temple might still be destroyed.

"Tomás called off the operation," Ammon said, trying to buy time. "You don't have authorization—"

"I have authorization from the faction that actually controls these matters." Konstantin's smile was thin as a blade. "Tomás was always a means to an end—a moderate voice to manage the politics while the real work continued. Did you really think a single priest's change of heart would stop an institution that's been doing this for two thousand years?"

Tomás moved forward, positioning himself between Konstantin and the others. His body shielding them from the direct threat—a gesture that was brave and futile and fitting for a man trying to atone for decades of moral compromise.

"I gave my word," Tomás said. "I told these people the Church would work with them."

"And your word was never yours to give." Konstantin's voice held a note of pity that was worse than contempt. "You were a tool, Father. The decisions were above your pay grade."

"Then let me make this decision now."

Tomás's voice found its strength, steadying with each word.

"I've spent my life protecting people from truths I thought would harm them. I told myself it was faith, but it was control. It was arrogance. It was believing that I knew better than the billions of people whose lives I was supposedly protecting."

He took a step closer to Konstantin. The fixer's hand tightened on the detonator.

"This place has been waiting for thousands of years to share what it knows. Waiting for someone with the courage to carry its flame forward."

Tomás's voice filled the ancient chamber, echoing off walls that had witnessed countless moments of transformation.

"I won't be the one who snuffs that flame out."

"Then you'll die with it."

"Perhaps." Tomás turned, his gaze sweeping across the bronze tablets, the astronomical device, the inscriptions that had waited millennia to be read. When he spoke again, his voice held a peace that seemed impossible given the circumstances.

"But I'll die having finally done something I believe in. Something that serves truth rather than suppressing it. I spent thirty years serving an institution. It's time I started serving the faith that institution was supposed to protect."

Konstantin's finger moved toward the trigger.

Ammon saw it happening—saw the micro-movement of muscle, the tightening of Konstantin's jaw, the slight shift in weight that preceded action. In the space between heartbeats, he knew they were out of time.

But Jeremiah Stone was already moving.

He launched himself from behind a column where he'd positioned himself during Tomás's speech—a flanking maneuver that spoke to his years of Consortium training, now turned to a different purpose. His trajectory was low and fast, aimed not at Konstantin's body but at his arm, at the hand that held the detonator.

Konstantin was faster than he looked. He twisted, trying to bring the detonator out of reach, but Jeremiah's tackle caught him at the elbow. The impact drove them both sideways. Konstantin's hand spasmed open. The detonator skidded across the stone floor, spinning end over end, coming to rest against the base of a tablet shelf.

They hit the ground hard, a tangle of limbs and desperate struggle. Konstantin's professional training met Jeremiah's raw determination. An elbow strike caught Jeremiah across the jaw. He responded with a knee to Konstantin's ribs that drove the air from his lungs. They rolled, each fighting for dominance, crashing into artifact displays and scattering bronze tablets across the floor.

Aspen moved first, sprinting for the detonator. Jonas was a step behind them, cutting off Konstantin's angle if he broke free. Agent Reyes shouted orders, and her team members—Martinez and Chen, who had been searching for explosives in the outer chambers—converged on the struggle.

Konstantin got an arm free, reaching toward his vest—toward a secondary trigger, Ammon realized—but Jeremiah caught his wrist and slammed it against the stone floor. Once. Twice. On the third impact, something cracked. Konstantin's face contorted in pain, but he didn't cry out.

Then there were too many hands for him to fight. Reyes's people pulled him and Jeremiah apart, secured the fixer with zip-ties reinforced with tactical cuffs.

Aspen had the detonator, holding it like it might bite them, their fingers nowhere near the trigger.

"The vest," Reyes said sharply. "Martinez—get those charges off him. Now."

Martinez approached cautiously, combat knife in hand. Konstantin lay still as the agent cut the straps securing the explosive vest, his eyes tracking the movement with professional detachment. When Martinez pulled the vest away and set it carefully against the far wall, something shifted in Konstantin's expression—the resignation of a man whose final option had just been removed.

"You should have let me finish it," he said softly. "Now we all die by inches instead of quickly."

"Nobody's dying today," Reyes replied. "Not if I can help it."

"The other explosives," Ammon said urgently. "Where are they?"

Konstantin laughed—a harsh, broken sound that held no humor, only the satisfaction of a man who knew his mission wasn't finished. Blood trickled from a cut above his eye, and his broken wrist hung at an unnatural angle, but his smile was serene.

"Distributed throughout the complex. The main chamber. The passage to the astronomical observatory. The entrance to the tablet archive."

He listed the locations with the calm precision of a man reciting a grocery list.

"Pressure triggers on some. Motion sensors on others. Redundant detonation systems with radio backup. You might find some of them. You'll never find all of them. Not in time."

"How much time?"

"Fifteen minutes. Give or take." Konstantin's smile widened, blood staining his teeth. "I told you—some things are worth dying for. The question is whether you're willing to die to stop them."

Fourteen minutes, forty-seven seconds.

The number burned in Ammon's mind as chaos erupted around him.

"We need to split up," Reyes said, already pulling up a schematic on her phone—notes she'd been making since they entered the temple. "Martinez, Chen—main chamber. Look for anything that doesn't belong. Kowalski, you're with me on the passage to the observatory."

"The tablet archive," Tanaka said, her voice tight with fear and determination. "That's where the most dangerous knowledge is. If we lose that—"

"Then we don't lose it." Thomas's voice cut through the panic, steady as bedrock. "Ammon, Aspen—help me move what we can. If we can't stop the explosives, we save what matters most."

Twelve minutes.

Ammon grabbed a stack of bronze tablets, their weight surprising—each one dense with the accumulated knowledge of a lost civilization. Beside him, Aspen was doing the same, their movements efficient despite the trembling in their hands.

"The social engineering tablets," Tanaka said, pointing to the alcove where they'd been working. "Those need to go first. If that knowledge falls into the wrong hands—"

An explosion echoed from somewhere deeper in the complex. Everyone froze.

"Controlled detonation," Reyes's voice crackled over the radio. "Martinez found one in the main chamber. Disarmed it. One down."

One down. Unknown number remaining.

Ten minutes, thirty seconds.

Ammon worked faster, his arms burning as he hauled tablets toward the chamber's far wall—away from the explosives, away from the collapsing passages. The main entrance was buried under tons of collapsed stone. They needed another way out, and they needed it fast.

"Got another one!" Jonas's voice, triumphant and terrified. "Observatory passage. It was wired into the door mechanism—would have triggered when we tried to leave."

Two down.

Eight minutes, twelve seconds.

Thomas stumbled, his injured shoulder giving out under the tablets he carried. Jeremiah caught him, took the burden without a word, and kept moving. Something passed between the two men—a recognition that transcended their complicated history.

"The astronomical device," Thomas said, his voice cracking. "We can't move it. It's too heavy, too complex—"

"Then we document it." Tanaka was already snapping photos with her phone, capturing every angle, every inscription, every gear and mechanism. "If we can't save the object, we save the knowledge."

Thomas stood frozen before an alcove they hadn't yet explored, his weathered hand pressed against the stone.

"The singing bowls," he said, his voice breaking. "My grandfather described these. Said the old ones used them to heal—that the sounds could mend what was broken in body and spirit. I thought they were legend."

Seven bronze vessels sat in careful arrangement, their surfaces covered in inscriptions that matched the visual dictionary's notation for sound and frequency. Tanaka planned to study them for months.

"We can't carry them," Aspen said gently. "Thomas—"

"I know." The old guardian's hand trembled as he pulled back from the alcove. "I know."

He turned away, and Ammon saw something shatter behind his eyes— the loss of something his family had protected for generations without ever seeing it.

Six minutes.

Another explosion—this one closer, loud enough to make the floor shudder beneath their feet.

"Third device neutralized," Reyes reported. "But I'm seeing wiring that leads deeper into the complex. There's at least one more. Maybe two."

Konstantin watched from his restraints, his expression unreadable. Blood had dried on his face, giving him the look of a man who had already accepted his death and found a strange peace in it.

"You're running out of time," he said. Almost helpful. Almost kind. "Some of my devices are better hidden than others."

Four minutes.

Ammon's lungs burned. His arms screamed. The pile of salvaged tablets near the chamber's far wall grew, but the archive was so vast, so impossibly rich with knowledge they couldn't afford to lose.

"The wall inscriptions," Aspen said, desperation in their voice. "We can't move the walls—"

"Record everything you can." Tomás had joined them now, his phone out, photographing inscriptions with hands that no longer shook. Whatever transformation had occurred in him was complete. He moved like a man who had finally discovered his purpose. "Every image. Every word. The stones may fall, but the knowledge can survive."

Two minutes, thirty seconds.

Another explosion rocked the complex. Dust filled the air, thick enough to choke on.

"Fourth device!" Agent Kowalski's voice was ragged. "There's one more—I can see the wiring, but I can't reach it. It's embedded in the ceiling of the main chamber."

"Everyone out!" Reyes shouted. "Now! Find another way out! Move!"

One minute, forty-five seconds.

They ran.

Ammon grabbed the last stack of tablets he could carry, felt Aspen's hand close around his arm, pulling him toward the passage. Behind them, Thomas and Jeremiah supported each other's weight. Tanaka clutched her phone like a lifeline. Tomás brought up the rear, still photographing, still recording, still trying to save what could be saved.

Reyes's people dragged Konstantin between them, his broken wrist jarring with every step, his face finally showing pain. He didn't resist—whatever resolve had carried him to martyrdom seemed to have cracked when they stripped away his vest. Now he was just a man with a broken wrist, being pulled toward survival whether he wanted it or not.

Fifty seconds.

"This way!" Aspen shouted, their guardian instincts pulling them toward an alcove they'd passed earlier without examining. Behind a collapsed shelf of tablets, a narrow fissure split the stone—not carved, but natural, widened over millennia by water and time. "There's airflow. It leads somewhere."

The narrow passage stretched before them, dark and raw—not the worked stone of the temple builders but natural rock, an escape route that the ancients might have used or might never have known existed.

Thirty seconds.

Light appeared ahead—the canyon, dawn, survival.

Fifteen seconds.

They burst from the passage into the cool morning air just as the final explosion tore through the complex behind them.

The ground shuddered. A sound like thunder rolled through the canyon, echoing off walls that had stood for millions of years. Dust billowed from the passage entrance, a choking cloud that obscured the sky.

Then silence.

Ammon set down the tablets he'd been carrying and looked at the others—exhausted, filthy, alive.

Thomas leaned heavily on Jeremiah, his tired legs finally giving out. Aspen stood with their hands on their knees, gasping for breath. Tanaka was already scrolling through her phone, counting photos, calculating what they'd managed to save. Jonas sat on a rock, staring at nothing. Agent Reyes was on the radio, finally able to reach the outside teams, calling for medical support and reinforcements. Robert rested against a boulder.

Father Tomás stood apart from the others, his gaze fixed on the passage they'd escaped through. The entrance had collapsed, sealing the First Temple once again under hundreds of feet of rock.

"What did we save?" Ammon asked, approaching Tanaka.

She looked at the scattered tablets, then at her phone.

"Thirty-seven tablets. Maybe forty. Two hundred photographs of the astronomical device, the wall inscriptions, the archive layout."

She paused.

"The social engineering tablets—the dangerous ones. Those made it out."

"And what did we lose?"

"Everything else." Her voice was hollow. "The astronomical device itself. Most of the larger tablets. The murals showing the transoceanic voyages. The star maps."

She glanced at Thomas, who stood apart from the others, his gaze fixed on the collapsed passage.

"The singing bowls," she added quietly. "Thomas's grandfather's stories—we'll never know if they were true."

She closed her eyes.

"Decades of work, buried in seconds."

Konstantin watched from his restraints, his expression impossible to read. The satisfaction Ammon had expected wasn't there—instead, something that might have been doubt flickered behind his eyes.

"You thought you'd win," Konstantin said as Ammon passed him. "But the institution I serve has been fighting this war for two thousand years."

"Maybe." Ammon stopped, meeting the fixer's gaze. "But we saved something. And we'll keep fighting for the rest. That's the difference between us—you're willing to destroy what you can't control. We're willing to protect what we can."

He turned away, leaving Konstantin to whatever thoughts haunted a man that was willing to die to keep the masses in ignorance.

The sun rose over the canyon rim, painting the sandstone walls in shades of gold and amber. They had lost the temple. But they had saved its heart—the tablets, the photographs, at least part of the knowledge that had waited millennia to be discovered.

The First Temple was sealed again. But this time, some secrets had escaped.

The question now was what they would do with them.

CHAPTER THIRTY

What Slipped Away

Ammon saw Konstantin slip his restraints in the moment before it happened.

The chaos of the evacuation had created an opening—a split-second when no one was watching the prisoner, when attention was focused on the tablets and the desperate race to save what could be saved. Konstantin's broken wrist, ironically, had given him the advantage he needed—the swelling had subsided just enough during their escape that he could work his hand free from the zip-ties, millimeter by painful millimeter.

He disappeared into the slot canyon before anyone could react, moving with the fluid efficiency of someone who had spent a lifetime learning to vanish.

"I'll get him." Ammon was running before he finished speaking, following the Vatican's fixer into the maze of narrow passages that cut through the sandstone.

"Ammon, wait!" Aspen's voice echoed behind him. "Let him go—"

But Ammon couldn't let him go. Not after everything. Not with the knowledge of the temple still fresh in his mind, waiting to be reported to whatever faction might still be listening. The man had destroyed millennia of accumulated wisdom. He had to answer for that.

The canyon swallowed his footsteps as he plunged deeper, navigating by instinct and the occasional glimpse of movement ahead. Dawn light filtered down through the narrow gap above, painting the sandstone walls in color and light. The air was cold—desert cold, the kind that bit at exposed skin and turned breath to vapor—but Ammon barely felt it. Adrenaline burned through him like wildfire.

Konstantin was fast, but he was injured. His broken wrist would slow him, limit his climbing ability. Ammon tracked his path by the scuff marks on the rock, the displaced sand, the occasional smear of blood where Konstantin's damaged hand had touched stone.

The passage narrowed until Ammon had to turn sideways to fit, the sandstone pressing close on either side. His shirt caught on a jutting edge and tore. His shoulder scraped against rough stone, leaving skin behind. He didn't slow.

A boulder field forced him to climb, hands finding holds in rock that crumbled under his grip, feet slipping on surfaces still slick with morning dew. His lungs burned. His thighs screamed with the effort of the ascent.

Ahead, he heard nothing. No labored breathing. No footfalls. Just the whisper of wind through the canyon and the distant cry of a hawk.

He pushed harder, faster, following the blood trail through a series of switchbacks that seemed designed to confuse pursuit. Konstantin knew tradecraft—knew how to double back, how to lay false trails, how to use terrain against a pursuer. Ammon was an academic chasing a professional. The odds had never been in his favor.

The blood trail ended at a junction where three passages branched in different directions. Ammon stood there, chest heaving, scanning each opening for any sign of which way Konstantin had gone.

Nothing. No scuff marks. No blood. No indication that anyone had passed this way in years.

He chose the middle passage and ran for another ten minutes before admitting what he already knew.

Konstantin was gone.

Ammon stood in the widening canyon, hands on his knees, gasping for breath as the morning sun bathed the canyon in shades of fire. Somewhere out there, a man who had destroyed humanity's greatest archaeological discovery was disappearing into the wilderness. A man with thirty years of experience evading capture, with connections to powerful institutions, with knowledge of everything they'd found in the temple.

A man who would not stop.

The walk back to the others felt longer than the pursuit. Every step was a reminder of his failure—not just to catch Konstantin, but to prevent any of this from happening. He had led them to the temple. He had been so focused on discovery that he hadn't considered defense. And now the temple was gone, its secrets buried under a mountain of stone, and the man responsible was free.

Agent Reyes met him at the canyon mouth, her expression confirming what he already knew.

"He's gone?"

Ammon nodded, unable to find words.

"I've got teams searching the perimeter, but..." She shook her head. "A man like that, with a head start in terrain like this? He could be anywhere by now. Heading for an extraction point we'll never find."

"He'll report back to his superiors. Tell them what we found. What we saved."

"Yes." Reyes's jaw tightened. "Which means we need to move the artifacts. Today. Before whoever Konstantin works for decides to finish what he started."

Ammon looked back at the canyon—at the maze of passages where Konstantin had vanished, at the landscape that had swallowed a killer as easily as it swallowed water. Somewhere in that wilderness, a man walked free who had just destroyed one of humanity's greatest treasures. A man who believed he was righteous. A man who would try again.

Some people can't be saved, Ammon thought. *Some people don't want to be.*

It was a harder lesson than any the temple had taught him.

The others were waiting where he'd left them, scattered across the canyon floor like survivors of a shipwreck. Thomas sat on a boulder, his weathered face carrying a grief that seemed to age him years in minutes. Tanaka clutched her phone, scrolling through photographs of things that no longer existed. Jonas stared at the collapsed passage, as if willing it to open again through sheer force of hope.

Aspen found him before he reached the group. Their hand closed around his, warm and steady.

"He got away."

"I know." They didn't offer false comfort, didn't tell him it would be okay. They simply stood beside him, their presence a reminder that he wasn't alone in this failure.

"The temple is gone," Ammon said. "Konstantin is free. We have— what? Forty tablets? A few hundred photographs? From an archive that held thousands of years of accumulated knowledge?"

"We have more than anyone else has ever had."

"And less than we should." He looked at the pile of bronze tablets they'd managed to save—so small against the vastness of what had been lost. "The astronomical device. The singing bowls Thomas's grandfather described. The murals showing the transoceanic voyages. The star maps. All of it, gone."

"Not gone," Aspen said quietly. "Buried. There's a difference."

"Is there? Hundreds of feet of collapsed stone. Even if someone wanted to excavate, it would take years. Decades. And Konstantin's people would fight us every step of the way."

"Then we don't excavate." Aspen turned to face him, their dark eyes holding something that might have been hope or might have been determination—it was hard to tell where one ended and the other began. "The tablets you saved—Tanaka says they describe other temples. Other repositories. If the First Temple is lost, we find the second. Or the third. Or however many it takes."

Ammon stared at them. "You're talking about years of searching. Expeditions across multiple continents. Resources we don't have, facing opposition we can barely imagine."

"I'm talking about not giving up." They squeezed his hand. "Isn't that what the sacred vein means? Not the victories, but the persistence? Not the discoveries, but the commitment to keep looking?"

He thought about Hathenbruck, who had found this temple and chosen to hide it. About the original guardians, who had preserved their knowledge through millennia of upheaval. About his father and uncle, who had searched their whole lives without finding what they sought.

All of them had faced moments like this—moments when the easier path was surrender, when the losses seemed to outweigh any possible gain. And all of them had chosen to continue.

"The tablets mention twelve major repositories," Ammon said. "We've found the first. If even a few of the others survived..."

"Then the knowledge isn't lost. Just scattered." Aspen's smile was sad but real. "Waiting for someone stubborn enough to gather it back together."

Thomas approached them, moving carefully, his walking stick finding purchase on the uneven ground. His face was drawn with exhaustion and grief, but his voice was steady.

"My grandfather used to say that the guardians' greatest enemy wasn't those who sought to steal sacred knowledge. It was despair. The temptation to believe that the fight was already lost, that protection was futile, that the darkness would win no matter what we did."

He looked at the collapsed passage, at the tomb that now held so much of what his family had protected for generations.

"Today feels like darkness. I won't pretend otherwise. But darkness is not the same as ending. As long as there are people willing to carry the light, the darkness cannot win."

"Even when the light is just... forty tablets and some photographs?"

"Even then." Thomas placed his weathered hand on Ammon's shoulder. "The flame doesn't care how small it is. It only cares that it keeps burning."

They gathered what they had saved and began the long hike out of the canyon. The tablets were distributed among them, each person carrying what they could, the weight a constant reminder of what they bore.

Ammon walked at the rear, watching the others move ahead of him through the morning light. Tanaka and Jonas walked together, their heads bent in conversation—already planning, already thinking about next steps. Thomas and Robert supported each other, two old guardians carrying the grief of generations. Jeremiah dawdled behind them, lost in thought. Agent Reyes spoke quietly into her radio, coordinating security, planning for threats that might already be in motion.

And Aspen walked beside him, their presence a steady warmth against the cold morning air.

"He'll come back," Ammon said. "Konstantin. Whatever faction he serves, they won't stop with this."

"No. They won't."

"We'll be fighting this war for years. Maybe decades. Maybe the rest of our lives."

"Probably." Aspen glanced at him, and something in their expression made his breath catch. "But we won't be fighting it alone."

They walked in silence for a while, the canyon walls rising around them like the pages of a book written in stone. Somewhere ahead, the world waited—a world that didn't yet know what had been lost, what had been saved, what battles were still to come.

Ammon thought about the inscription they'd found in the temple, the warning about fire. *Knowledge is fire. It can warm or destroy. Choose wisely who receives this flame.*

They hadn't chosen wisely enough. Konstantin had found them, had destroyed what they'd discovered, had escaped to fight another day. The fire had burned them all.

But fire, Ammon reminded himself, could also forge. Could temper. Could transform weakness into strength.

The sacred vein ran through all of them—not just the blood of ancestry, but the choice to continue. To protect. To seek. To hold onto hope even when hope seemed foolish.

Hathenbruck had understood that. The ancient guardians had understood it. And now, walking out of a canyon that held both triumph and tragedy, Ammon understood it too.

Some truths were worth protecting, even when protection seemed impossible. Some secrets were worth seeking, even when the search might never end. And some people—the ones who chose to carry the flame—were worth more than any treasure buried under stone.

The search wasn't over. It was just beginning again.

CHAPTER THIRTY-ONE

The Weight of Truth

The FBI mobile command post sat three miles from where the temple lay buried. Equipment thrummed. Satellite arrays pointed at a sky that didn't care what they'd lost.

The evidence crates stacked along one wall looked pathetically small. Forty tablets. Two hundred photographs. The remnants of a library that had held thousands of years of human knowledge.

Ammon looked at the faces gathered around the folding table: Thomas and Robert Colorow, guardian elders carrying grief in every line of their weathered faces. Father Tomás near the door, his presence still uncertain. Agent Reyes with her tablet, ready to record decisions that might never matter. Tanaka with her laptop, scholarly passion dimmed but not extinguished. Jonas against the wall, arms crossed. Aspen beside Ammon, their hand brushing his.

"We all know why we're here," Ammon began. "The question is what we do with what little we saved."

The question hung heavy. What they'd found was so much less than what they'd lost. Memories of knowledge that now existed only in their minds, buried under a mountain of stone.

"What we do?" Thomas's voice carried generations of weight. "My grandfather died protecting secrets his grandfather protected before him. Five generations. And now—" He gestured at the crates. "This is what's left."

"It's more than anyone else has ever had," Tanaka said quietly.

"And less than we should." Thomas turned to face her. "You academics think peer review makes something safe. But you don't understand what happens when sacred knowledge becomes public property. Ceremony songs on YouTube. Sacred sites as tourist attractions. Our stories twisted into entertainment."

Robert Colorow leaned forward. "The tablets describe rituals tied to ceremonies we still practice. You want to publish those? Let anyone with a library card read what our medicine people spent lifetimes learning?"

"And how many problems could we solve," Tanaka shot back, "if we actually engaged with what the ancients learned? Medical treatments. Agricultural methods. Knowledge that could help people right now."

"Our ancestors built a civilization that lasted millennia," Thomas said coldly. "Yours built one that's destroying the planet in centuries."

Silence. Thick enough to cut.

"Perhaps," Father Tomás said, "we should acknowledge that everyone here has reason to distrust the others."

Thomas's eyes narrowed. "You tried to blow up the temple."

"I stopped Konstantin from doing that."

"After you sent him."

Tomás absorbed the blow. "Yes. I spent thirty years suppressing evidence, discrediting researchers, burying findings. I told myself it was about protecting faith." He paused. "But faith that requires ignorance isn't faith. It's fear."

"The Church has been stealing our sacred objects for five hundred years," Thomas said. "Why should your conversion matter to us?"

"It shouldn't. But I can tell you what happens when institutions try to control transformative knowledge. It leaks. Fragments. Gets twisted into conspiracy theories. The Church learned this with Galileo. We're still paying for that suppression four centuries later."

Agent Reyes cleared her throat. "From a federal perspective, we have immediate concerns. Three organizations tried to steal or destroy these artifacts in the past week. Word will get out. Treasure hunters, foreign governments, religious extremists—they'll converge on this site."

"So we hand it to the federal government?" Robert's voice carried an edge. "Let me tell you how that's worked for us historically."

"No one is suggesting—"

"Aren't they? Protection. Controlled access. Federal oversight. I've heard this speech. It ends with our sacred objects in museum basements and decades of legal battles to get them back."

Ammon felt the conversation slipping toward an edge from which there might be no return. Centuries of trauma crystallized into this single moment.

"My ancestor found this temple over a century ago," he said, stepping forward. "He could have revealed it then. Become famous. Instead, he hid it. Created clues that took generations to unravel."

"And you think he was wrong?" Thomas asked.

"I think he was doing the best he could. But Hathenbruck didn't just hide the temple. He left a trail. He wanted it found eventually. He believed there would come a time when people were ready."

"And you think that time is now?"

"I think that time is whenever we decide it is. Not because humanity is perfect. But because waiting for perfection is just another way of saying never."

He looked at each face in turn.

"The guardians have waited thousands of years. The Church has suppressed for centuries. The academics have demanded for decades. How much longer do we let fear make our decisions?"

"It's not fear," Thomas said, but his voice had softened. "It's wisdom."

"Then help us not profane it." Ammon faced him directly. "You're right that academics have mishandled sacred knowledge. That governments have exploited indigenous peoples. That the Church has suppressed truth. But the answer isn't more hiding. It's real partnership—where you have actual power, actual veto authority, actual control."

"Pretty words," Robert said. "We've heard pretty words before."

"Then don't trust words. Trust structure." Ammon pulled out his notebook. "Nothing published without tribal council approval. Guardians maintain physical custody of all artifacts. Academic access requires indigenous partnership—not consultation, but actual co-authorship."

"That would slow everything down," Tanaka said.

"Good. The tablets waited millennia. They can wait a few more years while we figure out how to share them responsibly."

Thomas and Robert exchanged a long look—decades of shared experience in that silent communication.

"What about ceremonial materials?" Thomas asked finally. "Some knowledge isn't meant to be shared outside our communities. Ever."

"Then it won't be. Full tribal authority over what's classified as ceremonial. No academic access, no publication, no discussion without explicit consent. If you say something is sacred, it's sacred. End of discussion."

Tanaka looked ready to argue, then stopped herself. "I spent three days being held by people who wanted this knowledge for themselves. Viktor didn't care about context or meaning. He just wanted the information." She paused. "I don't want to be that person. Even in academic form."

Father Tomás stirred. "The Church could help. Not as controllers—but as historical consultants. We have archives going back centuries. And frankly, there are elements within the Vatican who will try to suppress this regardless. Better to have allies inside arguing for engagement."

"You're asking us to trust the institution that sent Konstantin," Thomas said.

"I'm asking you to trust that the institution isn't monolithic. If my superiors decide suppression is safer—" Tomás paused. "Then I'll resign and work with you anyway."

Reyes spoke up. "I can offer federal protection for the artifacts. Funding. Legal backing. But I need transparency about threats. If someone comes after this discovery, I need to know immediately."

"Agreed," Ammon said. "Security cooperation. But oversight of the knowledge stays with the partnership."

"I can work with that."

By sunset, they had a framework. Imperfect. Contentious. But real.

Thomas still harbored doubts about academic intentions. Tanaka still chafed at research restrictions. Tomás still faced uncertain reception from his superiors. Reyes still worried about threats they hadn't anticipated.

But it was a beginning.

"One more thing," Ammon said as they prepared to leave. "The inscription in the temple—the warning about fire. 'Knowledge is fire. It can warm or destroy. Choose wisely who receives this flame.' Every decision we make should be measured against that standard."

"The guardian tradition will adapt," Thomas said, "but it won't disappear. Someone still needs to watch. To protect. That responsibility doesn't end because the temple was found. If anything, it becomes more important."

"Then we continue." Ammon looked at the evidence crates—so few of them, so small against the magnitude of what had been lost. "We carry what flame we have. We find the other temples. We rebuild what Konstantin destroyed, piece by piece, repository by repository. And we never forget that he's still out there. That his faction is still watching. That this war isn't over."

It was a gamble—not on human perfection, but on human capacity to grow. To learn. To handle difficult truths with something approaching wisdom.

The work of revelation had begun. But so had the work of rebuilding from ashes.

CHAPTER THIRTY-TWO

Homecoming

In the months that followed, the scattered pieces of their lives found new configurations—not returning to what they had been, but settling into shapes marked by what they'd lost. Some called it homecoming. Ammon wasn't sure. Home implied safety, and safety seemed like a lie they told themselves between glances over their shoulders.

Konstantin was still out there. The temple lay buried under a mountain of stone. And somewhere in the world, other temples waited to be found— or to be destroyed before they could reach them.

But life continued, as it always did. And in the continuing, something unexpected emerged: not triumph, but belonging.

The evening light fell soft and golden across Clara's porch. Jonas had made tea—chamomile, because Tanaka had mentioned once that it helped her think. He'd remembered. He found himself remembering a lot of things she said these days.

That itself was strange. Jonas had spent most of his adult life training himself not to remember. Names, faces, details: in his old world, they were liabilities. Attachments that could be used against you.

Now he was sitting on a porch in Denver, making tea for a woman whose favorite flavor he'd memorized without meaning to, and the vulnerability of it didn't terrify him the way it should have.

They sat in the old wicker chairs Clara kept on the porch. The air smelled of pine and coming autumn. A wind chime near the door offered an occasional note, gentle and unhurried.

"Stanford wants me back," Tanaka said, cradling her cup. "They're calling it the opportunity of a lifetime. Leading the translation team."

Jonas watched her face—the way her brow furrowed when she was thinking through something complex. "And what do you want?"

She was quiet for a moment, studying the mountains as they turned from gold to purple. "I want to understand what we found. All of it. That's going to take years. Decades, maybe."

She turned to look at him. "Thomas has offered me a position as academic liaison at the cultural center. Working with university partners, coordinating research protocols. I'd be based in Utah most of the time."

"That sounds convenient."

"It does, doesn't it?" Her smile widened, and she reached across to take his hand. "Almost as if someone planned it that way."

They sat like that as the first stars appeared—not speaking, not needing to. The tension that had defined their early interactions had transformed into something Jonas hadn't expected to find again. Connection. Trust. The quiet certainty of two people who had faced danger together and emerged intertwined.

"For what it's worth," Jonas said, "I think my hacking days are finally behind me. The cultural center offered me a permanent security position. Legitimate work, proper salary, benefits."

"The reformed hacker goes straight?"

"Turns out there's more satisfaction in protecting knowledge than stealing it."

She leaned her head against his shoulder. "So. Utah."

"Utah," he agreed.

Jeremiah Stone's hearing lasted less than an hour.

Agent Reyes testified about his cooperation—the intelligence that had made the rescue possible, the tactical support that had saved lives. Father Tomás, via video link from Rome, confirmed that Jeremiah's information about Vatican operations had been accurate. Even Thomas spoke on his behalf, describing the transformation he'd witnessed in the sacred chamber six months before.

The judge's ruling was measured: sentence reduced to time served, followed by five years of supervised release.

The financial intelligence he'd provided had proven equally valuable. Federal prosecutors had frozen over forty million dollars in Consortium assets—funds that would be held in trust for indigenous cultural preservation programs. The Vance family's dark legacy, transformed into something that might actually heal.

Ammon met him outside the courthouse. Winter sunlight made everything feel sharper. The air was cold and clean.

"Thank you," Jeremiah said. "For everything."

"You earned it."

Jeremiah looked at the sky—really looked, the way you do when you've spent months staring at ceilings and walls. A hawk circled in the distance, riding thermals. His eyes tracked it automatically—old instincts—and then he caught himself and simply watched. No agenda. No calculation.

"I've been thinking about what comes next," he said. "I spent decades exploiting sacred places. Taking from them, profiting from them. I'd like to spend whatever time I have left doing the opposite."

"The guardians could use someone with your skills."

"Skills acquired through crime and violence."

"Skills are tools. It's what you do with them that matters."

Jeremiah nodded. "I'd like that. The chance to prove I'm more than my worst choices."

They shook hands. Jeremiah's grip was firm, his eyes clear. Whatever darkness had driven him before, something else lived there now. Something that looked like hope.

Ammon thought of Konstantin—how things went the opposite way. Konstantin brought his whole world crashing down and rode off into the sunset—in literal fashion. Not everyone can be saved, he reminded himself. But some people can. And Jeremiah proved which kind he was.

The federal courtroom was austere. Margaux Vance stood before the judge in a simple gray suit, her posture composed, her hands folded and still.

Ammon watched from the gallery. He'd debated whether to come. In the end, he'd decided that bearing witness was its own form of closure.

The prosecutor outlined the charges: conspiracy, abduction, obstruction of justice. Her cooperation had earned consideration, but she had still participated in violence against people who trusted her.

"Five years, minimum security," the judge pronounced, "with eligibility for early release based on continued cooperation."

As the guards approached, Margaux found Ammon in the gallery. For a moment, the mask slipped—and he saw a woman confronting the consequences of choices made in her father's shadow.

Thomas had warned him about her. Aspen had warned him. He'd overruled them both. The five-year sentence was his reminder: trust was a gift that could be weaponized.

The heavy doors closed behind her with a finality that sealed more than just her fate.

Viktor Semenov received no such consideration.

Ammon attended the sentencing because Tanaka had asked him to. She needed to see it end—to watch the man who had held her captive face consequences.

Viktor entered in orange, shackled, flanked by marshals. The urbane professional who had orchestrated kidnappings was gone. In his place stood someone diminished—a predator finally understanding the cage was permanent.

When the judge pronounced the sentence—life without parole—Viktor simply nodded. His eyes found Tanaka in the gallery. Not remorse. Not anger. Just recognition that the game was over.

"It's done," she whispered as they led him away.

"It's done," Ammon agreed.

But they both knew "done" was relative. Viktor would spend his life in maximum security. The scars he'd left would take longer to heal. Some might never heal at all.

Father Tomás returned to Rome to face the consequences of his choices.

The hardline faction was furious—a carefully planned operation disrupted, decades of secrecy compromised, one of their own standing with the opposition at the critical moment. There would be hearings. Investigations. Possibly worse.

But Tomás walked into those meetings with something he hadn't felt in years: peace.

"I'm not afraid of what they'll do to me," he told Ammon during their final video call. His hands, Ammon noticed, were still. In previous conversations, Tomás had always been in motion—the restless energy of a man managing more secrets than any one person should carry. Now he sat with his hands folded, the stillness of someone who had finally set down a weight.

"What about Konstantin?" Ammon asked.

Tomás's expression darkened. "Vanished. The hardliners are furious—not about his actions, but that he was exposed. They'll distance themselves publicly while hunting for him privately."

"Hunting to silence him?"

"Hunting to redirect him. He's a liability now, but a useful one." Tomás paused. "Watch your back, Ammon. He knows what you saved. He knows about the other temples. And he has nothing left to lose."

"What will you tell your superiors about the temple?"

"The truth. That what we found doesn't threaten faith—it expands it. That a civilization predating Scripture doesn't invalidate Scripture, but provides context for understanding how human spiritual development occurred across cultures."

"They won't like it."

"No. But perhaps some will listen. And if they don't—" He smiled. "Then I'll have done what I believed was right. That's all any of us can do."

The cabin was quiet in the early morning light.

Aspen had been awake for hours, watching the sky shift from black to gray to soft pink through the bedroom window. The new security system blinked green on the nightstand—one of many changes since they'd returned. Motion sensors on the property. A direct line to Reyes's team. The quiet vigilance that had become their new normal.

The mountains stood as silent witnesses beyond the glass, their peaks touched with the first gold of sunrise.

Beside them, Ammon slept peacefully—the first truly restful sleep they'd seen him manage in weeks. They didn't want to wake him, so they simply watched him breathe, marveling at how much had changed.

They had a secret. One they'd been carrying for three days now, confirmed and reconfirmed, waiting for exactly the right moment.

Their hand drifted to their stomach—a gesture that had become automatic, protective, though there was nothing to show yet. Just the knowledge of what was beginning.

Not here, they'd decided. Not in the quiet privacy of their bedroom. This news deserved a different setting—one that would tie their personal future to everything they'd fought for.

The ceremony was tomorrow. They could wait one more day.

Ammon stirred, his eyes opening. He smiled when he saw them watching—that soft, unguarded smile he only wore in quiet moments. His hand sought theirs beneath the blankets.

"You're thinking loud enough to wake me," he murmured.

"Just counting my blessings." They leaned down to kiss him. "Go back to sleep. We have a big day tomorrow."

He pulled them closer instead, and they let themself sink into his warmth, their secret held safe for just a little while longer.

Clara Lundquist closed the last box of family documents and surveyed her attic with satisfaction. What had been chaotic jumble was now organized archive—properly catalogued, professionally preserved, ready to be integrated into the broader record of the Hathenbruck legacy.

Late afternoon light slanted through the small window. The smell of old paper and cedar had become familiar, almost comforting.

"It's strange," she told Ammon when he visited. "I spent my whole life running from this history. Convinced the search had destroyed everyone it touched."

"And now?"

"Now I understand the search wasn't the problem. The problem was that no one ever found what they were looking for." She gestured at the organized boxes. "You found it. Even if you couldn't keep it, you proved it was real. That's more than any Lundquist before you managed."

"The temple is buried under a mountain of stone. We saved fragments when we should have saved everything."

"Fragments are more than nothing." Clara's voice was gentle but firm. "Your father died chasing shadows. Marcus died without ever seeing his research validated. You found the shadows and proved they were real. That matters, Ammon. Don't let grief convince you otherwise."

He was quiet for a moment. "Konstantin is still out there. The man who destroyed the temple—he escaped, and we don't know where."

Clara's expression darkened. "Will he come back?"

"Almost certainly. His faction won't stop because of the tablets we saved, the information they contain. And they describe other temples. Other repositories scattered across the world."

"So the search continues."

"The search continues. But it's different now. We're not chasing ghosts anymore. We're racing against people who want to bury the truth before we can find it."

Clara touched one of the boxes, her fingers tracing the neat label. "These papers tell our family's story. I want to make sure it's told properly—so that whoever comes after you understands what they're inheriting."

"A war."

"A responsibility." She met his eyes. "There's a difference. Wars end. Responsibilities are passed on."

Uncle Silas called that evening, his voice lighter than Ammon had ever heard it.

"I visited Marcus's grave today," he said. "First time since the funeral."

"How did that feel?"

"Like setting down a weight I didn't know I was still carrying." Silas's voice caught. "I told him what you found. That you proved him right—the temple was real. That it was destroyed, but you saved what you could."

"The search isn't over," Ammon said.

"I know. I told him that too." A pause. "But it's changed, hasn't it? We're not failures anymore. We were steps in a process that needed to happen across generations. Each of us contributed something, even if we couldn't see how it fit at the time."

"Dad. Marcus. You. All of you kept the trail alive long enough for me to follow it."

"And now you'll keep it alive for whoever comes next."

The conversation continued until the sun set and the first stars appeared. For the first time in his life, Ammon felt the full weight of his family's history—not as a burden, but as a foundation.

The sacred vein ran through all of them. Through Silas visiting his brother's grave. Through Clara organizing the family archives. Through Jonas making chamomile tea on a Denver porch. Through Aspen carrying a secret that would change everything.

And through Ammon himself, standing at the intersection of past and future, loss and hope, the temple that was buried and the temples that might still be found.

The flame was smaller than it should have been. But it was still burning.

CHAPTER THIRTY-THREE

The Bridge

The clearing in the Uinta Mountains held the late afternoon light like a vessel, golden and amber pooling between the ancient pines. Ammon stood at the edge of the natural amphitheater, breathing in air that carried the sharp sweetness of pine resin and the deeper, earthen scent of needles decomposing into soil.

At the perimeter, barely visible among the trees, Reyes's people held position. Two at the access road. Two more on the ridgeline. Armed rangers who dressed like hikers and smiled like tourists while their eyes tracked every movement in the forest. A reminder that even sacred moments now required protection.

Konstantin was still out there. They couldn't forget that. Not even here.

A creek babbled somewhere nearby. A woodpecker drummed against bark—the same sound, perhaps, that Hathenbruck had heard standing in this exact spot over a century and a half ago.

This was where F.W.C. Hathenbruck had first met Kwiyaghat—whose name meant "hawk" in the old tongue—a descendant of the great Chief Walkara and the guardian who would become Hathenbruck's closest ally. Where a German physician, thousands of miles from home, had recognized something in the young Ute warrior's eyes—a shared understanding that some knowledge required protection, that some truths demanded guardianship.

Ammon had read his ancestor's account of that meeting so many times the words had become part of him: *"He looked at me as if he had been expecting me all along."*

Now, standing in the same clearing over a hundred and fifty years later, Ammon finally understood what Hathenbruck had meant.

The others were gathering. Thomas moved across the carpet of pine needles, his walking stick finding grasping the soft ground with each careful step. The parade of dangerous ordeals had aged him—his shoulders carried a new stoop, and pain flickered across his features with movements that would have been effortless months before. But his eyes remained sharp, and when they met Ammon's, they held a warmth that spread through Ammon.

Robert Colorow walked beside Thomas, matching the elder's pace without making it obvious. The two men had been guardians together for decades, their friendship forged in the same fires of secrecy and responsibility that had shaped the tradition itself.

Behind them came the tribal council representatives—six men and women whose faces Ammon had come to know well over the past months. Some had supported him from the beginning; others had opposed his involvement with an intensity that bordered on hostility. All of them had chosen to be here today.

And Aspen stood beside him, close enough that he could feel the warmth of their body against his arm. They combed their hair today— something they rarely did—as they preferred to wear a hat. A small surrender to ceremony—and it caught the slanting light like dark water catching sun. Their free hand kept drifting to the medicine bag at their belt, the one their grandmother had given them.

When they slipped their other hand into his, their fingers interlaced with his own as naturally as breathing.

"Are you ready?" they asked.

Ammon looked at the gathering—at Thomas settling himself on a fallen log positioned like a seat of honor, at Robert arranging ceremonial items on a flat stone that served as a natural altar. A bundle of sage. A small clay vessel holding water from a sacred spring. A worn leather journal that Ammon recognized as one of the guardian tradition's oldest surviving texts.

"I'm not sure," he admitted. "But I don't think that matters."

The ceremony began as the sun touched the western ridge, spreading color and warmth. Robert lit the sage bundle, and its smoke rose in lazy spirals, carrying prayers older than memory toward the darkening sky. The scent wrapped around them all, sharp and purifying, and Ammon felt the magnitude of the mantle settling on him.

Thomas spoke first. His voice had lost none of its power despite his body's frailty—it carried across the clearing with the resonance of someone who had spent a lifetime speaking truths that demanded to be heard.

"We stand in a sacred place," Thomas said, his weathered hands resting on his knees, palms upward in the traditional posture of receiving. "A place where two traditions merged, where the old ways met the new, where the bridge between worlds was first constructed. The ground beneath our feet remembers what happened here. The trees witnessed it. The mountains hold that memory in their stones."

He paused, and in the silence, a bird called from somewhere in the pines—a single note that hung in the air like an offering.

"Today we honor that bridge. And we honor the people who have carried its weight across the centuries. The ones whose names we know—Kwiyaghat, who first recognized Hathenbruck as worthy of trust, and F.W.C. Hathenbruck himself, who proved worthy of that recognition. And the countless others whose names have been lost to time but whose faithfulness made this moment possible."

Robert stepped forward, holding the worn leather journal open to a page covered in faded handwriting. The council members shifted, some leaning closer, others bowing their heads in respect.

"These words were spoken over a hundred and fifty years ago," Robert said, his voice carrying the formal cadence of ritual. "The original agreement between Kwiyaghat and Hathenbruck, written in both Ute and German, pledging mutual commitment to the protection of sacred knowledge."

He read the words in Ute first, the syllables rising and falling like water over stones. Then he read the German, and Ammon felt a chill run down his spine despite the warm evening air. These were his ancestor's words, his ancestor's promise, spoken aloud in the place where they had first been given.

"These words created an obligation," Robert said, closing the journal with reverence. "An obligation that has passed from generation to generation, binding descendants who never knew each other across time and space. Today, we acknowledge that obligation—and we welcome a new generation into its keeping."

The tribal council members spoke in turn, each rising from their place in the circle to add their voice. Ammon listened to each one, holding their words carefully, feeling the texture of their acceptance—some generous and warm, others measured and cautious, all significant.

Mary Appawoo, the eldest, spoke of her grandmother's stories about the "German doctor who understood." Daniel Wanassay talked about the skepticism he had felt when Ammon first appeared, and how watching him in the First Temple had changed his mind. Louise Colorow—Robert's niece—simply said, "You have proven yourself. That is enough."

Then silence fell, and every eye turned to Ammon.

He stepped forward, feeling the soft give of pine needles beneath his feet. In his hand was a copy of Hathenbruck's testimony—the document his ancestor had hidden in the guardian codex, the words that had started this final leg of the journey. The paper trembled in his grip, and he steadied himself with a breath.

"My ancestor wrote something in the codex," Ammon said. "A testimony he kept secret even from his family. I'd like to read part of it now."

He opened the document, found the passage he'd marked, and began to read:

"The sacred vein runs through all of us. It connects us to those who came before—the builders, the preservers, the guardians who sacrificed so that knowledge might survive. It connects us to those who will come after—the seekers, the scholars, the protectors who will carry the flame when we are gone. And it connects us to each other, binding us in shared responsibility for truths too important to be left to any single tradition or perspective."

Ammon looked up from the text. The faces around him were lit by the last of the sunlight, and he could see his own emotion reflected in their expressions.

"For most of my life, I thought the sacred vein was about a lost mine he said, a giant gold vein hidden deep in these mountains," he said. "My family was obsessed. It was also about bloodlines. About the Hathenbruck family, the Lundquist legacy, the genetic inheritance that made me part of this story."

He paused, feeling the weight of his father's absence—the man who had searched his whole life and died still searching. Who would have given anything to stand where Ammon stood now.

"I was wrong. The sacred vein isn't about gold, and it isn't about blood. It's about responsibility. It's about the choice to carry something forward—not because you were born to it, but because you recognized its importance and decided it mattered."

He looked at the people gathered in the clearing—guardians and academics, rangers and hackers—united by everything they had endured together. Jeremiah Stone stood apart but present, his face bearing the complicated expression of a man still learning how to belong. A man who had chosen redemption when another had chosen escape. The contrast wasn't lost on Ammon.

"Anyone can become part of it, regardless of where they come from or what they've done before. All that's required is the willingness to bear the weight."

He took a breath, feeling the mountain air fill his lungs, feeling the presence of everyone who had stood in this clearing before him.

"I came to this place six months ago as a seeker—someone chasing answers that had eluded my family for generations. I found those answers. And I watched them get buried under a mountain of stone."

His voice caught, but he pressed on.

"Today I stand here as something different. As someone who has learned that finding answers is only the beginning. That the real work is deciding what to do with them. That the greatest treasure isn't knowledge itself, but the wisdom to protect it—and the courage to keep seeking when what you found has been taken from you."

He turned to face Thomas directly. The elder's eyes glistened in the fading light.

"The guardian tradition has survived for millennia because each generation found people willing to carry it forward. I want to add my name to that chain. I want to commit myself—and whatever years I have left—to the sacred responsibility of protecting knowledge while helping humanity prepare to receive it."

Thomas let the silence stretch. The clearing had grown hushed, even the creek seeming to hold its breath.

Then he reached for his walking stick and rose to his feet, Robert moving to support him but Thomas waving him away with a gentle gesture. He crossed the space between them with careful, deliberate steps.

When he reached Ammon, he placed both hands on Ammon's shoulders—his grip surprisingly strong, his palms warm through the fabric of Ammon's shirt.

"The guardian tradition doesn't accept members lightly," Thomas said, his voice thick with emotion he didn't try to hide. "We've seen too many seekers who wanted the knowledge without the responsibility, the discovery without the burden. We've been betrayed by those we trusted. We've buried secrets because the world wasn't ready for them."

His hands tightened on Ammon's shoulders.

"But you've proven yourself different. You found the First Temple—and you watched it fall. That kind of loss breaks most people. It didn't break you. You've carried the weight without breaking. You've made choices that put the tradition's needs above your own. When you could have claimed glory, you chose partnership. When you could have demanded control, you chose trust."

Thomas turned to face the council members, his hands still on Ammon's shoulders, presenting him to the gathered witnesses.

"I speak for the guardian tradition when I say: Ammon Lundquist is one of us. His testimony is accepted. His commitment is acknowledged. He stands in the line of succession that stretches back to the First Temple builders and forward to whatever future we help create."

He paused, his voice taking on new weight.

"The First Temple is lost. But the tablets speak of others—repositories scattered across the world, waiting for guardians to find them. That is our mission now. Not just to protect what we have, but to seek what remains. Before those who destroyed the First Temple can destroy what's left."

One by one, the council members rose to their feet.

Mary Appawoo nodded, her weathered face creasing into a smile. Daniel Wanassay stepped forward to clasp Ammon's forearm in the traditional warrior's greeting. Louise Colorow pressed her hand briefly over her heart, a gesture of acceptance that needed no words.

Robert came last, embracing Ammon with the warmth of a man welcoming family home after a long journey.

"Your ancestor would be proud," he murmured. "And so am I."

The sun slipped below the ridge, and the clearing softened into twilight. The sage smoke had thinned to wisps, rising to join the first stars appearing in the darkening sky. People began to talk quietly among themselves, the formal ceremony giving way to something warmer and more human.

At the perimeter, barely visible now in the gathering dark, the security team held position. Vigilance that didn't rest, even for ceremonies. Even for sacred moments.

Aspen found him at the edge of the clearing, where the pines gave way to a view of the valley below. The mountains were purple shadows now, their peaks catching the last light of the vanished sun.

"How do you feel?" they asked, slipping their arm through his.

"I'm not sure I have words for it." He turned to look at them, at the face that had become more familiar to him than his own. "I couldn't have done any of this without you. You know that."

"We couldn't have done it without each other." They held his gaze. "That's what partnership means, isn't it? Neither of us complete alone, but together—together we're something more."

Ammon pulled them close, feeling the warmth of their body against his, the steadiness of their presence that had anchored him through everything.

"Whatever comes next," he said, "we face it together."

"Whatever comes next."

They were quiet for a moment, their head resting against his chest. Then they pulled back, looking up at him with an expression he couldn't quite read.

"Actually, there's something I need to tell you. About what comes next."

"What do you mean?"

Aspen took his hand and pressed it gently against their stomach. Their eyes never left his face.

"The sacred vein," they said softly. "It's going to have another link."

For a moment, the words didn't register. Ammon stared at them, his mind struggling to catch up with what his heart already understood. Then the meaning broke through, and something cracked open in his chest—a flood of emotion so overwhelming he couldn't tell where joy ended and terror began.

"You're—" His voice broke. He tried again. "We're—"

"Yes." Aspen's eyes were bright with tears, but they were smiling—a smile that transformed their whole face, that made them look like someone standing at the edge of a great adventure. "About three months along. I wanted to wait until today to tell you. Until this moment."

Ammon felt tears streaming down his own cheeks, and he laughed—a broken, joyful sound that seemed to come from somewhere deeper than his throat. He pulled them into his arms and held them as tightly as he dared, his face buried in their hair, his body shaking with the force of everything he felt.

"A baby," he managed. "We're having a baby."

"We're having a baby." They were laughing too now, crying and laughing together. "The next generation. Another link in the chain."

He pulled back to look at them, cradling their face in his hands. The first stars were reflected in their eyes, and he thought he had never seen anything so beautiful in his life.

"All this time," he said, "I thought the sacred vein was about looking backward. Honoring the past. Protecting what came before. But it's not just that, is it? It's about looking forward too. About building something that will outlast us."

Aspen nodded, pressing their forehead against his.

"That's what the guardians have always done. Preserved the past so the future could learn from it. Protected knowledge so that someday, someone would be ready to receive it."

They placed their hand over his, where it still rested against their stomach.

"Now we get to be part of that future. All three of us."

They stood together as night settled over the mountains, wrapped in each other and in the magnitude of everything that had changed. Behind them, the sounds of the gathering continued—quiet conversation, occasional laughter, the clink of cups being raised in celebration. The sage smoke had faded entirely now, but its scent lingered in their clothes, in their hair, marking them as participants in something ancient and ongoing.

The stars emerged fully, the same stars that had guided the First Temple builders across oceans, the same constellations that Hathenbruck had used to encode his secrets. Ophiuchus the serpent-bearer, Orion the hunter—their ancient patterns wheeling overhead as they had for millennia, as they would for millennia more.

Ammon stood in the sacred clearing, surrounded by people who had become his family, holding the person who carried their future within them. For the first time in his life, he understood what it meant to belong—not the absence of danger, not the end of struggle, but the certainty of purpose.

Konstantin was still out there. Other temples waited to be found or destroyed. The war wasn't over.

But standing in this clearing, holding the person who carried his future, surrounded by people who had become family—he knew they would face it together.

This search was over—the search for the First Temple, the quest that had consumed his family for generations. But a new search was beginning. Other temples. Other guardians. A race against forces that would bury the truth forever if they could.

The sacred vein ran through all of them. And it would continue running, carrying knowledge and responsibility and hope, for as long as there were people willing to carry the flame. For as long as there were children yet to be born, ready to inherit the light.

EPILOGUE

One Year Later

The Guardian-Academic Alliance Cultural Center rose from where the old tribal center had once stood, rebuilt from the ashes of Viktor's attack into something stronger and more secure. The new structure honored the original design while incorporating layers of protection that weren't visible from outside—reinforced walls, hardened server rooms, and security systems that would make another assault far more costly.

Dr. Yuki Tanaka paused at the observation deck each morning, still struck by how the ancient and modern had learned to coexist here on the reservation.

Climate-controlled chambers purred with equipment while the sounds of the reservation drifted in through carefully shielded windows. Life continuing, as it always did, indifferent to human loss.

Security was discreet but thorough—and more extensive than it would have been a year ago. Biometric scanners disguised as decorative stone pillars. Motion sensors concealed along the perimeter fencing. Armed guards who dressed like maintenance workers and smiled like staff members while their eyes tracked every unfamiliar vehicle on the access road.

Konstantin had resurfaced twice in intelligence reports: once in Rome, once in Athens, both times vanishing before anyone could confirm the sighting. The knowledge that he was still hunting, still watching, still opposed to everything they were building, cast a shadow over even the brightest discoveries.

The main translation room occupied the center's central chamber, a space deliberately designed to echo the proportions of the First Temple—a memorial as much as a workspace. A reminder of what they'd lost and what they were fighting to recover.

Tanaka walked through rows of workstations where an international team of scholars—linguists, archaeologists, historians, astronomers— collaborated on the bronze tablets they had carried out in their arms during those desperate final minutes, before the mountain came down. The work was painstaking—forty tablets and two hundred photographs to reconstruct knowledge that had filled chambers. Like reassembling a library from a handful of pages that survived a fire.

The visual dictionary tablets had been among the first things Tanaka grabbed during the escape—instinct or providence, she still wasn't sure which. They were proving to be exactly what their builders had intended: a key that unlocked understanding for anyone willing to make the effort. She had spent the first three months just cataloging what they'd saved, cross-referencing the physical tablets with her photographs to build a translation framework from ruins.

The discoveries, even from fragments, had been remarkable.

A single tablet had described a surgical technique for removing cataracts—a procedure ophthalmologists confirmed matched modern methods almost exactly. Another had contained astronomical observations so precise they'd quietly corrected a three-minute error in global navigation software. Fragments of genius, hinting at the ocean of knowledge now buried under stone.

Some discoveries had required more delicate handling. The social engineering tablets—techniques for mass manipulation that had chilled them when Tanaka first translated them in the temple—remained in the most restricted archive, accessible only to a small committee that included tribal representatives, academic ethicists, and a Vatican observer whose presence represented the fragile alliance Father Tomás had helped forge before his reassignment to quieter duties.

The protocols for managing dangerous knowledge had evolved organically over the year, balancing transparency with responsibility. Peer-reviewed papers appeared in academic journals, each one vetted through a process that prioritized accuracy over speed. Public lectures drew crowds eager to learn about humanity's hidden past. But some tablets remained in the restricted archive, their contents discussed only in rooms swept for surveillance equipment.

It was the final section of tablets that had captivated Tanaka most—not the revelation that other temples existed (they'd known that since the escape), but the painstaking work of extracting actual locations from astronomical references and geographical descriptions.

She pulled up the relevant translations on her laptop, her heart racing with the implications she had confirmed just that morning.

The First Temple had been part of a system—a network of twelve major repositories scattered across the ancient world, each preserving different aspects of accumulated wisdom. Some had been deliberately destroyed during periods of upheaval. Others had been lost to natural disasters, their locations now beneath ocean waters or buried under volcanic ash.

But a few, the tablets suggested, might still exist. Hidden in remote locations, protected by guardian traditions that had survived in isolation for millennia, waiting for a world that might finally be ready to receive what they had preserved.

Or waiting to be destroyed by those who believed the world should never receive it.

Tanaka picked up her phone and called Ammon.

"I need you to see something," she said when he answered. "The Temple of the Southern Stars. I've confirmed the coordinates. We know where it is."

She heard the intake of breath on the other end—the sound of someone processing information that changed everything.

"I'm on my way."

Twenty minutes later, Ammon and Aspen arrived at the center.

Tanaka met them at the entrance, struck as always by how the past year had changed them both. Ammon moved with a quiet confidence now, though his eyes still swept every room he entered—a habit he'd developed since Konstantin's escape and hadn't been able to break. Gray had appeared at his temples. Stress or wisdom, perhaps both.

And Aspen carried their six-month-old daughter in a traditional cradleboard on their back, the baby's dark eyes alert and curious. There was a softness in their expression that hadn't been there before, though their eyes still held that watchful quality of someone trained to notice what others missed.

They'd married shortly after the ceremony in the Uinta clearing, and little Anna—named for Ammon's great-grandmother—had arrived in the spring. New life against destruction. Future against the buried past.

"Show me," Ammon said.

Tanaka led them to a display room where the relevant tablets had been arranged in sequence, bronze surfaces gleaming under carefully calibrated lighting. The text described a system of interconnected repositories—twelve major temples and dozens of smaller sites, positioned across continents and connected by the maritime routes the First Temple builders had established over generations of seafaring.

"We knew about the network," Tanaka explained. "But the location data was encoded in astronomical references—star positions as they appeared thousands of years ago, before stellar drift changed the night sky. It took months to work backward through the precession calculations."

She pointed to a passage on the central tablet.

"The Temple of Earth Sciences—that was the First Temple, here in Grand Staircase-Escalante. Geology, metallurgy, the properties of stone and metal. The Uinta chamber was connected to it, a satellite site, but not one of the twelve primary repositories."

She moved her finger across the ancient map etched in bronze.

"The Temple of the Eastern Waters—somewhere in the Mediterranean basin, possibly the Aegean. The astronomical references suggest an island, but I haven't pinpointed which one yet."

"And the Temple of the Southern Stars?" Aspen asked, one hand reaching back to touch the baby.

"That's the one I cracked this morning." Tanaka's voice carried barely controlled excitement. "The text describes it as 'the place where the sky wheel turns opposite'—a reference to the southern hemisphere, where constellations appear to rotate in the opposite direction from our perspective here."

She pulled up a map on her laptop, overlaying the ancient coordinates with modern geography.

"Patagonia. Southern Argentina, near the Chilean border. A region so remote that significant portions remain unexplored even today."

"We're talking about a repository built by the same civilization that created the First Temple," she continued. "Potentially containing knowledge that neither the Utah sites nor anything we've found here preserved. Different guardians. Different traditions. Different secrets."

Ammon stared at the translations, feeling the familiar quickening in his chest—the pull of mystery, the call of undiscovered truth that had driven him since he first opened his great-grandmother's locket.

He thought of Hathenbruck, who had carried this same feeling across an ocean and into the wilderness. Of the guardians who had kept faith for generations, never knowing if anyone would come. Of his daughter, who would inherit a world where these secrets were finally emerging into the light—or being buried forever, depending on who found them first.

"How long before we can mount an expedition?" he asked.

"Months, at least. We need local contacts, permits, cover stories. The region is politically complicated—indigenous land rights, national park restrictions, competing claims."

"And Konstantin?"

Tanaka's expression darkened. "If he has access to the same tablets we do—if he photographed anything before we escaped—he might already be looking. He had hours in the temple before the confrontation. We don't know what he saw."

The weight of the past year pressed against Ammon's chest—the triumph of discovery, the agony of loss, the knowledge that somewhere out there, Konstantin was watching. Waiting. Planning.

The First Temple was gone. But another temple waited to be found. Another race against those who would bury the truth.

"I guess we're not done yet," he said.

Aspen leaned into his shoulder, and he felt Anna stir against their back—a small sound of contentment, life continuing its ancient work. Three heartbeats. Past, present, and future, linked by blood and choice and the responsibility they had chosen to carry forward.

"Were we ever done?" Aspen asked softly.

Through the center's windows, the reservation stretched toward distant mountains—a landscape that had kept its secrets for millennia and would keep them for millennia more. But Ammon's mind was already elsewhere. South of the equator, where the sky wheel turned opposite, where another temple waited in the dark.

Waiting to be found. Or waiting to be destroyed.

The race had begun.

The sacred vein, running through all of them. Running toward whatever came next.

THE END

The Sacred Vein series will continue in

Book Three: The Hidden Network

AUTHOR'S NOTE

Thank you so much for reading. Truly.

When you picked up this book, you took a chance on an independent author, and that means more to me than I can properly express. Writing has always been my way of making sense of the world, of processing life's questions through story, and knowing that my words found their way to you—and that you stayed until the end—is a gift I don't take for granted.

If this story moved you, made you think, or simply gave you a few hours of escape, I'd be incredibly grateful if you'd consider leaving a review. For independent authors like me, reviews are everything. They help other readers discover books they might love, and they give authors like me the encouragement to keep writing.

It doesn't need to be long or polished. A sentence or two about what you enjoyed is more than enough. Your voice matters, and sharing it helps more than you know.

Thank you again for your time and your trust. I hope we'll meet again in the pages of another story.

With gratitude,
Brian Young

ABOUT THE AUTHOR

Brian Young grew up in Utah hiking, camping, and searching the High Uintas—the same mountains that provide the dramatic backdrop for The Sacred Vein Series. Those formative years exploring wilderness trails and hearing legends of lost Spanish gold planted the seeds for his debut novel.

Young now lives in Chicago, where he works as a Software Engineering Leader by day and pursues his passion for writing in his spare time. The Sacred Vein Series represents the culmination of years of research into the real history of the Lost Rhoades Mine, combined with his deep love for the Utah landscape and its indigenous heritage.

"The Uinta Mountains shaped who I am," Young says. "Writing this book was a way of honoring that landscape and the stories it holds—both the historical record and the legends that have grown around it. I wanted to create something that felt true to the place, even as it explored questions that feel urgent today: Who owns the past? What do we owe to the cultures whose heritage we study? And what really matters when we strip away the glitter of gold?"

Brian welcomes hearing from readers. Whether you have questions about the series, are interested in a speaking engagement or book club visit, or simply want to share your thoughts on the story, you can reach him at brianyoungauthor@gmail.com.